D0028366

daisy

cooper's

rules

for

living

NO LONGER PROPERTY
OF ANYTHINK
RANGEVIEW LIBRARY
DISTRICT

daisy cooper's rules for living

TAMSIN KEILY

PARK
ROW
BOOKS

If you purchased this book without a cover you should be aware that this book is stolen property. It was reported as "unsold and destroyed" to the publisher, and neither the author nor the publisher has received any payment for this "stripped book."

PARK
ROW
BOOKS™

Recycling programs
for this product may
not exist in your area.

ISBN-13: 978-0-7783-0974-1

Daisy Cooper's Rules for Living

Copyright © 2020 by Tamsin Keily

All rights reserved. No part of this book may be used or reproduced in any manner whatsoever without written permission except in the case of brief quotations embodied in critical articles and reviews.

This is a work of fiction. Names, characters, places and incidents are either the product of the author's imagination or are used fictitiously. Any resemblance to actual persons, living or dead, businesses, companies, events or locales is entirely coincidental.

This edition published by arrangement with Harlequin Books S.A.

Park Row Books
22 Adelaide St. West, 40th Floor
Toronto, Ontario M5H 4E3, Canada
ParkRowBooks.com
BookClubbish.com

Printed in U.S.A.

For Mum,
who taught me the power of a good pen and a pile of notebooks.

daisy cooper's rules for living

Rule One

Anything Can Happen

IN THE BEGINNING, THERE is life. And it's wonderful. But persistent. It grows like a weed and it wriggles into every corner of the world, expanding and changing. And space is limited. So there becomes a need for death. We've all heard it before, right? The necessary evil. The unexplained, unavoidable end to everybody's story. Everybody gets their turn at life and everybody gets their turn at death.

You're all very good at pretending that you accept that, but I know you don't really. It's in your eyes. At funerals, at hospitals, when you watch those soppy documentaries on television. Part of you wonders why we can't just try a world with immortality, just to see what happens.

Of course there's a real reason why you can't get that thought out of your head: it's because you're hoping that if you keep thinking it, it will happen and you won't have to die. You'll be the first, the one and only, the miracle. The one to cheat death.

But you won't. I'm not trying to sound ominous here. I'm not waiting behind your door with a knife or something. I'm just speak-

ing from a position of authority and clearing away any misconceptions you might have. In the end, it will happen. In the end, it will be your turn. There's billions of different choices being made by people across the world every day and one of those will, no matter how unknowingly, be the one that guides you toward your final hour. Someone offers you your first cigarette, someone doesn't check the brakes on their car, someone passes on their genes. Anything can happen and I suppose I'll be waiting for you when it does.

And yes, I'm aware that you've had to leave behind your family and no, I can't change that for you. Boxes have to be ticked, quotas have to be met.

Life has to end and I have to arrive, sooner or later.

❋ ❋ ❋

It starts around seven. The snow that is. Predictably, London grinds to a halt as the ground is dusted with the lightest smattering of the stuff, so much so that I'm twenty minutes late for dinner. Honestly, you would have thought the bus driver was driving across an iceberg, the speed he was going.

Despite the snow, the restaurant is still packed. Then again, it is a bit of a sanctuary. The combination of candles and radiators and people is enough to raise the temperature significantly, which I'm grateful for when I'm really not dressed for the arctic winter. Tonight's date night, after all and Eric has been texting me all day about how much he's looking forward to it, so I sort of felt that sweaters and jeans weren't really going to cut it.

He sits across from me, fingers tapping incessantly against the wood. One leg jiggles under the table, causing my cutlery to tinkle softly as they hit against each other. A tiny earthquake.

"Eric, you're acting like this is our first date." He glances up from his plate of carbonara, eyes wide so I can see every little speck of toffee brown in there. "And now you look like you've just been caught pissing in the shower—what's going on?" I say, laughing. But he doesn't join in. Something is definitely up.

"Sorry," he replies after a beat of silence. He looks genuinely apologetic. "Just got a lot on my mind."

"Anything you want to share?" My voice is light, like I'm not bothered, but I've got a slight fluttering of fear in my throat. Things have been great between us for a decent amount of time now—but of course there's the inevitable paranoia that I've only just not noticed all the signs and this is him about to break up with me. I'm already considering how I'll tell my parents without causing a complete shitstorm when I notice that he's speaking again.

"...and you know how much I love spending time with you, Daisy, but I want more..."

Here it comes. He wants more. So he wants someone else. He wants someone who knows how to have a serious conversation without injecting sarcasm into it every five seconds. Someone who's a proper grown-up, not one who doesn't really understand how her taxes work. I'm preparing for the inevitable, holding back the tears and the misdirected anger, when Eric pulls something from his pocket and places it on the table.

I'm so floored by the action that it takes me a whole five seconds to register what it is. There's the predictable, heart-stopping moment when I think it might be a ring, but a closer look dispels that idea. Instead, it's a key with a smart pink leather keyring attached to it, embossed with a golden "D"— for Daisy, I presume. I look back over at Eric with a frown.

"A key?" I ask, realizing that I'm probably being incredibly slow.

Eric laughs, warm and confident. Clearly, now he's started

with his big announcement, he doesn't feel quite as nervous anymore. Well, bully for him. "Yeah, a key. It's a key to the flat, Daisy."

"Your flat?"

"Yeah." He leans across and takes my hand, squeezing it firmly. "We've been going out a while now, Daisy. And you're really special to me. So I want to take things further." He draws in a deep breath, like a ringmaster about to announce the main attraction. "I want you to move in with me."

I wonder distantly if the entire restaurant can hear my thudding heart. It takes me a second to take in his words, to fathom the fact that he's just asked me to live with him. Me. The grumpy marketing assistant who only met him in the first place because he needed nagging about a late piece of paperwork. Anything can happen, I suppose.

"Wow," I say finally, once my voice has found its way back to my throat again. "Eric, this is amazing, I mean—wow!"

Eric raises an eyebrow, still holding my hand. "So…is that a yes?" Big brown eyes watching me, drawing me in to the big next step on the ladder of life, if you can excuse that atrocious cliché.

It's easy to accept the offer. I can feel a ridiculous grin on my face as I nod, squeezing his hand back this time. "Yes, of course! I mean, it will take a while to move out and get my shit together. But yes, let's do it. Let's move in together."

Eric beams at me, sitting back in the chair with that big old grin. "Brilliant," he says. "That's just brilliant." He looks like the cat who just caught the mouse, though perhaps I should think of a slightly lighter metaphor. Trust me to go dark.

It's a little difficult to continue with a normal meal after that. We try, though; time doesn't stop just because you make a big decision and this food is fancier than our usual chain-restaurant pizza. So we go back to our food, exchange little smiles across the table, like we have this shared secret. We'd be terrible spies.

He orders pudding and I order a massive cappuccino (it's been a long day). We talk about storage solutions for all my stuff and possible decor changes (definite decor changes, but he doesn't need to know that yet). We get the bill; he takes it in an automatic motion and pulls out his card. He glances over to me, sensing my dislike of the action.

"Just this once, Daisy? I know it goes against your 'independent woman striking out on her own' vibe but this is a special occasion."

I roll my eyes, considering it before conceding with a nod. Well, mainly conceding. My stubbornness doesn't quite allow me to sit there and be paid for, so I pull out my purse and tug out a few coins. "Just for the tip," I explain as Eric begins to complain.

He lets it go with a slight shake of his head. We may not be living together yet but he certainly knows me well enough to pick his battles.

We leave the restaurant sometime after ten. The snow has stopped but the chill outside bites at any exposed skin, quickly and efficiently chasing away any warmth still lingering from our time inside. To add insult to injury, there's not even any proper snow on the ground. Just a slushy, slippery mess from hundreds of feet trampling through it.

"So…wanna bunk up at mine?" Eric asks, as he's buttoning up his coat, eyes squinting slightly against the wind.

It's tempting, but I find myself shaking my head. "Probably shouldn't. If I've got to tell Violet that I'm moving out, it probably shouldn't be right after a night at yours." Eric smiles with a slightly knowing smile, which I'm grateful for. Violet Tucker is my best friend and current flatmate. My unofficial sister, that's what everyone says. And I wouldn't disagree with that. It took Eric a grand total of three dates to work out that she was as ingrained in my life as salt is in the sea, and another few dates to accept that fact. Two years down the line and it seems he also understands that this new living arrangement will take delicate explaining.

"Fair enough, thought I'd give it a try." He rubs his hands together, blowing on them in an attempt to warm them up before he pulls his gloves on. "You busing it?"

I nod, shivering. The gray blazer I'm wearing over my dress really isn't doing me much good, even when paired with a scarf. "Are you cabbing it?" Eric lives in the opposite direction to me, by the river in one of these glass-and-metal creations where successful and, let's face it, smug city slickers live. On the other hand, the lowly marketing assistant here has to settle with a basement mold-farm of a flat. And a bus rather than a cab.

Eric already has his phone out, opening up the appropriate app and searching for a ride. As he's doing this, he nods. "Cabbing it," he confirms, tapping the screen a moment later with a triumphant smile. "You going to be all right?"

As usual, my instinctive reaction to his concern is to roll my eyes. I can't help it. I've survived on my own for years after all, even if most of those years haven't been in the "big city." Somehow, having a boyfriend seems to mean I lose all those skills. Maybe a little harsh, so I soften my response with a smile and a squeeze of his arm. "I'll be fine. I've got my polar bear Taser and I'm sure the bus driver will have a spare sled."

Eric grins, leaning in to kiss me. When he pulls away, he gives me a jaunty wink, eyes all twinkly with excitement. "See you soon then—roomie."

It's such a cliché that we both have to laugh. "You dork. See you soon."

With one final wave, we part ways. I glance back as I make my way toward the bus stop, watch him duck into a car. Even from a little distance away, I can see a lingering smile on his face. Happiness and triumph emanates from him, unhampered by the cold. That brings a smile of my own to my face as I step onto the just-arriving bus. Who would have thought that Eric Broad, the golden boy of Bennington & Moore Insurance, would be so pleased by giving little old me a key?

The journey home isn't too long, but I spend it trying to get some sort of plan of delivery straight in my head. After eighteen years of friendship, since day one of primary school, I know Violet's ways pretty well by now—and big news has to be shared with great care.

By the time I get home, it's almost midnight. Despite this, Violet is still stretched out on our slightly threadbare sofa, swathed in the fleece blanket I got her for Christmas. I don't blame her; our flat either does freezing cold or boiling hot. Judging by the way my breath still crystallizes in front of me, I'd say it's currently the former.

She doesn't turn around from her phone but does deign to wave a hand vaguely in my direction. Standard Violet behavior. "One of these days it's not going to be me coming through that door but some burglar. Then you'll be embarrassed," I comment, as I kick the door shut, wedging it into the slightly warped door frame with a grunt.

Violet sniggers, plopping her phone down on the coffee table, narrowly avoiding knocking over the ridiculous New York snow globe my mum bought us as a flat-warming gift. Once she's satisfied it's safe, Violet twists around to look at me. "Yeah, 'cause embarrassment is going to be my biggest concern. So, how was dinner? Did he pop the question?" she asks, resting her chin on the back of the sofa as she surveys me with eager curiosity.

"No, he didn't. I promise you if that ever happens, I will call you up literally as he's doing it, so there's really no need to keep asking." Moving to sit beside her, I kick off my heels and let out a sigh of relief at the feeling of having my toes free once more.

"Wuss," Violet teases, prodding me with one finger. "I danced in higher heels than that for six hours today."

"The difference being that you got paid for it."

"If you can call those wages getting paid." She mutters this with a huff, though there's a grin lurking in the corners of her mouth anyway. Violet might complain about the pay but this is her biggest professional dancing job since we moved to London together, three years ago. She can't quite hide her pride, even if she's got bruised and battered feet.

I don't reply and perhaps that's how she knows there's something on my mind. That's the trouble with having a friend like Violet; she knows me better than I know myself sometimes. She can predict when I need to say something before I've even got the words together. "So, he didn't pop the question, but something else happened?"

I nod, automatically worming my finger into the large hole on the arm of the sofa. As if I might find the answer in there. "He asked me to move in with him." The words slip out after a moment of silence, in which I realize that there's no easy way to tell her the news.

The sofa creaks slightly as Violet shifts, so she's facing me a little more directly. Out of the corner of my eye, I catch her chasing away a small frown. By the time I'm looking at her properly, though, she's smiling. "Wow, Dee. That's amazing." She obviously spots my concern, because she prods me with her finger again. "Oi, don't get all droopy on me. I'll be fine. You know I only put up with you in this flat for your tea."

Her voice is steady and her eyes are bright. It doesn't exactly fool me, but, for now, it will do. So I grin, leaning across to hug her tightly. Her wild curls tickle at my nose, just like always. "It won't be for a while, I'm sure. Plenty of time to get used to the idea."

Violet makes a thoughtful noise, appraising me in that examining way she often does. It makes me shift uncomfortably, an insect under the microscope.

To escape this examination, I clap my hands together and stand up. "Anyway. Tea?"

Violet's turned back to her phone now I've stood up, but spares me a guilty look. "You'll need to go to the shop for milk, then…"

Typical. "You promised me that when we lived together you'd stop consuming a damn dairy every day."

She shoots me a grin, one finger tracing an invisible halo above her head as she watches me hunt around for some better shoes. "Love you, tit."

"Love you, dickhead," I reply automatically, following our usual routine.

So a moment later I'm stepping back out into the night, with stupid heels back on because my trainers were buried somewhere under Violet's vast collection of shoes. Gripping my keys tightly in my hand (I don't want to be outside for any longer than I need to be), I start down the street.

Tugging my coat tight around me, I quicken my pace. The night is silent—or as silent as London nights can ever be—which is a nice change. No buses hissing to a halt, no planes roaring across the sky and nobody else mad enough to be out in this weather. Just me and the stars. Perhaps I should stop and appreciate this moment. But it's too cold.

Just as I pass the bus stop, that's when it happens.

I don't know what's going on at first, just that the pavement seems to disappear beneath me. My foot tries to go one place, but the frozen ground has other ideas, sending it sliding out to the left. For a moment it feels as if my balance has saved the day, but then the other foot skids against the icy patch I've stumbled onto and the world tips. Like somebody has trapped me in a snow globe and turned it upside down.

There's a brief second when all I see is the sky, burnt orange from the streetlights and scarred with the fuzzy trails of unheard airplanes. Then gravity grabs at me and drags me down to the pavement in one swift, heartless motion. I hear—no, *feel*—a crack somewhere on the back of my head.

Distantly, I hear a whistle. Like an old-fashioned kettle boiling on the stove. And then everything goes black.

Rule Two

We Can't Be Prepared For Everything

THERE'S A DANGER TO be found in complacency. Maybe you've heard this before. Don't become complacent, don't settle, don't get comfortable. Prepare for the unexpected.

Of course, this is fine when the unexpected is a new job offer or a surprise trip to Lapland. We all can learn to adapt to that. The human brain is remarkably well built for adaptation, like it's still preparing to evolve into something else. You shoulder new responsibilities, you settle into new routines.

Sometimes, though, change leaves no room for adaptation. It creeps up behind you in the shadows, smirking to itself as it hides its nasty secret. It waits until the opportune moment; until you're happy, cozy, settled. It waits until you're just feeling like life is heading in the right direction.

Then all it takes is one unsteady paving stone, one patch of ice, and everything goes to shit. Change washes through your life like the cruelest tsunami and you can bet there will be casualties.

So, really, the saying "prepare for the unexpected" is a whole load of crap. You can't prepare for it. You can just hope that when the wave of change is coming by, it somehow leaves you be.

So, death goes like this. First comes unconsciousness, from the pavement. Then it feels like being shoved in the back, but instead of tumbling forward, there is a distinct sensation of tumbling out. There is no moment of looking back and seeing your body below, floating away from you (or you away from it). Instead there's simply an awareness that you're no longer on the Earth.

Then comes the white. So bright that it feels like it will burn right through your skull. Until suddenly, it clears. No pearly gates, just a desk in a flat gray office that could have been anywhere in the world.

Except somehow, I know that this is it. That I, Daisy Cooper, am dead.

I was only twenty-three. Was that really it?

On the desk is a slim manila-colored file, and a red telephone with one of those old-fashioned spin dials and with three squat lights on top that are all flashing red. A chair sits on either side of the desk. There are three doors; one door directly behind the other side of the desk while one is off to the side. Another stands just behind me and I think I came through it, but my memory feels like it's been put in a blender. Behind the desk is a calendar on the wall, with countless tally counts squished into each day's box, in dainty pencil marks. And that's it.

Instinctively, I know I need to sit. But I can't move; is there even anything *to* move? It feels like I've been vaporized, and now I am nothing but smoke in the wind. I hear the side door open with a slight huff as it gets stuck on a bit of threadbare carpet, and I'm struck by how ordinary this all is. Perhaps I'm not dead.

"Hello, I'm Death."

Bang goes that theory.

Death, then, comes to sit on the faded office chair that waits on his side of the desk, adjusting its position with a scowl of concentration. I distantly feel my toes curling tightly in my shoes. Like I'm getting ready to run. A tight feeling starts in my throat; running probably won't do much good here. I force myself to focus on this newcomer, try to stop my hands from shaking.

He is tall and lean, though not, as you might expect, skeletal. His skin is definitely present, and even comes with a smattering of freckles and precise dimples in his cheeks. He wears his hair, which at least attempts to stick to the stereotype by being jet-black, in a precisely mussed style, with carefully selected wisps falling just above his eyes. A pointed nose, and then eyes the color of the morning grass, a moss green that darken slightly as he glowers at the file on his desk. Is it wrong to call the Grim Reaper attractive? Undecided.

He wears a periwinkle-blue shirt with the buttons done right up to the top, tucked into a pair of black skinny jeans. He could have been any guy in a bar, except for the white tag on his chest that says "Death," with a cartoon skull doodled beside it. Someone's idea of a joke, perhaps.

"Sit, sit please Mrs. Aberdale."

I don't know why he's calling me that. I stare, and I'm sure if I do have a body, my mouth is hanging open. He looks up, raising an eyebrow before beckoning with a hand I note to be covered in flecks and smudges of pen. "Come on. Today's a busy one and you've been a right pain to locate. We weren't expecting you for another hour."

I try to walk. I find the process to be reassuringly unchanged and a moment later I've managed to seat myself in the chair.

In the somewhat cold reflection of his eyes, I can see something resembling me. A silhouette, the curve of my hair. I wonder if it's matted with blood; I suppress a wince as the crack of pavement hitting head rings through my ears.

He looks at me for a good two minutes, or at least it feels like that. Then he rests his chin on his interlaced fingers. "Blimey, they do get younger every century—did he sweep you off your feet? Or was he just very rich?" I have a horrible feeling he's trying to be funny. "Hey, at least you got to wear the dress before you came here, eh?"

I have been typically quiet up to this point, but Death's final words bring a halt to that. Irritation always manages to do that for me it seems. "What are you talking about?" I ask, and then let out a sigh of relief at hearing my voice, shaky but still existent.

Death watches me with amusement, then glances down at the file on his desk. He picks it up and gives it a little wave in a way that's presumably supposed to make everything clear (it doesn't).

"This. It says: Tiffany Aberdale. Recently married. Beaten to death in a robbery." He reads this from the white sticker stuck to the top. I notice that a bubble of air is trapped in its edge, and I wonder distantly how the afterlife still has such menial problems. More consciously, though, I'm concerned by what he's just said.

"That's not me."

"What?"

"Tiffany Aberdale, that's not me. I'm Daisy. Daisy Cooper. I—I think I tripped."

"You did what?"

"Yes, I tripped on—on the ice." I swallow, finding it difficult to talk under the intensity of Death's gaze. He looks utterly perplexed and I feel a strange sense of pride: I, average Daisy, have flummoxed the Grim Reaper himself. He flicks open the folder, flipping through the sheets with gathering speed. Then he drops it back onto the desk and dives down to pull open a drawer.

"Daisy Cooper, you say?" he calls up from the depths of the drawer, and I make a somewhat dazed noise of agreement. Maybe this is all an accident, a big mistake? Maybe I can go home.

But that doesn't happen. Instead the time ticks by until Death reappears, holding an identical folder in his hand. The phone trills on the desk, a harsh sound for the almost eerie silence around us. At the very same moment, a mobile phone hums a bizarrely jaunty ringtone until Death pulls it from his pocket and furiously taps the screen a few times. Then he turns back to the file, opening it up and scowling at its contents. "Daisy Cooper, you say? Daisy Cooper of 1b Brownview Road, London? Daughter of Claire and Gary Cooper? Sister to Oliver Cooper? Currently living with Violet Tucker?"

I nod mutely and he smacks the folder down on the table, the action making me jump. "Well then, Daisy Cooper of 1b Brownview Road, London—what the hell are you doing here?"

It's not quite the response I was expecting. I was thinking he might give me a pat on the shoulder, apologize for any inconvenience then send me back. That would be professional at least. Instead, he drops the file and comes around the desk to examine me more closely, as if I'm a wriggling bacteria under a microscope. "Well," he states, after a long, uncomfortable moment in which he simply stares, "you look pretty dead to me."

He lets out a sigh, ignoring my small whimper of despair, and moves to sit up on the top of the desk. As he leans across to grab the red phone's receiver, I notice distantly that he's wearing white Converses like the ones I myself own. *Owned.* Except his are still dazzlingly white, while mine were the gray of an English summer.

Then he starts speaking again and my gaze snaps up. But he's just on the phone. "Right, listen. I want to know which half-brain, sham of evolution sent me Daisy Cooper when she's not meant to be dead yet. No. Sorry, do I really have to repeat myself? Daisy Cooper isn't meant to die for another sixty-nine years. Yes, I've read it right!" He hangs up then, dropping the receiver down onto the handset with a look of impatience. When he turns back to face me, however, he's all smiles.

I know that look, though. It's the look my boss gave me when I asked if I was ready to move on from just being a marketing assistant. It's the look that the real estate agent gave Violet and I when we asked what we could afford in London with our budget. It's the look of "hold your nose because here comes the shit." This is why my breath stops—and I wonder for a moment why I'm even bothering to breathe anymore? And how?

As if he can see my thoughts scrolling above my head, Death grimaces. "Force of habit," he explains with a careless wave of his hand. Then he stands and walks back around to his side of the desk, rubbing his jawline thoughtfully.

"Let me break it down for you, Daisy."

"Break it down?" I raise an eyebrow quizzically.

He doesn't seem to notice my little interruption, though. Instead, he shuffles his papers and adjusts his collar. "An admin mix-up has meant that the major life event which was meant to leave you with severe concussion has left you dead instead. Do you see my problem?"

I shake my head. Honesty is most definitely the best policy in this situation, even if it causes Death to rub small, irritated circles around his temples before going on.

"You can't go onward because you're not due yet. You can't go back to your life because you've seen too much. The cutoff time for when a dead person can return to their body is during the whiteout—that bit when all you saw is white," he clarifies, as clearly my expression of bemusement gets too severe, before continuing. "Somehow, some cretin allowed you to wander up here without checking your status in the system. And now, Miss Cooper, you're stuck in the middle: you cannot go forward, and you cannot go back."

I stare. What else can I do? He's spoken to me as if I understand the intricate workings of postlife, when, funnily enough, it's not my area of expertise. From the way he's tapping his fingers rhythmically against the desk, I think I'm meant to respond.

"I…" I begin, and then trail off again. "Sir, uh… Mr. Death—"

"It's just Death."

"Right. Uh…if I can't go forward, and you don't want to let me back, where the hell am I meant to go?"

He shrugs a little. "You don't go anywhere. Not until you're due. You're stuck in the middle, in Administration, as we call it, until your time comes. In sixty-nine years, according to your file." His phone goes off, the mobile only this time. Sighing, he stands and moves toward the door to the side. "Please, wait here. I've got to deal with this. Someone will find a solution, probably." He turns away without another word, already interested in his phone call. Before I can mutter what I think is meant to be a thank you, he's gone.

Suddenly, there's just silence. Total silence like I've never experienced before and it takes me a moment to work out why it feels quite so crushing. It's because, for the first time ever, I don't hear the distant sound of my heart beating. My body is frozen, stuck. Dead.

Sometimes realization hits you all at once like a car colliding into your side. Or a pavement hitting your head. Wham. All in one go, panic sets in. The silence is broken as a groaning sob escapes my mouth. I'm confused, because I didn't even know my body could make that sound. But it's a passing reflection because my mind is filled with one all-encompassing thought.

My life is over.

I've been working toward this imaginary future where my current slogging away at the bottom of the work rung would finally pay off. I'd get a job that actually seemed to have a point. Violet and I would visit New York together. Eric and I would make his flat our home. But now that future's gone. All I ever achieved was a moldy flat and a pointless graduate job. Shit.

It feels like someone's stabbed me in the stomach. I didn't think the dead could feel pain like this; surely that shouldn't be possible? And yet here I am. Crippled by the dreadful agony of realizing that I've just entered the past tense. Daisy Cooper *was.*

I find myself stumbling onto my feet. There's a sudden, desperate need to escape. Maybe somewhere around here is an exit back to my home, my life, my world. I run, straight out of the door behind me.

Before me is a corridor that stretches onward in a long straight line, seemingly endlessly. The walls are slightly off-white, the floors are slightly off-white and the lighting gives everything a slightly off-white quality. It feels like stepping into a blizzard and it certainly doesn't help with the feeling of dismay rising up my back. The more I stand in this utterly silent, utterly empty corridor, the more I feel like I need to scream. No! *Keep it together, Daisy.*

One foot moves in front of the other until, ever so slowly, I begin to walk. I have no idea where I'm going; there doesn't seem to be anywhere *to* go. This corridor is empty, and the few doors I pass are firmly shut and unmarked. Until suddenly I'm at a junction. There are two possible turnings and a crisp, clean sign on the wall. According to the sign, the left turn leads to "Fire, Alcoholism, and Poisoning" while the right turn leads to "Life."

Well, there's only one way to go from here, it seems. I stumble off to the right, where I'm met with a set of lift doors. So innocuous…there's even a little paper sign next to it with a scrawled message on it: "Please do not press the button more than once, it will break the mechanism!" The mundaneness of this somehow makes me feel even worse. There's a world up here with people and problems and I'm not ready to be a part of it.

The lift opens as I step toward it, which sort of figures. This whole place has a definite creepy vibe to it and automatic lift doors fit perfectly with that. Inside, I'm greeted by the rather unnerving sight of my reflection. Not usually unnerving, I should add. But when you've just been told you've died, all sorts of things start running through your mind.

My first instinct is to try and see the back of my head. I have this visceral, stomach-churning memory of the crack it made when it hit the pavement. I really don't want to spend what is shaping up to be a rather long time with a visual reminder of that. But, fortunately, I'm spared. With a bit of twisting and turning, I can see that the back of my head is just the usual mass of strawberry blonde hair. I can't help thinking that perhaps the afterlife should come with automatic detangling and antifrizzing...

My tight and rather uncomfortable dress from date night is gone, however, and in its place is a white dress that is loose enough to be comfortable but fitted enough to not look like a dustbin bag. In fact, it fits perfectly.

As I've been taking in my appearance, the lift doors have smoothly closed behind me. The rest of the lift walls are covered, floor to ceiling, with buttons. Small, circular white ones, like you'd find in any ordinary lift. Except these ones are devoid of any numbers, or any helpful markers at all. I get the sense that the lift hasn't started moving yet, probably because no buttons have been pressed, so I find myself pressing a random button near to my elbow. Immediately, the lift shudders beneath my feet, then begins to move downward in a smooth and steady motion. It continues like this for around twenty seconds then stops with a rather abrupt jolt that causes me to grab on to the nearby railing.

There's a moment of pause, then comes the ding, before the doors slide open.

It takes me less than a second to work out where I am. The faint smell of damp is unmistakable, along with the sight of a sunken blue sofa strewn with enough blankets to smother an army (if that was your chosen method of getting rid of said army). No doubt about it. I'm home.

Stumbling out of the lift, I let out a small sob of relief. Maybe I'm going to be OK. Because now I'm back in my flat, nothing will take me away from it.

I hear footsteps behind me and I turn, grinning at the sight of my best friend. Violet is now swathed in her gray fluffy dressing gown, dark curls peeking out from beneath the hood. Her eyes are glued to her phone, the light from it casting an ethereal glow over her dark skin as she wanders across the weird linoleum tiles that cover our entire flat. I'm about to say her name, preparing to give her the fright of her life then tell her about my crazy trip to get milk. But then she looks up. And she looks right through me.

Rule Three

Love Has Its Downsides

LET'S TALK ABOUT LOVE. *I'll be honest with you, it's not something I completely understand. Why would I? Nobody loves death. Even those who think they want me to arrive don't welcome me with the sort of song and dance you see between reunited couples across the world.*

Don't get me wrong, I'm not jealous. Do you know what love is? It's vulnerability. And it is completely illogical when you really think about it. Why would you ever allow someone to become such an integral part of your world when you can guarantee them leaving it, one way or another?

I know what you're thinking. You're thinking that I must have never experienced love and that's why I'm so against it. And maybe I haven't. But that doesn't mean I haven't witnessed it, and the way it can so easily destroy you.

I once visited on the morning of a wedding.

I stood in the corner and watched as the bride meticulously zipped up her glittering white dress, hands fumbling as dizzy excitement stole her dexterity. I watched her soft smile as she took hold of her carefully chosen bouquet, kissed her father on his cheek as they left for the church. And then I watched their car skid right off the road.

I tried to avoid the aftermath, tried not to notice the arrival of her husband-to-be. But some sounds, like the desperate wails of grief, even I cannot ignore.

See? Love is for fools. For every heart swoop, every glimmer of joy, there's an ugly, gnarled and twisted downside. I've had to rip the hands of lovers apart, I've been forced to tug the foundations away from families, I've sat and watched that blasted love blossom, knowing that it's blossoming below an unstoppable ticking clock.

So, in conclusion, I'd advise you to go nowhere near it. Let somebody else have their heart broken. Steer well clear.

❋ ❋ ❋

Have you ever had someone completely ignore you? Pissed off somebody and they've taken the childish route of dismissing your existence. Or you've been at a party where everyone else knows someone and you're stuck in the middle, waiting desperately for your one friend to return from the toilets and speak to you so you can reassure yourself that you do indeed exist.

But that's not really being ignored. No matter how much somebody tries, they can never completely ignore you. Not when you're still a visible living being interacting with the same world as they are. In order to know what it's like to be properly disregarded, with absolutely no acknowledgment of your existence, you'd have to be good and dead. Except I don't recommend that—because it is a truly painful and heartbreaking experience. Especially when the person ignoring you is your best friend.

As I'm standing there, feeling like someone has punched me in the gut with a concrete glove, she's merrily gathering the supplies together for tea. She's still waiting for the milk I went to get her. She doesn't know; she has no idea that her best friend has just been ripped from her life.

Then there's a knock at the door. That weird tinny sound of someone's knuckle against the glass because we never bothered to get a proper knocker. Violet pauses, glancing back toward it. And I can almost see her thoughts scrolling above her head, like subtitles. She's thinking that I must have forgotten my key. She's thinking that it's about time I'm back because it's been a while. She's thinking that we live in an all right area but you can never be too careful, not at this time of night.

Another knock. Then: "Uh... Violet?" A somewhat familiar voice who knows Violet's name and that's enough to convince her. She steps forward and tugs open the door, with the usual amount of force required to pull it from its slightly warped frame.

It's the young woman who lives across the road from us, the one with the three kids and the postman husband. She's wrapped in her thick coat, expression stricken. Foreboding grips at the back of my neck, like icy fingers digging into my skin. Here it comes.

Violet blinks. I watch the way her fingers hold the door a little tighter, hear the wood creak. "Um, hi?" she begins, and all of a sudden she seems so small, so young.

The neighbor shifts, adjusts her coat. "Violet... I—I was just going to get some cat food, we'd run out...and, um, I thought you should know..."

She's not saying it right, she's not making sense. That's all I can think. I need this to be done properly, and I don't care if she's finding it difficult because this is Violet and I need her to get through this. And this woman won't know that Violet hates any sort of suspense and that she needs clear information, and I know I could do this so much fucking better than her.

If Violet would just look at me.

Her eyes crinkle into a bemused squint. "Uh,…? What? What should I know?"

The neighbor, Nina her name is, bites down on her lip before stepping away a little. "Your friend Daisy, She—she's had a fall."

I can see Violet's shoulders stiffen, like someone has injected cement into her veins. Does she know, instinctively, that this is it? Or does she think that there's just a few broken bones, a concussion? "What?" she replies. "Is she OK? Where is she? What happened?" The questions tumble thick and fast from her mouth, causing Nina to grip her coat tighter around herself, a makeshift shield of sorts.

Hesitantly, she gestures for Violet to follow her. "I—I called an ambulance, it's just arrived. I think she fell awkwardly…" She trails off, glancing back to Violet as she reaches the top of our steps and moves back onto the street.

"Awkwardly? What does that mean?" she demands.

Nina shakes her head, gently beckons her up the last few steps before leading the way toward the corner shop. Down at the other end of the street, by the bus stop, an ambulance is parked. In the intermittent flashes of blue, I catch a glimpse of a shadowy form sprawled on the pavement.

Violet starts running, then. I want to stop her, in case *she* slips as well. Though at least I wouldn't be alone anymore.

I shake that unpleasant thought from my head before it can get too comfortable.

"DAISY?" Her yell cracks through the air like lightning. I half expect the houses to crumble at the sound, or the trees to topple down around us.

I don't want to go any farther. I don't want to see the scene of my own death. But I can't leave her on her own, not Violet. I made sure she wasn't alone at her most recent dentist appointment, for fuck's sake. I can't leave her now.

And there it is. My body. Crumpled on the pavement, a small pool of blood staining the ice around my head. It's brutally real and I feel something inside twist, cruel and painful. We run around, thinking we're going to make our mark on the universe, but really, all we are is this: a body with a finite end that can so easily become an empty shell, an abandoned doll.

Violet has skidded to a halt, staring as a paramedic begins to work on trying to revive my body. I feel like screaming at them, to warn them how pointless their attempts are. Especially when I can see Violet's shoulders hitching up by her ears, just like they do when she's waiting to hear back about an audition. She's hopeful, she still thinks I'm coming back. She's still hoping for a miracle. But I don't want her to get her hopes up, not when they've got so far to fall.

The paramedic sits back, takes my pulse. As if it isn't already obvious that there's nothing to be done. She looks up a moment later.

"I'm sorry—she's gone."

Violet's shoulders crash back down and I hear her voice tremble as she finally manages to speak: "What the hell are you talking about?"

"I'm sorry," the paramedic says again. "We can't revive her...there's nothing we can do. She's gone."

It only takes a second for Violet's legs to give out from beneath her. For her to drop to the freezing ground.

"Woah, woah it's OK, sweetheart." The paramedic sounds so kind, but I know that Violet hates that term of endearment because it's what her father always called her.

"OK?" she snaps. "OK? My best friend is *dead*!" she yells,

and that seems to trigger some further realization in her. "Oh my God, my best friend is dead!" Her head drops down to her knees, her curls seeming to cocoon her, protecting her from the world. But I can still hear her desperate, broken cries. I think the whole street can hear them.

I find myself stumbling forward, coming to kneel beside her trembling form. "I—I'm sorry, Vi! I'm so sorry…"

But we've become two parallel lines and there's no chance of us interacting, not anymore.

Violet's head swoops up. I think, for a desperate second, that maybe, somehow, she can feel me there, but she continues to ignore me, as she looks across to the paramedic. "What do I do? I don't know what to do? I'm sorry, I don't know what to do."

The paramedic hesitates, then gently helps her up. "We'll take you to the hospital. Do you have the numbers for her parents?"

Violet nods mutely. She's starting to go a little blank, like a computer crashing. I know that look; I know that it doesn't bode well for her mental well-being at all. But I'm helpless, invisible. Stuck. All I can do is trail after her. Violet takes each step slowly, cautiously. She leans on the paramedic like a crutch, hitched sobs escaping from her mouth. Each one feels like someone's sticking a pin into my heart.

I try to block them out. I glance back down our street. That blissful quiet and darkness I remember is gone. All because of me. The houses look like some strange art installation, with the blue lights of the ambulance flashing on them, over and over. People are peering out of windows, some are on the steps, all of them watching with that sick fascination that everyone has, rubbernecking car accidents because we find some sense of safety in knowing that, this time, we were the lucky ones. Except now it's they, not we.

I can see the ambulance, doors open and one other paramedic inside. He hops up, moves to help Violet sit down in the ambulance before helping his colleague lift the gurney down onto the street. Violet stumbles as if her legs have gone to jelly, pressing a hand to her face as she practically howls with grief.

This is the problem with loving someone so dearly. It will break you when they're gone.

I can't be in this chaotic street anymore. Everything's too bright, too loud, like the very edges of the world are starting to press closer and closer. I have to get out. Now.

But as I hurry down the street and back into the flat, I'm horrified to find that the lift that inexplicably transported me here has now, equally inexplicably, disappeared.

"No, no, no! Come *on*!" I rush forward, my fingers floundering through thin air, desperately searching for a button, a door, anything. "PLEASE!"

"Over here."

I turn toward the sudden and jarringly calm voice. There, ten paces to my left, is the lift. Somehow the walls of it seem to seamlessly blend into the very fabric of the world. No wonder I couldn't find it. Without the opened doors, there's no hint of it being there. But the doors are opened now. And Death stands there, framed by the warm glow of the lift's single light. His expression is inscrutable but then he sighs, taking in the surroundings somewhat wearily, as if this is all a great inconvenience to him. Then he steps to one side, gesturing inward.

"Come on. I think you've seen enough."

Perhaps too quickly, I comply. Maybe later I'll regret how quickly and easily I step away from my flat and my life. But right now it feels so hostile, so unwelcoming.

I step into the lift, and I don't look back. Not until the doors have swooshed shut behind me.

I can feel Death staring at me as heavy tears roll down my face. I can also feel myself bristling under it, preparing myself for a barrage of platitudes about this being a blessing in disguise or whatever crap he's going to come out with.

But his first words, a long few seconds later, are not quite what I expect.

"Soooo—there's no need to warn you about visiting your relatives now."

I stare for a moment, then manage to find my voice again. "What?"

He gestures around the small space, though he keeps his eyes on me. Like he's expecting me to combust if he doesn't keep a close watch. "Going in the lift. Down to your relatives. Not a good idea."

"I—I'm dead." The words slip out of my mouth in a weak, croaking imitation of my usual voice.

Death blinks. "I did explain that already."

"What?"

Death sighs, fiddles with the buttons on his shirtsleeves. "I told you that you were dead. Remember?"

I'm flabbergasted. "It's not... I didn't mean..." I grit my teeth, trying to get my thoughts straight. It's not like me to be unable to get a good rebuttal out when necessary. "I know you told me, but funnily enough it's not something that I can get my head around just like that."

"Oh."

I stare at him, as he looks away and toward the doors with an air of complete disinterest. "Oh?" I echo. "That's it?"

"Yes. That's it. What else did you expect?"

The lift doors ding, then slide open. We're back in that off-white corridor, but I make no move to leave the lift just yet.

"I expected you to have some understanding of what dying does to someone's head."

"Well, in your case, I know quite well what death did to your head!" A small grin slides up his face as he gestures to the back of his own head with an unpleasant cracking sound coming from his mouth. Clearly he's rather pleased with his little pun. I, on the other hand, am not.

"Is that supposed to be funny?"

He shrugs. "I found it funny." Then he gestures one hand out of the lift, a silent invitation for me to get out of it. But I still don't move.

"They were going to ring my parents." The words leave my mouth all of a sudden and without much warning.

"That is the general procedure, yes."

His coldness feels like a slap in the face. I force myself to push on. "I want to be with them. I *need* to be with them."

"Why? They can't see you, you know."

"That's not the point."

Death looks at me for a long moment. "Did you not hear me before? About seeing relatives? Do you really think that's something you want to do again?" he asks, though he doesn't sound as if he's particularly interested in the response.

"It doesn't matter. It's not about me seeing it. I need to be there with them." It alarms me that this man in charge of our mortality seems to have no idea what we as humans are actually like.

His eyes narrow, then he checks his watch. Silently calculating whether my parents' grief will fit into his schedule. Finally he looks up again, meets my gaze. "You can have ten minutes. That should be enough, right?"

I watch as he steps back into the lift and turns away, apparently not that interested in my response. His fingers skim expertly over the dozens of buttons until he selects one and presses it gently, almost respectfully. Then he looks back to me, hands returning to his pockets. "Done," he says simply.

The lift shudders as the button lights up. Then I feel that familiar falling sensation as the doors close and we're dragged back down to the world once more.

Rule Four

Some Things Should Never Be Seen

I ONCE WATCHED A woman give birth.

I should mention that I wasn't there for a death. I mean, I could have been; these things can happen and unrelentingly do. But not this time. My schedule was kind to me this day and let me see the beginning of a life instead of forcing me to end one.

Someone in animal-related deaths requested it; their granddaughter was having a child and they wondered if I could escort them to see the moment the child was born. Apparently I was having a soft moment because I said yes and, the next thing I know, I'm in a maternity ward, seeing something no person should ever see. Honestly, someone needs to have a good think about the biological process behind childbirth, because that seems unnecessarily gruesome.

Anyway, this is all a somewhat long-winded way of me telling you that, in life (and death) there are some things we should never see. The business end of childbirth being one. Your own dead body is another.

The list goes on, of course, but perhaps one of the most important *moments to avoid ever witnessing is the moment when a person's sleep is interrupted by an unpleasant, unwelcome phone call. When the peace is shattered and they're dragged out of their dreams to answer it. When they're greeted with an unfamiliar voice saying a sentence that doesn't make sense at first. Until their brain catches up.*

Some things should never be seen, because once you've seen it you will never be able to unsee it.

The moment a heart breaks, for example.

❋ ❋ ❋

The lift spits us right out into the upstairs landing of my parents' house.

It's been more than a month since I last came home. Why did I leave it so long? Why didn't I somehow guess that time was short?

I kept saying I'd come back for a weekend. But it's an hour train journey out of the city, work had been so busy, and they both get funny about coming into town. Mum grew up less than ten miles away from where she lives now (in the deep, dark hole of suburbia) and Dad came down from a tiny village up north, so neither were particularly equipped for coping with prolonged time in London. I'd said I would finally come home at the end of the month whatever happened with work, and force Violet to see her mum at the same time. But that's off the cards now.

As I step from the lift and onto the overly plush carpet of my home, I glance briefly back at the lift. The impossibleness of this particular mode of transport is making my head hurt; how can only a couple of hundred buttons take you to such specific places? Where does it actually go in between? So many questions, though I suspect my brain is generating these as some strange form of self-preservation.

Of course, Death steps from the lift like he's stepping off a bus, though I guess this is his usual mode of transport. He's probably despairing of me the same way I do with the tourists who stand and gawp at the Tube.

The landing is silent, dark. I squint through the gloom and spot the clock that hangs by the bathroom door. Just past midnight. My parents would have been asleep for a good hour by now. About the time I've been dead for.

Suddenly, the silence is shattered by the merry trill of the house phone. It makes me jump, which in turns makes me feel a little sheepish. I'm expecting to feel the back of my neck heating up like it always does when I get embarrassed. But there's nothing.

"Well, come on. You'll miss it at this rate." Death doesn't sound impatient or irritated, just a little bored.

"Oh…right," I reply, trying my best not to lose my temper with him. I don't know how long I'm going to be stuck with him so best not burn any bridges just yet. I stumble forward, hesitate at the door to my parents' room as the phone continues to ring, and I begin to hear the gentle sounds of movement inside. "Won't they notice their door opening and closing on its own?" I whisper.

Death shakes his head. "I've been doing this for thousands of years, Miss Cooper—trust me, they won't notice. It's just not on their radar." He steps around me, opens the door and then gestures me inside.

A second after I've crossed the threshold, perhaps a second too late, I wonder if this is maybe a bad idea. If perhaps there are some things you shouldn't witness.

But there's no going back now. A scene is beginning to unfold before me that I cannot rip my eyes away from.

Dad's answered the phone, of course he has, because Mum will sleep through an earthquake, or at least stubbornly pretend she's sleeping through it. Clearly her curiosity has got the best of her now, though, because she has opened her eyes and rolled toward Dad. I want to scream at her to turn over and go right back to sleep. I want to snatch the phone from Dad's hand and throw it against the wall. Let them have tonight, just one more night of normality.

But, of course, I can't do any of that. I can only watch as Dad places the phone to his ear, settles back against the pillow and fumbles around for his glasses. "Hello?" His voice is husky with sleep. "Violet? Slow down."

That's got Mum up. She heaves herself up to sit beside her husband, brow furrowed and eyes immediately sharp. "Is she OK?" she whispers, and it's impossible to tell if she's asking about Violet's welfare or my own. Mum used to joke that we were interchangeable in her eyes. It always made me strangely proud when she said that.

Dad doesn't answer, staring straight ahead. From my spot by the door, I can hear the faint, garbled voice of Violet. She's still speaking at top speed and I can't work out what she's saying, exactly. I can guess though, of course.

Since Violet's started talking, it's like someone has begun to drain the color out of Dad's face. He becomes almost unrecognizable. At least he's hearing it from Violet and not some police officer going through a procedure, I tell myself. As if that might make it better.

He stays like this for a minute or so, asking a few general, clarifying questions but mainly just listening. I wonder if Mum can tell what's happened already, if she's noticed the way his grip has tightened around the phone.

"OK," he says finally. "OK, Violet, we'll see you soon— I've got to go. It's going to be OK, sweetheart."

He hangs up, turns to Mum.

"What's going on?" she asks.

"Something's happened."

"With Violet?" Mum's question doesn't surprise me; Violet has had her own trials over the years that have inevitably spilled into my family's life too. It hasn't been the first time Violet has phoned my parents in a panic. Her own parents don't really cut it, what with her father being distinctly absent and her mother being like a red flag to a bull with Violet. So Mum doesn't sound particularly worried. Yet.

"It's Daisy, love. Something's happened to Daisy. She's had a fall." As Dad's words leave his mouth, I find myself backing right up against the wall in the vain hope of going right through it and escaping this dreadful scene.

"Can we go?" I hiss across to Death, trying desperately to ignore the scene now playing out in front of me. "I—I can't do this."

Death raises an eyebrow. "I did warn you," he mutters, glancing back over as Mum stumbles out of bed and rushes for the wardrobe.

"Please!" I snap, a little louder this time. I can hear snatches of Dad's words across the room, no matter how hard I try to block them out. Something about keeping calm and needing to get to the hospital. He comments how it's not looking good and I can't decide if I want to scream or laugh. *Of course it's not fucking looking good.*

As Death is begrudgingly stepping back to let me out of the room, I hear Mum slam the wardrobe shut. I can't help it; I look back.

"What do you mean, it's not looking good?" she breathes. Dad crosses the space between them, pulls her into a hug. But Mum is having none of it, wriggling free with an almost growl. "Gary! Tell me what the hell is going on!"

"Claire, I don't know. Violet just said Daisy has had a fall. And it's not looking good." Dad's voice is steady right up until the last word. I hear it shake, even from my spot on the other side of the room. He draws in a breath, pulling himself back together. "We need to go."

Mum's shoulders tremble as she pulls on a sweater, tugs it over herself. A protective layer against a new reality that she's not ready for. "My girl…" she whispers.

"I'm here," I find myself whispering back. "I'm here, it's OK."

A clearing of the throat from my companion. "I mean, you're not really…" It's a quiet mutter, like he knows he shouldn't say it but just can't help himself. It's enough for me to be able to drag my gaze away from my crumbling parents, just so I can glare at the cause of this unwanted interruption.

Death shrugs, looks a little awkward. "Just stating the facts. It's a different world, despite appearances. Weren't we leaving?"

Mum has dropped back to sit on the bed. The reality of the situation has caught up with her it seems, stealing her ability to stand in the meantime. Her head drops down to her knees and she lets out a strangled, fragmented sob. I've never heard her make a sound anything like that before. My head snaps back to Death. "Leaving…yes," I croak, my feet tripping over each other a little as I make for the door. Shame settles on my shoulders like a winter's chill but something won't allow me to stay. Call it instinct.

By the time we're stepping back into the lift, Mum's crying has stepped up. It sounds like someone's stamping on her heart. Who knew there was a sound for that? Who knew a human being could make a noise that hurt so much to hear? I squeeze my eyes shut, resist the urge to press my hands to my ears because I should hear this. I owe them some attention, if just for a few more seconds.

Then the doors whoosh shut and, just like that, complete silence settles over us, like snowfall.

We're joined by the hum of the lift's mechanics starting up a second later. So ordinary... I could be in the lift at work, nursing my thermos of tea and trying not to think about the infuriating day ahead. But I'm not. I'll never go in that lift again. I'll never have the satisfaction of opening a thermos of tea and feeling the steam rush onto my face. And I'll never enjoy those snatched moments of texting my mum while waiting for the lift to reach my floor. It's all gone.

I give myself ten seconds. I count them out, slow and careful, as if that might somehow help. It doesn't. That scene seems to have become permanently imprinted on my eyes, stuck in a loop. Guilt looms over me, heavy and cruel.

Finally, after those ten seconds, I open my eyes. I can still feel my body shaking. "Maybe—maybe I shouldn't have seen that."

Death makes a thoughtful noise. He's watching me from the other side of the lift, a little warily. Maybe he thinks I'm going to start crying again. Not a completely ridiculous notion, it has to be said. "Maybe," he says finally. He glances at his watch again. "But on the bright side, we were only gone seven minutes. So no harm done."

"No harm done?" My voice is so cold it feels like it might freeze my tongue. "Are you serious?"

He nods. "I usually am. It sort of goes with the job description." There's a small glint lingering in the corner of his eye. Almost like he's inviting me to keep fighting back.

At that moment the lift rumbles to a stop and the doors slide open. Then we're swiftly greeted with the sound of an outraged gasp coming from the corridor beyond.

I turn. An older woman is standing there, arms crossed with a fierce glare on her face. She's dressed in white like me, though instead of a white dress she wears a rather severe-looking white suit. Her hair is pulled into a tight and severe-looking bun that matches the severe expression on her face.

"Death! What the hell are you doing? I've been looking everywhere for you."

I glance over to the man now dealing with two furious people. "Well, I'm honored," he states. Then he glances back to me. "This is Natasha, my head of Admin. She keeps everything running smoothly and makes sure nobody's having too much fun," he explains, before turning his full attention to this new arrival. "Natasha, I hope you're going to be polite to Daisy. She's had a very stressful day." He moves to inch around Natasha, rather pointedly giving her a wide berth. To avoid being stuck inside the lift, I reluctantly follow him.

Natasha places her hands on her hips, lips pursed. "What *are* you talking about? You were due in Moscow ten minutes ago and yet here you are, conversing with a human who…" She pauses, looking me up and down. Then a glitter of realization sparks in her eyes, followed by a little grin. "Oh dear, did you screw up again?" she asks, her tone at a perfect level of condescending. Beside me, I see Death stiffen.

Natasha seems to take rather a lot of joy from this, throwing back her head and crowing her laughter to the ceiling. "Oh, this is just brilliant! Maybe you'll be fired at last!" she exclaims a moment later.

Death crosses his arms. "I did not screw up, as you so delicately put it. I chose her."

"Chose her?"

"Yes. I chose Daisy from the millions I see to be my personal assistant."

"What?" I splutter.

"You heard, come on," he says through gritted teeth, taking me by the forearm and tugging me away from the lift.

Natasha doesn't give up that easily, though, and is chasing after us immediately.

She follows us around the corner and then down the corridor, bouncing questions off our backs: "How is she your assistant? What makes *her* so special? Have you asked if it's OK? Did you get permission?" Suddenly, we're back at Death's door.

Pushing down on the handle and swinging the door open, Death propels me inside, one hand on the small of my back. Then he turns around to face Natasha as she brings her stream of questions to a halting end: "You can't shut me out, Death! Everyone needs to be accounted for!"

"Quite right, Natasha. But now, we're closed." The door clatters shut and he turns the lock.

All of a sudden it's silent. Death turns to face me, expression back to what seems to be standard for him: generally uninterested.

"She's…nice," I finally comment, because the silence is starting to be replaced with my mother's cries, ringing in my ears.

Death sniffs. "Natasha was knocked over by her own car when she left the handbrake off," he says, in apparently a way of an explanation.

I raise an eyebrow, meeting his gaze stonily. I've not quite forgiven him for his recent comments in the lift. "That killed her?"

Death winks. "She was by a wall. Natasha sandwich."

"Did she die at the wrong time too? Is that why she's stuck here?"

"Oh. No. It's a big team here. Me and then a hundred others in different departments. You know—murders, traffic accidents… There's even a team who decide which near-death experiences will end with death after all. But they can move on when they want to. You can never have enough help up here, so I tend to keep an eye out for people with the right skills. Natasha's been here about fifty years. She had spent her life working as a receptionist so I thought she'd be a good bet to replace my previous head of Admin."

"Do you pay her?"

Death blinks, considers this for a moment. "No. What would I pay her with? It's not like she needs to pay rent. Besides, for most people the opportunity to delay the inevitable..." He pauses to gesture at the door behind his desk. "... is pay enough."

It's probably the longest time Death's spent talking since we met. I just wish I knew what to say to any of it.

The phone on his desk rings. He ignores it at first, eyes still fixed curiously on me. But then the mobile phone starts ringing as well. He pulls it from his pocket and answers it, after he's sent the device a scathing glare. "Yup? Yes, going now. No, really I am... I will. Bye." He hangs up, and casts his gaze back to me.

Then he asks his next question: "So...do you fancy it?"

Rule Five

Pain Has A Right To Be Felt

THE CRUELEST TRICK THE Universe ever pulled was giving you free rein of your emotions. It opened up a whole can of worms, in my honest opinion. You weren't ready for that sort of freedom. And so you all end up finding the smallest things to worry about and then letting your brain go into meltdown mode: no sleep, no appetite, no ability to stop and just think for a minute. It makes no evolutionary sense to let you get yourselves into such ridiculous states. And yet, here you all are, panicking at the drop of the hat, as if the fact that your train's been canceled is cause for complete and utter despair.

And now who has to deal with that mess? Me, that's who. Because, funnily enough, death can be pretty anxiety-inducing. I suppose, if I was being charitable, I could accept this as being reasonable. But reasonable or not, it causes me a huge amount of difficulty when it comes to bringing you up here.

I know, you have a right to your emotions, your pain. They're what make you human, or whatever. But trust me, a guy who has witnessed a lot of death: feelings are overrated.

✳ ✳ ✳

There are those moments, you know the ones, where the air seems to spark with anticipation. Where the entire universe seems to hold its breath and wait. When he asks her to marry her, when she's seconds away from winning a world record, when the bomb is about to go off. We've all felt it, felt the laws of nature suspend themselves in respect of a moment that demands attention.

And here, in this bland office, I can feel it. Time frozen, poised in expectation of my answer to Death's question. *Do you fancy it*, like he's asking if I'll go down to the store for a packet of potato chips.

"Really?" You can't blame me for being skeptical: the role of Death's assistant doesn't sound entirely appealing, especially when Death has shown, at best, ambivalence toward me so far. Like a moth on his windowsill.

Death shrugs, hands resting loosely in his back pockets. "I mean, it's not like there's anything else for you to do."

"Am I... I mean, I'm not sure I'm completely qualified..."

Another shrug. "You seem somewhat intelligent; I'm sure you'll manage."

Somewhat intelligent? Nice. Good to know all that hard work to get top grades in school and university has really paid off.

He hasn't exactly sold it to me. And there's a million and one questions raging around my head, unsurprisingly.

However, Death doesn't seem interested in giving me an appropriate amount of time to mull things over. One foot taps against the floor, and he flips his phone over and over in his hand. If that wasn't an obvious enough sign of impatience, a moment later he gestures to the door and says, "Shall we?"

"Shall we what?"

"You're my assistant, I'm Death, someone's dead—see how this works?"

No, no I don't see how this works. But, despite the fog of confusion filling my head, one question comes out before I can think about it properly. "You said before about departments...so you don't go to every death?" Death tilts his head, examining me with almost scientific curiosity.

"No," he says finally. "No, I couldn't go to them all. I'd have to be in countless places at once. Most of you don't get the pleasure of my company. You just get one of the other chaperones." He pauses, and there's a flash of something across his face. Almost sadness, but it's gone before I can get a proper look. "I just go to the unfair ones."

Maybe it's this moment of seeing Death display something other than cold indifference and sarcasm that brings a decision out of me. Or maybe dying has made me lose all sense. Either way, against my better judgment, I find myself nodding. "Fine, OK. I'll—I'll give it a go."

Death nods, then breezes past me. "Good. Come on then, we'll be late. You lot don't really wait around when it comes to snuffing it."

With that charming remark, he's back out the door again and, without much of an alternative, I find myself hurrying after him. He heads confidently for the lift, looking at the screen of his phone with a thoughtful expression. "Jennifer Montgomery," he reads out, though he doesn't look back at me so I'm not sure if this is for my benefit or just something he always does. "Fourth victim of a killing spree—oh look, England. That will be nice for you."

I'm not sure what to say to this. What do you say to somebody who thinks it will be nice for you to visit a murder in your home country? "So...you visit the unfair ones. That must mean quite a lot of murders?"

Death shrugs. "Some don't quite qualify. It's a complicated system." He shoots me a searching look then, clearly trying to decide if he thinks I could possibly keep up with such a system. It's the sort of look that sets my teeth on edge, because I've been dealing with those looks at work since I started there. As if the fact that I'm generally quiet and, God forbid, a woman, meant I couldn't handle a simple budget sheet.

"Jennifer lives in a shitty part of a shitty town, has very little prospects and doesn't get on with her family," Death goes on, unaware of the irritation he's caused me. "If she'd died a month ago I wouldn't have been giving her my time. But, according to this," he pauses to wave his phone as he comes to a halt by the lift before continuing, "she's just met a guy who could be her ticket up and out. If she wasn't about to die, this would probably be a positive turning point in her life. But no such luck. Ergo, she's my business."

His careless attitude is rather difficult to hear. He's talking about a young woman who is about to be tragically murdered, not just a trying pile of paperwork. Clearly my thoughts show on my face because, as we step into the lift, I can feel him watching me carefully. But if he wants some sort of understanding from me, he's not going to get any.

"Just like that," I finally say, and there's a definite edge to my voice.

This edge seems to bounce right off Death, though. He just gives me a brisk nod of confirmation. "Just like that." We fall into silence for a moment, as the doors close and the lift thrums into life. Then Death holds up three fingers. "There are three categories of death that I visit. You ready for these?" He gives me a half second to nod, then goes on.

"One: your death causes a child to be left without a parent or significant guardian. Two: your death happens right before your life was about to significantly change for the better.

Three: you're a wholly innocent person and you're killed by someone else—that last one is the rarest. You don't get many truly innocent people these days."

Apparently satisfied, he turns away. But I'm nowhere near finished. "That's—that's it?" I splutter. "That's your complicated system?"

Death shrugs, then holds up a hand to bring this conversation to a definitive halt. "We're getting close and there are some things I should probably tell you." He turns and fixes me with an intense gaze. "Now, this is important: you're not to interfere. We are here to ferry her from her world to ours, not to stop or avenge her death. You stand back, you watch, and you do nothing."

"Nothing?" I echo. "What's the point of me being here, then?"

Death smooths his collar as the lift begins to slow down a little. "Undecided. Just follow the rules," he says simply, as the lift comes to a halt.

The night is dark, and the street we step onto is relatively quiet. A few passing cars, dark houses, a nearby park with stationary swings. But it's life. Ordinary and yet so fascinating when you're no longer a privileged member of the club. The little things draw me in: the glittering red of the rain-soaked car parked beside the road, the warmth of the lighting within a pub, the muted sound of a television in someone's house nearby.

Distantly, I feel my feet moving forward.

"Woah there." Death comes before me, his face stark in this vibrant, living world. His eyes meet mine, holding my gaze. "Life is like that kid offering pills at the party—you have to step back and ignore it, especially when it's early days for you. It can draw you in, and then you'd be lost forever down here."

I scowl. "Would that be so bad?" After all, I am from this world—unlike Death who clearly never belonged here.

He smiles bitterly, awkwardly pats my shoulders. "You are not one of this lot anymore, Daisy. You would be forever lost at a party which you weren't invited to."

"Sounds just like life," I mutter, before returning to the matter at hand. "So, where is she? Jennifer—where does she die?"

In response, Death takes my arm again and tugs me across the street. A bus draws up and a stick-thin girl stumbles from it. She looks underfed and exhausted. She secures a clutch bag in her armpit so that she can hitch up the dress she wears, dusting it down with a critical eye. Like she knows that it's not quite clean enough but can't do anything about it. Beside me, I hear Death check his watch again and I glance at him with a small scowl. "She's going to die, have some respect."

Death frowns. "What's her dying got to do with anything?" he asks, as if it simply does not make sense to him. I just shake my head, looking away. Now is not the time.

Jennifer is now leaning against the wall of the pub, one leg bent beneath her while she taps rapidly on her mobile phone. The faint smile on her face makes it clear who she is texting, and I can almost smell the fresh new love in the surrounding air.

But then a shadow dislodges from the pub wall, and a young man appears. He is totally average looking, except for a pair of piercingly cruel blue eyes that light up as they fall on Jennifer. For a moment, I wonder if this is the man Death mentioned, the one to turn her life around. Then I see the scornful look he receives from the girl, and I realize it's quite the opposite. She does not know him, but now she will probably never forget him.

Beside me, Death nudges my ribs. "Don't interfere," he reminds me, and I feel myself scowl as I notice that I've taken an instinctive step forward. I'm a perfectionist and it bothers me that I'm getting a reminder already. I force myself to step back again, as the man finally breaks the silence.

"Going anywhere special tonight, love?"

Jennifer laughs, cold and sharp. "Nowhere with you, sweetheart," she shoots back, quick as a whip.

This guy is undeterred, though. He laughs back, his own laugh a touch warmer than hers. Still determined to disarm her with charm. He steps forward, hands jammed in his pockets. "Aww, come on…"

But Jennifer is a girl of the real world, and she's not going to be so easily swayed. She glares, shoving her shoulder deftly into his side as she pushes past him. "Piss off," she calls back, sending a rude gesture his way. From where we stand, we can see this man's, this killer's, face. He smirks, and he twists his neck until it clicks eerily. Like the safety catch on a gun. Then he turns and walks after Jennifer.

I start after them, but Death catches me, squeezing my arm tight. I glance back at him, confused. "What?" I demand when he simply shakes his head.

"You don't want to see it. The cause of us being here. You don't want to see that." Death looks like he's trying to be helpful for once, but his words send another bristle of irritation through me. I tug my arm free and point a finger at him.

"No, I'm sure I don't. But I bet she doesn't want to see it either. Or feel it. No one does, but we have to. So if someone can be there at that moment, they should be, right?" Death says nothing. I roll my eyes, but then a screaming whistle pierces the air, so loud that I have to grip at my ears. I look around, certain that everyone will be out of here in a moment, because surely the whole world will have heard that. But there's nothing. No one comes.

"What—what is that?" I demand as Death walks past me.

"It does that."

"What does?" I hurry after him, my hands still clutching the side of my head even though the screaming, dreadful sound has stopped. It sounded like a kettle whistle when the water has reached boiling point, mixed with the wailing of a hungry baby. It makes me terribly afraid, and I don't know why. It hits me a moment later, makes me stumble to a halt. I've heard it before. As my head smacked into the ice-covered pavement in the dark, empty street where I died.

Death glances back, stops, then walks the short distance to stand before me. "It's life. When it leaves, it screams. It usually doesn't want to go." I open my mouth to say something back but he stops me with one raised hand. "No. No, Daisy. Whatever it is you're dying to say, it can wait. We can't miss her."

He barely spares me another glance as we round the corner into the pub's car park. And there she is, Jennifer Montgomery, the girl who was about to feel her life shifting beneath her feet, about to have fortune smile upon her weary face.

The girl who now lies in the puddles with her hands clutching at her throat. Blood spills between her fingers and she coughs, over and over. The culprit is already gone, blade in a back pocket as he strolls into the pub. I bet they'll never suspect him; not the young man with the twinkling eyes.

Death stands beside me and for once his face is devoid of anything mocking or joking. But there's also no sympathy. He is shadowy now, and so terribly blank.

"What do we do?" I whisper, and he looks to me with

some surprise, as if he has forgotten my existence entirely. It wouldn't surprise me.

"We can only wait."

It's possibly the worst thing he can say. I do not want to wait for the light to leave Jennifer's eyes, second by second.

Before Death can stop me, I have stepped over to her body, splashing through the rainwater that fails to soak my simple white plimsolls. "Daisy…" he begins, sounding almost weary. But I shoot him a glare as I tuck my feet beneath me and sit down at Jennifer's side. I have never experienced death before, except my own. And even that was so much cleaner, so much simpler. Other than that there's been nothing. My grandparents aren't dead yet. I had a fish but I was only five when it died, and I was told it had been sent on to a bigger tank. I believed my parents until thirteen-year-old me recounted the tale and my brother teased me mercilessly for about a week.

Silly old me. Somehow, I know what to do now though. I feel it within me, like the instinct to breathe. My hand reaches out and takes hers, tugs it away from her throat and holds it tight. She stares at her hand, tears clumping in her mascara eyelashes. Then she meets my gaze.

Terror rages through her eyes, in a way that I've seen only once before. When I held Violet's hand in the emergency room and waited for them to either pump her stomach or pronounce her a lost cause. I remember how she looked up at me, half-conscious, and all I saw in her eyes was fear.

It's the same now. It burns through the tears pooling in the corners of her eyes and almost seems to burn right through me. Distantly I feel her hand grip back, her fingers scrabbling for purchase. Maybe she thinks she can use me to hold on to life like this, and suddenly I'm filled with guilt for somehow misleading her.

"I can't help you, I'm sorry," I find myself whispering.

As if my words have had some sort of magic power, I feel her hand go slack in mine. I watch her eyes go blank, lose signal with the life within, then flutter shut. In other words, I witness the death of Jennifer Montgomery.

"Daisy." It's Death; I'd almost forgotten about him, which is ironic considering this is his big moment. "Are you done getting in the way?" Apparently he's not interested in an answer for this though, as he half nudges me out of the way a second later. "Honestly, it's like having a puppy," he mutters to himself, as he places one hand on Jennifer's forehead.

Deciding to let that comment slide for the moment, I shuffle back a little. "What are you doing?"

I get a grunt in return. With his hand now on her forehead, Death has closed his eyes and seems to be concentrating greatly, judging by the deep frown on his face. He doesn't reply for a moment, fully immersed in his task. Then his eyes snap open and he hops up, dusting off his jeans a little critically. "She'll be here soon," he states, apparently satisfied.

"What did you do, Death?" I demand, standing up as well.

"I guided her…well, you'd probably call it her soul. I guided her soul. The essence of her, the thing that makes her Jennifer. A bit like what makes you Daisy is apparently a busybody who can't keep her beak out of my business."

I cross my arms, shaking my head. "Why are you acting like me comforting her was so horrifying?" I demand, eyes narrowed.

"Because you're messing with emotions that you don't understand."

But before we can carry on, a voice speaks out from behind me. "Um, excuse me?"

Death and I turn. Standing beside a silver Ford Fiesta is Jennifer Montgomery, in a white dress very similar to mine.

Except hers is floor-length, floaty. It looks beautiful on her, but I can't help thinking that it won't be very practical as something to wear for eternity. Her spots are gone, her hair is shiny and even her skinny little wrists seemed to have gained some meat to them. It's like in death, she's gained a new lease of life. Except, as our silence continues, she grows increasingly anxious.

"Did—did you say his name was Death? Am I…am I dead?"

I hear Death heave a sigh and mutter something that sounds like "denial." "Yes, Miss Montgomery, I'm afraid you are dead. Let's talk away from here, shall we?"

"That's it?" I whisper across to him. "That's how you're going to break it to her?"

Indeed, Jennifer looks like the bottom has just dropped out of her world. "I'm *dead*?"

Death places a hand on her shoulder. "Yes. But no need to worry, you're in safe hands now." The moment his hand touches her shoulder, she seems to relax a little.

"Right…um, OK, OK." Death gives her an approving smile, already guiding her toward the lift. She stumbles a little, legs seeming a little shaky.

Something doesn't quite sit right with me, and I tug Death back a little.

"What's going on?" I demand in a hushed voice. "Why is she so calm? Shouldn't she be freaking out?"

"And delay my schedule? I don't think so. There's this little trick I have. It's like a—a magic touch, just to calm them down."

"You mean, like sedating them?"

Death gives a little shrug, already turning away. "I guess."

"Take it off."

"What?"

"Reverse it, whatever. I don't care how. It's not right. You need to let her feel her own damn death!"

I can practically see the cogs whirring away in his mind. Then a sly smirk slides up his face. "Fine. You *clearly* know better after all." He tugs his arm free and moves to place a hand back on Jennifer's shoulder. "Sorry, Jennifer, where were we?"

It's like somebody has thrown a switch. Complete panic immediately takes over. "Please! You don't understand! He killed me! Oh my God, that man killed me!"

Death looks over to me. "Well, perhaps Daisy can help you."

I know a challenge when I hear it. I just wish I knew what to do. But if Death wants proof that the recently deceased don't need to be bloody bewitched, I will just have to show it to him. Somehow.

I offer Jennifer my hand. "It's going to be OK. You're safe now."

Jennifer immediately shoves me away. "I'm dead! That's the fucking *opposite* of safe! Don't you take me anywhere!"

"We have to, Jennifer. I'm sorry, but we've got to leave."

I might as well have told her to dye her hair pink, the good it's done. She shakes her head again, her whole body seeming to collapse into itself.

To stop her from simply falling over, I pull her into a hug. It's like hugging an earthquake. And she cries and cries, not listening to anything I've got to say to her.

All the while, Death leans against the door of the lift and watches, expression inscrutable.

After a good few minutes of this, I manage to hobble her into the lift. Jennifer seems to have become almost primal in her grief. And nothing that I can do seems to help.

I'm so lost in helping calm her down that I barely notice the lift moving, then stopping, until Death clears his throat.

"Jennifer," I try, as Death steps smartly back into the corridor then turns around to watch us. "Jennifer, it's time to move. We're here."

Jennifer shakes her head, sobs a little louder again. Death looks at his watch, then clasps his hands behind his back. I can feel time ticking away relentlessly. How many people die in a minute? How many people like Jennifer need fetching? How many people are we holding up?

He's watching me expectantly, as if he knows exactly what I'm thinking. Can't give up, not yet. I find the fingers that are clutching at my dress and pull them away. Miraculously, she releases her grip, lets me start to lead her down the corridor toward Death's door.

By the time we've made it to the office, Jennifer is a little calmer. But that doesn't stop me feeling the wasted time like a weight on my back. Death finally takes over, gestures to a filing cabinet behind his desk. "Her file will be in there, Daisy. Jennifer, please sit." His words are as wooden as his desk.

There's a bitter taste in my mouth as I drag myself around the desk and pull open the cabinet. I do it with more force than necessary, though, just so he knows I'm still not happy. I'm expecting rows and rows of files; I'm expecting the drawer to keep opening and opening like in a film I saw once. But it doesn't. Instead, it opens as far as my arm goes, and it's empty except for one gray file. Jennifer Montgomery is stamped across the top.

Death takes the file from me and sits himself down at the desk. "Right, Jennifer. Let's get this sorted out, shall we?"

Once Death has handled the paperwork and ushered a panic-stricken Jennifer through the official door, he turns to me, expression one of supreme frustration. "What the hell was that?" he asks and, despite his expression, his tone is eerily calm.

"Excuse me?"

"Do you realize how much time you've wasted now?"

For a moment, I can only stare at him. Outrage has stolen my voice, but not for long. Soon, I am stepping toward him, arms crossed defiantly across my chest. "At least I'm not robbing people of understanding their death, just so you get an easy ride!"

Death shakes his head slowly with disbelief, eyes hard. "She was traumatized, Daisy. Death is shit enough without having to be terrified about it. There's a time and a place and a dirty car park next to her still warm body was not Jennifer's place. These sort of things need careful handling." He slides his hands into his pockets, shifts a little. "Besides. There's not time. Don't pretend you weren't thinking it. I saw you. I saw you consider it."

"I don't know what you're talking about," I snap. It's a lie, of course, and I think he knows it, because he shakes his head, looking away.

"Next time I'll wear my cloak and bring my scythe, shall I? Would that make you happier?"

That does it for me. "Yes! Yes it would! At least then something would actually fit with my *bloody expectations!*"

I find myself pushing his chest with all my might. He hardly budges, a wall of inflexibility. Huh, just about sums him up, really. We're standing glowering at each other; two immovable forces that just won't stop colliding.

But then, after a few seconds of this silent fuming, the phone rings, and he moves to answer it. "Yes?" A pause then he nods, hangs up. "I'm overdue. You. Just. Stay. Up. Here." He takes a step toward the door, then turns back. "When I come back, we're finding a way to get you out of here. This isn't working."

And with that, he leaves. I'm left alone with those words hanging over me, unable to work out if I've just been offered a lifeline, or an execution.

Rule Six

Anger Has Its Uses

CAN I TELL YOU *a secret?*

You are allowed to be angry. Yes, really. People might see it as some terrible sin but those people tend to be the ones expressing their feelings in other, far more damaging ways. Like tweeting (honestly, just turn the computer off and have a good shout at your pillow or something).

Anger is an emotion that was once heralded. Anger has been used to fix famines, to cure diseases. Trust me when I say that smallpox would still be around if Edward Jenner hadn't got so pissed off with all the rashes and decided to do something about it. Vaccination made, disease eradicated. Solution found.

And yet we're not allowed to be angry anymore. It's dangerous, apparently. You should just dig a deep pit and pop all that rage in there, before anyone notices. Well, I'm here to say that such an idea is bordering on lunacy. Rage keeps us strong. Anger keeps us fighting.

Maybe you think I'm biased, because from the outside it looks like anger is a permanent resident in my psyche. But you're wrong.

In fact, for someone running an entirely unrewarding system, day in and day out, I'm not sure I'm quite angry enough.

✵ ✵ ✵

He's gone for about two hours. I think it's two hours, anyway. The clock on the wall has moved steadily around from four o'clock to six o'clock but I can't be sure that it is governed by the same structures of time that clocks back home are.

It feels long enough to be two hours, though, that's for sure. After a painful stretch of time sitting staring at the walls around me, I decided to give up waiting in his office. I could feel all sorts of big and scary thoughts tickling at the edge of my subconscious and I had no interest in opening up that particular can of worms.

So I wandered off. Out the side door and into those horribly blank corridors. There had to be something else, after all. Something other than Death's office, a lift and lines of locked doors. For a while it seemed as if that really was all there was, until finally I rounded a corner and found one door that was actually open.

Inside was a kitchen. The stark mundanity of it almost made me laugh. And perhaps that was why I decided to stay. Or perhaps it was just because it was a room that had more than one color present (if you can count beige as a color). All I know is I found myself sitting there for the next two hours, flicking through the pile of dusty and hefty recipe books on the table. Each one had a different name written in different handwriting and I couldn't help but wonder how they had ended up there. How had Otto Sundberg's book on *Quick and Easy Curries* ended up here, in an empty and lonely kitchen in the middle of a maze of deserted corridors?

But then *he* arrives. I don't know how he's managed to find me and I try not to think about it too much. Either he can somehow track me, or this place is made up of very limited rooms, and I'm not sure which one of those reasons is less appealing. He opens the door, pausing on the threshold as he looks at me idly turning the pages of the curry book. When I look up, he's got a rather surprised expression on his face.

"What are you doing?" he asks finally, sounding genuinely bemused.

I stare at him. Considering that last time I saw him, he was furious and talking about sending me away, this isn't quite the conversation starter I was expecting. "Um," I begin, before glancing down at the book in front of me, "I was just looking. While I waited."

Death comes forward so he's standing a little to my right. I sense that he's hanging back, giving me some space. "You know you don't need to eat anymore, right?"

"If I don't need to eat, why is there a kitchen? And recipe books?" I can't quite believe I'm going along with this bizarre conversation but if it stops us shouting at each other, then fine. The past few hours have washed away the blinding screen of my own anger and I'm painfully aware that neither of us handled things well earlier.

Death drops into a chair, picks at the edge of the table with fingernails still stained with spots of pen. "People missed eating. So I made a kitchen."

"So we can eat?"

He nods. "If you want to. You don't have to, obviously. But you can."

"Oh. Right."

An uneasy silence settles over us as both of us consider whether there's something else to say other than the somewhat difficult conversation we both know needs to happen. Finally, though, Death seems to buckle. Clearly he's not as comfortable in silence as I can be. "So. Earlier you seemed sort of...upset."

"Observant of you."

Death frowns, then his expression clears. "Oh, you're being sarcastic. I thought maybe you were giving me a compliment. I don't know, to clear the air or something."

"Not really my style," I admit, because it's true. Compliments aren't worth anything if they're not genuine, in my opinion.

Death makes a thoughtful noise. He's tugged a pen from his pocket and he slowly twirls it over his fingers. The pen lid taps against the table at the end of every twist. Like a ticking clock. "Why were you so upset? Did you know her? It wasn't in your file."

I stare, confused and a little suspicious because I can't quite work if he's joking or not. But his expression is entirely serious. "No. I didn't know her."

"So why did it matter so much?"

"Are you seriously asking me that?" I receive a slow nod, his eyes fixed on me intently. "Because it's really shit to die. And maybe you don't see that when you're dealing with it all the time. It's awful and scary and lonely. But that doesn't mean we shouldn't be allowed to feel it. It's when we don't feel things properly that the problems start."

Death's gaze sharpens even more. "Like Violet?" He shrugs at the surprised look I'm sure I'm now wearing. "In your file. She features. Heavily."

I look down at the table. Hearing her name hurts like a slap in the face. "I'm sure she does," I mutter eventually. "She never quite got the hang of feelings." I don't want to say any more, not to this man who doesn't understand the first thing about humans. He won't understand how depression grabbed a hold of my best friend's brain and twisted her emotions into terrifying, unmanageable monsters. How she would cry herself to sleep at night or, even more alarmingly, sit on the sofa and stare into space for hours. How, even now, I feel responsibility for her weighing down on me like a box of lead. So I move on, swiftly. "I'm just saying that I don't think it's your place to take the trauma of death away from people."

The pen has paused in its twirling. Death stares into space, the cogs whirring at top speed. Then his gaze snaps back on me. "Perhaps."

"Perhaps?"

"That's all you're getting. Don't push it." He watches me carefully for a moment, then carries on. "Do you want to go back, then?"

I'm starting to realize that Death doesn't really seem to understand the relative gravity of his different questions. He asks them all in the same, casual way, regardless of how earth-shattering they may be and then looks bewildered when I seem flummoxed by this.

"Back—back to Earth? How?"

Death stretches, a small smile appearing on his face at the prospect of being able to explain himself and, presumably, show off his cleverness. "I've been thinking about that, actually. You're not properly dead, see? It's not your proper time yet and you've not passed through the door yet. So *theoretically* you should be able to get back. If we do it properly."

"How? How do we do it properly?"

Death's grin suggests this is the right question. He hops up, beckoning me toward the door. Out of some sort of desperation, I follow him.

"Where are we going?"

"You're not going to be able to get back home from that kitchen."

I falter, pausing hesitantly in the corridor. "Wait! I—I don't think I can go back to my flat. Not yet…not until we're sure I can stay. I—I can't do that to her."

Death has stopped too and he turns back to me, badly hidden impatience in the crinkle of his brow. "We're not going back *there*, come on." He's one moment away from an eye roll, I can tell. But somehow he manages to restrain himself.

Somewhat reassured, I catch him up and we make the tiresome walk back through the corridors to the lift.

Death seems lost in his thoughts, until the doors close, and he finally seems to remember I'm there. "So, this is how we're going to do this," he begins, like we're planning a bank heist. "You're not fully dead, like I said before. This version of you here, standing in the lift, hasn't crossed through my door yet. That, plus the fact you arrived early, should work in your favor."

"Should?"

Death shrugs, eyes flicking away from me. "It's the best I've got."

I suppose I should be grateful that there's a chance at all, but my natural preference for order and organization does not approve of this vague, fingers-crossed attitude that Death is showing. Still, no time for that now. The lift has shuddered to a halt, signaling our arrival. I can't help but be a little apprehensive and I glance over to Death again. "Where are we?"

Death smiles maddeningly. A little kid hiding a secret that he's just dying to tell. I think he's quite enjoying himself. It's a little jarring, but it's a nice change from the blank-faced robot that took me to fetch Jennifer.

The doors open and we step out into the world once more. I take a second to get my bearings in the wholly unfamiliar landscape, blinking in the sudden sunlight. Wherever we are, it's morning. I can tell from the way the sun is peeking over the mountains off to our left and the anticipatory silence that lingers around us. A day is hatching, potential seeping through the cracks.

"Rachel."

It's my turn to look bewildered. "It's Daisy."

Death rolls up his sleeves with a sigh of exasperation. "Rachel is the name of the town. Well, not really a town. More just a—a collection of houses and people."

I look around again and I can see his reason for the clarification. There really aren't enough houses here to qualify as a town. And between the few buildings, all I can see is flat ground stretching out for miles and miles. Middle of nowhere doesn't begin to cover it.

"Right. And dare I ask why we're here?"

Death stops adjusting his sleeves and places his hands in his back pockets. "Rachel is the nearest settlement to Area 51. You know—the one with all the aliens and crap?"

"Is it crap?" I interrupt, suddenly wondering if he'll know the answer to this.

Death glances at me, trying to decide if he can waste any of his precious time on this question. Finally, he seems to decide it is. "Put it this way: if they exist, they're not coming through my department."

A surprisingly sensible and courteous answer. "Right." A pause, which Death doesn't fill, so I give him a gentle verbal nudge: "Go on."

"Well, I figured that people living near Area 51 won't bat too much of an eyelid if you appear out of thin air."

"But if I appear here, won't I just be stuck in the middle of a desert, finding my own way home?"

Death shoots me an indulgent look. "Daisy, if you manage to appear here during your first attempt, for long enough that you need to get yourself home, I will personally find a UFO to fly you there."

Well, that puts me in my place. "So this isn't going to be a quick process?"

"No, Daisy. Returning from death is not a quick process."

Deciding that I can ignore his withering tone for the moment, I move on: "Fine, OK. How do I return from death, then?"

Death clasps his hands behind his back, straightening his posture somewhat. I smell a lecture coming. I'm not disappointed. "Despite what you might think, I actually believe certain emotions to be incredibly important." I raise an eyebrow at this, but he carries on. "In fact, it has long been said by the wise philosophers of the universe that emotions are what make us truly alive."

"Which philosophers said that?"

Death squints at me and my incredulous tone, sensing a trap. "Plato?"

"Don't think so."

"The other one."

I can't help but laugh at that, crossing my arms. "The other one, right. I forgot there were only two wise philosophers of the universe."

"It's really not important, Daisy. May I?" Smirking a little, I gesture for him to continue. Clearly my grilling has exhausted him so much so that he feels the need to sit down, which he does on a nearby rock. "Emotions are closely linked to your being, your essence. Your living soul. All those different and complicated emotions make us true, living humans."

"Us?"

It's a question asked out of pure curiosity but I notice a slight tightening in his jaw as Death corrects himself. "You. Them. Whatever. Anyway, I think that is what could bring you back to the living world. A strong emotion and a shove."

"A shove?" I'm trying hard not to sound too disbelieving

but a shove just seems far too simple to be involved in the process for bringing me back to life.

He shrugs. "That's the idea. The line between life and death is fragile. It's old and stretched. If you've got the right amount of ingredients, the recipe is pretty simple."

I watch him for a moment, trying to decide if I really trust him. He sounds fairly confident and relaxed, but that does seem to be his general state. Then again, I can't really see how it could go wrong. Either it will work or it won't. There is one more thing nagging away at me, though. "Have you tried this before?"

Death shifts a little on his rocky seat, then shakes his head. "But I checked with Natasha and she said my theory was sound. She questions my approach to paper clip storage, so if she thinks it's all right, I must be pretty close."

I have to smile a little at that. Then I nod. "All right. Let's do this."

Grinning, Death jumps up and moves over to my side. "Cool. OK, you're going to need to think of something that makes you angry."

"Angry?"

Death nods. "Really angry. Steaming at the ears angry. I feel like that's something you've experienced before."

Can't argue there. "Why anger, though?"

"Because, as much as people like to pretend that happiness or love are the most powerful emotions, you can't really deny that angry people get a lot more shit done."

I want to argue but I have too much evidence in my short life to support Death's claim. For someone naturally quiet, rage has always been a surprisingly comfortable place for me to visit when necessary. When you're called Daisy, people like to assume you're a bit droopy. And sometimes those people need to be put in their place. Clearly some of these thoughts show on my face because Death shoots me a small, knowing grin.

Sighing, I take a step away from him and turn my back. I need to concentrate and I can't do that with him gawping at me. I close my eyes, force myself to think of a time when I've been truly angry.

Well, there's one that comes to mind immediately. One where anger seemed to lodge itself right in the core of my bones, seemed to rot away part of my heart.

It was only about a year ago. Violet had been going through a rough patch with her depression and had taken a few days off from a dancing job to get herself back on track. It had been days filled with weary tears and bitter arguments as I tried to help her out of bed and out of her own dark thoughts, as she clawed her way back into rational thoughts and fought for the right to a day not filled with utter lethargy and hopelessness.

Finally, after four days, she managed to pull herself out the other side. The next day of work for her was a Saturday so I said I'd go in with her, so she didn't have to face the Tube and the other dancers' stares and the director's glare alone. She did so well, kept her head up high as she marched back into the theater. I was watching her make this confident beeline for the director when I heard them; a small group of other dancers loitering by the door with matching sneers.

I heard she was off because she went mental. That's what Denise told me. Apparently, she was sending her texts all Wednesday night. Whining about how she couldn't see the point anymore, or whatever.

Such an attention seeker, probably just wanted an excuse for dancing like shit last week.

And that was all it took. For my protective instincts to rear up and roar. Because they hadn't seen how hollow Violet's eyes had been all week; they hadn't heard her desperate, exhausted sobs in the middle of the night; they didn't understand what it was like to be attacked from the inside.

My fists have clenched, I can feel my nails digging into my skin. A tingling feeling begins, then spreads, from my chest right to the tips of my fingers. Somehow I know that this is it, the moment I'm aiming for. I take a deep breath, nodding rapidly in the hope that Death sees this and takes it as the sign that I'm ready. I can't open my eyes, can't risk losing the threads of the deep, painful rage, because I know they're so fragile that the smallest distraction will send those threads fluttering away in the breeze.

It seems he gets the message, though, because a moment later I feel a firm hand on my back which then shoves me rather forcefully forward. I stumble, almost falling to the ground. Then I feel something within me, like a little shiver deep inside. My eyes snap open and I look around me, desperate for some sign of my shift from death to life.

There's a glorious moment when it's just me on the dirt ground, alone. Death is no longer standing beside me, confirming my shift from his world to mine. But then comes the shiver again and, like a television with bad reception, Death reappears, his appearance slightly hazy and jittery for a second. Then the tingling on my skin is gone and he's standing there, clear as day.

"I had it, I did!" I gasp, somehow out of a breath that I no longer even require.

"I know," Death says. I can see he's impressed, but he's trying to hide it. "Pretty good for a first try, well done." Wow, actual praise. Clearly my pleasant surprise is showing on my face because he clears his throat and turns away a little. "But obviously we need to keep practicing."

So that is what we do. We keep practicing until the sun is high up in the sky and the flocks of alien conspiracists start arriving. Then Death moves us on somewhere else, deciding that appearing in front of so many people, even people with a healthy attitude to the paranormal, is not a good idea. We visit the middle of the rain forest, in the dead of night with a moon glowing high above us. We practice trying to appear again and I manage to do it for long enough to startle a loitering bird, but then I'm gone once more. Death blames it on the humidity, takes me to a tiny alpine village and tries to get me to appear in front of a field of sheep by the side of the road. But this time I can't even manage a second.

We practice for hours. We visit another three places: a sleepy village right out of a fairy tale, a Japanese shrine on the edge of a tranquil lake, an ancient-looking fort atop a hill that overlooks an overcrowded town. But I don't ever appear for more than a few seconds.

Death gets a slightly desperate look in his eyes, then. He's already rejected about six phone calls and he knows he's running out of time, but I don't think failure is something he deals with very well. I feel emotionally drained. The act of reliving a moment of intense anger over and over is beginning to take its toll on me.

But Death is not giving up. And with a still slightly wild look in his eyes, he drags me from the dusty courtyard of this strange, faraway fort and back into the lift.

"We're trying something else," he mutters through gritted teeth. "Last try, then I've really got to get back." Yes, I imagine he does. I'm sure Natasha will be furious at him for being gone so long.

Then the lift doors open and all thoughts of Death's deadlines leave my head. Because of all the places in the world, did it really have to be here?

We're standing on my street. It's a wintry midafternoon, judging by the fact that the sun is almost behind the row of houses. A bus whooshes past, a plane screeches through the sky. Far away I hear a siren, off to another scene of changed lives. But here, on my street, everything seems the same. There's still the cracked wall by number nine, there's still the lazy tabby cat stretched out on number thirteen's fence. Number seven's letter box is still wonky, the hedge is still haphazardly trimmed from that one weekend of sun a few weeks back when the old man living there got a little over-excited. For a moment, it's like I'm alive again. Standing in front of the iron railings after a long day at work, ready to go inside and enjoy my evening with Violet. An evening of laughing ourselves to tears, usually at something inappropriate, while the simple joy of being together chases away the cold sneaking through the cracks in the walls.

As if she's sensed my wistful imaginings, Violet arrives.

It can't have been more than a day now since I left her, but the change in her is clear. Her hair is scraped back off her face and tightly confined to a bun, which is something Violet never does as she owns her curls with intense pride. She's dressed in her old jogging bottoms and her huge netball team sweater from university, which is half covered up by her fluffy dressing gown. Rings circle her eyes, and her face is devoid of any makeup. Another complete rarity for her. Her feet are bare, even though there's still a definite February chill in the air. She clutches a small bunch of flowers in her hand, knuckles prominent from how tightly she's gripping. Like she's afraid someone is going to take those from her too.

She comes up from our basement flat, then makes her way down the street toward the corner shop. But she stops before she reaches it, instead kneeling down to one spot on the pavement. I think this must be where I died.

For a moment the world around me fades to nothing. It's just me and Violet, lost in two entirely different forms of grief.

Then I feel it. That weird tingling sensation all over my skin but this time it's stronger, and there's a tugging feeling in my abdomen as well. Like someone has wrapped rope around my stomach and is pulling with all their might. But I don't understand; I'm as far away from angry as I could possibly be. There's just cold, visceral grief now. And yet I feel like I'm inches away from breaking through from death to life.

Death clearly senses it somehow because a second later I'm shoved forward with the usual suddenness and ferocity. I stumble, coming to a halt right in front of her. "Violet?" I call, my skin feeling like it's covered in frantically moving ants.

Nothing.

I turn around to Death, feeling desperate frustration welling up inside me. "What the hell were you thinking, bringing me here? This isn't fair! I can't be here, not yet!"

Death runs a hand through his hair, ruffling it up with a grimace. "Maybe not," he sighs. "I thought it was worth a shot..."

I want to shout at him some more, to make him see that this isn't some fun experiment. This is my life.

But then I hear a gasp.

I turn, not quite ready to hope yet, but at the same time feeling a lifting sensation in my chest.

The gasp, of course, has come from Violet, as she sits among the paving slabs, bathed in the last scraps of winter sunshine. Staring right at me.

Rule Seven

The Universe Does Not Play Fair

THE QUESTION IS ALWAYS there, and it's always asked eventually: "Why do good, innocent people die?" And I'm sorry, but I don't have a very good answer for you.

It's not part of a plan. Small children do not starve to death in the midst of a crippling famine because some higher being decreed it so (not that I know of anyway)—they die because we have a quota to meet. Don't look at me like that—it's better this way. Just think what would happen if I left you to it. Overcrowding, fighting, bitterness, endless starvation. Because without death, you can suffer for a really long time.

But I know that doesn't really answer the question. Because there are plenty of bastards in the world roaming around while people like Daisy, who haven't ever really done anything significantly wrong, are snatched from their lives all too prematurely. And I don't know why. I told you, I don't have a very good answer for you.

Except to say that the Universe, like many things, is not always *fair.* Sometimes good people have to deal with tragedy, sometimes bad people are treated to rewarding days.

What matters is what you do next. Because the Universe has been unfair for a really long time. But sometimes, by sheer will and determination you manage to tip the scales. So take this as a reminder: sometimes injustice only exists as long as you allow it to.

✳ ✳ ✳

Violet stares for ten seconds. Ten long seconds while I'm just standing there, wondering how long I've got until I suddenly disappear again. Then she stands up, takes a cautious step toward me. "Daisy?" she asks, her voice a whisper.

Fifteen seconds. I nod mutely.

"Daisy, is that *you*?" She's standing right in front of me and she reaches out, tentatively. "Wow, that's good! I mean, that's impressive," she whispers, as her fingers graze across my chest. Then she gives me a good hard prod, enough to make me stumble a little.

"Hey! Jesus, Violet! It's me, it's Daisy!" I steady myself, shooting a wary glance at the pavement for understandable reasons.

"Oh shit! Sorry, I thought you were fake or something. Or like…a hallucination. But you're not!" Realization seems to finally arrive and she jumps back as if she's been electrocuted. "Shit! You're here? But you're dead, Daisy! I saw you! I saw you on the pavement!"

I bite my lip, wondering how on earth to explain this. I find myself turning instinctively toward where Death's standing. But I can't see him anymore. It's just me and Violet, and I have no idea where to begin.

"It's…complicated. But it's me, Violet. It's really me." It's not a great answer in the end, but it will have to do. "Are—are you OK?"

Something about the concern in my voice seems to reso-
nate with Violet, because her face crumples and she lets out a
small sob. "Oh my God! It *is* you," she breathes, then crashes
into my arms. She's crying so loudly that I'm sure we're going
to draw attention from the neighbors. So I take Violet's hand
and gently tug her toward our home.

We stumble over each other's feet, down the stairs and
through the door. Foreheads bump against each other, arms
wrap around. It's so familiar. It brings me back to when she
was in hospital after she tried to see Death for herself. I remember her shaking then, just like she is now. She doesn't
feel quite as frail as she did then, when it was she who was
brushing against the line between life and death. But the
hitching sobs, sounding bruised and cracked, are pretty much
the same. It fills me with fear.

Finally, though, we have to pull away. Time is ticking on
and for me every second could be my last one visible to her.
Can't waste it crying, as tempting as that is. We stand staring at each other for a moment, tears blotching up her face.

"Tea?" Violet croaks finally and I laugh, before shaking
my head.

"Well, I'm not sure what will happen..."

Violet's eyebrows quirk with curiosity. "Just, uh, run that
one by me again."

I shrug. "Apparently I can still drink, even though I don't
need to. But I haven't actually tried it yet."

Violet tilts her head, looking at me for a long moment.
"You're still dead, then," she states, rather than asks. She's
saying it calmly, like how you might state the weather. But
I know better. So it's with a great deal of caution that I nod.

Violet steps forward and touches my cheek, prodding hard.
I wonder if this would hurt if I had any nerves left to tell
me so. I can just about feel her fingers on my skin but it's as

if I'm encased in plastic wrap not quite in contact with her. "But I can touch you! How—how can you be dead? I can touch you and see you and you're talking to me. It doesn't make any sense." That calm she had grasped at a moment ago is rapidly fluttering away and her shoulders rise, cinching up by her ears. I know what's coming. Call it experience.

"Vi," I say gently, reaching forward and taking her by the shoulders. "Breathe." She shakes her head, lips pursed together as tears well up in her eyes. "Violet, breathe!" I repeat, a little more firmly, before deciding to try some humor: "One of us has to for Christ's sake!"

A strange, cracked laugh tumbles from her mouth. She presses against me, shaking her head as she does so. I can feel her trembling again and it fills me with guilt. This is all so unfair. One patch of ice and suddenly I've left my best friend alone in this flat. "I'm sorry, Vi, I'm so sorry. I should have paid more attention."

Violet finally lifts her head after a few moments, eyes red raw. They are still blazing as she dares me to refuse her next request: "Tell me, Daisy. Tell me what happened."

How can you tell someone what happens after you die? Even without any guidance from Death, I know it's not for her to know. But Violet and I aren't the sort of friends to cope without knowing every intricate detail of each other's lives. So I sit her down on the sofa, curl my feet up under the blanket (try to ignore the fact that it offers me no warmth), and tell her what I can. I tell her how I tripped, how I felt no pain after the initial smack on my head. I tell her that I'm not alone (though I don't go into details about who I've got keeping me company) and tell her that I've been learning to appear to the living again. It all comes out in a garbled mess that probably makes no sense, because part of me is convinced that, any moment now, Death is going to reappear and drag me back to his office.

But he doesn't. And with my half-story told, the conversation inevitably turns toward the life I've left behind.

Violet pulls her curls free from their bun, lets them explode outward in their normal way. "Oh Daisy, it was *awful*," she sighs, tugging at the bags under her eyes. "Your mum, she wouldn't stop crying and your dad…your dad kept shouting at the doctors to keep trying, to not give up."

"And Eric?"

Violet hesitates, looking at me warily. It's a look I don't exactly like and I frown, leaning forward a little. "And Eric, Violet?" I ask again, more firmly this time.

She sighs, twirling one curl of hair around her finger. "You know what Eric's like, he doesn't really know how to handle the big emotions. I think he struggled that time you got all weepy at the Attenborough documentary."

Despite the situation, I feel myself smiling. I remember that, baby turtles and Violet and I yelling with anguish at the television as some predatory bird just doing its job swooped down on these tiny turtles. I was sitting beside Eric, tucked into his side, while Violet was balanced precariously on the arm of the armchair, like always. I remember the tears welling up in my eyes and Eric looking positively terrified until Violet told him to harden up and get me a tissue. So I could imagine that all the grief floating around right now was difficult for him, especially when he was grieving himself.

"He met us at the hospital, with your parents," Violet begins, voice hushed as if that will stop me hearing the way it shakes. "But then he wouldn't stay. Once it was all…official, he said he had to get home and left. I think your mum was considering skinning him on the spot but your dad managed to convince her otherwise."

I find myself wincing a little. Eric is the living embodiment of "all talk and no trousers." People assume he's got his whole self sussed out because he comes across as this super-confident person on the outside. But really, he's as vulnerable as the next person.

"Anyway, I called him this morning and told him that you would never let him live in peace if he didn't pull himself together."

"He is grieving too, Vi," I reason, my voice gentle. "It hasn't been that long."

Violet shifts a little on the sofa. It feels slightly defensive and I watch her carefully, trying to gauge what's coming. "Yeah, well. Nobody else was around to put him in his place."

There it is. The simple sentence that comes loaded with hidden, painful meaning. "I'm sorry." The apology feels so wrong, so out of place. Violet's expression suggests she feels the same way, just for a moment, but then she seems to brush it away and forces a smile.

"It's fine; you're here now. So it's fine."

I bite my lip, knowing I need to be honest with her. But how can I be? How can I tell her that, at any moment, this could all come crashing down? I can't. Not when she's looking at me with such hope in her eyes. She thinks this is a reset, a start over. A miracle deletion of the previous day's events. Call me a coward, but I can't be the one to set her straight on that one. Not yet.

"So. Tell me." I'm not going for delicateness here, not when my time is limited. Violet shoots me a suspicious look that she tries to hide in confusion, like she doesn't know what I'm referring to. Which is, of course, bullshit. So I don't say anything, just let her squirm in the firm knowledge that I can sit in silence for longer than her.

A minute later, she cracks. "Ugh, you're the worst," she

grumbles, as she rests her head on my shoulder. "Um, about two hours sleep, five panic attacks, think I ate a banana this morning…anything else, doc?"

I nudge her with one elbow in an almost automatic motion. "That's normal—probably."

She laughs bitterly, lifting her head to meet my gaze. "Daisy, nothing about this is normal. Honestly, if it wasn't for the lengthiness of this conversation I'd be convinced this was a side effect."

"Of?" I can't help the sharpness in my voice, though I do shoot her a somewhat apologetic look for it. But if she's mentioning side effects that either means she's on different medication or she's not taking it. Both of those are causes for concern with Violet; the last time she was put on different medication, she stayed in bed for three weeks straight—and the last time she wasn't taking it, she ended up in hospital on suicide watch.

Violet shoots me a gentle look. It has enough clarity and understanding to settle me a little. "Of very little sleep and a significant trauma, Daisy." Her hand finds mine, squeezes it tightly. The purple friendship bracelet on her wrist that I made for her ten years ago brushes gently against my skin. I can't feel it, of course, but I can pretend I can. "Try not to worry. I mean, I know you will, but try not to worry too much."

I don't know what to say to that. She's right, I will worry. Particularly when I know the truth, that any second here could be my last one before I'm whisked away. But perhaps that's all the more reason not to worry. Perhaps it's best just to make the most of being visible, before it's cruelly ripped away from me.

So that's what we do. We sit and try to just be us. We talk about helping my parents, sorting out Eric. Then we move away from such serious topics and instead share little, price-less moments of laughter about stupid things, like how she went to get coffee at the hospital and then lost me for half an hour, and all she could think about was how much I would haunt her if she wasn't there to stop anyone throwing away my clothes, bloodstains or no bloodstains. Humor is dragged out from the cracks of a mainly horrific experience and it feels almost healing.

Eventually, Violet falls asleep. We've given up on chatting and we're watching one of our favorite documentaries, when her head droops against my shoulder. Smiling at the oh-so-familiar sight, I tuck her up in the blankets, close the curtains and shut off the television, preparing to spend the night sorting out my room a little.

First, though, I drift into Violet's room. I know the clues to look out for and it worries me how many I see already: her medication isn't in its usual place but stuffed into a drawer where she can pretend to have forgotten about it, she's covered up the photos of us on her bedside table with a scarf, left her bed unmade, not cleared away the mugs of coffee. It's only been a day, I force myself to remember. This is normal.

I'm just pulling her medication back out of the drawer when it happens. Suddenly, like a switch being turned on, every single inch of me begins to tingle angrily. I crumple to the ground, letting out a little gasp of surprise and horror. "No, no, not yet," I find myself whispering, because I know what's coming, no matter how unfair it feels. My time is up.

And the minute I think it, it happens. There's a tug in my midriff, a lot more violent this time. It's as if the longer you stay, the more force is required to get you back. Distantly, as I'm knocked onto my back, I hear the box of pills leave my hand and clatter to the ground.

For a moment, I can only lie there, in total shock. Instinctively, I know I'm back in the world of the dead again but my mind doesn't want to quite accept it.

"Violet?" I call as I slowly sit up, stumbling out of the room and over to the shadowy shape of Violet, asleep on the sofa. "Violet!" I yell it, just once more. Because I know it's no use. I'm gone, and Violet is going to wake up alone.

"I'm sorry," I murmur, kneeling down beside her. What else can I do? Or say? I know nothing is going to make it better. A little smile lingers on her cheeks, neatly breaking my heart in two. "I'll be back, I promise." My voice catches in my throat as I say this, and I turn to leave before it gets worse. Before I have to think any more about what this is going to do to her.

But it seems like fortune isn't going to be quite that kind to me. I should have guessed, considering recent circumstances. The universe has made it very clear to me that it doesn't play fair. So, as I turn to leave, head down and tears imminent, I hear a sound that makes my stomach drop. Violet shifts, groans and then murmurs my name.

I should just keep going, I shouldn't stay to see this because no part of it is going to be good. But I can't help myself. I turn, I watch helplessly as Violet sits up and blearily looks around. "Daisy?" she says again, and her voice is still calm because I don't think she's quite woken up enough to really fathom what's happened. But she'll get it in a second.

Just like clockwork, she suddenly stands up with a gasp. "No," she whispers. "No, no, no! DAISY?" She rushes through the flat, stumbling over the blanket she was still half cocooned in until she kicks it away. Doors open with enough force to crash loudly against the wall as she tears through her bedroom, my bedroom, the bathroom. Desperation covers her face. "DAISY, COME BACK!"

Up to this point, it's been easy to forget that Violet has

suffered the grief of me dying because all I've seen is her relief and happiness at seeing me back. It's easy to forget anything that came before because I'd fixed it. Now it's all broken again.

I close my eyes, determined to get myself furious again. I imagine those awful dancers over and over, I blow it up to be something greater and more dramatic than it really was in the hope that that somehow helps. But it doesn't work. Frustration wells inside of me and I yell out as loud as I can. Violet hears none of this. My yells hit a wall that they cannot penetrate and all she gets is silence, the dripping tap, her own heartbeat.

Unable to take any more, I find myself stumbling out of the flat, numb from the injustice of it all. Outside, the street is deserted, quiet. The buses have stopped for the night and it's a couple of hours too early for most people to be going to work yet. It's just me and the pavement.

Then I hear a soft ding, the creaking swoosh of doors sliding open. I turn, knowing what I will find waiting for me and yet somehow hoping it's something else. A miracle, a ticket back home. Anything.

But it's not. It's just the lift, its innards warmly lit but not in the slightest bit inviting. And there's Death, hands in his pockets and eyes fixed steadily on me.

"So," he says finally. "How'd it go?"

Rule Eight

Play Your Part

SOME PEOPLE LIKE TO think this job is easy. Where's the challenge? You take the person in the lift, you check their file, you send them on. Simple.

But of course it's not. Because you're not taking a parcel, you're taking a person. A person who has just lost everything they cherished, who is being taken from everything they know. How can that ever be simple?

Once upon a time, I too thought it was easy. Back when things weren't quite so tight for time and you could spend a moment consoling, chatting, reassuring. I used to find out so much about these people, way behind their files. I was an eager young boy who had no idea about the world he was cleaning up and I had countless brains to pick (figuratively speaking before you start panicking). I found ways to make people smile, despite everything they were going through, and it felt wonderful.

Then the rules changed. Too many people, too many deaths. It was made very clear to me that it was not my role to connect with *these people or to help them feel better. Find the person, take them in the lift, check the file, move them on. Done.*

I have to play my part. I am Death and if I'm not doing that right then there's not much point in me existing. So I stick to my role like glue.

Even if I know, deep down, that I could be so much more.

❉ ❉ ❉

I can tell that Death would rather we stood in silence and just pretend that nothing had happened. But I can't do that. Violet's heartbroken cries tumble around my head constantly as the lift takes us back up, and I feel like I'm going to go mad if I don't say something, if I don't do something with them.

"What happened?" I blurt out all of a sudden, after a few seconds of mute standing in the lift. "How come I lasted so long this time?"

Death shrugs. "Beats me."

I snort angrily, needing something to take my feelings of sorrow and guilt and frustration out on. "Well that's fucking great that is…what an expert you are."

Out of the corner of my eye, I can see Death frown a little, clearly taken aback by my words. "Look, it's not exactly a tried and tested art, OK?"

"You brought me there. You clearly had something in mind."

I've got him there and he knows it. He rubs his forehead, eyes closing for a moment. "I know," he mutters finally. "I was thinking that perhaps anger wasn't enough. That there needed to be something else as well, like your rather pervasive desire to protect Violet from anything and everything."

"So you thought you'd let me break my friend's heart all over again to test your little theory?"

Another frown. But this time it swiftly turns into an ir-

ritated scowl. "We were going to have to try it with someone you knew eventually, Daisy. That's the entire reason for
you going back. Are you telling me you didn't enjoy being
with her?"

I could slap him. I almost do but he's already turned and
moved out of the lift, back down the corridor toward his office door with an arrogant confidence that I'll follow. The
frustrating thing is that I do; after all, where else am I going
to go?

"That's not the point," I snap, as we step back into his office. "It's not about me and my enjoyment. It's about Violet
and her now being in pieces all over again!"

"We're going around in circles here." Death pinches the
bridge of his nose, looking thoroughly fed up with this conversation. He moves to sit down, places his hands flat on the
desk and stares mutinously at his telephone. Like he's hoping
it will ring and interrupt this unpleasant moment. "Am I to
assume, then, that you won't be trying that again?"

This takes me by surprise somewhat. I don't know why;
isn't this what I've been heading toward? But his words make
it seem so final.

Then again, when all I can see in my head right now is
Violet's distraught face and all I can hear is her heartbroken
sobs, I know there isn't another option. So, after a few long
seconds of silence, I nod. "You'd assume correctly," I murmur. Defeat sits heavy on my words, almost muffling them.

Death watches me for a moment then nods, stands up and
begins shuffling through his papers. I get the odd and not
altogether pleasant sensation that I'm no longer required or
wanted in this office. So I turn, intending to leave and find
a dark corner to hide in until further notice.

"Daisy, wait." With a sigh, I spin myself back around to
face him. "If you're not going to try appearing anymore then

you're stuck up here. And we're back to square one. So perhaps we should train you up a bit. I mean, being my assistant isn't just some little shop job you can do on your Sundays with a hangover. It takes serious skills. And I don't carry deadweight up here." Despite my still lingering frustration and pain, I can't help but smile slightly, hiding it with one hand as his eyes appraise me with open suspicion. Clearly he hasn't grasped the concept of puns. "You can smile if you want, Daisy," he goes on, somewhat haughtily, "but there's a reason I don't have an assistant already."

He looks so determined to impress me that I decide to concede. Anything to distract me from my best friend's broken sobs. "OK, so train me."

Death watches me silently for a long few seconds. It drives me mad that he has no issue doing this, doesn't care that I'm standing here squirming under his gaze.

Finally, he speaks, clearly satisfied that I'm now taking him seriously. "OK, we start tomorrow. Take some time to recover from...everything."

I'm not sure how I feel about him reducing the extreme trauma of what just happened to one careless word, but I don't get a chance to voice this complaint. Death's phone starts ringing and all three lights on his desk start flashing. He glances at the lights, then comes around the desk, taking my arm and propelling me toward the lift. "Change of plan," he says, "training starts now."

So, before I really have a chance to fully comprehend what's happening, we're back in the lift and we're heading back down to the surface. And there's a highly cynical part of me that wonders if this is some complex trick of Death's to get me to try appearing again. I really wouldn't put it past him.

But, when the lift doors open, I can see we're definitely here for the dead.

Wherever we are, something has gone horribly wrong with the balance of nature. We step out of the lift, and I immediately have to yank Death back to stop him getting flattened by a palm tree that has just now decided to buckle. He tugs his arm free and shoots me a look, as if he can't quite believe I would think a tree would ever pose such a threat.

I send him a scowl right back; I can't help that my "mumfriend instincts" (as Violet used to affectionately call them) are still alive and well.

But a rumble of thunder above forces me to focus on my surroundings instead of my frustrating company. We're somewhere tropical, that much is obvious from the number of palm trees lying on the ground and the sticky heat I can feel passing through my semi-present body. I think there were homes here once, but now there is just rubble everywhere. Piles of shredded-up wood and crumbled bricks, with somehow still intact bits of furniture sticking out of them. A cricket ball rolls past my feet, coming to rest in a rust-colored puddle. I turn back to Death, an uncomfortable lump forming in my throat.

"What happened here?" I ask, not entirely sure I want to know.

Not that Death is anywhere close to giving me a straight answer. "Tuesday," he replies.

"What?" My voice is sharp because I have this horrible feeling that he's trying to be funny.

He sighs. "Daisy, in my line of work, chances are there's going to be somebody dying near me. If you're going to have some moral code about being somber at all times then this is going to be a very long afterlife for you."

I don't answer, refusing to admit that he's probably right. Death as a concept is most likely going to become a normality soon, something that I will barely blink at. But it terrifies me that, one day, I will be so jaded by the endless sweeping up of the dead that I will start laughing at Death's jokes. That I will forget what death does to a person's family and friends. I think Death notices fear in my expression because he decides to be kind and reluctantly answers my original question. "A typhoon hit. Don't think they got much warning." He doesn't get a chance to tell me any more because the air begins to fill with the eerie whistling that apparently signals the passing of life. "We need to go, time's running out."

He starts off at a brisk, confident stroll and I'm forced to trail after him. But not silently. If I'm stuck being his assistant, then he's going to have to deal with all my questions. "How do you know where to go?"

"Just do."

"Elaborate—please," I add hurriedly, paired with a smile for good measure.

He turns away again, still leading me through the jungle of shattered houses. "You just get a feeling, like radar. You'll pick it up soon enough, the less alive you get."

"What do you mean?"

Death comes to a halt beside what looks like a destroyed café. "Well, the less like this lot you are, the more you'll be able to sniff out the anomalies, the ones on the cusp of becoming like you. Plus I get directions." He shrugs with a small, sheepish smile, as he tugs out his phone and gives it a little waggle. For a second, he almost seems normal with that smile. Almost seems likable.

I turn my attention back to the world around me, force myself to take it all in regardless of how horrifying it is. I think it used to be a tourist trap around here, because the flyers fluttering around this particular pile of debris are all in English, even though this looks nothing like any English-speaking country I know. A nearby café's tables somehow still stand proudly among snapped beams of wood and shredded glass, and I'm sure I can still smell overcooked burgers and ketchup. Just as I'm thinking this, a blotchily tanned man in baggy board shorts and one flip-flop (the other is held loosely in one hand) runs past. "Grace?" he screams, his desperation filling the air.

"Is it Grace we're here for?" I ask, not able to keep the dread out of my voice.

"No," Death replies and I'm halfway toward a sigh of relief when he spoils it by going on. "She's being picked up by one of the admins. Doesn't make the cut for us."

Death is looking expectantly at me, almost buzzing with anticipation at whatever silly human thing he thinks I'm going to say, so this time I stay silent, stubborn to the end of my life and beyond.

He turns away and hops forward over a smoldering oven that has been ripped away from whichever wall it was once attached to. "Over here," he calls, beckoning me to follow him.

Our subject lies underneath one of the tables. At first, I can't work out what has killed him. But then we get closer and I realize that there is a significant portion of his leg missing. It's a mangled mess and blood pools around him, dripping from a deep cut in his stomach. I remember how the café smelled like overcooked burgers and my stomach churns. I turn away, try to heave.

Nothing happens.

Death tuts. "Really?" he groans, shooting me a look of disbelief.

"Half of his leg is missing! I'm not used to that sort of thing just yet!"

"A quarter."

"What?"

"It's more like a quarter missing. Now stop having a hissy

fit and concentrate. Training starts with this guy, even if he isn't all here."

"Why is *he* unfair? You said you only go to the unfair deaths. There must be children here—surely you should be going to them?"

"Kids have their own department, apart from the really extreme cases." He hunkers down, watching this man take his last few, effort-filled breaths. "Remember my three categories? His son—he's going to be an orphan now. This man was all he had in the world. So we go to him."

A tear slides down my cheek, too quickly for me to catch it. "Why? Why does he have to die?"

All I get is another shrug. When I open my mouth to argue, to get more from him, I get a hand held up in my general direction. Shut up Daisy, the hand says. Death turns to face me a moment later. "That doesn't matter. I don't decide that—there's a quota to be met and it's this guy's turn to step up to the plate. He's lucky—he gets to be picked up by us." He falls silent, watching me intently. When I finally nod, he gestures for me to join him on the ground. I do, trying not to look at the bottom half of the man.

"OK, first step? What did I do with Jennifer?" he prompts a moment later.

"Um…you put your hand on her chest. You found her soul and guided it to the other side." I blink, surprised for a moment at how automatically this knowledge has come to me. I'm not sure I like it.

Death seems surprised too, though pleasantly so. "Exactly. We're dead. Or rather, you're dead and I'm Death. Either way, we're now this man's kindred spirits. So we can guide him to our side. Without us he'd get lost and we can't have that."

"What about me?"

"Hmm?"

"When I died, there was nobody guiding me. What happened? Why wasn't I lost?"

Death considers it for a moment. "Well, you were an anomaly. Nobody expected you. As for why you didn't get lost...well, I suppose you can call it luck."

Finally, an explanation, of sorts. Bolstered by that, I shift a little closer to our subject. "So, what should I do?"

Death considers the man for a moment, then rests his hands firmly on his chest. "We can guide him together. Find his soul and bring him to us. Two guides will definitely be easier than one." He looks so alert now, he's almost unrecognizable. "OK, hands on," he urges and I obey, hands coming to rest next to his. Our little fingers are skimming alongside each other and I'm distantly surprised by how warm he feels. But then I force myself to focus on his words: "Close your eyes, feel your way after him," Death instructs, eyes already drifting shut.

It takes a moment, then it all happens rather quickly. Within the darkness behind my closed eyes, I suddenly see a flash of white, hear a man's cry, glimpse a shadowy version of our subject. Then my eyes snap open and I'm greeted with the sight of our subject now standing next to his own mangled body, dressed in a white vest with white cargo shorts.

"W-w-what?" he stammers.

Death leans across the now deceased body, smiles at me. "Just like that. Now we calm him." He stands up but I grab his arm, pausing him.

"You're not doing that magic touch thing."

Death looks at me for a long moment, as if he's trying to decide if this is worth a fight. Finally, he concedes. He hops up, pulling me with him. "Name first," he murmurs, leaning in close. "Look at him closely, carefully, and it will come to you."

After a long and painful few seconds, I shake my head. "I... I don't know"

He sighs then turns back to his current client. "Jao Amudee, I'm Death."

The man shakes Death's hand with understandable hesitancy, then his eyes slide across to me.

"Oh, I'm Daisy. Nice to meet you."

"Daisy's my assistant, *Khun* Amudee—she's still learning," he explains, using what I assume is some form of Thai formality.

Death comes back around to my side. "Find the lift," he mutters in my ear.

Keen to get something right, I glance around me, squinting for the telltale flicker of an illuminated button. But I don't see anything. What a surprise. "How?" I ask, feeling helplessness seeping into my bones. "I don't see anything!"

Death shoots Jao a look of apology, then comes around to stand in front of me again. "Concentrate. The lift appears when it is wanted. Reach out to press the button and focus on it being there, waiting for you."

"Did a shitting yoga instructor design this stupid afterlife system?"

Death responds by taking my hand, tugging my index finger forward and jabbing it into the air. A lift button immediately appears. A second later the air ripples in front of me, and then the ripples slide away to reveal the interior of the lift.

Death turns back and gives Jao a smooth smile, before placing an arm around the man's shoulder and gently coaxing him toward the lift. "Apologies, we may seem a little chaotic today, but don't worry. *I* know exactly what I'm doing."

"Well, he likes to think he does." I blurt the words out before I can stop myself, shooting Jao a grin.

The man hesitates, then returns my smile. "Oh, it's quite nice really. It's like you're just...normal."

Death narrows his eyes. I get the sense that he doesn't like the idea of being called normal. So I decide to end this particular conversation abruptly. "Well. That's good to know. Um...into the lift?"

I receive a nod from Death, then a gesture to indicate I should continue. Clearly my small moment of confidence means I'm in charge all of a sudden.

I can't say the processing of Jao is perfect after that, but I'm fairly sure it's not a disaster. There's a tricky moment in the lift when I can't find the right button (and Death watches silently from a corner) but then Jao somehow finds the button for me, like the place he belongs in now is calling to him.

That stings a little, because I'm not sure where I belong anymore.

Once we're done with the paperwork I show him to the door, behind Death's desk. He pauses at the threshold, turns back to me and nods his head just once. "Thank you, Daisy. You did just fine," he assures me with a certainty that I wish I shared.

Then he disappears through to the other side. The door closes behind him and I lock it, before flopping back into Death's chair with a heavy sigh.

Almost instantly, I hear a creak as Death sits down opposite me. By some miracle, he actually has a small smile on his face. "Well, it was a close call but you did it. Thought I was going to lose you in the lift but you pulled through."

"You could have stepped in to help, you know."

"No fun in that. Anyway, there's a few things we'll need to work on but for a novice, you weren't too bad."

"Such as?"

Death shrugs. "You talked too much to him during the file check—you've got other people waiting."

"He'd just died, just left his son on his own. I wanted to make sure he was OK."

"Lovely, but that's not our job. We stick to our job, Daisy. Like glue."

I roll my eyes, stand up. "Why can't that be our job, too? What's the point in being there otherwise?"

Death's eyes are hollow as he meets my gaze across the desk. "There are rules, Daisy. And not wasting time is one of them." Conversation apparently over, he nods toward the Admin door. "Go, have a break. I'll come find you when I need you."

"Can't wait." I tuck in his chair, walk around his desk and make for the door. Then I turn back, not wanting to leave this important topic. But I'm stopped in my tracks by the sight now before me.

Death's slumped a little in his chair, clearly thinking that I'm out of his hair and he's out of my sight. It takes me a moment to place the look on his face, perhaps because I haven't seen it before. But I get it eventually.

For the first time since I've met him, Death looks truly sad.

"It still upsets you, doesn't it?" The words are out before I really realize it.

Death swallows. "What does?"

"The deaths. They still upset you. That's why you don't talk to them properly. You don't want to get too close."

After a long moment, he stands up and turns away. "You've got it all wrong, Daisy. But nice try." He doesn't give me a chance to go on; he's reached the other door, the door that leads out to the lift, and has left the room a second later.

I stare at the now shut door, before finally turning and leaving out my own door. But it's with a small smile on my face. Because I've learned something new about him. No matter how hard he tries to hide it, he's just like us. He's got his own baggage, his own trauma. And he doesn't know what to do with it.

Maybe there's a role for me here after all.

Rule Nine

Don't Get Stuck In The Days That Suck

I'M SURE YOU KNOW *that life is a balancing act. But life is also like a wave coming into the shore. There will always be glorious rises and crippling falls.*

And some days will always suck.

Maybe you'd like to convince yourself against this. Maybe you think that every day is a gift. And maybe every day is. But not all gifts are a blessing; I once received an envelope full of nail clippings from a particularly disgruntled customer. I still don't know how they managed to get that back to me. The Universe truly is miraculous.

Anyway. Sometimes you will open your eyes and realize that today is not your day. Maybe it's a little thing, like a broken heel or a missing wallet. Maybe it's a big thing like a lost pet or a date on the calendar you've been dreading all year. Maybe, like Violet Tucker and the Cooper family, you spot the black clothes hanging from the wardrobe door and you remember that today is the day you put someone treasured in the ground.

It's OK, you know. To accept it. To accept that sometimes we

*will be delivered a day that is the equivalent of an envelope filled
with nail clippings. As long as we remember that there's always tomorrow. That's the trickier part.*

※ ※ ※

I think a week has passed since my death. I say "think," because it's really hard to tell in this place. There's no night and
day to help you, no real sense of a routine like breakfast and
dinner and bedtime. It's just random, sporadic moments of
doing the job and then crushingly empty periods where the
reality of my situation hits me once again.

Meanwhile, Death has built up a careful wall around himself. Since I called him out on his own emotional baggage,
he has been determined to ensure I never see any evidence
of that again. We don't mention it again and he deftly avoids
any conversations about his past or, indeed, his present. He
learns lots about me and my life, he hears many stories about
my antics with Violet (he particularly enjoys hearing about
the first night we spent together in London, when we couldn't
get the fire alarm to stop). But all I learn about him is that
he's been doing this job since it was created and his favorite
place to visit is anywhere near the ocean.

Over this week, I probably visit about ten deaths. Death
goes to more but he doesn't take me along to them all. He
says he's easing me into it, but I'm not so sure. I see the way
he carefully examines the circumstances of each death, brow
furrowed. Maybe he's protecting me, but my cynical side
thinks he's considering whether bringing me along will allow
me to see some more of his vulnerabilities.

Still, a week goes by, one way or another. We visit a road
accident, two hospitals, houses of all shapes and sizes. We
bring in all different people too. An elderly lady who died
in a fire; a guy in his twenties who died from an accidental

overdose; a woman in a traffic accident. Sometimes they're relatively relaxed and accommodating, other times they're full of panic and terror. I continue to stop Death forcibly calming them, even if their screams and cries seem to weigh heavier and heavier on me. Death seems to give up trying to push the matter. Perhaps, like me, he sees no point in us arguing. We're stuck together for the foreseeable future, after all.

Besides, sometimes I'm sure I catch a glimpse of something like triumph when he sees me calm someone down yet again.

When the week comes to an end, I can tell something is bothering him. I can see it in the crinkle of his brow when I catch him staring at me during those rare down periods. Finally, I decide enough is enough.

"What's up?" I'm trying to be nonconfrontational but I still get a now-familiar frown from him.

He shifts in his chair, shrugging as he puts down the pen he's been fiddling with. A real habit of his, I've noticed. "Nothing."

"Nothing?" I'm trying to give him the opportunity to explain himself without an interrogation, which I think he spots, because he hesitates and I can almost see the thought process whizzing around inside his head. I don't picture Death's head as cogs; that's far too logical. He's more like fireworks, popping off every few seconds in random places.

Finally, after a moment's silence, he sighs. "Fine, but don't now berate me for saying this after you dragged it out of me."

I shoot him a look to suggest that I would never dream of it, though it's delivered with a good deal of humor. Something I've found makes all of this a great deal easier.

"I was digging around through some paperwork," he goes on, back to fiddling with the pen, "just tying up some loose ends, when I came across it, and I wasn't sure whether it was something you'd be interested in or not. I mean, it might be a bit much…"

"Death, could you get to the point please?" I'm a touch gentler than I'd normally be.

Death blinks, kneading his forehead so exuberantly that I'm surprised he doesn't rub the skin away. "It's your funeral today." After all that hesitating, he ends up just blurting it out in one slightly rushed sentence. But I hear the words, just about. And I feel…how do I feel? A little sick, a little numb. And a little touched that Death thought this was something I'd want to know about. I think that might be progress.

"Oh," I say after a few seconds, feeling that I need to say something but not yet knowing what.

"I think they're burying you."

"Right." Again, not exactly something I can answer easily. Though at least my parents listened to my rants about how freaky I find the idea of cremation. Death bites his lip, his gaze fixed on me intently. Finally, he spits out what's really on his mind.

"Do you want to go?" he asks a second later, leaning forward and fixing me with one of his customary piercing looks. "Might be fun."

"It might be fun?" I echo a little incredulously, as I'm not sure I see the appeal myself.

"Yeah. I mean everyone will be weeping over you and going on about how much of a tragedy it is and what a shining light you were, blah, blah. And there's always someone who turns up wearing something inappropriate."

I look at him with disbelief. I've not been to that many funerals, but I can't imagine that being a genuine pattern. "That's bullshit. Besides, you've not met my mother. She'd not let them in the place."

Death stands, stretching out his arms a little stiffly. "I once went to a funeral and there was a guy in a dressing gown. Never quite got to the bottom of that one."

Despite my best efforts to be serious and disapproving, I feel a smile on my face. "That would be my Uncle Dennis," I murmur, half to myself.

I get a small, slightly hesitant chuckle from Death, but then he's silent. He's waiting for my answer.

So I force myself to think about whether it's something I'd actually like to go to. Unsurprisingly, there's not an obvious or easy answer. I'd get to see my parents again and, of course, Violet and Eric. That would be nice, but I would be seeing them in a situation of mourning. Mourning *me*. That doesn't sound so great.

Then Death, rather surprisingly, comes to my rescue. "Why not give it a go? If you hate it, we leave. But you only get one funeral and not many people get the chance to see it for themselves."

I can't really argue with that. If it turns out to be a mistake we can leave, but I can't go back to this day if I change my mind later. As far as I know, Death's skills don't extend to time travel. So, after a moment, I make my decision. "Fine, OK," I sigh, standing up as well. "But if I want to leave, we go. No trying to reason with me or whatever."

Death nods, looking unusually somber. "Deal."

I've never been particularly religious. Curious, more than anything. And my family have been the same: a healthy dose of skepticism mixed with that innate human desire to believe that life isn't all there is. So I'm not surprised to find us arriving for my funeral at somewhere that doesn't resemble a church. Instead, there's a clean and crisp-looking brick building with large windows, surrounded by neatly raked gravel with trees and grass spreading out from this spot. It's quiet, except for the distant and occasional whoosh of a nearby passing car.

"Where are we?" I whisper to Death, who stands beside me with that usual, maddening expression of calm and nonchalance.

"A cemetery? Your file wasn't particularly specific. Do you recognize it?"

I turn a full circle, trying to spot any clues. In the distance I can see the faint steeple of a church. "I think we're back near my parents'," I murmur, and I can't quite hide my disappointment. I spent my whole life getting out of this dull-as-ditchwater town and now I'm back. Though I can imagine my mother not giving anyone much choice on that matter, considering how I practically had to sneak myself and Violet out to London.

"Well, that's nice," Death says. He doesn't sound entirely convinced, to be honest. He takes a step forward, then beckons me on impatiently. "Come on, it will have started already."

I'm not sure I particularly like Death's eagerness, not when I can't place the reason for it. I give him a mild look of disapproval before moving past him, heading for the main doors that stand closed and imposing in front of us. I reach them, hand coming to rest on the handle. But something is whirring away in that irritating, worrisome part of my head, and I find myself stepping back. "What—what if nobody came? Your funeral is kind of a big deal, and if there's nobody there… well, it just means that my life really wasn't worth anything. It just…happened. Like a—a passing cloud."

Death's face crinkles in thought and then, in a moment of supremely surprising forethought, he steps forward and places a hand on the handle. "I'll go check. Then at least you can have some warning." He obviously notices my surprise because he rolls his eyes, shaking his head. "Yes, sometimes I do feelings. Call the papers."

I decide that, on this occasion, it's in my best interest not to comment. I do quite want him to go and check after all and I feel like any teasing will push him right off that idea. So I just gesture for him to get a move on.

He opens the door and steps inside. For a second, I get a sneak peek at my funeral. Gentle piano music (hardly my preference) and hushed voices. I'm sure I catch a glimpse of a white rose and I can't help but roll my eyes. So far, this has my mother written all over it. Pretty and floral and safe, which has never really been my style. If I'm going to accept flowers, they have to be bright and tropical. As far away from my namesake as possible. The only daisy reference I accept in my life is the bracelet Violet got me for my eighteenth, which she handed over with tongue firmly in cheek. I glance down at my empty wrist and wonder what happened to it. Did they take it off and give it back to Violet, or did they keep it on my body? I'm not sure which I'd prefer.

I'm pulled out of this reverie by the door opening once again. Death tries to look somber for a second, but quickly takes pity on me and smiles. "You're all good. More filled seats than empty, which I always count as a success." He watches me and my obvious hesitation, then holds out a hand. He looks almost surprised at his action but then quickly recovers, shooting me a jaunty wink. "Come on, or you'll miss the juggling."

Instinct seems to take over and I find my hand reaching for his. "As if there's juggling," I mutter as I push past him to get inside.

"No, but it got you in, didn't it?" he whispers, his words tickling against my ear.

Despite my best efforts, I can't help but smile at that. I've noticed over this strange week that, when Death wants to, he can be quite good at cheering me up. Perhaps it's thanks to our equally dark sense of humor.

But my smile doesn't last long. We're inside now and the reality of being at my own funeral has hit me like a strong gust of wind. I spot my mother at the front and immediately feel a sensation akin to a kick in the stomach. She's not wailing as she was in her bedroom anymore, but she's still not OK. Funny how I can tell that from all the way back here. It's all in the twisting of her hands, the way she fusses with her hair every few seconds. She's clearly stressing about something. Knowing Mum, she will be claiming it's the caterers or the lack of parking or something completely unrelated to the reality of this moment. Mum diverts her feelings on regular detours until they all arrive in one sudden explosion. I've seen it happen before, more than once.

Regardless of how much diverting she is doing, there is no denying that she looks exhausted. Rings haunt her eyes and her black dress hangs limply from her thinner-than-usual frame. I can feel Death's palm suddenly pressed tightly against mine and I realize that I'm squeezing his hand, hard. I hastily let go, tugging my sleeves down over my hands instead.

As I'm staring at her, my mother is joined by my father. It's weird to see him in such a smart suit. He's a caretaker for the local school and has been for years, so he usually does paint-splattered jeans and old shirts. But now he's in a brand-new black suit and a crisp white shirt and, if that wasn't jarring enough, he's got rid of his usual bristly stubble too. That would have been Mum again. *It's your daughter's funeral, smarten up.* I spent my childhood loving how those bristles would tickle against my cheek.

So there they are, suited and smartened and standing united. Waiting for their dead daughter. Feeling a little shaky,

I take in the rest of the room. I spot my grandparents nearby, my aunts and uncles, shaking their heads and murmuring to each other. Then there's the headmaster from my secondary school, looking as uncomfortable as I'd expect him to look at the funeral of an ex-pupil he probably barely remembers. I spot some people from my school and from university. Some of them I would expect to be here, but there are some who I can't help but raise an eyebrow at.

"What the hell is Laura Thatcher doing here?" I hiss, and Death glances at me, eyebrow raising quizzically.

"Enemy?" he whispers back.

"That would require her actually acknowledging my existence. How the hell did she even find out about this?"

Death sniffs with amusement, smirking a little. "People will do anything for free sandwiches."

I have to smile at that, but then the background music fades gradually, causing people's conversations to cease as they twist in their seats expectantly. I feel Death hesitate before he takes my hand again and steers me toward a back corner, with a gentleness that I haven't really seen from him before. Now's not the time to quiz him on that, though.

As we come to a halt in our new spot, the doors open again. And there I am. Boxed up, ready for delivery. It could be anyone inside that coffin and maybe that's why I'm not freaking out. I can just pretend it's someone else. But then I see my brother, and Eric is just behind him.

Reality smacks me pretty hard in the face then.

I notice in a distant sort of way that Eric's got his hair all combed back. Another change. He usually wears it carefully styled to look like he's just rolled out of bed. I wonder if he made that decision himself or if Mum told him. Or if Violet warned him that turning up with uncombed hair would be a dire offense. Not that it matters anymore, I suppose. It's not like he needs to impress them; they're not his girlfriend's parents now. That ship has sailed.

They carry the coffin down the aisle at a stupidly slow pace and all I keep thinking is that they need to hurry up, that this is too awkward and somber. I watch as they pass by the telltale explosion of hair that is Violet in the second row, watch as her head dips down and there's an audible sob that makes it all the way back to us.

It hurts. It hurts to hear her cry and it hurts to see the way my brother's arms shake a little as he carries me. The pain doubles when I see Dad's head coming to rest against my mum's shoulder and his own shoulders trembling as he clearly tries to hold back whatever emotions a father has at seeing their daughter coming down the aisle in a box rather than a wedding dress.

Guilt gnaws away at my insides. This is all on me. Everybody's here and hurting because of me.

I feel a shoulder bumping against mine. I glance to my left to Death, who jerks his thumb toward the door with a questioning look. Do I want to leave? A little bit, yes. But that doesn't mean I should. I think maybe I owe it to everyone here.

So we stay. We stay through all the somber waffle about going on to a better place and the meaningless words about how much joy I brought my parents. As if that matters when I took it away again.

Then my brother gets called up. I notice the way Ollie seems to skirt around the edge of my coffin a little, as if touching it might somehow make it all real. He looks so small in his smart black suit. We've always teased him for looking so young, it doesn't seem quite so funny now. He looks like he's dressed up in his father's clothes. My death has shrunk him.

I've been doing OK so far, but the moment Ollie opens

his mouth to speak, I know I'm in trouble. I can feel that heavy, crushing feeling of guilt again and it makes me feel like I'm drowning.

"I'd like to thank you all for coming today. It's been a hard time for the Cooper family but your support has been really appreciated," Ollie begins, his voice husky and soft. Ollie has always been more outgoing than me, has always been a confident, sporty type. But he seems unsure and almost shy now. I guess it's a lot easier to talk about workouts than it is to talk about feelings. "Daisy—Daisy was my little sister but she was also my friend. She knew how to make me laugh and gave the best damn advice ever. She was kind and clever and so determined to help those she loved. I know I speak for us all when I say we're really going to miss her."

He carries on, but I can't listen anymore. I find Death's arm and squeeze it tight, glancing to him and shaking my head. I don't wait to see his response because there's no time to waste, not when it feels like someone is jumping up and down on my chest. Pushing past him, I stumble out the door and keep going until fresh air hits my face.

The sobs erupt from me like some sort of volcano and my knees hit the gravel of the driveway as I fall to the ground. All the denial crumbles down, paving the way for the crushing realization of my death's impact. There I was selfishly hoping my funeral wouldn't be empty, hoping that as many people as possible would be broken by my departure. What the hell does that say about me?

As I gulp the tears down, I'm distantly aware of Death coming to sit beside me. Unsurprisingly, he says nothing. And, to be honest, I'm glad of that. I don't want to be reasoned with or consoled. I just want the whole weight of this pain to be felt without distraction, as it's been quietly waiting to do for days.

I don't know how long it takes until the calm begins to arrive. But, finally, it does. "Sorry," I whisper, forcing myself to look across at my companion. "I just… I couldn't do it anymore. I couldn't face up to all the hurt I've caused."

Death is looking determinedly at the trees directly opposite us. But at these words he glances back at me, albeit briefly. "*I've* caused," he corrects, voice soft. He shrugs, quirks an eyebrow with a small, bitter smile. "Technically speaking."

I sniff, rubbing at my nose and wiping at my eyes. "Well, we can't both feel guilty. At least, not at the same time."

Death smiles distantly, looking out across the grass once more. "We'd never get anything done," he murmurs.

He looks distant, almost exhausted. For the first time since we met, I can see how heavily the job he does weighs on his shoulders.

The main door opens again and two people stumble outside, drawing my attention away. It's Eric and Violet. Eric is supporting Violet at the waist and, even from here, I can sense her utter panic and despair.

They manage to drop down onto a bench, a few feet to the right of us. Violet's crying hard, her hands clenched so tight that I know her fingernails will be breaking skin. Eric seems better composed but you only have to look a little closer to see that he's only keeping it together for her benefit.

Death shoots me a questioning look, but I shake my head. I'm transfixed by this scene and I can't leave it, not yet. I owe it to them, somehow.

"What a mess," Eric finally mutters after a few minutes of his silence and her tears. Violet looks at him sharply, and he hurriedly backtracks, as one hand fumbles around for his pocket. "I meant the whole thing, not you, obviously."

I can see Violet holding back an eye roll. "Yeah. Well, I think it's reasonable to apply it to me too. I mean, look at me," she groans, rubbing at the bags under her eyes. No more than three hours' sleep a night, that's what those bags tell me.

Eric has pulled out a pack of cigarettes and a lighter. This fills me with a quiet outrage because I told that idiot to quit months ago. Then he offers one to Violet and I narrow my eyes. "If she takes one of those, I'm going to kill her," I hiss, and Death smirks a little.

To give her credit, though, she shoots Eric a glare. "I'm a dancer, Eric. Do you know what those things do to your fitness? Besides, didn't Daisy tell you that if she ever caught you smoking again, she'd shove one up your backside? And light it?"

With a small smile, I shrug under Death's curious look. "I don't like smoking."

Meanwhile, Eric sighs, tapping the lighter against the box of cigarettes but not opening them yet. "Yeah, well, this is sort of a desperate time."

Violet looks away, staring out across the driveway and to-ward the car park. "I just—just can't believe she's really gone."

"I know," he whispers. He's silent, then: "Violet, I'm sorry I haven't been around much for you."

It's barely a whisper but we all hear it. Violet glances over to him, clearly confused. "What do you mean?"

Eric shakes his head, kneading at the corner of one eye. Determined not to cry. "She—she would want me to look after you. I know you're struggling and I should be helping you. It's just... I don't really know how."

Violet's expression is one of surprise. I can understand that. I remember feeling that surprise myself, when Eric first showed his softer side to me. After a moment, she sighs and shuffles a little closer, pats his leg. "Eric, as sweet as that sen-timent is, you're really not going to be able to do much for me. I just need...time."

A quavering sigh comes from Eric and he watches her worriedly for a moment. But then he nods, accepts her words (far too easily in my opinion). "Time. Right."

The door opens again. This time it's my dad who steps out. He's loosened his tie a little and his neatly combed hair is already starting to mess itself up. Mum will be flattening that down soon, I'm sure. "There you are, we were looking for you." He pauses, noticing Violet's damp cheeks and puffy eyes. "Are you all right, Vi?" He asks the question with ease, familiarity. It's not the first time he's asked Violet that, after all.

But the fresh air seems to have helped Violet and she stands up slowly, helping Eric up as he surreptitiously pockets the cigarettes again. "I'm fine, Gary. Just needed some fresh air; it was getting a little much in there."

Dad places a bracing hand on her shoulder. "Well, we're almost through now. The hardest bit is over. We just need to put our Daisy to rest. Then we can all have a stiff drink, eh?" My dad is doing his usual thing of hiding everything behind humor and practical speeches, but he's not convincing anyone.

Still, the three move inside and then it's just us again. The air seems colder without the warmth and the noise of the living around us.

"How are you doing?" Death asks, after a moment.

"Pretty shit." Honesty seems like a good policy right about now.

Death makes a small noise of agreement. "Yeah, some days are always going to be shit. But you can't get to the next day without going through them…"

He speaks with a strange sense of authority and I find curiosity burning through my cold sense of loss. "Death. Why did we come here? Really?"

For a moment, Death looks like he's going to find a way to avoid the question. He's been doing that to me a lot of the time, after all; I've learned the signs. But then he sighs, rubs at the back of his neck. "Back when Natasha joined us, she asked if she could go to her own funeral. Begged me. I told her no, said it would be too hard on her. I mean, that's always been the rules. Don't make it harder than it needs to be, avoid excessive contact with living relatives. I thought seeing your own funeral would definitely fit into that. I was just following the rules but I think she thought I just couldn't be bothered. Because after that...well, you've seen what she's like around me. I thought I was helping to make it all a bit easier for her. But I think I just made it harder. So I didn't want to make the same mistake today." A darkness settles over his gaze for a second but when he looks at me a moment later it's gone.

"Oh." I fall silent for a second, then another question arrives, almost out of nowhere. "You've done this job for a long time, haven't you?"

Death gently pushes the gravel around with his foot. Then nods. "It's all I've ever known. No life, no file for me—just this. Forever."

"That's a lot of shit days to work through." He shrugs, but I know that he's agreeing with me. "So, maybe there should be room for just a little more compassion? You don't *have* to rush each person through. You choose to. And if you didn't, maybe it would be a little easier."

Death considers this. "I think I've...always been a little scared. Of—of getting attached," he finally murmurs, each word slow and considered.

"I know," I reply, then shoot him a weak grin.

Death hesitates, then smiles back. It's the most natural smile I've ever seen from him and it transforms his face completely.

He bumps his shoulder against mine again, but this time he doesn't move it away. I hesitate, then find my head coming to rest against his shoulder. Two people, drained by a day that was always going to take its toll, even on the unsleeping dead. There's a warmth and comfort to be found in this position and, right now, I need that more than anything.

"So…home?" he asks a moment later.

The word doesn't quite sit right and I find myself glancing back toward the building currently hosting my funeral. I think I know what I need to do next, but now is not the time to voice it. So I nod, pull my head away.

"Yeah. Time to go."

Perhaps we can survive each other's company after all.

Rule Ten

Give Grief The Respect It Deserves

DO YOU KNOW WHAT *always really irritates me? And no, the answer is not everything. It's the way you lot portray grief. It's defined as intense sorrow, especially caused by someone's death. Intense sorrow, you see? But when I catch glimpses of your films and television shows, your books even, grief is this tidy and neatly packaged emotion that lasts for a finite amount of time before it gets magically swept aside, usually by some saccharine and highly unlikely life-changing event.*

Well, grief is nothing like that. Grief is that mean kid in the playground who won't leave you alone. It's big and it's ugly and it will keep on prodding you until you snap. People who have been bullied snap in different ways, right? Some fall to pieces, some fight back, some come and visit me. But do you ever just see them letting a few tears travel artfully down their face before moving on? No. Grief doesn't move on. Just like that bully, it's always there. Yes, the principal might get involved and give them a warning or a disciplinary action but you never stop looking over your shoulder for it.

So don't give me this tidy packaged crap. You owe yourselves more than that. Grief should be respected and feared like the lion standing by its open cage door. Don't ignore it, or before long you'll find it chewing on your leg.

✳ ✳ ✳

I leave it two days. Two days for me to recover from the funeral so I can be certain about my choice and two days for my family to recover too. Because I know what I want to do next. I need to see them. I need them to see me. And perhaps then I can stop thinking about my mum's shaking fingers, my brother's broken voice, my dad's bristle-free chin.

And maybe they'll help me stay longer, I don't know. All I know is I have to try and I have to see them. There's that desperate, hollow feeling of homesickness in the pit of my stomach, like that time when I went on a residential trip with my school for a week and every night I went to sleep with tears stuck to my cheeks. But I also know I have to be kind to them and let the soil atop my coffin settle.

After two days, I broach the subject with Death. We've just finished helping a traumatized young woman through to the other side with surprising success and so Death is in a fairly good mood. "Death," I begin, a touch tentatively, "I've been thinking…"

He looks up, his startlingly green eyes narrowing with clear suspicion. "Thinking what?" he asks.

"I want to try again."

It takes him a moment, then he glances back toward the doors to the lift. "Try appearing to them again? Are you sure?"

I don't need to think for that long; I've had two days to stew and I know I have to do this. For one reason or another. So I nod. "Yes. I'm sure. I want to try again. With my family."

Death purses his lips, considers it for a moment. "You remember what happened with Violet, right? It will probably be worse."

"I know, but I think it could also help."

He looks at me thoughtfully, trying to decide whether I really do know what I'm talking about, but he accepts my words with a nod a moment later.

We're doing this.

We stand outside my family home, my cul-de-sac. Where I grew up, or did the majority of my growing up. We moved here when I was five, from Cornwall, because my grandma got ill and Mum didn't want to be too far away. I don't remember much from that first place. Just the salty smell that clung to everything and the sense of freedom from being able to rush down to the beach from the garden. Everything was so battered by the wind and the sea that you didn't try to make things look too perfect.

Here, though, everything has its place. Hedges are trimmed with rulers and curtains are twitched whenever a different sounding car engine comes into earshot. It drove Violet and me mad. I think it secretly drove Mum mad too, but she always pretended she liked it, to make Gran feel less guilty. But Violet and I dreamed of getting out for years, right from the moment we first got on the train and visited London. The irony of me coming all this way, back to this suffocating little corner of England, hasn't escaped me. But I'm here to see my family.

Death is unusually quiet. He hasn't spoken much the entire way down, lost in his own thoughts. It's weird to see him looking this troubled compared to his perpetual state of nonchalance.

"So this is it," I murmur.

"Yep."

"Are you OK?" I ask, curiosity getting the better of me.

Death nods, rubbing his chin with one hand. "Yeah, fine. I'm just…thinking. Still sure about this?"

"Still sure. I have to try, Death. You saw them at my funeral…"

Death purses his lips, something flashing across his expression for just a second, too quick to place. He nods briskly. "Yes, I did. OK, fine. Let's do this."

It's a little jarring, to suddenly be told to do something that is hardly the most simple of tasks. But I push that to one side, force myself to focus. I close my eyes, bring myself back to that now all-too-familiar-feeling of anger. Except it's harder today, because I can't picture anything to do with Violet without also picturing her crying outside my funeral.

After a moment of trying desperately to feel angry and getting nowhere, I open my eyes again with a huff of irritation. "It's not—I can't do it! I can't get angry about that memory anymore."

For a moment, Death says nothing. It's almost as if he hasn't heard me. Finally, though, he responds: "Well, perhaps anger didn't get you there last time, perhaps something else did. Get thinking." He takes a step forward, places a finger on the doorbell.

"What are you doing?" I demand.

"Giving you some incentive. Wind in your sails. Chop-chop." Then he presses the bell.

"Are you crazy?" I hiss, taking a step toward him. "I can't do it! I just told you!"

Death steps toward me. "Well then, your mother is about

to open the door to nobody. She'll probably think it's some-one pranking her or maybe she'll think she's going mad. Ei-ther way, it won't be very nice for her."

I can feel myself panicking. Death steps around me, places a hand on my back. "I think I can hear her. I'd say you've got ten seconds…" His hands find my shoulders, squeeze them gently. "You can do this, Daisy."

I close my eyes, desperately trying to feel that burning rage I had before. But all I've got is fear and worry at the thought of my grief-stricken mother opening the door to an empty step. It builds inside me, bigger and bigger, spreading over me like wildfire.

I hear the latch click. I feel Death shove me. Then the door opens.

Mum's standing right in front of me and, judging from her expression, it's worked.

She can see me.

There's a second, maybe two, of calm. Silence in which we both appraise each other with trademark Cooper suspicion-meets-concern. She's still looking so tired and thin, and now she's a little gray-faced as well.

"Hi, Mum," I try, each word feeling like a step across a battlefield. I don't know when the bombs will drop, just that they will.

Indeed, a second later, Mum lets out a piercing scream and slams the door shut. I hear her yelling for Dad and I have to resist the urge to turn and run. Maybe Death was right; maybe this wasn't a good idea after all.

But then I hear heavy footsteps approaching the door and the door is pulled open and once again I'm revealed to a fam-ily member. Dad shares the same skin tone as Mum right now, like a rain cloud, but his expression is a touch calmer. He's always been the calmer member of our family, the peace-maker. I just hope he can rise to the occasion now.

"Oh my God!" he whispers initially. Then he leans forward a little, eyes wide with shock. "Daisy?" he asks slowly, gently. Like he's afraid his words might blow me away. I nod mutely, my throat feeling a little tight as I fight back the tears. "Daisy, sweetheart, what are you doing here?"

It's such a simple question, so out of place with this highly complicated situation. Maybe that's why I can't hold back anymore. Or maybe it's just because I really missed my parents. Whatever the reason, his words trigger something in me and I let out a desperate sob. "I came to see you." The words feel like toffee in my mouth, sticking to my teeth.

Mum makes a soft sound of almost longing. She's been standing behind Dad but seeing her daughter in this state seems to have chased away her initial fear, because she steps around him and comes to give me a tight, almost possessive hug. "My poor girl, we've missed you much," she whispers against my ear.

"I'm sorry, I didn't mean to—to…" I trail off, spluttering out another round of painful tears. "I didn't want to leave you."

Mum strokes the back of my head. It feels like she's wearing protective gloves, thanks to that cruel and unmoving barrier between me and them. Dad's arms come around the pair of us and we stay enclosed in this embrace for a moment, until Mum speaks again. "What happened, Daisy? What happened to you?"

I pull back a little, looking at her and then over to Dad. Both look like they're trying so hard to hold it together, for my sake. Even after my death, they're still trying to protect me.

"I—I can't really say. I'm sorry, I'm so sorry." I stumble over the words, too choked up with tears.

Mum holds my cheek, runs a thumb under my eye. "Come inside, we can talk."

Yes, the last thing we need is Mrs. Clarke from next door spotting me and reporting it to the police, like the time she spotted Violet and I trying cider at the bus stop (we were six months shy of eighteen, God forbid). So I nod, shakily step into the house.

Home smells the same: washing detergent and cooking. I can't decide if the unchanging nature of my parents' house is comforting or smothering. Eighteen-year-old me definitely found it smothering, but now it's not so easy to decide. There's definitely something soothing in knowing that, even beyond my death, home stands firm.

Except when you look closer, you can tell that's not really the case. There's a pile of unopened envelopes on the hall table, closed curtains in the adjoining sitting room, abandoned shoes by the stairs. All little things but if you knew how house-proud my mother was, you'd be feeling the same level of concern.

Mum carefully leads the way down the hall into the kitchen. That, at least, is tidy. A semblance of normality in a house that already feels crooked, out of place. She comes to a halt by the table that sits in the center of the room. For a second I can see Violet and me, gangly nine-year-olds with matching French braids doing our homework together. I can see Ollie and me spraying the table with flour as we help Mum make Christmas cake.

But then it's empty again.

"How..." Mum begins, then stops as she tries to construct a sentence and apparently finds it harder than expected. "Are... are you back? Properly?"

Dad has come to stand near me, resting against the kitchen

counter. "Claire, give her a second before you start with the interrogation," he says gently.

Mum stiffens a little as she looks across at him, then back to me. "I need to know. I need to know what's going on. Can you blame me? I—I can't get my hopes up for nothing I'm...not strong enough for that."

Her voice breaks a little toward the end. It sends a shiver down my spine. "I'm not back," I whisper. Who knew three simple words could be so difficult to say? Mum stares at me for a long time and I can see a flurry of emotions passing through her eyes. Despair, fear, anger, bitterness, heartbreak. The gang's all there.

"I see." Her words are barely audible as she turns away, moves toward the kettle. From my position, half-frozen by the door, I can see her fingers trip over the handle of the kettle, made clumsy by a persistent trembling.

"Claire..."

At Dad's gentle warning, Mum lets out a small sound, almost like a moan of pain, back curving over like she's trying to curl up inside herself. "Mum?" I'm trying so hard not to be scared by this display of grief; I know she has every right to be like this. But it just feels so wrong. Seeing your own parent cry shatters every illusion that you had of them being an untouchable superhero. They're just human. Fragile and finite like the rest of us.

And that scares the hell out of me.

"Mum, please—it's OK."

I watch her head shake slowly as she rests her forehead against the nearby kitchen cupboard. "OK? You were my baby girl! I held you in my arms and I watched you grow and then...then you were just gone."

There are tears blurring my vision as Dad moves over to her. She shakes her head again, steps away from his comfort before turning back around to me. "Did you go and see Violet?"

I'm a little floored. "What?"

"Violet? Did you go and see her? She called me, the night after you—you left us. She was in bits because she said she had seen you."

I nod slowly, trying to work out where she's going with this. "I—I wanted to see if I could."

"Middle of the night it was, ranting on about spending the evening with you. We thought she'd had a breakdown or something, thought she was going to end up in hospital again. But she was telling the truth?"

Another nod. Inside me is a real fear that every word coming out of my mouth has the potential to cause irreversible damage. So I keep quiet. Mum sighs, looking away. Even from across the kitchen, I can see the shake of her shoulders as she tries to hold back tears.

"Mum, please," I try, desperate to somehow fix this train wreck of a visit. I was meant to be making things better, not worse.

"We've just buried our *daughter*! We've just buried *you*, Daisy!"

"This—this isn't my fault, Mum. It was an accident."

Mum's hands tremble a little as she picks a mug from the mug tree, trying to lose herself in routines. "How much had you drunk?" she murmurs, not quite able to look over at me. "You did ice-skating lessons until you were fifteen, so why did you forget how to balance that one time?"

I stare at her, stunned.

"Tell me how you managed to die tripping over a pavement! Because I don't understand it. I don't understand and it is *tearing me apart*."

Her grief has transformed her into someone I barely recognize. This isn't the woman who would pick me up from school when I was ill, even if it meant leaving an important meeting. This isn't the woman who learned all the moves to my ice-skating routines so she could practice them with me at home.

And maybe this is why the dead aren't meant to cross the paths with the living. Because you will come face-to-face with grief, and grief is not to be trifled with. Grief brings anger, bitter and dark. It brings blame. Why did you have to get cancer? Why did you not look properly before crossing? Why did *you* have to be the hero?

I shouldn't have come.

Dad is trying to soothe Mum, murmuring words about low visibility, black ice and how really the method does not matter, not now. This just makes her more upset though. "No, Gary, none of it matters. Because she's still sodding *dead*!" The words tumble out, paired with that strange, animalistic sob I heard from her that night in their bedroom. Her hands shake with the pure emotion of it all, which in turns knocks the mug from her hands.

The clattering smash makes us all stop.

Mum stares at the mess, then at me, and I can see the regret in her eyes. I sigh, the sound fluttering around this oppressively awkward kitchen. "Mum… I don't know what to do."

The doorbell rings. We all turn to stare down the hall in perfect unison. There's a pause, then it rings again. Another pause, then again.

The mail slot creaks open. Through the small gap, I spot a pair of familiar, startlingly green eyes.

I'm out of the kitchen so fast that I almost fall over (at least that would prove to my mother that I wasn't drunk, that I really am this fucking uncoordinated). I run down the hall, and wrench open the door so hard that I hear the hinges squeak. And even though I know exactly who is there, I still feel shock smack against my rib cage.

Death straightens up, hands sliding into his pockets. Then he winks. "Surprise," he states. "Now, are you going to let me in?"

Rule Eleven

Families Come With Complications

I'VE OFTEN WONDERED WHAT *makes a family.*

As somebody who never had parents and who never technically had siblings, the concept was always a little alien to me. Why would you want to spend your time with people who are similar to you and so are inevitably going to clash with you? Why would you place such importance and value on a group of people who are as frail and finite as the rest of humanity? Isn't that just setting yourself up for a loss?

I've met a lot of families over the years. Traditional nuclear families who paint me a perfect picture of their home life, forgetting that I've got their files and know about the visit to the divorce lawyer or the son's dealings with the police. Families who can't stand to be in the same room together. Families full of "steps" and "halfs" that determinedly hold themselves together despite the intricate web of interwoven histories that follow.

But there's one thing that's always the same. They all come with complications. An elephant in the room, an unspoken secret, or perhaps just a memory of an event that left an unfixable scar right in the middle of the family portrait. It's messy and confusing and that's before I've even got involved. They fight and break and mend and adapt and sometimes break again. They drift apart, they grow new branches.

So, why bother? I asked a mother that once. She smiled to herself, a silent secret hidden in the corners of her mouth. She was a painter, and she told me how her best paintings were the ones with the biggest messes around them. And that was like her family—messy all around the edges but with this masterpiece in the center.

I'm still not sure whether I agree with her.

But I'm hopeful.

❋ ❋ ❋

For a moment, I just stare at him. Can you blame me? It's not every day that Death turns up on the doorstep of your childhood home. Even if Death is someone you've become somewhat acquainted with.

Of course he takes full advantage of my surprise. He sidesteps smartly around me, pats my arm, then strides confidently down the corridor and into the kitchen.

For a moment, I stay frozen in shock. Then I remember who else is in that kitchen.

"Oh shit," I hiss, then hurry after him to find that he has already shaken hands with both of my parents and is now rooting through the cupboards. Mum and Dad stare at him, but strangely make no effort to ask what he is doing, and who he is, as if some deep part of them already knows. Perhaps not who he is *exactly*, as there would probably be a great deal more screaming, but they certainly aren't treating him like some sort of random home invader.

Finally, after a moment of stunned silence, Death finds what he's looking for—a large bag of "flaming chili" tortilla chips, according to the lurid logo splashed across it. "Oh, these look fun," he crows triumphantly, moving over to my side, whereupon he takes me by the arm and leads me to a chair. In a slight daze, I squish up on one side to allow him to share. He sits, knees bumping against mine, and finally my mother snaps out of her temporary silence.

"Sorry," she says, and then blinks at how sincere her apology actually sounded. "Who is this?" she asks, looking to me for an answer.

Death looks to me as well, his eyes burning into the side of my face. "Uh," I begin, then swallow to see if that will help me work out what to say. It doesn't. So I go for a lame, "He helped me come back."

Next to me, Death snorts as he pulls open his bag of tortilla chips, shaking his head. "Help is a loose way of putting it. I mainly just watched." Then he makes a rather troubling gagging noise as he sniffs the bag. "Are you all right?" Mum asks, as Death proceeds to glare furiously at the packet of tortilla chips.

"These are not even remotely flaming chili," he whispers, as if the tortilla chips were actually fried spider legs.

My mother puts a hand to her mouth, and lets out a gasp that sounds incredibly genuine. "Oh I'm sorry—let me find you some better ones." She hops up and I watch with bewilderment as she moves to ransack the cupboards with a bizarre urgency. Instinct takes over, and I turn to scowl suspiciously at my chair partner.

"What have you done?" I hiss, and Death leans in until his words can only be heard by me.

"Nothing. The subconscious mind is aware of the importance of my very existence, here in this room, but the conscious mind is never quite able to work out exactly who or what I am, so all it can do is heighten every emotion, and give humans an intense urge to keep me happy, lest I drag them to the abyss," he whispers, before his head snaps back around to face Mum as she returns with the bag of high-end chips she usually reserves only for special guests.

"Here, try these," she murmurs, passing them over before moving back to her husband's side. They both stand silently with a very distinct sense of expectation in their expressions. It's a little weird, to say the least, and yet I find myself turning to Death as well. After all, he did come across the worlds to be here and I assume it wasn't just to sample our snack selection.

Death opens the bag, takes a chip and bites into it tentatively. Apparently satisfied, he gives my mother a thumbs-up before turning to the business at hand. "So," he begins, and I recognize that calm, professional tone that he uses with his customers, "I imagine you've been finding this is a little difficult?"

Mum shifts uncomfortably, causing Death to shoot her an indulgent smile. Dad bites his lip, taking her hand. "We're just...confused," he whispers.

"It's perfectly normal," Death goes on, his voice confident and knowledgeable. "There's really nothing to feel guilty about. You've been through a great trauma and this probably shouldn't have happened—my bad. Grief needs time, it doesn't need...disturbance. So, Daisy and I will leave, and when the door shuts behind us, you're going to find that you have completely forgotten that Daisy was ever here. Just like that."

I don't want to leave, regardless of how badly this reunion has gone. I lean close to Death again, until his ear is practically in my mouth. "Do—do we have to?" I whisper, and I am certain I have never sounded this desperate. "Maybe I can fix this."

He turns to meet my gaze, grimaces a little. "Time to go, Cooper," he says gently.

The sudden new nickname doesn't really do much to convince me. But there is a sadness in his voice, and it seems almost weighed down with an understanding of how I'm feeling. This floors me, because I can think of no reason why he would understand this feeling. It's not like he has a family.

I find myself standing. Death smiles with relief, then stands as well, shooting my parents a reassuring expression. I catch Mum brushing at her eyes, watching me almost longingly.

She steps forward, rests her hands on my shoulders. "I just—just wish you weren't gone." Pressing a final kiss to my forehead, she turns away, busies herself with the washing-up. Like she's already trying to forget what's happened. Her soft crying floats around the room in cruel, unrelenting echoes.

On the other side of the table, Dad seems to be hesitating, not quite ready to give up.

I look over to Death, hopelessness weighing heavy on my shoulders. I don't know what I'm asking him, but he shakes his head anyway. There's a heavy, reluctant finality to that shake. I can't argue against it somehow. "I'm sorry. I'm really sorry," I croak, turning back toward Dad.

Dad smiles back at me, his eyes a little hollow. "It's OK. You—you be safe."

When I hear Dad's voice shake, that's when I know I have to leave. I can't even bring myself to hug him, or say another word. Everything feels sharp and cruel and I just need to escape. I stumble down the corridor on unsteady feet, the door ahead seeming to grow, shrink, and warp before me, like I'm in one of those wonky corridors you go through at a carnival, until suddenly I'm outside.

I find myself taking big, panicked gulps of the fresh morning air. As if it might somehow help. I'm so involved in this that I barely hear Death coming out behind me, so when his arm touches my shoulder, I jump with surprise and have to stifle a small yell of shock with one hand. He hurries around to stand in front of me, hands out and expression steady.

"Easy, Daisy. It's just me."

I want to be angry with him. I want to rage and scream at him and make this all his fault. But I know, logically, that it's not. I chose to come here; he gave me the chance to change my mind and I didn't. I thought I knew best.

Maybe that's why I don't shout at him. Maybe that's why, when Death's arms suddenly wrap around me, I don't resist. I just let my head drop to rest against his chest. "I—I thought I could make it work."

I feel a sigh brush against the top of my head. I can sense that Death is a little awkward around all this emotion. But, to give him credit, he sticks with it. He keeps his arms around me, even gives my back a few awkward pats. You could almost believe he's done this before. A moment later, he pulls back, but only a little bit. "Maybe we should go somewhere else that isn't outside your family home. I'm not sure how helpful it is to be here."

Eventually we end up back in his office. I can't quite stomach sitting at his desk so I slide down to the floor, resting against one wall. Death hesitates, then drops down beside me.

Silence descends. Our natural habitat. Except I don't think I can do this anymore. Silence will not work right now, not when grief is prickling against my skin like a hideous rash. I have to say something, anything.

"Why did you come?" I find myself asking, watching as Death pauses in his fruitless pen fiddling.

"I was…worried."

"You were…?"

"Worried, yes. I was trying not to be nosy, so I was just popping in and out. You were doing all right for a bit but then—"

I sniff with bitter amusement. "Then I fucked it up."

Death tugs at a stray strand of jet-black hair. "I wouldn't say it was you," he says slowly, as if he's choosing each word incredibly carefully. I don't blame him because I feel like if he says anything against my parents, I'll be saying something right back. Understandably, they're a sensitive topic right now.

"Look, Daisy. I'm not an expert on families. But I am an expert on grief. It takes its toll, Daisy. More so than your own death, in my opinion. It needs careful handling. I should have warned you about that." He meets my gaze for a moment but then doesn't seem able to hold it, and looks away. That strikes a chord with me and I lean forward a little.

"Why do I get the sense that you're talking from more than just professional experience?"

Death chews at his lips. I can tell that he's really carefully considering whether to tell me or not. A few days ago, he probably would have brushed it off but there's something different about him today. Something softer, less guarded.

"Lucas," he murmurs. "A long time ago, there was Lucas. I hired him, back when I was still…young. I thought it would make things easier, if I didn't have to be alone." His hands clasp together and, for a moment, I'm sure I see them trembling. But then a second later they're steady and I can convince myself that I imagined it. "He was a good kid. An idiot and annoying sometimes, but he was kind—and he was company. I came to think of him as a brother, in a way"

A sense of foreboding settles around me like a winter's fog. "What happened?"

Death's green eyes are dark, clouded over. Usually they remind me of a forest on that first day of summer but now it looks like midwinter in there. "He got taken away. He was… too kind, I guess. And he tried to help this girl, this terrified little girl. He spent hours with her because he wanted to be sure she was OK and—and he missed his next appointment. It wasn't the first time, either. He broke the rules, Daisy. And, then the next day, he was gone. Just like that. And I was alone." Instinctively, I reach for his hand. He doesn't tug it away, which is a pleasant surprise. Instead, he squeezes our hands, tight enough to make his knuckles flare white. "That was when I began to understand what grief was."

In this moment, he seems so *human*. And while part of me wants to allow him to move on, to be freed from reliving what was clearly a painful moment for him, I can't let him go just yet. "So what is it? What is grief?"

Death sighs. "It's dark and angry and cruel. It can't be packaged into tidy little emotions and it certainly can't be reasoned with. It's like being possessed by the damn Devil himself." He finally meets my gaze again, slowly retracting his hand from under mine. Slow enough for me to know that I don't need to be offended. "All I'm saying, Daisy, is that you shouldn't take your parents' actions personally. It's not that simple."

I sigh, finding comfort in picking at the edge of my sleeve as memories whirl around my head. "My brother. Ollie. When he was little, he got hit by a car." The words slip out, a little clumsily. Almost as if they weren't quite ready. "He was ten, I was six. He wasn't concentrating, typical Ollie. I didn't think things could change so fast—one moment he was laughing at my joke, the next he was on the ground."

I can feel Death's gaze stuck on me, focused like a laser. No going back now. "Mum and Dad, they told me to say goodbye to him, at the hospital. I remember how weird their voices sounded, like they were pretending to be someone else.

They weren't sure he was going to make it, he had lost so much blood and his lungs were really bad. But then he pulled through and they were so happy, so relieved. They kept saying how they couldn't bear to bury their own child…" I feel my voice shake as I reach the crux of this little trip down to memory lane. "And now they have."

Death tilts his head, expression incredibly thoughtful. "So you feel guilty?"

"Well, yeah. But it's more than that. They used to drive me mad with their overprotectiveness all the time, and even though I knew why, it still frustrated me so much. And now, seeing them like that, I just wish I could go back and do it differently. Not go out in the middle of the night for bloody milk. I think I've always felt like I've let them down, one way or another, and this just sort of proves it," I mutter, voice bitter as I find myself shuffling down a little against the wall.

Death shifts a little more so he's facing me more directly, considers me with a thoughtful expression. "Daisy, I'm pretty sure families never listen properly to each other. Lucas and I never did. But somehow we all manage to take in the important things. And that made you who you are today. Sure, if you listened to them and stayed safe all the time, you might still be alive. But you wouldn't have gone with Violet to London and found your own life there. You wouldn't have looked after her like you did. That's worth something, right?"

I shake my head, let out a sigh. He takes this as a cue to go on.

"We can't stop families being messy, Daisy. No more than we can stop death." I find myself smiling because Death really is as unpredictable as the wind. So obtuse sometimes and then he comes out with nuggets of wisdom like this.

I don't reply, but I don't need to. I can tell he knows that he's got through to me. We sit in a now rather comfortable silence, both lost in thoughts that, at least for my part, feel a great deal less intimidating. "Thank you," I finally say. "For telling me about Lucas. It helped."

Death rubs at his nose, that more familiar smirk of sarcasm returning. "Well, I'm glad my traumatic experiences are of use to you."

I sit up a little straighter again. "So, what now? Traumatize my aunts? Or Eric?" I'm only half joking, which Death seems to pick up on after a few seconds.

He shoots me a weary smile, stretching out his arms before twirling his pen deftly over his fingers. "Maybe give it a few days, eh? Although, I suppose we should be celebrating in a way."

I tilt my head, curious. "Why?"

Shrugging, Death points the pen at me. "Because, Daisy, you have now appeared to the living for a significant amount of time, twice. That is pretty impressive."

I smile, feeling a rare moment of warm pride in my chest. He's right, and that's good, because I'm not ready to give up on getting back to my life one day. And this is a step in the right direction. Even if it is a step on a thorny, painful path.

Just as I'm considering this and what it could potentially mean, the room fills with a dull and droning alarm. It wails loudly, causing me to instinctively cover up my ears. Death stands, returning the pen to his pocket and adjusting his name tag with a heavy sigh of exasperation. "Really? Now?"

"What is it?" I ask, standing as well.

"MDS," he replies and, when I continue to look blank, he grimaces and goes on. "Mass Death Situation. Or, in other words: get your umbrella because the shit just hit the fan."

Rule Twelve

Don't Let Fear Win

FEAR IS A POWER like no other. Sometimes it can do extraordinary things. It can be the extra kick of strength you need to swim to the surface, or the extra determination to lift a car and free your child. But sometimes fear can be the sly hand that slips around your middle and tugs you away from where you need to be, and whispers that next time you'll do it, but not today. Next time.

When people arrive up here, they seem to assume that fear is a curse reserved for the living. Like the moment you die, your brain cleverly shuts that part of you away. A reward for a lifetime of quickened heartbeats and sweaty palms.

Well, that would be nice.

Fear has long since traversed the gap between life and death. It might not feel the same when you have no heartbeat or no need to breathe, but it just finds more devious ways to settle on your shoulders.

Fear found me when I was small. That much I know. I don't remember not feeling scared so I must have been pretty tiny. It shrank the room I stood in until it felt like the walls were crushing me. It *whispered in my ear that I was a failure. It made the faces in front of me twist into sneers of disgust.*

I tried to be brave. I remember that. I tried to be brave.

And for a while it worked.

✻ ✼ ✻

Outside Death's office, there is a frantic hive of activity. I've never seen it this busy before, nor even seen anywhere near enough people around to believe it could be this busy.

As we squeeze past a gaggle of particularly stressed looking workers, I catch sight of Natasha. When she spots us, her eyes narrow, then she races across to block our path.

Death lets out a heavy groan beside me. "Oh God, here we go!"

"You employ me to do a job—I am trying to do it. Would you like me to or not?"

Death clasps his hands and raises them heavenward. "Oh please, by all that is good and gracious in this world, tell me the news. Or did you fake an MDS just so you could see my face?"

"It's a plane crash, weather-related it would seem," Natasha replies with a scowl. "Numbers are looking high at the moment."

I find myself frowning. "But how is this Death's business? I mean, how does it fit into your criteria?" The words sound terrible coming out of my mouth but Death shoots me an almost congratulatory smile.

"MDS is an exception to the usual rules. The number of deaths in a Mass Death Situation means that one department cannot deal with the processing alone, regardless of its cause, so it doesn't matter about it being unfair or not. All departments drop everything and deal with it. It's first priority," Death explains, as we start down the corridor.

When we reach the lift, Natasha presses the button then turns back to us. "We'll need it under control within the hour please," she says, voice clipped.

"Will try my best! Try not to miss me too much!" Death steps into the lift and I follow him inside, trying to find comfort in the fact that Death and Natasha are clearly relaxed enough to continue to insult each other. Then again, I'm pretty sure these two would argue their way through the apocalypse.

"Stay close," Death says, once we're in the lift heading down. He's reassuring me. The fact that he's making such an effort to do this does the opposite of what he's probably aiming to do. A flutter of worry settles itself at the back of my throat as the lift comes to a halt. I think Death senses my concern, because he gives me a small, slightly wonky smile.

Then the doors open.

Death sucks in a deep breath, gathering himself. Then he steps out and I have to say that for a second I seriously consider staying in the lift. But he looks back and shoots me a meaningful look. *Stay close.*

So I step out into the madness.

We're in the middle of a field. In front of me is the burning carcass of what was once a functioning jumbo jet plane. Acrid, angry smoke billows from almost every possible gap and spirals up into the sky. Debris is scattered across the field in random clumps, blurred by the smoke. In the distance, I can see the pinprick lights of the approaching emergency services, but for the moment we are alone.

A scream rips through the silence. It sends a shiver down my spine, makes my legs bend slightly as the instinct to run kicks in. Another scream joins it a second later, then another, then another. Like some unholy chorus of banshees. Slowly, they are replaced by the whistling sound of death arriving.

It gets louder and louder as more join the fray. Next to me, Death says something but it's barely audible. Then he's off, striding toward the carnage.

I hesitate, only for a moment. Then I chase after him.

The second the smoke engulfs us, the world disappears. There's just swirling, billowing blackness. It brings crushing panic to press against my chest. Death scrabbles around for my hand and squeezes it tightly. Really tightly. I try to tug myself free, but Death doesn't let go, doesn't even loosen in the slightest. "Death!" I snap.

The smoke suddenly clears as we reach the center of the crash.

It's not Death holding my hand. Death is nowhere to be seen. Instead, the owner of the pincer grip is a little boy, probably about eight years old. And his all-white attire tells me that the crash has already claimed his life.

"Where's my family?" he asks in a small voice. When I don't (can't) answer, he squeezes my hand even tighter and screams the question again. "WHERE IS MY FAMILY?"

I try to kick my brain into action. This little boy has just died and he has nobody except me to help him. It's time to do my job, however daunting that might be.

Kneeling down to his level, just like Mum used to when I was upset, I fix this petrified child with what I hope is a confident expression. "Hey, shhh. It's OK. My name's Daisy. I'm here to help."

The boy's shoulders are shaking uncontrollably. I gently place my hands there, steadying them slightly. "Peter. It's Peter, right?" He nods, and I feel a brief sense of relief that I've finally got the knack of working out the recently deceased's name. "Do you think you can tell me what happened?"

But Peter seems almost frozen in shock and it takes him

about two minutes before he finds his voice. "It got really loud," he whispers. He takes a shuddering breath, glancing around at the awful scene he's trapped in. "It was so bumpy... Mum told me to hold on, she was c-crying. Then... I—I don't remember!"

I can sense his panic rising again, a second wave roiling up inside him. So I draw him carefully into a firm hug. Again, just like Mum used to do. "You're safe now, Peter. You're safe."

Peter stays pressed against me for perhaps a minute or so, and I feel his shaking subside as he manages to calm himself down a little. Maybe he's ready to hear the truth.

"Peter, you need to listen carefully now, OK? Something's happened. You're...you've died."

Peter looks up at me with a solemn expression and for a moment I think he's going to be able to handle this. But then he whimpers, face almost crumpling as he cries out desperately, "Where's my mummy? Where's my daddy?"

"I'm—I'm sorry, I don't know."

Peter shakes his head, trying to refuse this new information. A rumbling echoes around as part of the plane collapses. It brings a terrified scream from Peter, who has now backed right away from me and the news I've just given him.

I don't know what to do. I'm stuck with this poor little boy and there's no Death to be seen; where *is* he?

Just then someone grabs my shoulder and tugs me around to face them. It's a woman, middle-aged and corporate, her suit dazzlingly white now. "You! Do you know what's going on? I can't find my bag. I'm not going anywhere without my bag."

Almost simultaneously, an older man joins us, clambering over a single row of chairs lying on their side. "We've crashed! Oh my God, we've crashed. The pilot, he's injured back there!"

Another man, this time around my age, joins us. "Are we dead? We're dead, aren't we?"

"OK, OK, everybody, just stay calm. As much as you can," I add hurriedly in the face of some rather disbelieving expressions. "Yes, I'm afraid you're right—Tomas, is it?" The younger man nods a confirmation. "Tomas is right. You've been involved in a crash and you've not survived. But I'm here to help you move on, OK?"

"So it's true? We're really dead?" the woman, who I think is called Marie, asks. When I nod slowly in confirmation, she draws her suit jacket a little tighter around herself.

A silence falls over the group. I can see an edge of terror in all their expressions but I think they're trying to stay calm for Peter's benefit. I feel a little hand slip into mine. I glance down, find Peter standing beside me. This sight gives me the boost of courage I need to go on.

"I'm sorry this has happened to you," I finally say, "but I know what to do next. I'm Daisy Cooper and I'm here to help."

Marie sniffs, brushes at her cheeks impatiently. But then she nods. "Right, OK. Lead the way then, Daisy."

After that, my little group prove pretty easy. Even the slightly belligerent older man goes off without a fuss eventually.

I leave Peter until the end; I feel like he's owed my full attention. He's sat very quietly next to me while I've processed everyone else, but now he's beginning to fidget a little. "Right, you saw me do everyone else. You know this isn't scary."

He nods slowly but I watch his eyes flick over to the door

that he's watched everyone go through. "Am—am I going to be alone in there?"

I follow his gaze over to the door. For a child, it must look exceedingly daunting, with its heavy latch and complete lack of clues about what's on the other side.

I wish I could offer him something. Maybe his parents are waiting through the door. But I don't know, not for certain.

What would I want someone to tell this kid, if he was mine? There's a question I don't have an answer for. But he needs something. So I squeeze his little shoulder, smiling weakly. "You might be. But not forever. Someone will come."

He gives the door one final look, full of suspicion. Then he slowly nods his acceptance.

We work through his file together and I try not to let him see how wrong it feels; to be confirming important aspects of his life, like the fact that he has dinosaurs on his bedroom wall and likes drawing spaceships when really all that matters to him is finding some way to make him safe.

Eventually, I have to guide him over to the door. I can feel him digging his heels in a little, so I come down to his level again, kneeling in front of the door. "Hey, listen. It's OK to be scared. It's just not OK to let it beat us, all right? That was my mum's rule. You just need to remember that, and you'll be fine."

That seems to bring him a bit of comfort, a touch of light to his eyes. I give him one final hug, open the door for him, and I hear him gasp. "MUM!" he bellows, voice cracking with an emotion that only a child finding their mother again can display. Then he's gone, racing across into a world that I'm not yet allowed to be a part of.

Finally, I'm alone in an empty office. I rest my head against the now closed door, allow my mind to slow back down to a walking pace, allow myself to comprehend what I've just done. There's sorrow, pride, shame, longing (because no child will ever yell for me like Peter did)—and anger at a system that cannot be reasoned with, not even when it comes to children.

Then Natasha walks in.

"So, by all accounts, not too bad?" She pauses, surprise on her face when she sees me and not Death. "Oh, Daisy. Where's Death?"

"I don't know. He was with me one second, then he disappeared."

Natasha hesitates, pursing her lips, then shakes her head. "He does that sometimes. Disappears."

"Oh... OK."

Natasha laughs at my obvious bemusement, though it's not entirely unkindly. "Don't worry, Daisy. You're not the first to be baffled by that man."

The laugh softens Natasha's usually severe expression a little, which gives me the confidence I need to bring up something that's been playing on my mind. "Natasha, I'm sorry but there might be a bit of a confusion in the paperwork. There was a child in that plane crash and I didn't know where to file him, and I didn't want to keep him waiting so I just filed him with the rest."

"So?" Natasha asks, when it's clear I've got nothing else to add.

"Well, Death said that children have their own department."

"He did? Maybe you just misunderstood..."

She looks like she's going to go on to explain all the complex reasons why such a thing would never be allowed but then Death suddenly steps into the office. He looks a little shell-shocked and one hand fidgets with his shirt buttons, but he's OK.

It surprises me how relieved I am to see Death all in one piece. But I hide this relief behind a scowl. "Where the hell have you been?"

Natasha sends him a knowing smirk. "Let's debrief later." With a nod at me, then Death, she turns and heads out.

"Well?" I prompt Death, eyes fixed firmly back on him.

Death gives me one of his trademark nonchalant shrugs. "I got hung up with the pilot. Wanted to take me through every damned detail of the crash to prove it wasn't his fault."

I think back to the crash and I know there's something not quite ringing true there, but now is not the time.

"I did four passengers. On my own."

"What?"

"I found four passengers. And I processed them."

"You…?" He's staring at me with what can only be described as shock. Then he nods toward his desk. "Show me."

So I do. I take him to his desk and flick though all four files. He looks at each one in turn, asks a few questions about what I've written. Then he shuffles the files carefully, places them in a drawer. "You need to make sure you label them as MDS. Just so the system knows they're part of the same group."

"Oh. Right."

"Daisy, I'm so proud of you."

There is an unusual gentleness to his voice. It immediately brings a lump to my throat.

"Um…" My voice is a shocked croak, until I hurriedly clear it. "Thank you."

"Pleasure," he returns, not missing a beat. I think he notices my surprise because the next sound to come from his mouth is a slightly awkward laugh.

"Follow me," he says, hopping up and moving over to the exit door.

"Where are we going?" I ask, he leads me into the lift and jabs one random button with confidence. But he just shakes his head with a smirk.

A moment later, however, the doors open. And I'm sure my gasp is loud enough for even the living to hear.

Rule Thirteen

A Dangerous Storm Starts Small

SOMETIMES STORMS COME IN an instant. I'm sure you've seen those happen before. Standing outside on a glorious day and then suddenly in a flash you're battling against gale-force winds and wondering what to do with a waterlogged barbecue.

Those storms can, of course, be dangerous, but perhaps not as dangerous as those that sneak up on you quietly, gradually. The storm you don't notice until it's too late. You adjust to the strengthening wind, the driving rain. You close your windows, you turn up the heating and forget about it, until suddenly it's taking off your roof.

Adjustment and adaptation is wonderful until it gets you killed.

Have we adjusted and adapted, Daisy and I? Possibly. I see it sometimes. The way she opened up to me after visiting her parents, the way she let me see her cry after her funeral. I see it now, as I go to all these lengths just to show her how proud I am of her.

Maybe this adaptation and adjustment won't be devastating for us. Maybe this is one storm that will pass off to the west and leave us be.

Then again, it only takes one stray gust of wind, one bolt of lightning. For everything to change.

❊ ❊ ❊

When I was six years old, Dad took me to the local museum in town. Usually it had pretty useless things that didn't interest me at all; facts about how our town came into existence, or a whole exhibition on the river and its ecosystem. So six-year-old me wasn't particularly enthused about going there on a sunny Saturday.

But they had this temporary exhibit on. A guy had come back from Oklahoma with all these photos and videos of the storms he had seen and, well, I was transfixed. Particularly with the photos of tornadoes. I just stood staring in awe at this inexplicable quirk of nature that seemed to have no purpose other than to remind us how small we really were. I stood for hours in that museum, watching every video, trying to read every bit of information and making Dad read the bits I couldn't. We were there all afternoon, until finally he dragged me home.

After that, I was hooked. Violet would tease me incessantly about my constant desire to research and talk about them, would roll her eyes when my turn to do show-and-tell came around and I'd sidle up to the front with my tornado in a jar and latest weather information book.

Even as I got older, I never quite stopped being fascinated by them. I became more aware of their dark side, of course, but that didn't put me off the idea of one day seeing one. I had it all planned out; one day I'd save up enough to go on a storm-chasing tour across the plains of the USA and I'd find myself a tornado.

Of course, it didn't happen. University and jobs and adulthood got in the way. I told myself I'd go there one day, before I had a family of my own, but then the pavement had other ideas and it became just another regret.

So now you understand the significance of Death taking me down in the lift, opening the doors, and popping us out, right in front of a tornado. Just like that.

I am speechless. Of course I am; I've waited my entire life to see one of these up close. And there it is. Towering above us, an almost blinding white color, like it's been made from snow instead of cloud. It spins around gracefully, collecting dust from the fields beneath it. We're in the middle of nowhere, no towns to worry about or people to collect; this isn't another job caused by this swirling mass of wind. It would seem that Death has brought me here, just to show me a tornado.

That fact is almost as shocking as the sight of the tornado. Then again, as I watch the beastly vortex of wind toss a tree into the air with the nonchalance of a child tossing a ball, I change my mind. Nothing can quite beat this. There's something to be said for being so close to something with that amount of power. It has no regard for anything in its path and in a way that's to be respected, though I'm sure the people who have been unfortunate enough to have their house in its path would disagree.

I turn to Death, eyes wide. He is standing as casually as ever, though he looks at the tornado with deep respect in his gaze. More respect than I've ever seen him give anything else.

"It's beautiful, isn't it?" he says after a moment, his voice soft yet somehow audible over the howling wind. The tornado is probably about a mile away, but the trees are still bending and creaking their complaint around us.

I find I can't actually speak. Shock and awe have stolen my voice. I just find myself nodding mutely, turning back

152 / Tamsin Keily

to stare at the tornado. I don't want to blink, I don't want to miss a second.

We stand in silence, watching the swirling mass make its carefree way across the field. Watching the dust it kicks up in its wake, watching the angry clouds above it rumble with thunder. Nature, undisturbed.

But, all too soon, the tornado begins to rope out (that's a technical term, by the way. I told you, I know tornadoes). Its solid funnel starts to weaken, gradually getting thinner and thinner until there's just a tiny thread of cloud, wavering in the air. Then it's gone. The dust cloud it's created drops to the ground, suddenly lifeless. The wind calms around us, and it feels like the entire world has given one great sigh of relief, and then relaxed.

It goes quiet. Then a bird, somewhere far away, chirps a joyful call to the sky. An all clear, maybe. When I look back to Death, I find that he's staring at me. I wonder how long he's been doing that for.

"You're crying," he states, almost kindly.

I press a hand to my cheek. It's damp. I don't know when that happened. I hurriedly rub at my cheeks. "How did you know—about the tornadoes?" I ask a moment later. One of many questions.

Death shifts beside me, looking a little sheepish. "I, uh, checked your file a while back. It said in your unfulfilled aims part that you wanted to see a tornado in real life."

I stare. "That's in my file?"

Death shrugs. "It's a big file. There's a lot in there."

"Yeah? Like what?"

"Like how you spent a whole afternoon geeking out in a tornado exhibition and how Violet always said you'd end up getting sucked up into one of them one day."

I have to smile a little at that. It sounds about right. Violet had a special expression she reserved for when I started going on about weather. A look of exasperation and somewhat disbelief that this was the best friend she'd been given in life. Although there was always a little hint of fondness there too. I imagine I wear a similar expression when she starts talking about the significance of that particular bar of music in that particular song in that particular musical.

"She used to pretend she didn't care, but she always found something related to them for Christmas," I murmur.

Death smiles faintly, scuffing a little at the ground. There's a touch of almost longing in his expression but he doesn't let it stay long. It ropes out as well. Then he gently nudges me off toward the right.

A few yards away, standing in the middle of this barren and arid field is a bench, its wood softened and worn from its years of duty out in the elements.

"What is a bench doing out here?" I ask, as Death leads me toward it.

"Patty Clearson," he replies, without a beat of hesitation. I frown, incredulous, and he laughs before pointing to the name I can now see carved into the back of the bench. "Patty Clearson's husband put this bench here."

"Of course. And here I was thinking we were in a place unrelated to death for once."

Death shrugs, drops down onto the bench. "I'm a busy guy, Daisy. I don't get much time off. If I've visited a place, chances are it's because someone died there."

Well, I can't really argue with that. Death sits down with a satisfied sigh, legs crossed and head resting back against the bench. After a moment, I find myself sitting down beside him. "So, how did she die?"

Death seems lost in his thoughts for a moment, which I've come to find quite common with him. I nudge him gently with my foot and he seems to stir from his daydream. "Oh, nothing that exciting. Old age, various illnesses. The general wear and tear of the human body. But she loved this spot. So, when she died, her husband bought her a bench and put it here."

I glance around, confused. "But we're in the middle of nowhere."

Death sits up a little and moves over until our shoulders bump. It feels surprisingly natural. "Over there," he says, pointing off to the left. "On the horizon. See those shadowy shapes?" If I squint, I can just about work out what he's talking about. "That's the Clearson farm. Their pride and joy. Think it's owned by a big corporation or something now. But Mr. Clearson wrote into his will that the bench had to stay if anyone wanted to buy the land after he died. Seems like they're honoring his wishes so far."

"That still doesn't explain why she liked this spot so much. There's nothing here."

Death shrugs. "You're the human. You should be an expert at finding meaning in nothing." I obviously look a little put out by this because he relents and goes on, "Look, I'm certainly no expert but I seem to recall that it had something to do with the sunset."

I glance up to the sky but the sun is nowhere to be seen beneath the dark clouds, so I suppose I will have to just take his word for it. "OK, next question," I say a moment later and Death rolls his eyes, though it seems rather good-natured this time.

"Shoot," he says, giving me a little grin. He could pass for human with that grin, that twinkle in his eyes. A fairly attractive one, if I'm honest.

"Why did you decide to suddenly bring me here?"

Death's grin slips slightly. "I thought it was obvious?" he says. "I'm thanking you."

I stare at him. "For what?"

"For what? For what you did, Daisy." He laughs, seeming a little exasperated. "You dealt with four deaths in an exceedingly volatile and unpredictable situation. It's incredible."

"Considering my previous record?" I quip.

He gives me a strange look, then flicks his eyes back out to the horizon. "You know what else it says in your file, Daisy, other than your love of tornadoes?" he asks, his voice a little piercing. More like the voice I'm used to, the one that could slice through a diamond if it wanted to.

"Shoot," I reply, echoing his previous response, and receive an eye roll for my trouble.

"It says one of your biggest problems is that you don't know how to respond to positive praise."

Ouch. "What?" I splutter.

He looks steadily at me. "What, are you going to tell me it's not true?" he asks. "Come on, Daisy. I take you to see a tornado to say thank you for sorting out a pretty big fuck-up in the universal balance, and you make a joke?" He shifts, until he's facing me even more directly. "Look me in the eyes, then. Look me in the eyes and tell me I'm wrong."

I stare, right into those stupid green eyes of his. Willing myself to find the composure to tell him that he's wrong, that I am comfortable with being praised, as much as I'm comfortable with being irritated by him. But there's no composure to be found. I know he's got it right. Dead-on. That's why it's prickled against my skin so much.

"I can't," I mutter, after a long five seconds.

"Exactly." He returns to facing the front again. Oddly, there is no smug grin upon his face.

"Does it bother you?"

"Of course it does. I'm not completely heartless, Daisy. When I see that you're unable to be proud of yourself, it makes me feel…" He trails off, clearly struggling to find the right word.

"Sad?" I suggest. He nods, pointing an affirming finger in my direction.

"Exactly. Doesn't it bother you?"

I consider it. "A little," I finally say. "When I was younger, I used to ice-skate. All the time. It was my…thing. And I was good at it. Could have gone professional, my coach said. But I *hated* all the attention that came with it. Eventually it got too much and I had this massive panic attack before a major competition and dropped out. And I never put the skates on again. I thought I could cope with that worry because it didn't seem that big, and then—boom!" I don't really know how I've ended up spilling all this to Death, but I can't stop now; I'm like my own tornado raging out of control. "I always felt I wasn't good enough to deserve the praise, but I didn't want to appear ungrateful for it. So I avoided it…"

Death laughs softly, causing me to send him a sharp look. But it's a kind laugh, I think. "You're good enough, Daisy. Trust me, a guy who has met a lot of people—you're good enough."

I don't reply. It's all very well him saying that, but it doesn't change the deep-set feeling inside my heart. Just like me saying to Violet that she has nothing to be sad about wouldn't stop her depression from telling her the opposite. But it's a rarity to have Death showing such a sensitive side and I'm really not going to be the one to shoo it away.

"Thanks," I say instead, probably with not quite enough sincerity for it to be plausible. I decide it's time to move on. His turn now. "The pilot on that plane…"

"What about him?" he asks, eyes abruptly looking away again. There's a small crinkle in the corner of his eyes.

"What was he saying, about the crash?"

"Just…things. Something about…sails."

"Sails?" I ask, eyebrows raising and allowing a little grin to appear on my face, because surely someone as ancient as Death should be better at lying.

"Why does it matter?" he snaps, scowling at me now.

I shift a little closer. "One of the people I processed. He said he saw the pilot, saw him injured. Injured, not dead. And now you're feeding me some bullshit about sails? What's going on?"

Death purses his lips, then sucks in his cheeks until I'm sure he's going to implode. "Fine," he snaps, "I wasn't with the pilot."

"Where were you?"

"Daisy…"

"No, come on. You left me alone. To deal with a child. A child, Death. I think I'm owed a bit of an explanation."

Death stands up all of a sudden, like the bench has spontaneously caught fire. A bolt of lightning crackles across the sky a few miles away but neither of us pay it much attention. There's an atmosphere between the pair of us that is far more intense than any lightning bolt. He doesn't speak, lips pursed together and eyebrows creased as he frowns out at the horizon. I almost give up, almost decide that this is just one of those things he's not going to tell me about, but then he turns around quite suddenly. "I get…" he tries, then trails off helplessly. "I… I don't really… I can't process children."

I stare at him. Right now, with his eyes flicked to the ground and arms wrapped around his chest, he looks so incredibly human. Like an awkward teenage boy trying to ask a girl out on a date. I would never have thought for a second that Death would be capable of any form of anxiety, of any type of fear. But here he is, admitting to me that some aspects of his job scare him so much that he has to hide and lie to his colleagues.

Clearly I stare for too long. He sighs heavily. "Are you done gawping yet, Daisy?" he grumbles.

"Sorry," I reply. "It's just—just you constantly surprise me with how different you are to my expectations."

He crosses his arms, almost hugging himself. "I know, it's disappointing to me too."

I slide off the bench and come to stand beside him. "That's not what I mean at all. You're not a disappointment. It's just... You should have told me, I wouldn't have minded."

"I have a reputation, Daisy. I have a role to play. Freaking out about dying children isn't part of that." Death's voice has a bitterness to it and it's not the first time I've heard that in him. It's a stark reminder that the job he does isn't necessarily one he does by choice.

"What happened?"

Death's jaw tightens. "It was a long time ago," he sighs, rubbing at the bridge of his nose. "Lucas... Lucas had just gone and I was still this young little thing but apparently ready to be left on my own. He had always taken charge when there were children. He knew how to calm them down, made it seem so easy."

It's strange, and a little sweet, to think of Death as a child. "Go on," I say, gently.

"It was my first job after he'd...been taken. There was this raid. A village got attacked by invaders and it was...messy. So many slaughtered. So many children... And there I was, just about big enough to reach the button for the lift, having to deal with it. Alone. They kept screaming, Daisy. Nothing would stop them. Screaming for their families. And I had no idea what to do…" He draws a rasping breath that hurts to hear. "Nobody helped me. I kept yelling for Lucas, for anyone. But he…of course he didn't…couldn't come. And those that did? They just kept shrugging and saying it was my job to work it out. I was begging for help and they turned away."

He falls silent, a curl of what I think might be anger traveling across his lip. I watch as his fingers grip tightly together.

"What happened?" I ask finally.

This seems to bring Death back to the present. He blinks, refocuses. "I stopped feeling it all. Just switched it off." He snaps his fingers, then looks down at his feet with a sigh. "Except, after that, I decided I couldn't deal with the children anymore. They remind me of Lucas. They remind me that the job I do is so cruel, so brutal. And if I have to do it for an eternity, I need *something* to ease the pressure of it all. So I hide from the children. Siphon them off to other departments. There's enough different departments for nobody to really notice and when I saw that kid coming toward us at the plane crash I panicked and sort of…ran off."

"And left me to deal with it instead? Look, you can't just avoid things you're afraid of forever."

"Why not?"

I turn and meet his gaze, expecting to see some level of sarcasm, some sort of attitude in his expression. But there is none. Instead there's just honest curiosity. He really doesn't know. At first, I'm not sure what to say. I'm hardly an expert in psychology; then I think about how Violet has kept all her feelings about her father's affair and abandonment bottled up, and how that didn't end well at all.

"Because…because it's like poison," I finally reply. I take a deep breath, take a moment to get my thoughts straight. "When Violet's dad had an affair and then walked out, she went through this period of time where she would have a panic attack about leaving her mum alone. She was so convinced that her mum was on the brink of some nervous breakdown that she was terrified about leaving her. She would make me literally drag her to school because she didn't want to fall behind but she couldn't get herself to go on her own. It was...well, awful."

I can tell that Death is trying to work out what this has to do with his question, so I decide it's best to cut to the chase a little more. "Anyway, that led to her getting properly depressed. But she still wouldn't accept that there was a problem, even when other things started piling up; her schoolwork, her dancing, the constant fighting with her dad. Then it all got too much and..." I close my eyes, trying not to let the painful memories back in "...and then she tried to kill herself." It was almost five years ago now. We were eighteen years old. Pretending to be grown-up but still just kids, really. That awful day still sits fresh in my mind. "After that we had to do something about it properly. She went on antidepressants, started counseling, and it helped. It's not perfect, of course. But it helped—I mean, look at her now, living on her own in London, working toward her dream..." The words feel bitter on my tongue, because she shouldn't be on her own. That was never part of the deal.

Death must see some of this on my face because he nudges me with his foot. "You miss her badly, don't you?"

I nod, tugging the sleeves of my dress down over my hands a little. "Always. And I worry about her. All the time."

"You don't trust her?"

I hesitate, feeling the instinctive shake of the head coming but somehow holding it back. "It's not that I don't trust her, it's just that I'm so used to being her safety net. I don't know what will happen without me." Shaking my head now,

I fix him with a rueful expression. "Stop trying to change the subject."

Death smirks. "Busted," he mutters with a little chuckle, before indicating with a wave of his hand that I should go on.

"All I'm saying is that these things can start off seeming like nothing. Like a tornado can start off just seeming like a bit of wind. But then, before you know it, it's controlling your life. This fear of yours might not be causing significant impact right now, but one day it will. So maybe you need to do something about it. And…this is me saying that I'm here to help, however I can."

"You'd do that, for me?"

I shrug, shoot him a small smile. "Well, what else is an assistant for?"

He holds my gaze for a few seconds but it doesn't feel uncomfortable, not like that piercing look he used to give me. Finally, he returns my smile, though it's still a little bitter. "Well then, Daisy Cooper, assistant to Death, what do you suggest I do? What I'm being impacted by is death and I can hardly get away from that. I mean, it's who I am."

"It doesn't have to be."

Death snorts slightly. "I'm Death. How can it not be?"

"Have you ever considered *not* being Death, though? I know you have all these rules to follow, but is there actually a rule that says you have to be called Death?"

He's as still as the air around us. "There isn't."

"Well then. That could be step one. If you weren't called Death, what would you be called?"

He falls silent, resting back against the bench and staring out across the field. He stays silent for so long that I begin to wonder if he's even considering the question anymore.

But then he straightens up a little, fiddles with the buttons of his shirt as he turns back to me. "When I was younger, Lucas used to call me Scout. Like a nickname, I guess."

I feel myself grinning. "Why?"

He shrugs. "Because when we were going to deaths, I would always be the one to go in first, scope out the situation. One day he said how I was like a scout for our little pair and then...then it just sort of stuck."

"Scout? I like it. You don't just take life away. You look for people and then you help them. It fits."

"So... I can just be Scout? And not Death?"

I nod. "Sure. It's your name, it's your choice."

"I choose Scout." I've barely finished speaking before he's shot back his reply and we share a little laugh.

We fall back into silence, a comfortable understanding passing between us that seems miles away from our first hours together. It brings a warm feeling to my chest, a feeling that I distantly recognize. Don't we all know that feeling, when we meet someone's eye and see that there's an understanding there? A connection with infinite potential?

Except. Except I'm not here to form those sorts of connections with Death (or, I should say, Scout). And this moment brings a sharp jolt of realization that somewhere in this world is Eric. Eric, who I haven't properly thought about for a while now. I'm immediately weighed down with a heavy sense of guilt.

"Daisy?"

"I think I'd like to go see Eric next."

I feel like I blurt the words out a little roughly and I can see that he is slightly taken aback by them.

"You know, maybe you should take some of your own advice." His tone is gentle as he shoots me a somewhat knowing smile.

"How so?"

He stands, stretching slightly before offering his hand. I find myself taking it without really thinking, until his fingers are wrapped around mine and I feel heat spreading through my palm. "You keep going for broke with your appearances to the living," he explains. "Maybe we need to take it slow. For both you and your relations."

I consider it for a moment. Maybe he's right, maybe this isn't the place for knee-jerk reactions. But there's something brewing inside me, gaining momentum. I don't want to be caught out, don't want to be stuck in a storm without a shelter. "Fine," I murmur finally, "we'll take it slow."

The newly named Scout looks out across the expanse of field, eyes drifting off toward the departing clouds. They're gathering strength again, perhaps brewing up another tornado. And in his expression, I see something brewing as well.

But I look away. Before I get sucked in and lost in a whirlwind of a completely different sort.

Rule Fourteen

Time Stops For No One

DO YOU EVER WONDER about time? I do. It's kind of important in my line of work. After all, a minute can be the difference between control and chaos up here. And not just up here, of course. As someone who has waited around for a death to happen on many occasions, I can tell you with great confidence that a lot can happen in a minute. One moment a shop is the most ordinary place in the world, the next it's a bloodbath thanks to one man and his illegally obtained handgun.

It also never stops. It's relentless to the point of cruelty. Sometimes I literally want to scream with panic as I feel the seconds slipping by with nobody able to stop them. I don't know why it scares me so much when there's no real end in sight for me. But it does.

Perhaps it's because I know that time can still affect me, one way or another.

Every day, I feel it pushing me through the endless cycle of deaths, forcing them to worm into my brain and weigh on my shoulders. Decades and centuries and even millennia have passed me by. All thanks

*to time. And while I don't have the wrinkles or the gray hair, I'm
still old. Time has still begun to cripple me.*

*If that's the case for me, then I can't help but wonder what time
will do to her.*

It only takes me three days before the desire to see Eric gets
too much. It would probably have been sooner but I manage to distract myself with getting use to Death's new name.
He takes to "Scout" like a bird takes to the sky, but for me
it takes a little longer.

Eventually, though, it's settled into my mind and, with
that sorted, I can't help but drift back to the idea of visiting
Eric. After some convincing from Death (Scout), I agree for
the seeing to be a one-way thing. He makes some impres-
sively well-considered points about Eric's well-being and my
own, which just about convince me that now is not the time
to appear to my boyfriend.

So I go down with the promise not to try and appear to
anyone.

When I first step out of the lift, Eric's flat is empty. The
lights are off, so the flat is only lit by the twinkling lights
of London coming in through the windows. Eric's flat is his
pride and joy, mainly because of the view. It is a good view,
though admittedly a quarter of it is dominated by the roof of
a supermarket. The rest of it, though, is impressive: a slither
of the river, shiny skyscrapers, the corner of Tower Bridge.

With Eric not home yet, I take some time to visit some of
my favorite spots in his flat. I spend some time fiddling with
all the ridiculously complicated gadgets in his glossy kitchen,
tentatively stoking the memories they bring to mind. Eric
bought them all at once in a fit of heady excitement after
getting a promotion. He couldn't get them to work properly,

because we couldn't find the instructions in English. I can still almost see the sprawling mess of parts on the kitchen tiles in front of me, can hear the hysterical laughter when, after slaving over them all evening, the coffee machine managed to spray milk foam all over the opposite wall. That was the moment we gave up and went for pizza.

My fingers graze over the faint milk stain still lingering on the wall and I feel longing tugging at my heart. We had the foundation of a good little life forming here. But not anymore.

As I'm trying not to literally cry over spilled milk, I hear the door. Instinctively, I tuck myself into a corner, which is bit ridiculous in hindsight, considering the fact that he can't see me.

Eric Broad has always been a classically handsome guy. At least to me. Well-groomed, good bone structure, warm eyes—the whole package. But now, as he steps into the kitchen, he looks gaunt, almost gray. His usually well-tailored suit seems to hang a little loosely off his body, like he's put his father's on by accident. Ironically, it's a bit like seeing a ghostly version of him.

He dumps his workbag on one of the kitchen stools, then sits down in the other one. Already a step out of his routine— usually Eric comes home ravenous and demolishes his fridge for a good ten minutes before returning to civilization. Now, though, he just sits and scans through his phone, brow furrowed. I take a step out of the corner, drift over so I'm standing directly opposite him. He doesn't look up, eyes fixed on the screen of his phone. It's an intensely jarring situation, to stand in front of your boyfriend and be completely ignored. I've been dead for weeks now, but it's not something I think I'll ever get used to.

After a moment of scrolling through social networks in a

half-focused sort of way, Eric's phone starts ringing. He answers it almost immediately, resting it against his ear while his exhausted eyes stare listlessly at the opposite wall.

"Hey, Violet. No, I'm fine—really. Well, I've had a busy day, that's probably why... How are you?" He pauses to listen to Violet's answer, fiddling with the strap of his bag. "Did you try eating? That might help," he says finally, which doesn't fill me with great confidence. "I'm aware I'm not one to talk, Violet, but it's true. And I'm not the one almost passing out in dance rehearsals. I'm sure I do sound like Daisy, Violet. The truth is the truth, though. Yeah, I know... Would you like me to come over?" He rubs at his forehead, eyes crinkling shut for a moment. "That's fine, I'll be around in like an hour, OK? See you soon, bye."

He hangs up the phone, places it down on the counter and then stares at it for a moment. Part of me feels a little proud that Eric has clearly taken on the responsibility of Violet and is taking it seriously. But that's somewhat overwhelmed by the sadness that comes from seeing my usually, almost exhaustingly energetic boyfriend, reduced to this: a still and quiet man, staring at a phone.

After a minute or so he manages to heave himself up. He passes the fridge and I feel something break inside me as his fingers gently graze past the photo of us pinned there. It's easy to tell that this has become some automatic part of his routine, like taking his newspaper from the vendor in the morning. That *hurts*. I don't want to be just a photo on his fridge, a memory with crinkled edges. I want to be here for real, nagging him to eat, reminding him to turn the kitchen light off when he leaves the room.

I can't hang around much after that.

I thought I wanted to see Eric, thought that perhaps it would help somehow. Being around Death and the dead so much has made my life feel distant, separate. I wanted to feel connected to it. But I don't. I just feel guilty all over again.

So I leave, before that guilt starts gnawing away at me once more.

When I get back to the office, Scout's nowhere to be seen. I don't particularly feel like sitting around waiting for him, not when the memory of Eric alone in his flat still lurks ominously in my mind. So I go for a walk, or perhaps an aimless wander is a more appropriate description.

The white walls of the corridors are just starting to sear against my eyes when I find a room that I haven't come across before which isn't just a locked office door. To my surprise and, yes, relief, it's what looks like a library.

OK, perhaps library is a little exaggeratory. It's a room with four bookshelves and three armchairs. But in a world of offices and blank corridors, it feels like an oasis in a desert. Because books have always been my "thing," as Violet would often say with an almost indulgent smile, as though enjoying reading was something to be pitied for. Needless to say, she didn't share my interest. About the only interest we didn't share—well, the tornadoes too, I guess.

I make a beeline for the bookshelves. The collection of books is a little haphazard but I soon find one that will be an adequate distraction.

I don't know how long I'm reading for until Scout appears. He knocks lightly on the door frame, bringing me out of the book with a jolt. Hurriedly wiping at my eyes (tears have been coming and going since I've started reading and I've just been ignoring them), I shoot him a small smile. "Oh, hello."

He grimaces a little at my somewhat bleary greeting, before stepping into the room with a slight tentativeness, as if he expects it to explode the minute he's inside it. He seems to consider me for a moment, no doubt deciding whether to mention the tears or not. Finally, he seems to decide to leave that particular can of worms: "Whatcha doing?"

"Playing a trombone."

He tuts, coming to sit in the chair beside me. "It's the lowest form of wit, Daisy."

I shrug, folding over the corner of the page and shutting the book. "It was the lowest form of question." He grins at that, a silent acceptance. "I'm reading. You never told me you had books here."

Scout peers around the room a little vaguely. "I forgot this place existed. I don't ever come in here. Think someone from the Household Accidents department set it up as a way to give people a break. Never really saw the appeal myself. Anyway—" he waves that away, twists in his chair to face me more directly "—how was Eric?"

I feel my nose wrinkling as I gesture at my still teary eyes. "How do you think?" I sigh, before pushing on, "He's... struggling. And Violet's struggling. And I don't really know what to do." I say the words lightly, trying to trick myself into thinking it's no big deal when really I can feel panic fluttering away in the corner of my mind.

He seems to mull over my words for a moment. Then shrugs. "Not much you can do," he replies, green eyes a little hollow as he meets my gaze. But then he blinks and they brighten, as he moves away from that tricky subject of feelings. "What's the book about?"

The change of subject is jarring but, if I'm brutally honest, rather welcome. Scout is right, even if it's a little bluntly put. There is nothing I can do. And thinking about it is just making me feel worse. So I go with it. "It's just a collection of old fairy tales."

"Old what?"

Frowning, I search his face for some sign of sarcasm. But there's none. "You don't know what fairy tales are?"

Scout picks at a loose thread of the armchair, then slowly shakes his head. He's wearing the expression of someone who has just been caught out. A boy admitting he hasn't learned his spellings for the test. And my guilt-ridden brain latches eagerly onto this opportunity for a full-blown distraction.

So I teach him about fairy tales.

We start with the simple ones, "Three Little Pigs" and "Little Red Riding Hood." This turns out to be a mistake, though, as Scout gets overly fixated on the negative representation of wolves, rather than the actual stories. I'm not sure I particularly help this by mentioning my own personal opinions on the poor treatment of stepmothers; the next thing I know I'm retelling "Cinderella," "Hansel and Gretel," "Snow White." Scout demands to know every detail, eyes wide with a childlike fascination.

Hours drift by like that until we're called away to a job. I'm painfully aware of how I've swept the problem of Eric under the rug with no clear solution to his pain, but it seems like the only option. Wallowing in self-pity certainly won't help, after all.

That's what I keep trying to tell myself anyway, as the days start to pass by at an increasing speed and we settle more and more into a routine. I begin to forget Scout was ever known as anything different, though he does quietly ask me one day that we keep that name between us, for the moment. I accept, smiling to myself because it's just another vulnerability that he's willing to share with me. Progress.

Another day passes and Scout tentatively suggests we visit the miniature library again after a particularly bleak job; a murder in the desert in which the man refused to accept he was dead and tried to fight us the entire way. I actually relented and let Scout use his calming touch after the man almost punched me in the jaw. After that, it feels like I've stepped away from my own humanity a little, and I'm more than happy to accept his request.

So we drift back to the room. We try one of the horror books but Scout finds it a little too close to home and we move onto lighter fantasy stories instead. Scout revels in tales of dragons and heroics—ironically, anything where normal people triumph over death. I think he likes the hope they offer.

It's easy for time to pass by when we're spending some of it reading. It's easy to forget I've died and left my world behind me, when I have this new world of books and comfy chairs and occasional hearty debates.

Time marches us right onto Violet's birthday. When I see that date on the calendar, reality once again smacks into me like a particularly heavy book. It doesn't take much convincing for Scout to let me go down to see her. It only takes slightly more convincing to get him to accompany me, which is good, as I have a feeling that I might need some company.

Violet's birthday has always been a big event in the calendar. For her at least; for me it's the day I brace myself for a whirlwind of partying and then tidying. Violet hates tidying at the best of times; hungover Violet is highly allergic to it.

By the time we've finished some top priority jobs that apparently cannot be missed, it's past eleven at night. We take the lift down and, while Scout chatters away in my ear about how he's never understood birthdays, I feel worry beginning to nibble away at my insides.

I always had a bit of a sixth sense when it came to Violet; didn't sleep the night she was finding out about her father's affair, felt sick with worry the day she broke her leg aged

172 / Tamsin Keily

nine, even before I knew about it. My death doesn't seem to be changing that; worry churns around inside me, just as we arrive at the flat to find a party in full swing, but with no sign of a birthday girl.

Music thuds throughout the flat, far too loud. Mrs. Morris upstairs will be on the phone to the police already, I'm sure. The flat is packed with people, a lot of whom I don't recognize. Violet's like one of those trawler nets fishermen use— she picks up all sorts without really realizing. I was always waiting for one of these new people to be the one who replaced me. After all, they always seemed far cooler, far more "Violet" than I ever did.

Among the strangers, I see Dean from her stage school, downing an obnoxiously colored drink, and Amie from the café Violet works part-time at, who is looking somewhat uncomfortable among so many dramatic artistic types. Amie and I would probably have got on if we'd had the chance to meet more than once.

But I see no Violet.

"I'm going to find Vi!" I shout across to Scout. Even though he's right beside me, he still only just hears me. He gives me a nod and a thumbs-up, before going back to watching this raw display of humanity with open bemusement.

It doesn't take me long to find her. She likes to think she's this wild, free spirit but she has routines and patterns just like the rest of us. And I know them better than anyone. So when I don't spot her in the main area of our flat, I head for the bathroom.

Lo and behold, she's there. My best friend, reduced to a desperate mess, sitting by the toilet. Mascara all over her face, drink knocked over beside her, tears everywhere. It sort of feels like stepping into the scene of a car crash. Carnage everywhere and nothing you can do.

To my surprise, Eric is also there. As Violet sits with her back against the bath, splitting between sobbing and retching, he's there rubbing her back or holding her hand. He looks a bit like a rabbit caught in the headlights but at least he's there.

"What the fuck are we doing, Eric?" she croaks. "She's dead and we're having a fucking *party*?" She tries to stand up, stumbles against the bath and almost cracks her head against the bathroom tiles. Fortunately, though, Eric has hurriedly stood up also and is there to steady her. "Everyone needs to fuck off, they need to go home."

"You want me to send everyone home?" Eric asks, sounding a little dubious. I can understand where he's coming from; some of Violet's friends can be a bit scary.

Violet staggers against him, tears pouring down her face and leaving streaks of makeup in their wake, stark even against her dark skin. "It's my fucking birthday and my best friend isn't shitting here. Why would I want a party? Why would I want to see other people when she's gone?"

"I did mention that when you were planning it…"

"Fuck off, Eric," she snaps, trying to push away from him. I could have told him he'd get that reaction, but I'm once again surprised by how he lets these words slide off him. Instead, he helps her to sit down on the edge of the bath.

"All right, OK. I'll start encouraging people to leave. You stay here, I'll bring you some water." He hesitates, pats her shoulder a little awkwardly. "I'll be right back, OK?"

He leaves, hurrying past me and back out into the party. For a second, there's a snatch of noise—laughter and music that is completely out of place in this bathroom. Then the door closes again and it's silent once more.

Violet slides back down to the floor, a low sob rumbling from her chest. Her legs come up to her chest, one hand instinctively adjusting her dress to keep an element of decency.

On her own like this, she seems so small. Maybe that's what brings me to her side. Or maybe there's just nothing that will stop me trying to look after her.

"I miss you," I whisper as I sit down beside her. "I really miss you. I wish I could make it better."

She doesn't hear me, of course. She's on her own and her head comes down to rest against her knees, her curls immediately hiding her face. Muffled but still painfully audible, her crying floats in slow circles around the small room. A constant, unrelenting reminder that time has been cruelly passing for Violet as well, and it's only made things worse.

The door slowly opens. Violet doesn't notice it but I do, which gives me a hint as to who might be behind it. Indeed, Scout is standing there. He has somehow found himself a little cocktail umbrella which he's twirling between his fingers but this stops immediately when he sees the scene before him. And I've never seen him move so fast, from his spot by the door, to right beside me.

"Daisy, this isn't helping—let's go."

He pulls me into a hug then. For a moment I want to fight it. But it's the first time he's properly hugged me, and there's something about the feeling of his arms around me which makes it easier to block out the world.

Maybe that's how he gets me back up to his office: by keeping his arm around me the whole time, gently coaxing me away from my best friend with the promises that we'll find a way to help her. I see Eric shooing people toward the door as we leave and perhaps that's another reason why I let us leave. Perhaps if I keep thinking of reasons, I'll be able to forgive myself for leaving Violet alone on the bathroom floor.

We sit at his desk, stuck in silence. He fiddles with his pen, I find myself tracing the empty space on my wrist where my daisy bracelet should be.

In the end, it's somebody else who brings us out of this stalemate of grief. Natasha knocks on the door, then breezes in, her confident footsteps faltering as she takes in the scene before her. Lifting my head, I catch her nonplussed expression.

"Oh," she begins, "is this a bad time? It's just... I think I've found something, something to help."

Rule Fifteen

Anyone Can Be Selfish

LET'S TALK ABOUT MOTIVATION. Let's talk about how everything we do comes back to a desire to please ourselves. No, don't try to argue with me; it's true. Even the most selfless-appearing act comes with an underlay of selfishness. We help people because we want to feel good about ourselves (or maybe because we expect some sort of reward after death); you give money to charity to enjoy a moment of smugness as you carry on down the street; you look after the elderly with the assumption that someone will one day do the same to you.

I should point out that I'm not judging here.

How can I, when I fall for the exact same trap? Selfishness does not stop at the edge of my lift. Selfishness does not come linked with the beating of your heart. It is undying, eternal. Look at Natasha. She works incredibly hard and goes above and beyond all the time. Maybe you think she's just a nice person (unlikely) who wants to do a service to the recently deceased. But I suspect she's hoping for some sort of VIP treatment when she finally moves on.

And look at me. Selflessly helping Daisy to calm herself down after seeing what grief has done to her best friend. Selflessly supporting her like a good, selfless companion should.

Yeah, right.

Let's look at that again. It's not selfless to help Daisy calm down because I'm not just doing it for her. Because if she doesn't calm down then eventually she won't want to stay here anymore. She'll drive herself crazy and run away and I'll be alone. See? It's not just her I'm looking after. Because this funny little human with her prickly self-righteousness and stubbornness has found a way to make my existence bearable. And I'm not prepared to lose that.

You can call it an act of kindness and compassion if you wish. But I know the truth.

❄ ❄ ❄

Scout steers Natasha out of the room almost immediately, like he's afraid one more word might send me over the edge. To be fair, that's not an entirely ludicrous idea. With Violet's sobs still echoing in my ear and Eric's gaunt face permanently seared against my eyeballs, I can feel that edge teetering right under my feet.

So I'm glad for the break, even if it leaves me in silence. Something that feels dangerous right now. I try to distract myself by sorting through the files on Scout's desk. We'd left for Violet's party so quickly that we hadn't properly filed our recent jobs. It surprised me at the time that Scout was OK with leaving his precious filing for later. He keeps doing that at the moment, surprising me.

Thankfully the pair are not gone long. Filing is an adequate distraction but not one that will last for long. I can already feel fluttery panic and sorrow squeezing at my throat again, just as Scout opens the door and steps inside, Natasha at his heels. Both look unnervingly somber.

"What's going on?" I ask, as neither of them make any move to speak.

Scout glances to Natasha with a meaningful glare that causes her to glare right back for a moment. Then she reluctantly steps forward and looks to me. "Daisy, I know you've been trying to get back to the living world and you kept getting yanked back. Well, something turned up in lost property today that I think might explain why. And might help you stay visible."

My mouth suddenly feels very dry. I can only nod at her, desperately waiting for her next words. Natasha digs around in her pockets, pulls something out, and then offers it to me.

It takes me a second to recognize what it is, perhaps because they're so out of place up here. They're my keys. The ones to my flat. As I somewhat tentatively take them from Natasha, I hear the daisy chain keyring quietly jangling. It immediately fills me with the desperate ache of homesickness.

"How? How do these help? And what do you mean 'lost property'?" I croak, looking between the two and willing one of them to make things clearer for me.

"Sometimes, when people die, things get brought along. I know a man who managed to get his bicycle up here," Scout explains, his voice surprisingly gentle. "But, as I'm sure you can imagine, they get in the way. So we tend to ship them off to lost property where we can decide if they can be returned to their owner without too much fuss."

"So how will my keys help?"

Natasha comes a little closer, hands pleated in front of her. "When you die, there's a huge amount of power transferal. Usually this all goes into bringing you away from your living body and into the form you're in now. Without it you'd just be a…haze. But you were holding your keys when you died. Not only that, but those keys mean something to you, right?" I nod mutely, and she smiles, buoyed by her correct guess. "I thought so. So they're an important object that you were holding when you died and, most importantly, when you died at the wrong time."

"So some of that energy went into the keys?" I ask, and receive a small smile of confirmation from Scout as he comes to sit down on the other side of the desk.

"Got it in one, Cooper. There's life energy trapped inside them and I think that if you tried our little getting emotional and pushing trick while holding the keys, there would be enough power to keep you there. For as long as you wanted, as long as you had the keys."

I glance down at them in my hand, trying to convince myself that something so innocuous can be so important, so powerful. "It wouldn't run out? Ever?" I ask, looking up at them once more.

Scout wrinkles his nose, which is usually his way of saying he doesn't know, because he doesn't like saying those words aloud. Natasha notices this as well and huffs a little, taking over the conversation again. "I would think that the life energy would run out when your life was planned to run out. Normally, when a person dies at the right time, the energy can't linger like it does in those keys, because there's not enough left. But with you—well, there's a whole lot of residual energy hanging around."

I can feel hope tickling the corners of my mouth, upturning them into a smile. "I could go home," I murmur.

Across the desk, I hear the sound of Scout's chair creaking as he shifts a little. He normally starts fidgeting when he's stressed, but when I look over at him, he seems his usual calm self. "You could go home," he confirms.

I think back to my poor best friend, drunk and heart-broken and alone in her bathroom. I think back to my poor boyfriend, trying his best to fix a situation that has no solution. I think back to my poor mum, driven to screaming at her own daughter as grief twisted its way through her heart.

I don't need any more convincing after that.

Natasha leaves us to try together. She gives me a warm smile and a slightly awkward hug before wishing us luck and heading back to work. She even offers to cover Scout's jobs until he's back, which Scout looks positively dumbstruck by. But then he's taking my hand in an automatic sort of way and leading me to the lift.

It's still night when we get back to the flat. We reach the door and I can hear voices petering through the thin and half-rotten wood. But only two. The party is well and truly over.

Scout has come to stand beside me, his shoulder bumping against mine. "Violet and..." He trails off, looks over to me with an eyebrow rising. "Eric?"

I nod, feeling a strange sense of unease from the way Scout says it, like he's solved some dark secret. Why wouldn't they be here together? "Violet probably needs company still."

"Uh-huh." Scout looks back to the door, but I catch the small frown on his face.

Still, if I'm going home, it doesn't matter what he thinks. Soon Violet will have me and Eric can go back to being my boyfriend and not Violet's support network. So, without another word, I open the door and step into the flat.

Of course, Eric and Violet don't bat an eyelid at our entrance. Violet is sitting at the kitchen table, while Eric busies himself in the kitchen. It can't be that long past midnight, but Eric seems to be making some form of breakfast. Probably a good idea considering how much alcohol Violet seemed to have consumed earlier. From the looks of things, it's not the breakfast that Eric would be vying for—the greasier the better is Eric's attitude—whereas Violet aims to use as many avocados as is humanly possible. Eric loves fried eggs but Violet will always insist on poached. And this is about Violet, so the eggs are being poached and there's already half an avocado carefully sliced onto a plate.

"What is it with this time period and avocados?" Scout mutters from beside me as he takes in the scene. "You treat them like the answer to everything—just have some fucking Cheerios and get lost."

I manage a smirk of amusement at that, giving him a brief smile of almost-gratitude because it's that sort of humor I need right now. It's good to see Violet's OK, but it's also disconcerting to see somebody else helping her. And, if I'm truly honest with myself, it's disconcerting that that somebody is Eric.

"So, what now?" I ask, tearing my eyes away from the scene and focusing fully on Scout.

He takes a moment to look away from the pair at the table, his expression a little strange. Almost like regret, but what is there to regret here? Unless this is just a reminder that his admin error caused so much heartache.

"Scout?" I prompt and he blinks, refocusing in an instant.

"Well, it should be just like usual. I think we can pretty safely say that anger won't be powerful enough for you—it hasn't seemed to work in the past. So I would go for…" He pauses, tries to find the right words before shaking his head and giving me an almost fond smile. "Just be you, Daisy," he finally finishes.

"Will—will I see you again?" I find myself asking. Scout looks away, placing his hands back into his pockets with a sigh.

"I'm not sure. We'll see," he replies, voice a little husky.

It's not much of an answer but I'm getting the sense that he is finding this a little difficult. We've grown close in a strange sort of way over the past weeks. This could be a big change for him.

But one look back to Violet and Eric and I know there's no choice in the matter. I have to go back to them. I'm suddenly conscious of that tingling feeling. It's spread right across my skin in one big rush, an out-of-control wildfire sparked off by that determined commitment to get back to my friends. In my hand, the keys begin to buzz softly, then glow a warm golden color.

I look over to Scout. "This is it, I think." He nods, places his hands on my shoulders. "Thank you for everything! I'll miss you!" My words come out just as he shoves me and I see, for a split second, his expression change into one of surprise. And then he's gone, winked out of view.

The nearest chair smacks into my thigh and I'm sure I even feel the pain of the collision. I'm here, I'm real. The chair makes a scraping sound as I hit it, causing Eric and Violet to whip around.

I know they see me because Violet gasps and Eric swears, loudly. They stare at me, the color draining from their faces in unison. I'm grinning, I can feel it tickling at the corners of my mouth. "I'm here! I made it! Guys, it's me!"

"Oh my God!" Eric croaks.

"You're back," Violet whispers, a tentative smile beginning to bloom. It's full of an almost blazing hope that seems to chase away the dark shadows of smudged makeup under her eyes. I can feel that hope somehow bolstering my drive to stay visible, a tether around my waist that anchors me firmly to life.

But it doesn't last. The tugging feeling returns, violently

and abruptly. I feel my whole body shiver and my living companions step forward. Violet wears fear on her face once more. This doesn't make sense! I've got the keys. Why aren't they working, why aren't I staying? I desperately reach out for Violet and Eric in the vain hope that they might help me stay.

"Daisy!" Violet calls, racing around the table toward me. "Don't you dare leave me again! Please!"

I feel her fingers graze against mine. She grips at my hand but it's like gripping an ice cube. I slip through her grasp and I know from the utterly defeated look on her face that I've disappeared once more. Desperate not to do this to her yet again, I try and force myself back into her world. But there's a heaviness around my midriff, a heaviness that has been there since everything started going wrong.

When I look down at my waist, I'm greeted with a shock. Scout's hands are there, and he's holding me back. I wriggle around, realization slamming into me like a forty-ton truck. "You! You stopped me." The words are heavy on my tongue because I don't want to believe it's true. But his refusal to meet my gaze is answer enough.

Behind me, I can hear Violet's anguished cries but for once they don't command my immediate attention. "What did you do, Death?" I whisper, his old name slipping out as anger begins to rise inside me.

He winces. "Can we...can we not do this here?"

"Screw that. I'm trying again. I could have done it!"

He steps forward. "I don't think you should, not now. I mean, look at them!" He gestures at my friends and I force myself to look over at them.

Violet's made it to the table and her head is down on it. Her shoulders are shaking so hard that I'm worried that they might just fall off altogether. Is that possible? To cry yourself to death? Meanwhile, Eric sits beside her with a face the color of concrete and eyes so hollow they could be made of glass. All Death's doing.

"You made them like that!" I spit, fury racing through my poor, deserted veins.

He doesn't deny it. "Regardless," he says after a long pause, "you can't try again right now. It could break them."

As much as it pains me to admit right now, he's probably right. And while he may not care, I certainly do. So, with extreme reluctance, I find myself nodding.

The moment we're back in his office (after an understandably awkward and frosty trip), I round on him. "Tell me. Tell me what is going on with you."

He pushes his hair from his face and I see a slight tremble in his fingers. Maybe this should be a sign to back off but I don't. I can't. Not after what he's done. So when he sighs and mutters, "Daisy, leave it, please," I just shake my head.

"No. Tell me."

"You're very emotional, this isn't the right time for this."

He's half right: I'm currently running on some sort of primal rage. Dad always said it took a lot to properly rile me up but when I snapped, I went all out. But we're not leaving this until later. "Don't you think I deserve to know? You have taken *everything* from me! My home, my family, my friends, my boyfriend! My freedom! And then you give me this chance, this—this beacon of hope. And you dangle it in front of my face before snatching it away again! What have I done to deserve that? Is this actually hell I've wandered into? Are you trying to punish me?"

"No!"

I find myself shoving him backward. He stumbles, not expecting it. "Then tell me! Tell me what the hell you're doing!"

"I... I..."

"I? I what?"

Death's face screws up as he steps back again. "I didn't want you to go," he croaks.

"Why? Why didn't you want me to go? Were you worried about the paperwork?" Sarcasm drips from my words, thick like syrup.

"Daisy, you know I think more of you than that."

"Then why? Why did you do this to me?" He's inching to the left, trying to see if he can get around me. But he's not going anywhere.

"I—I just didn't want you to leave!" It bursts from him like some massive confession, despite the fact that this sentence is almost identical to what he said before, except... Except it's not. There's something about the way he says it this time that makes each word so much heavier, so much more meaningful, somehow.

My anger has been snuffed out by his words. Just like that. "Scout," I begin, my voice low, "why don't you want me to leave?"

The forest that seems to reside within his eyes is dark now, as if dusk has come and stolen the green away. "Because," he begins, and I can tell that the prospect of saying these next words is terrifying for him. His hands fiddle around with his name tag, then the buttons on his shirt. He moves forward, takes one of my hands in his own. The heat from his anxiety spreads across my palm and down my fingers. "Because I don't know what I'll do without you."

There's no nonchalance in his tone this time. I know he means every single word he has just said. Perhaps it's the shock that makes panic take flight inside my chest. Perhaps it's the realization that, despite all his grandstanding, Death is just like the rest of us: selfishly heading toward his own goals and desires. Or maybe it's something else.

All I know is that Death has just told me that he can't imagine being without me and I have no clue what to do next.

So can you blame me when I turn and run?

Rule Sixteen

Pain Changes Us All

CAN I GO BACK to grief? I'm sure you remember what I said about it previously, about how the pain of it twists people into unrecognizable shadows of themselves.

Well, that's just the start. After the fierce onslaught of the initial shock, grief turns sly. Like damp, it sits in the corner and bides its time. Quietly growing and changing the world around it. Nothing escapes grief. And that's when we start making mistakes. That's when we start hurting people we love, even if we didn't mean to.

Some people can fight it. But some people can't. Perhaps the walls that your grief sits on are already slightly compromised. Then it's really only a matter of time until things start crumbling down.

Violet Tucker has walls that were once carefully held together by Daisy Cooper. With her gone, the damp has taken hold and everything has begun to crumble, just a little. Soon you won't be able to recognize her anymore. She'll be someone new.

I'm trying hard not to care so much about this. But grief affects us all. And Violet Tucker is not the only one changing into something unrecognizable.

❋ ❋ ❋

I don't expect Scout to come after me because he's never seemed the sort to chase after anyone. But it seems that he's fully committed to this apparent aim of surprising me as many times as possible in one day. I've barely gone ten steps down the corridor to the lift before he's chasing after me. I speed up but he's on my tail and showing no signs of giving up.

So I decide confronting him is the best option. Even if I really would rather not. I stop, whirl around and fix him with my best piercing glare. "I need you to leave me alone."

He stumbles to a rather uncertain halt. I can see he's wrestling between honoring my request and wanting to satisfy his own wants. He takes a step back, slowly and hesitantly. "Daisy... I didn't mean to freak you out. I just wanted you to understand."

"No, Death. You need to understand. You fucked this all up. *You.*"

I see him flinch at his old name but he wisely chooses not to comment on it. "Not deliberately!"

I laugh. It sounds hollow and cruel. This whole stupid situation has twisted me into something I never wanted to be and that just makes me angrier. I'm so sick of seeing how my death has changed things, usually for the worse. "Oh, right. Because that makes it all better."

He grits his teeth with what seems like frustration. Like he's trying desperately to get the right message through to me but he just can't. Well, he needs to hurry up because my patience is wearing exceedingly thin. "I just wanted you to understand how important you've become to me. You've made this job so much easier for me and I—I didn't want to lose that."

"Well, you're going to." He winces at my words and part of me regrets saying them. But the other part vividly remembers being tugged back from my friends and really doesn't care. "I don't belong up here and you can't force me to stay just because you'll miss me. It doesn't work like that."

I can see him trying to process this. It's like watching a toddler working out how to walk down stairs. Finally, he speaks again. "I thought…thought maybe you wouldn't mind staying here too. I thought you were happy up here."

"I'm dead. I'm away from my entire life, everything I love and care for. How could I be happy?"

I know I'm being a little harsh. I *have* enjoyed being up here with him in a strange way. We've found an odd sense of comfort and companionship. But it's not my life. It's not laughing until it aches with Violet, it's not the warmth and comfort of Eric's arms around me at night. This is something different. And they have to come first.

So when Scout hangs his head and turns to leave, I can't bring myself to go after him.

Left alone, there seems no other choice: I go back home.

It hasn't been that long since we left but the sun is just beginning to pull itself into the sky. Spring is on the way—you can feel it in the air, a sense of hope that doesn't match my mood in the slightest.

Pushing this rather dark thought away, I march purposefully down the street, heading toward my flat. I keep my speed up because there's a part of me that knows that if I think too hard about any of this, I might stop. If I can just get back to my world, where the weight of Scout's words will hopefully be far away, then it will be like none of this ever happened. A blank slate.

I'm moving with such determination that I almost slam my front door off its hinges when I open it. But, of course, nobody notices.

The kitchen is empty now. Poached eggs and avocados lie abandoned on twin plates by the sink. The chair I bumped into is still slightly askew. For a moment I wonder if they've gone out or something, but then a thumping sound comes from the other side of the flat. I squint through the darkness and I just about spot Eric banging on Violet's bedroom door.

It's a sight that fills me with terror, because the last time Violet locked herself in her bedroom she was brought out on a stretcher after the door was kicked down. I can't handle going through that all over again and I'm pretty sure she can't either.

"Violet, please open the door!" Eric calls out and I find myself racing around the sofa to come stand beside him. Though I'm not entirely sure what I can do to help this situation. "Come on, Violet. We can't deal with this through a door."

"I just want to be alone!" Violet calls back and I can hear the cracks in her voice. But at least she's answering.

"Don't give up that easily Eric," I find myself muttering. I'm willing Eric to do the right thing here because I know that appearing now won't necessarily help anyone. Violet needs to be a little calmer first; she's on the tightrope and any sort of disturbance could send her tumbling down.

So it's up to Eric. And he does me proud. He shakes his head, thwacks his palm against the door again. "No, Violet. You don't. You never really want to be alone. You just don't want people to see how hard this is for you."

I'm impressed. Clearly he's been paying attention over the past months. I've certainly never divulged any of that to him. Violet must be a little impressed too, because after a second or so, the door opens. She leans against the frame, face blotchy from the tears and a tissue screwed up in one hand. Despite the tears still welled up in her eyes, she manages to give him an appraising look. "Well, aren't you the knowledgeable one. Did Daisy tell you that?"

Eric shakes his head vehemently. "She would never say anything but praise about you to me. It was a little intimidating, if I'm honest…"

Violet's mouth twitches with a hint of a smile. "I'm sure it was." She moves past him, dropping down onto the sofa. She's silent for a moment, eyes staring at a spot straight in front. "At least you know I'm not crazy now—I told you she had come."

Eric moves to sit beside her. "I never doubted you," he replies, but he's grinning to let her know that he's not being serious. At her exasperated look, he shrugs. "Well, maybe if you didn't keep skipping your medication, I'd be more inclined to believe you weren't hallucinating."

Violet sniffs. "How do you know that?"

Eric rolls his eyes. "You told me last night, after your fifth rum and Coke."

Violet sighs, shrugging away the sentence with weary shame. Unaware of the invisible person standing watch with ominous fear now in their heart, a fear that seems to freeze me in place. She's silent for a moment, calming herself down a little more before allowing herself to speak. "They all keep leaving me, Eric. Dad left me and Mum even when I begged him not to, now Daisy's gone too. And I just… I don't know who I am anymore. I'm stuck, Eric. The world is spinning on and it's not like everything can stop just because my best friend died—but I sort of need it to. And then she appears, but she always leaves! Why won't she just stay? Where has she gone that's so hard to come back from?"

Eric's hand comes to sit atop Violet's, finding her fingers and squeezing them tight. "Violet, I can't explain what happened today and how we saw Daisy. And I certainly can't explain why she doesn't stay. But wherever she is, she wouldn't want you to be getting yourself into a state like this. We have to do her proud." I hear a crack of emotion in Eric's voice and wince inwardly. What has my death done to my poor friends?

"I—I don't think I know how," Violet mutters, frowning. "It's been Daisy and me since first year of primary school… I'm not sure I know how to just be…me."

Eric lets out a soft snort of weary amusement and understanding. "It's been Daisy and me for a lot less time than that and I think I know what you mean. She—she has a pretty large impact."

Violet nods at that, a tiny smile of agreement on her face. "Yeah, she does that. She marched into my classroom on her first day, just five years old, and immediately told the teacher she didn't like the way the crayons were arranged," she murmurs and the hazy childhood memory brings a little laugh from her. "She wouldn't talk to any of us kids for ages. Then I got my foot stuck in the railings of the playground and she helped me get free. And that was that."

I'm enchanted by her words, so much so that I can't quite find the drive to start trying to appear. I want to hear more, want to hear what impact I've had on their lives. Is that selfish? I don't know. But it's a rare moment where I find a benefit to being dead and perhaps I deserve to enjoy it.

Eric sighs a little, shakes his head fondly as he sits back against the sofa. "She walked into my office and saw right through all my bullshit. Apparently I was overdue on some paperwork for her department so I tried to give her the smooth-talking act and she cut me right off. Told me to just fix it, not explain the mistake. Then added this 'please' like she'd suddenly realized she was this newbie and she possibly shouldn't be talking to me like that. She always went on about how brave and outspoken you were, never realized she was just the same, in her own Daisy way..." His voice cracks again and I watch as he hides his face in his hands, determined not to let Violet see that firmly hidden vulnerable side of his.

"Eric?" There's a gentleness to her voice, which I've never heard Violet use with Eric before. I should be happy at this understanding that they've reached but I'm suddenly feeling strangely fluttery, unnerved. Do I want Violet to see Eric's sensitive side? A side that only I've been privy to up to this point? I mean, even his mother doesn't think her son knows how to cry. But I do. And now it seems like Violet's going to know it too. My death just keeps changing things.

I remember when I saw this side for the first time, and how alien it was to see cool and confident Eric Broad break down in front of me, back when we were having a break in our relationship, because things were going too fast for me, and he came around to apologize for pushing me too quickly. As he cried, he spoke these words of apology with so much care it was like each one was made of glass. That's when I realized there was something special about this guy.

When he speaks now, though, it's like the glass is broken and it's cutting his tongue. Every syllable seems to bring a grimace of pain. "I keep telling myself that I can do it. That I have to move on from this because my life is still so...unfinished. But it's impossible. She just won't get out of my head."

Violet's looking at him like it's the first time she's seen him. I recognize that look. I remember wearing it myself when he dropped down on the sofa that morning and begged for one more chance.

With a heavy sigh, Violet shuffles closer and pulls him into a hug. I see Eric stiffen, hesitate. He's not quite sure whether this is OK. But then, like clockwork, Eric relaxes and rests his head against her shoulder, his own arms coming around hers. They stay slotted together like jigsaw pieces, silent but comfortable.

I have a sudden, quite painful sense that I'm intruding. That this isn't something for me to see. They're mourning me, without even knowing that I'm here witnessing it. It's like watching someone planning a surprise birthday party for you—you want to hear what they're going to say but you also know you shouldn't. But I also don't feel like this is something I should just barge into. Here they are talking about trying to move on and finding their life without me; how can I just drop into their world again? Even with this newfound solution, it feels wrong. Grief has once again twisted things around and I'm not sure where I belong in this world anymore.

But where else can I go? Not back, not to Scout and his confusing words. I'm stuck somewhere in between.

Then Eric lifts his head and meets Violet's gaze and my chest tightens because I suddenly have a terrible feeling about what's coming next. I've seen enough movies to know what comes in these moments of heightened emotions and close body contact and met gazes. And I want to scream. I want to storm into this moment and shake the enchantment from it. Because that's all it is, right? A moment of sorcery caused by their anguish that has no place in the real world. And yet I'm frozen. The keys are only in my pocket but somehow my fingers will not move toward them. All I can do is watch and hope that somehow I'm wrong.

Then their lips meet.

It's like a tidal wave. I don't know how else to describe the feeling of watching your best friend and boyfriend kiss. There's a force that slams into you at 100 mph and all you can do is surrender to it. Let it sweep you away.

It's like my friends have morphed into dark, shadowy versions of themselves. I don't want that to be my lasting view of them, so I turn away before it can become permanently etched into my mind. As if it hasn't already! There's voices behind me, they're saying something to each other but it's muffled, as though I've gone into another room. And I don't make any effort to listen to it because I'm not sure there's enough strength left in me to take another hit.

Suddenly, I've stumbled outside. I don't really remember moving, I can probably blame that on that tidal wave for sweeping me along, away from its point of impact. I half expect to see Scout waiting on the pavement with one of his usual smug grins—he does seem to like loitering around and waiting for things to fuck up for me, after all. But he's not there. There's nobody and nothing. Just one dead girl, trying not to lose herself in the whirlpool of dark and painful feelings.

Should I be feeling this upset? Is it really a betrayal when the previous girlfriend has snuffed it? Yes, a voice snarls in my head, yes it is. I think of Violet and her father who she discovered was having an affair when she was sixteen. I think of how long I've spent helping her through that over the years and resentment sears through me. She should know how much this could hurt a person. She should still have those scars.

Behind me, there comes a soft and almost tentative "ding!" It's so familiar to me now that I feel a sob rising up in my throat. I wish I could explain why the sound of the lift has brought tears to my eyes. Is that what home is to me now? A lift? Or perhaps I'm hoping there will be someone waiting inside, ready to make this better somehow.

But the lift is empty. It's arrived all by itself. Scout says that sometimes it does that, as if it has a mind of its own. It spat us out once in the middle of Mumbai, on a silent and apparently uneventful night, when we were meant to be in the Norwegian town of Bergen. I remember how I told Scout that his lift must be broken and then he told me, in a voice with a surprising amount of fondness (considering he was talking about an inanimate object), that it must have brought us here for a reason.

"It always takes us where we need to be, even if that's not where we were expecting," he had murmured, watching with a small smile as the lift doors closed and left us there.

Indeed, not a minute later, an undocumented and unexpected death occurred just feet from where we are. And if we hadn't been there, that person would have been lost and alone, trapped in between death and life.

So maybe the lift knows that I need it. Maybe it heard an echo of my desperate, heartache-ridden cries and came running. It looks so inviting inside that I don't hesitate. I stumble in. It feels like walking into a cocoon or into the arms of my mother and, as the doors close, I feel a sense of relief wash over me. I'm safe in here; nobody can spring any nasty surprises on me from inside this little box. Time can rumble on outside and I can stay in this lift and ignore it all.

I don't press any buttons. I wouldn't know where to start with those right now. A second later, I feel the lift shudder and begin to move. Like I said, mind of its own. There's a gentle humming beneath my feet and it's oddly calming. It reminds me of the absentminded humming of my grandma when she baked. I used to sit in her kitchen, drawing with the special crayons she brought out for me when I came to stay. I'd watch her wander around the kitchen and hum to herself and I would giggle when she forgot the tune, paused, then just made it up.

The lift keeps going for what seems like ages. In that time,

I keep replaying their lips meeting over and over again, each time feeling more like a punch in the gut. I wonder if I'll forget what this feels like? I don't know if I want to. Part of me wants to never forget how this feels, so I can make sure I never forgive them.

Suddenly, the lift stops. A second later the doors open and the calm silence is blown straight out by a wild, roaring wind. My hair is immediately blown into a frenzy, mainly getting in my eyes until I push it out and tuck it behind my ears. Somewhat tentatively, I stumble to my feet, move to the edge of the lift and look outside.

I'm near the edge of a cliff and that cliff is weathering a mighty storm. Funny how you can go from London's morning sunshine to here, where it feels like the entire Earth is howling. I can hear waves crashing incessantly in the distance, pounding against rocks with an apparent glee that I can pick up from all the way up here. The clouds are low, whirling and thundering, hiding the horizon behind a dark and angry blanket. But it can't hide the cottage that stands in front of me, grimly holding strong on the edge of the steadily eroding cliff. I think I know that feeling.

The cottage is exactly how you'd imagine a cottage on its own on the edge of a cliff to look. Its walls are exceedingly weathered; they look as if one firm push would bring it all tumbling down. Meanwhile, the roof is somewhat lopsided and the windows are covered in grime. It looks a mess, and perhaps that's why I find myself taking a step toward it. We messes need to stick together after all.

As I'm moving toward it, I hear that familiar "ding!" behind me once again. I whirl around and watch as the lift doors smoothly close. And maybe it's my imagination, but it almost looks like it's winking.

Rule Seventeen

We All Need A Sanctuary

IT IS WIDELY BELIEVED that survival relies on five key things. There's water, food, sleep, air. And then there's shelter. Or, as I like to call it, a sanctuary. There's something innately comforting about the word in my opinion.

And I love the idea that whoever deemed it appropriate to create life decided that we couldn't do it if we didn't have somewhere to go when we needed to feel safe. When the rain begins to fall or the wind begins to howl or perhaps a predator begins to lurk.

Some of you call this home. Some of you call it "my friend's." Some of you call it the classroom at school with the kind teacher. Wherever and whatever it is, we all have one. And if we don't, then that's when the problems will start. Guaranteed.

The question, then, is this: Do the dead need a sanctuary too? They don't need to eat or drink anymore, neither do they need to sleep or breathe. So why would they need a shelter? The logical answer is that we don't. Nobody can hurt the dead so there's no need for us to seek safety.

And yet, on the edge of a cliff stands a cottage. A cottage once inhabited by a doting father and his daughter. The walls are crumbling, the floor is rotten. Except for the crash of waves and the call of gulls, you are alone.

And when your world seems to have become only rain and wind and predators, alone in a dusty and abandoned cottage seems like a pretty good sanctuary to me.

Stuck on the cliffs, there seems to be only one possible way to go. If the lift is insisting on abandoning me here, I may as well get out of the wind before the darkening clouds burst open above my head. My dead body does not suffer in the cold like the living but that doesn't mean that standing in a biting wind is any less unpleasant. It just means you can do it for longer without hypothermia arriving.

The door to the cottage is incredibly stiff. All the years of salty seawater and relentless wind have warped the wood and I know my caretaker father would be shaking his head disapprovingly at it. The handle creaks, almost screams, with complaint when I turn it and I have to give the whole door a hearty push before it finally relents and opens. Immediately, the wind tugs it from my grasp and slams the door fully open. Not quite the surreptitious entrance I was envisaging.

Still, no sense in filling the cottage with wind and rain for longer than necessary. I hurry inside and push against the gale until, finally, the door is shut once more. In an instant, as if someone has grabbed the wind and stuffed it in a soundproof box, there is silence. The walls of this cottage must be extremely thick, because now I'm inside, I could be fooled into thinking I'm in the middle of a tropical lagoon.

There's a light switch next to me. I try it and, unsurprisingly, nothing happens. So I'm left to squint in the gloom, trying to work out where I've ended up. I can make out a large table with a tablecloth made purely from dust, a somewhat chaotic-looking kitchen and a few other doors leading to other rooms. On the wall there is a photo in a pretty frame made from shells, clearly homemade. Oddly enough, it's the only thing in this place that doesn't seem to be covered in dust. Within the frame is a man and a young girl. The girl has a tube going into her nose and seems unnaturally pale, but the man beside her presents her to the camera with a pride that can only belong to a father. It brings a small smile to my face, though there's a bittersweetness to it. I wonder if this girl has already passed through Death's office. Judging by the state of this cottage, I'd say the chances were pretty high.

It's as I'm looking past this photo at the rest of the cottage that I notice that one of the doors is somewhat ajar, while all the rest remain firmly closed. It could just be a coincidence but it's enough to pique my interest. I take a step toward it, then freeze when I hear a creak of movement from within the room. It's enough to send a shiver of fear down my spine, which is strange when you consider the fact that there's not much in this world that can hurt me.

"Hello?" I call out tentatively, mentally berating myself for such a stupid act. It's not like anyone is going to bloody hear me.

Of course this idea goes right out the window when a voice answers back: "Hello?"

I'm about to turn and race from this cottage without looking back when something makes me pause. I know that voice. I can't quite believe I'm hearing it here, but I know it nonetheless. I move forward the rest of the way, pull open the door and stare at the sight before me.

Scout is sitting on top of a squat chest of drawers, back

against the wall. He's half turned toward the window but has twisted around to watch me enter the room. His Converses have been unlaced and tossed rather carelessly across the floor, leaving his feet bare except for a pair of dark blue socks. I notice, because I'm trying to avoid looking at his face for as long as possible, that there are tiny white stars dotted across them. He's also unbuttoned the top of his shirt which, like his socks, is something I've never seen before on him. There's a whole sense of vulnerability coming from him that brings me to a slightly shaky halt. I feel like I'm intruding on something here, like I've put my foot through a rabbit's warren or stumbled upon somebody's secret den. While I've been finding safety in a curious old lift, Scout seems to have found his own sanctuary.

"Daisy?" he asks and he sounds as surprised as I feel. I'm finally forced to look at his face, before it becomes painfully obvious that I'm avoiding his gaze, and I inwardly wince at the hollow look in his eyes. Surely that can't all be from me walking out? But then he goes on and the resentment in his voice answers that question for me… "I thought you were gone."

After what I've just been through, this is enough for me to drop to tears. Again. They spring from my eyes before I've even really realized, and by the time I start trying to stop the flow, it's too late. My cheeks are sodden in seconds and all I can do is turn away because I don't want him to see this. I don't want him to think I'm coming back to him with my tail between my legs because that's not what this is. I didn't even know he'd be here.

But there's no stopping me now. The sense of being alone, of being stuck between two difficult situations couldn't be stronger, and desperate sobs break loose from between my lips. In the lift I could control the tears because I felt safe. Now, seeing him, it's as if I'm out in the storm again.

I hear the floorboards creak and I know he's moving. There's the soft padding of his socks on the wood and then he's there, behind me. "Daisy?" he asks, and this time his voice is devoid of all emotions except concern. "What happened?"

The words are there, on my tongue. But I just can't. I'm too scared to hear his reaction, because I'm sure it's going to be full of sympathy but also laced with a thousand tiny "I-told-you-so's." So I don't turn around. I stay away and bury my face in my hands, try to find my own sanctuary in the darkness of my palms.

Distantly, I hear him mumble something, then move away, the sound of floorboards creaking getting fainter and fainter. Alone, I find myself pulling my hands away from my face, then dropping down onto the bed that sits in the corner of the room. God knows how dirty and old it is but right now I couldn't care less.

I can hear Scout crashing about in the kitchen but I tune it out, focus instead on trying to hold back the flow of tears and calm myself down. Easier said than done. I still can't scrub the image of Eric and Violet from my mind.

But then my gaze lands on the wall opposite me and the sweet mercy of a distraction arrives in the form of a mural. I had thought, at first, it was just some sort of pattern but it's far more than that. The sea has come to life inside this poky bedroom. Painted waves dip and rise elegantly and, beneath their foaming tops, there's a whole world of marine life. Clown fish dart between coral, a shark loiters in the shadows by the plug socket, an octopus propels itself proudly across the center of the wall. It's so detailed, so complex, that I'm sure I could stare at it for hours and still find something new.

"It was for Coraline."

I don't know how long I've been examining the painting when Scout announces his presence with these rather ambiguous words. Tearing my gaze from the wall, I look to him instead. "What?"

He's leaning on the door frame, looking at the painting with a thoughtful expression. "This bedroom. It belonged to a girl called Coraline. Her father built this house."

"The girl in the picture?" I ask, nodding out to the hallway where I saw the photo of the girl and her father.

He nods, his fingers drumming gently against the wood of the door. It sounds like rain. "She wasn't very well. She couldn't go very far without feeling exhausted but she adored the sea, more than anything. So her father built her this cottage."

My eyes flick back to the painting, the way it seems to live and breathe off the wall. The visual equivalent of putting your ear to a shell. "He brought the sea to her."

Out of the corner of my eye, I see Scout nod. But he says nothing and when I look at him properly, I see wistfulness in his eyes. Perhaps that's where my question comes from. "Why were you here?"

Scout shifts, moving to sit on a small chair in one corner of the room. I notice that one hand is holding a small green-and-blue bag. "Because I always come here. When I'm confused."

They're simple words but they still make me shift awkwardly. I also can't help silently cursing that damn lift, because it must have known what it was doing, somehow.

"Coraline was one of the few people I've considered bending the rules for. She was clever, she was kind, she was her father's only family. She was only nineteen. It didn't seem right at all. I came for her myself, even though she technically didn't fit my criteria. And when I came, her father tried so hard to hold onto her that I seriously considered just leaving her behind." He draws in a deep sigh, starting to unwind the top of the bag. "But you can't. The rules have to take priority above all…" He doesn't sound entirely convinced by his own words, and shakes his head a moment later. "Anyway, after she was gone her father moved away and I found myself coming here when I needed some space to think. It always feels safe here… So why are *you* here?" he asks, directing the bag in my general area in what I assume is an offer to take it.

It's a bag of frozen peas. This would be unusual enough on its own, but I have an odd history with frozen peas. Yeah, trust me to have a history with frozen peas.

It all stemmed from the time that Violet's father was caught out and his affair was brought, kicking and screaming, into the open. As I'm sure you can imagine, Violet was distraught. Her father had been a bit of a hero to her prior to this point and then the cape was ripped away rather unceremoniously. It broke her. We would spend hours talking it through, stumbling through the murky mire of her feelings and trying to find a way out of it. Riding the ebb and flow of panic attacks, trying to keep ourselves afloat. One day, I went to find our snack of choice in my freezer and found that the ice cream tub was empty. Probably thanks to my greedy brother, though to this day I don't have any proof. Regardless of who did it, there was no getting away from the fact that we didn't have any ice cream. All we had was a bag of frozen peas.

Violet had looked at me like I was crazy, when I returned with this bag. She told me as much when I tried to suggest it was a suitable snack, but I persevered and before too long, we were sitting on my windowsill, bag in between us, and a single frozen pea cooling each of our tongues. It didn't take long for the pair of us to decide we quite liked them. And it didn't take much longer for us to decide it was worthy of becoming a tradition. Over the years we've got through quite a few bags of peas, which shows how many trying times we've needed them for.

I have a sneaking suspicion that Scout knows some, if not all, of this history. Why else would he have a bag of frozen peas at this precise moment in time?

"Daisy?"

"Oh. Um…the lift dropped me here. Maybe it thought I needed to feel safe…" I hear his chair squeak, as he leans forward a little. I take a pea and gently roll it over my palm. It's not exactly freezing cold like it would normally be, but the barrier between death and life does allow a slight cooling sensation to trickle through. It's nice.

While I'm pondering this, Scout stands up, moves around and sits at the foot of my bed. His hand reaches across and he delves into the bag of peas. He retrieves three and places them flat on his palm, before trapping them with his other hand. I see a small shiver cross over his face as their icy chill takes hold but he soldiers through and a moment later he's ready to speak again. "I wasn't sure whether I'd see you again—or, more precisely, whether you'd see me again."

I don't say anything. Scout stays silent for a moment, waiting it out. I'm not giving him any easy ways out here, which he picks up on after another few seconds of silence. "What happened, Daisy? Please, I want to help. I thought you were leaving me…forever. But now you're here, in my cottage."

I consider questioning him on the ownership of this cottage, but instead I roll my pea slowly between my fingers, watching its movement somewhat absentmindedly. "Eric and Violet," I finally say, hoping that that will be enough.

Of course it's not. I glance over at Scout and he's squinting at me as if I'm a particularly difficult equation. Groaning, I go on, "They kissed."

"Oh." His voice is heavy, weighed down with shock. "Shit."

"Yeah. Shit," I agree, eyes fixed back on the wall.

"Why did they do that?"

My gaze rips off the wall and is back on Scout in a flash. If he's mocking me, he's getting a pea up the nostril. But he looks genuinely curious. "Well," I finally say, "I wish I could help you there. But I have no clue. Some people are just jerks."

"No, that's not it." He sounds mighty decisive about the matter, despite having just admitted to having no real insight into it.

"Oh? You're an expert?"

"In affairs? No. In love? Not really. But in your friendship with that Violet girl? Well, I'm getting there. You burble on about her enough. Don't give me that look—it's true. And I'm gambling here on you not making it all up, but from all you've said, I don't think it's that simple. I don't think she would ever do that to you. Not in a normal situation."

I can see what he's getting at. "But this isn't normal."

Scout nods and grimaces. Like he's glad I've reached the crux of the matter but he wishes that there was a different one for me to find. "Remember what I said about grief?"

I do. It's hard to forget when it came at the end of a particularly painful lesson on the effects of that particular emotion. "So that's it? I'm gone and they're all moving on without me?"

"You are dead, Daisy." He says it with a real gentleness, eyes full of concern as he watches me, waits for my reaction.

"I guess... I just thought they were better than that." It's been there on the tip of my tongue for a while now and, as it leaves my mouth, I feel a sense of relief. Because sometimes saying the horrible thing is a lot better than not being able to work out what the horrible thing is.

Scout sighs, flopping back on the bed, frozen peas clutched to his chest. "Yeah. That happens a lot." He's silent for a moment but there's a tension around his mouth which makes me think he's not quite done yet. I'm right, though the words that come out of his mouth are a bit of a surprise. "About earlier? I'm sorry."

"You're...?"

"Sorry. Yes. I'm sorry."

"Oh. Right." I feel myself stiffening up a little; I've never liked apologies, even when it's not me doing the apology. My instinct is to apologize myself, or feel bad as if I'm somehow responsible for getting the other person into this situation. "It's OK," I say, even though it really isn't.

Scout shakes his head. "No. It isn't and it wasn't. It wasn't fair of me to expect you to give up everything for me like that. Not when you've lost so much."

"Wow! When did you get so sensitive of others?" Scout shoots me a weary look and I immediately feel bad for trying to make light of this moment. It's a nasty habit of mine. "Sorry."

He shrugs, a smile twitching at the corner of his mouth. "We can't both be apologizing. Wait your turn, Cooper."

I hear myself laughing. It's nice; a bandage on the big, gaping wound that's been exposed by the last few hours. Scout seems to notice that his laughter has helped me somewhat and looks intensely proud of the fact. A painful thought enters my head. Perhaps Scout has never experienced cheering someone up like this before. And certainly not someone he actually knows. A strange sensation of sympathy washes over me then. Perhaps that's why I stand up and offer him a hand, smiling down at him. "Come on."

"Come on what?" Scout asks, looking up at me from his sprawled position.

"Let's get out of here. Let's get out of this...lonely cottage and do something fun for once in our lives—"

"Deaths."

His automatic correction is infuriating but not exactly un-expected. "Deaths, lives—whatever. Moping about in the bedroom of a dead girl isn't going to help either of us."

Scout huffs derisively. "Who says I need help?" But he smiles a moment later, just in case I thought he was being serious. He stands up slowly, all the years of service seeming to weigh heavily on him in that moment, until he shoulders them up and away again. "So, where shall we go?"

The question is big and open and a little intimidating. It's not often you get the chance to go anywhere you want, even when you're Death's assistant. There's too much work get-ting in the way. I've visited a lot of places over the months and many of them have been beautiful, astounding. But I don't want to go back there now because they'll just have a little invisible flag marker there, reminding me that some-one died there.

"I want to go somewhere where I can just forget I'm dead. Just for a bit."

Scout's expression twists with deep concentration. Then his eyes light up. "You know what? I think I've got just the place."

Rule Eighteen

Find The World's Magic

HAVE YOU EVER THOUGHT about how extraordinary our world is? I mean, really thought about it. A spherical world with just the right amount of land and water and just the right temperature (for now, you destructive people) that life is able to flourish on it. It's sort of hard to believe when you put it like that. And that's before you really, properly look at it.

There's a part of the world where lights literally dance across the sky. There is an ocean so deep that part of it has simply never been seen, while caves lie under the ground that twist and turn like the coils of a snake. Stones move on their own across deserts and ice forms structures larger than islands.

When you're clearing up the dead, it's easy to forget that such magic exists. But it does. In little pockets across the world it can be found. In the way that spring comes back every year and the way that people continue to come into existence despite the chances being so small. In the way that a whole storm of crabs can all simultaneously migrate to the same place to lay their eggs, and the way that *people just quietly accommodate it. Murmurations of starlings, the courting dance of the male puffer fish. The list goes on.*

I like to think that we can all find a little bit of magic somewhere in the world. We just have to remember to look.

When Violet and I were small, we made a bucket list. Being eight, we didn't call it that. We called it our "Non-Negotiable" list. Mum had been using that term with me a lot in regards to homework and ice-skating lessons, so we decided to use it for our means. We made a list of things that we would do one day, no matter what. Number one was move to London (even back then we felt a desperate need to escape the cul-de-sacs of our nondescript town). Number two was join the Spice Girls, which admittedly was a little optimistic for a non-negotiable.

Number three, though, *that* we thought we could one day achieve. Number three was to visit New York. We both had our reasons: Violet was desperate to visit Broadway and be swept off her feet in Central Park, while I wanted to visit the Public Library, Grand Central Station, see the view from the top of the Empire State Building. We'd grown up being fed all these romanticized scenes of New York in movies and we couldn't think of somewhere more perfect for us to go together. When we finally moved in to our London flat we started saving up straightaway. All our little bits of loose change were stored in a ceramic Statue of Liberty piggy bank that Mum bought us. One day we were going to go there.

Well, that never happened. To be fair, though, I think that was my doing more than hers. I didn't give us much time for saving before I cracked my head open and left for the afterlife. So I wonder if Scout knows how monumental taking me here is, or whether he just thought New York was the sort of city even the dead could feel alive in.

Whatever the reason behind it, we're here. In New York City. And even when there's a painful association with Violet attached to it, I can't quite pull back my wonder. Traffic roars in my ears, huge pavement vents drift steam across my vision, and a nearby cart wafts the smell of hot dogs and pretzels into the air. It's a million miles away from that tiny, lonely cottage. Here, life hits me, heavy and thick like pollution. It's everywhere, clinging to my skin and making my head spin. People are all around me, living their lives, texting, chatting, hopping over murky-looking puddles. Doing those little things that I crave so desperately.

"This is amazing!" I exclaim.

Scout sniffs. "Yes, amazing. Amazing how humans can take up so much space." But then he glances at me and grins. "Kidding. Come on, I know somewhere we can go."

I follow him, drinking in every little detail around me. The infamous skyscrapers stretch luxuriously into the clouds, and I've never felt so small. I like it, though; Scout's offices seem so tiny, so claustrophobic, even when they wind on forever. You feel as if you're stuck in an anthill while not being ant-sized. Here I feel tiny and insignificant and it's wonderful. Wonderful to finally feel like I'm not making a crater-sized impact on somebody's well-being. I become so lost in the sheer volume of life and the vast complexity of the city that I begin to lag behind until Death impatiently calls my name from ahead.

Hurrying to catch up with my companion, I bump my shoulder against his arm. "So, where are we going? You look like you're on a mission," I comment, because he does; he's paying no attention to his surroundings, except for the street names.

"We're going somewhere that every self-respecting dead person should visit when they come here."

My mind fills with a thousand different possibilities. I imagine climbing the Statue of Liberty in the dead of night when there is nobody else to disturb us, or watching the sun rise from the Empire State Building, where the city will sprawl out beneath us and we will have the view to ourselves. But when I voice these ideas to Scout, he laughs outright.

"Not quite. We're not just tourists, after all. When you come to New York City invisible, the city is completely open to you. Why go visit the tourist traps when there are tiny corners of the city that nobody else gets to see?"

Suddenly, we steer down a small alleyway. I step over a pile of garbage bags, wrinkling my nose as the smell manages to sneak through the barrier of death, into our world, and up my nostrils.

"This looks lovely," I declare.

He stops at a door, or rather half a door as the other half seems to have been ripped off. "You of little faith," he tuts, shaking his head. "Didn't anybody ever tell you not to judge a book by its cover?"

"I'm not sure that saying counts if there isn't even a cover to judge." I gesture at the half-destroyed door to prove my point, smirking as Scout rolls his eyes. There's a comfortableness between us once more, which I appreciate. I haven't completely forgiven him for tugging me back (after all, one could argue that that kiss would never have happened if I had been there still), but I'm willing to put it to one side. I want this to be fun. We could both use a bit of that.

"Just open the door and trust me, OK?" he asks, nodding to the door.

Sighing, I step forward and gingerly pull the half-door open. Inside is a simple staircase, as grimy as you would expect. The second step is cracked, the third step is missing all together. It's not looking particularly promising.

"Is this some trick? Are you just taking me to a job?"

Scout doesn't entertain that notion. He squeezes past me and hops nimbly up the steps, somehow managing to avoid the gaps and broken pieces of wood. I am really tempted to turn and go and visit the Statue of Liberty on my own. But I am too curious. Besides, the worst that could happen is I trip and fall to my death and, well, I've already done that.

So, with a groan, I start after him. We climb flight after flight of stairs. I count ten and then give up. I would ask about a lift, but this place barely has walls. Finally, we reach the top, which consists of a dead end and a door marked "DO NOT ENTER."

"How welcoming..."

"Right? Nothing better than a 'do not enter' sign," Scout replies, almost gleefully, as he gestures for me to keep going. Pushing open the door, I step gingerly outside, expecting to see a building site or some sort of hideout for criminals.

But I am pleasantly surprised. And not just because there's no crime going on or builders demolishing walls. But because I have just stepped into an enchanted world.

It takes me a moment to work out what I'm seeing, as a sparkling, iridescent light is dazzling my eyes. Then my eyes adjust and I realize that the glorious and glittering color I am looking at is being caused by thousands and thousands of pieces of colored glass stuck to the floor of the flat roof. A mosaic of sorts, but there does not seem to be any order to it, just a glorious mess of vivid, glimmering colors. I feel as if I have stepped into an ocean, but an ocean that has been flooded with a paint factory, or merged with the rainbow.

I step out from the gloom of the staircase and let the tiles' reflection bathe my arms in a blur of different colors. My fingers turn blue while a pink strand snakes up my arm, meeting a slowly twisting starburst of green light settled on my shoulder.

"How...?" I begin, because surely this light should just pass right through me? But Scout gets there first, clearly having read my mind:

"It's an anomaly. A chink in the world's armor. For some reason, up here, we are allowed to feel the light of life upon us."

I want to cry, because my previously deathly pale skin is now a patchwork of color and, what's more, I feel warmth from the sun seeping into my skin. It's completely impossible and it's completely wonderful.

After a few moments, I find myself drifting to the edge of the roof and sitting down, looking out across the city with feet dangling over a stomach-churning drop. Heights have never bothered me particularly and certainly don't bother me now I'm dead. Especially when there's a view to admire. We're not quite high enough to have a full view of the whole city, but I can see the unmistakable flash of green that is Central Park peeping through a gap in the towering buildings and tiny taxis buzzing along the road below. "It's perfect," I declare, and I'm treated to a rare noise of approval from Scout.

"I agree. It is. A little slice of perfection in this mad city."

Scout comes to sit beside me, though he leaves a little gap between us, just like he did in the cottage. An odd sign of respect for the still quietly present divide between us. His legs swing gently over the edge, clearly not bothered by the height either. "How did it get here?" I ask curiously.

"A woman, named Amelia Burtscott. She owned this building about twenty years ago. Had a business making ornate glass bottles, I believe. Her company went bust and she had to sell the building. But before she left, she took all the glass left over, smashed it up, and stuck it up here. She wanted to create a beautiful thing out of a horrible circumstance. And here it is."

I smile, struck by the magic of the living and the world they inhabit. I wonder what happened to her after she left, if she's still alive or if she's somewhere up in Death's offices. Maybe I can find her, tell her how her name lives on in the shimmering light of a New York afternoon.

"Did she…?" I begin to ask but Scout shakes his head.

"Not yet. She was an art teacher for a bit. Had a few kids, had a husband, had a house. Think she's probably retired now. Living in Vermont."

He rattles this off with such ease that I can't help but wonder if he's just making it up or whether he truly knows this much about one person. "How do you know all of that? You can't know that about everybody, surely?"

Scout shrugs. I think he's considering pretending that he does indeed know this much about everybody. I mean, he could try; I'd end up having a lot more fun than him, I'm sure. He obviously comes to a similar conclusion because he shakes his head a second later. "No, I don't. But when people do things like cover an entire roof with colored glass, just for the hell of it, I like to see how they turn out."

That makes sense. "Anyone else you're keeping tabs on?"

Another shrug. "A few. There's a guy in Sochi trying to teach his pet weasel how to fetch chicken eggs every morning. I'm kinda intrigued to see how that turns out."

He sounds like a little boy watching a butterfly emerge from a cocoon for the first time. In awe and amazed by the world around him. I can't help but find it endearing. "Well, do let me know how that goes."

"If I can." He says the words so quickly that I know he didn't think properly about them. Indeed, when I look over

216 / Tamsin Keily

at him, I can see regret creased into the corners of his eyes. "Sorry, that was uncalled for," he goes on to say almost immediately. "And I didn't mean for it to sound so...harsh."

"I wasn't leaving because of you," I blurt out, the words surprising me a little.

A plane roars above our heads, heading toward the Hudson River. Scout watches it for a moment, then meets my gaze. "I know," he says. But I don't believe him.

"No, you don't. You think it was all your fault. But it wasn't. And I'm sorry for what I said back in your office—I didn't mean it, not really. I am happy with you. And leaving you would *never* be an easy decision. I mean, I'd really miss you. But they're my family. My friends. Most of them I've known my entire life and if there was any chance of going back to them, it would be madness not to take it, even if leaving you would hurt."

"It...would hurt?"

I nod. "Sure. I've spent the last few months with you and only you. You might be an ass half the time but the rest of the time you're all right and, well, we've grown close."

"Yes, I suppose we have." Scout states this carefully, thoughtfully. "Like friends?"

The word doesn't quite sit right and I don't quite know why. I'd call the girl I do my book club with a friend, I'd call the people I sit with at lunch my friends. Scout doesn't quite seem to fit into that quota for some reason. It feels... too small. But I'm not sure what word I'd use instead so, for simplicity's sake, I nod. "Sure. Friends."

He grins at that, pride beaming from him like he's just won his first Sports Day. It settles on him like snow and he sits back a little, legs still swinging merrily over the drop. "So... New York City. Tell me."

I glance over at him. "You've read my file," I reply, a little hesitantly. I'm not sure I want to go into the backstory right now, when even saying Violet's name feels like a challenge.

Scout shifts so he's looking at me more directly. "I know the story. But the file doesn't tell me why you and Violet got so obsessed by the idea."

I shrug, feeling the memories prickle against my skull. "Who doesn't want to go to New York?"

Scout's shuffling means that his legs now bump against mine. The contact feels strange, charged almost. "I mean, I have a list if you'd like one?"

"Funny."

"Come on, Daisy, tell me. Why here?"

I can see that this isn't going to be a conversation I'm going to be avoiding easily. "We thought it was magic," I say simply, before going on a moment later. "We grew up in this gray little suburb with identical houses and identical-looking people. Can you imagine someone like Violet growing up there? She hated it—so I hated it. We wanted to go somewhere with color and excitement and unpredictable days."

Instinctively, as the flash of that kiss arrives again, my side comes to rest against Scout's, seeking some sort of comfort from his presence. I feel him hesitate, then wrap one arm around me. "Do you wish I hadn't brought you here?" he asks after a moment of almost somber silence.

I shake my head slowly. "No," I murmur, lifting my head briefly to shoot him a reassuring look, while also hiding my surprise at this unusual show of insight. "This is amazing, truly. And hard, of course. But there's always going to be something reminding me of her. Or Mum. Or Dad. Or Eric… I can't hide away from the world just because of that. Not when the world can look like this."

Scout nods at that, smiles as he gazes out across the city again. The sun is beginning to set behind him, causing his jet-black hair to light up a little. A night sky dappled with stars. "Lucas was good at that. Finding pockets of magic. Once he found this waterfall that could make a rainbow—and a pretty awesome waterslide."

I grin at that, the image coming to mind easily. "I think I would have liked Lucas."

Scout makes a small noise of agreement, a little weighed down with sadness too but not entirely. Certainly less heavy than the last time he brought up his lost friend. "Yeah, you would. He had all the heart I'm missing."

"Stop fishing, you've got plenty of heart," I reply, almost automatically. Once the words are out, I find myself silently considering how confidently I uttered them. That's certainly a change from those first few days in his company. Scout grins at me proudly, before looking back out across the city, obviously deciding to drop that particular line of conversation. Which is fine by me; there's something to be said for silence when you're in a place like this.

I follow his gaze, basking in the kaleidoscopic sunlight and the sense of well-being that is so different to how I was feeling a few hours ago. The magic of New York, viewed from a glittery rooftop at sunset, has chased the darkness away. There's no place for it up here, where the sound of life fizzes around us like fireflies: sirens wailing, chattering people on their way home from work, the hiss of a bus as it stops. Across the wind, there's even the sound of a saxophone—from some street performer, I guess. They could be miles away, but the sound is so clear it's like they're right next to us.

"There's a good echo up here," I comment, my foot gently tapping to the rhythm. I see Scout nod in agreement, before he suddenly hops up with the confidence of a mountain goat traversing an impossible cliff. He brushes himself off, then holds out a hand. "You're kidding, right?" I ask, because I know what he's getting at and I don't dance. Not unless I'm incredibly drunk.

"Come on. When else are you going to get the chance to dance with Death on a rooftop in New York?"

"We can barely hear the music!"

"Not if you keep complaining over the top of it," he shoots back. Sighing, I take the offered hand and allow him to tug me up and into the middle of the roof. He comes to a halt and turns to face me, raising an eyebrow with a challenging smile. That smile of his that never fails to drive me mad. "What? Does the world explode if Daisy dances?"

Groaning with defeat, I pull his hands from mine and then move them into the right place, one on my shoulder, one on my waist. "Do not move those," I warn fiercely and he nods, looking incredibly serious about the matter. I take a deep breath, then begin to sway. For a moment, his body is stiff and unmoving, but then he seems to get the idea and matches my movements. I have to smile as I glance up at his face and see concentration deeply set into it.

"I'm guessing you haven't done this before?" I ask after a moment of this swaying, the music just about audible enough for us to keep time.

"Danced on a rooftop?"

"Danced, full stop."

Scout's grip on my shoulder shifts a little. "Oh. No. Not really. Well, not at all. It's not something I really get much chance to do."

That makes sense, of course. It's hardly going to be a part of his job and that takes up a great deal of his time. "Well, you're not bad considering all that."

He looks rather pleased at that, and his pace seems to pick up a little. Almost as if my words have given him a little boost. Of course, it means we're no longer in time with the music so it's up to me to gently coax him back into the right tempo. The minutes pass by and the saxophone continues, allowing us to keep on dancing, or just swaying. I'm not sure when it happens, but at some point I stop noticing his hands on my shoulder and waist. And somehow we shift a little closer to each other. I tell myself that it's just so we can have better movement, but I sort of know that's not true. I know that I'm finding an odd solace in being so close to him. Something about us both having shown each other's vulnerabilities over the past few hours. It's made us equals, and there's certainly something comforting in that.

The sun begins to dip behind the buildings, dulling the glittering of the glass somewhat. The combination of the pink sky and this more subtle glimmer gives the whole place an ethereal glow. I feel as if I've put on a pair of rose-tinted spectacles. Then the music stops. The saxophone player must be heading home, back to his life and his friends and family. We are left without a melody. Just the thrum of the city. It's peaceful, but I find the thoughts in my head wriggling back to the surface, demanding to be noticed.

"Scout?" He glances down at me, continuing to sway to a song we can no longer hear. "What do I do now?"

Scout brings the dancing to a slow halt, standing back a little but not taking his hands away. "You're asking me?"

I shrug. "You're all I've got, really. Do I go back? Even after what I saw happening? I mean, I just feel like there's no place for me anymore."

Scout watches me carefully. "There's a place for you with me," he says softly, moving his hands until they rest gently in mine.

His hands feel so comforting, so natural. It would be so easy to just hide away in his offices and forget the world. And yet I also know it's entirely impossible. I can't forget *them*.

Besides, there's something else bothering me about that idea. Biting my lip, I look down at my feet, as if I might find some answers there. "Remember that first death you took me to? With Jennifer?" Scout nods but says no more, and I can feel him watching me closely. "I was so scared and horrified and you had to keep telling me off for meddling…"

Scout smiles a little. "Yeah, I remember. You were a nightmare, if I'm honest."

"Exactly. I *was* a nightmare. But I don't do any of that anymore. I go along, I find the dead person, I do the paperwork, I send them through the door. And I don't even blink an eyelid at it…" I step back, away from his grip as I feel tightening in my chest. The unmistakable sensation of panic, caused by voicing a fear that has been creeping up on me for weeks now.

Because it's true. This world has changed me. I used to cry at the death of a person, regardless of who they were. I used to waste time finding out minute details about their lives. I used to fight against Scout using his calming influences. Their friends and families left behind would haunt me. Now it's all just paperwork and procedures and time management. How can I even call myself a human when I view our mortality as nothing more than admin?

I don't expect Scout to understand this—why would he? He's been part of this process since the beginning.

But he surprises me, yet again, by getting my point instantly. "You worry about losing your humanity?" he asks.

I nod. "I've only been here a few months and I already feel as if I've forgotten what dying really means… What am I going to be like if I'm stuck here for fifty or so years?"

"You won't."

"How can you be so sure?"

Scout comes a little closer again, places his hands on my

shoulders. "Because if you were losing your humanity, you wouldn't care about losing it. If you were losing your humanity, you wouldn't come back from each job with a new story, you wouldn't be standing on this roof with wonder in your eyes because of a few bits of glass and some sunlight. Daisy, this job isn't changing you—I think it's the opposite. You're changing the job. Somehow, without breaking the rules for the dead, you're changing it for the better."

I stare at him as his words sink in. They're completely sincere, without a shred of doubt in them, and maybe that's why I find myself pulling him into a tight hug. My head comes to rest on his chest and I feel him take a sharp intake of breath.

When I pull back a moment later, he is grinning proudly, boyishly. "Wow. Daisy Cooper giving me a full-on hug—now I've seen everything," he says.

"Not another word, or I push you off this roof." He knows, of course, that I'm joking but he still doesn't say anything. Instead, he turns away with a little smile, focusing back on the view. "You know… I think it's because they're not just for the dead."

"Hmmm?" He glances back to me, eyebrows crinkling with admittedly understandable confusion.

I let my gaze drift across to him as well. "Your rules," I continue. "The reason I can follow them and still make a difference is because I've lived with those rules for years. They're not just rules for dying. I think they can be rules for living too."

Scout mulls this over for a second, then grins. "I think you could be right."

We share a little laugh, turn back to the view. As we're standing there, soaking it all up, Scout's phone rings. He glances down at his pocket, then to me. "Well, that was fun while it lasted. Natasha will be wringing my neck soon enough…" He sounds truly regretful and I have to agree with him there. These moments of freedom have made me really wish for more of it. But he's right; there's a job to do.

"Thank you, Scout. For taking me here and—and all of the other bits. It was just what I needed. I feel a lot better."

Scout rubs at the back of his neck, a sheepish expression of real pride on his face as he nods and accepts the thanks. "I just wanted to make it up to you. For everything. You deserve a lot better."

He holds out his hand, fingers waggling a little. A silent question about whether all is OK between us again. The answer to that is easy, really. Because it *is* OK between us. His choice was dumb, but I'm not sure it was cruel or worthy of prolonged berating. This evening has shown me that, really, he cares a great deal about me. Which fills my heart with a warmth as I realize that that caring is pretty reciprocal.

But there's something else. My eyes meeting his eyes, our heightened emotions in the air. I've seen this before. I know what comes next.

And there's a moment, a solid and real moment, where I consider letting the magic we've found have its effect. Consider accepting that perhaps Eric and Violet weren't entirely to blame for their own moment. But I can't. It wouldn't be fair to them, to Scout.

Scout leans in, just a little. And, for once, I wish he hadn't improved his social skills these last few months. Because it hurts. It hurts to watch a moment come toward you when you know you have to turn away.

Rule Nineteen

Show You Care

BACK WHEN I WAS this puny little scrap of a thing, I used to dream about Christmas. It was still pretty simple back then, not the commercial tsunami it is these days. Just people showing they loved other people in the smallest of ways. A little box of chocolates here, a carefully purchased clockwork toy there. It seemed extraordinary to me that people could find such joy in such small things.

Lucas and I snuck down to watch it once. I remember how I had to stand on his back to reach the button we wanted. I remember how we laughed the whole way down, high on the rebelliousness of it all. We were so damn small. Two kids trying to make sense of a nonsensical world.

We watched a family decorate their tree on Christmas Eve, then carefully place a few neatly wrapped parcels underneath. I can still recall how Lucas's hand was squeezing mine so tight, like he wanted to check it was all real.

We watched them for hours. We worked out eventually why we found it so magical, worked out that the family had somehow found *a way to show just a little fraction of their deep love for each other in physical form. And that was enchanting.*

I didn't fully fathom the importance of this display until a year later, when Lucas left a neatly wrapped box on my desk. There was a pen inside, somehow perfectly made for the incessant fiddling he knew I did. A little gift to show he cared.

It hurts a little to look at it now. But it also helps me remember that, even if my entire existence has been centered around taking people away from their lives, there was still someone who cared enough about me that they found a way to make me truly happy, if just for a while.

So now it's my turn. To show her I care.

✳ ✳ ✳

"I'm sorry, I can't do this."

There is it is. A sentence said by thousands, millions maybe. A sentence guaranteed to cause someone pain. A sentence Violet said to me the night before I got her readmitted to hospital on suicide watch. A sentence I said to Eric when he took a step too far toward a serious relationship. And now a sentence I'm repeating to someone else taking a step toward something I can't accept.

Scout, to give him credit, does not react nearly as badly as I was expecting. He pauses, then takes a small step back. "Sorry... I didn't mean..." he tries, frowning with deep confusion. I can see him struggling to work out this complex interaction and it hurts as much as it did to say that sentence.

I shake my head rapidly, feeling my eyes widening. "You don't need to be sorry. You didn't do anything wrong. It's just, with Eric and—"

He holds up a hand, bringing my rambling to a thankful stop. "Let's not. Let's not say anything. Let's just say that this was a nice time and—and not spoil it with trying to work out what *that* was. It won't get us anywhere."

It all gets a little awkward after that. I shouldn't be surprised; any chance to make things awkward and I'll bloody leap into action. After his rather heartfelt and considerate mini-speech, my ability to put together a coherent sentence seems to disappear. I end up rambling some nonsense about that being a good idea before declaring that maybe we should get on with those jobs before Natasha comes down for our guts. I know it's not fooling Scout in the slightest, that's obvious from the slight slumping of his shoulders. It makes me feel awful, but I'm also thinking about Eric. So I decide that I'm just going to ignore the feeling of disappointment rumbling through me like a discontented tiger.

I'm going to pretend I didn't, for a second, consider kissing Death.

We go to one job, then another. Just like old times. Our roles are clearly defined these days: Scout makes notes, I ask the right sorts of questions. Scout explains the jargon, I supply the emotion. His words about how I've changed the job for the better rest comfortably around my shoulders and, despite everything, I find pride in my work.

Another couple of jobs trickle by. We visit a fire and help a family (all except one child, hence our involvement), then we process a couple killed by a drunk driver. Like clockwork. It still scares me a little, because it's still somebody's death, still somebody losing everything. But it's also hard to be completely connected to the trauma of it all when you're on the other side, stapling and filing papers as though nothing has changed. I hug the poor mother as she sobs for her now-orphaned child, squeeze the father's hand. But when the door closes behind them, it's troublingly easy to move on. We put the file in the drawer, go to the next job. Or, if we're lucky, spend a few moments in the library. Scout has settled into a long historical series while I push through a weighty thriller, but despite the comfort of this routine, it doesn't take long for the temptation to visit home to grow again. A young woman waxes lyrical about her own best friend and my heart aches for Violet. A man killed in a traffic accident has the same dry humor as my father and it sends tremors of homesickness through me.

At first, the need to return is outweighed by a fear of what I might see, but eventually the longing takes over. I need to see them. I don't want to freak Scout out and make him think I'm leaving for good, so I don't tell him. Instead, I sneak out while he's in a meeting with Natasha. He decided very early on that he didn't need to torture me with those and they usually go on for hours so it's a perfect opportunity. I take the lift down and try not to think too much about what might be waiting for me.

By now, we're fully settled into spring. I died in February, Scout's calendar now tells me it's May. Three months have gone by, just like that. The planet continues to spin unrelentingly with no consideration for anyone it might be leaving behind.

As is typical of London, there isn't much of a sign of spring when I arrive. The sky is overcast, with thick and heavy clouds looming down in a rather oppressive way, as though they've all come to cast judgment on the people below. The unimpressive weather has caused the streets to be fairly empty. Everyone is inside, waiting impatiently for the sun to come back. A bus crawls past me, a few people staring gloomily out and, of course, staring right through me.

When I step into my flat, I'm greeted immediately by loud music, which thumps through the small space and makes the rotten window frames clatter a little in complaint. The flat is a bit of a mess, which makes me wince a little. Violet has always been the messy one out of the pair of us and now I'm not around to govern her, she seems to have let things go a little bit around here. Plates are piled up in the sink, the trash can looks full to bursting, and the dining table is covered in various bits of her life. There's makeup, magazines, random charging cables, laundry that could be clean or dirty.

It also fills me with fear. We've been here before. I remember so vividly how I almost had to drag her from bed because her depression had slurped up her energy like a greedy child with a milkshake. Her bedroom became steadily messier because the idea of making her bed literally made her weep. Seeing the flat like this makes me afraid that a dark monster has returned to Violet's mind and is now invading every inch of her sanctuary.

When I finally find Violet, she's in her bedroom, all bundled up in her duvet with only the top of her head visible. Even with the noise of the music, I can make out her quiet and desperate sobs. And I can see the whole cocoon of blankets tremble with her body's violent shaking.

This is meant to be my wonderful, fiercely determined and strong-willed friend. Now, though, it seems as if my friend is broken. The longing to return to her grows strong in my chest. I just want to make her better.

But I can't risk it. My last visit has knocked all confidence in the idea. But I also can't just sit here, watching her suffer. Frustration wells up inside me because there's no solution here. Nothing I can do. Useless.

It makes me feel small and helpless. Childlike. Maybe that's why I don't go straight back to Death's world but, instead, drift off to my parents' house. It's the first time I've felt brave (or desperate) enough to go there since my rather traumatizing experience but I need *something*. Some sort of silver lining.

I find them all at home, which makes sense considering it's the weekend. Mum's doing the bills at the kitchen table, pen stuck behind her ear like always. Dad's out in the garden, checking on the spring arrivals, no doubt. I could almost trick myself into thinking that they haven't experienced any sort of trauma, but it's easy to see the cracks on closer inspection. Mum keeps her head down and frowns overly hard at her laptop, keeps pausing to look out the back windows to the garden where Dad is. And she doesn't look with fondness. She looks with fear, as if she's waiting for him to disappear too. Outside, Dad is silent. There's none of his silly humming that he got from his mother. The lines around his eyes seem deeper too, like trenches dug into his skin.

Looking for something positive, I go and find my brother. Ollie has always been the glue in our family. Mum and I bicker because we're alike, Dad tends to retreat within himself until someone remembers to bring him out. But Ollie brings us back together with his calm, logical thinking and quick sense of humor.

He's in his bedroom, door shut. Not necessarily a bad sign with him, but it feels weird inside his room. I've never felt unwelcome in there but now I do. Something about the way the curtains are still shut and the way he hunches over his laptop as though he wants to jump inside it. He's so still—unheard-of with Ollie, who got put into every sport club possible by Mum just so he'd be worn out enough to fall asleep at night.

As I'm watching him, I hear Mum yell up the stairs to him. Her voice sounds cracked, fraught. But Ollie barely blinks, jaw tightening a touch as he ignores her. When she shouts again for him, he rolls his eyes and stomps over to the door.

"I'm busy!" he yells down the stairs. "I'll be down later, all right?"

Instinctively, I wince. I've never heard Ollie talk like that to Mum. Ollie was always the one nudging me to calm down, or muttering something to make me laugh and stop picking a fight. This isn't the Ollie I remember at all.

I have to leave after that. I don't know why I came here, really; I was never going to find anything to cheer me up. And now I'm scared. Scared that it's already too late to make this better.

When I arrive at Death's office, feeling thoroughly miserable, he's at his desk. At first, I worry how he's going to react to me sneaking off. But he doesn't seem in the least bit bothered.

"You're back," he states, once I've dropped into my usual chair with a heavy sigh. He's stacking papers into three different piles with apparent randomness, but if I know him, which I believe I do these days, there will be a highly complicated process behind it all. However, as I sit down, he pauses. He places the paper that he's currently holding back into its original spot and surveys me carefully. He needs a pair of glasses to look over, really. That would cement the whole stern-librarian vibe he's giving off right now. "Are you OK?"

It's the closest we've got to starting a proper conversation since New York and I feel instinctive, inexplicable panic fluttering about in my chest. Stupid, really—he's just asking me a question, showing he cares.

And yet, I'm still wary. "Yes, fine."

"Are you sure? You look like you've just been smacked

with a rotten fish." I catch Scout's little smile at his own words and roll my eyes. Of course he's proud of that.

"Thanks. That's the sort of thing that will definitely cheer me up."

Scout has inevitably found a pen to fiddle with and he now jabs it in my general direction with triumph. "Aha! So you *aren't* fine."

I have to give him that one. "We'll make a detective of you yet. No, I'm not."

Leaning forward and resting his chin on his hands, he looks at me with concern. "Why not? What happened? Did what's-his-name kiss Violet again?"

"You know perfectly well what his name is, Scout. And no, he didn't."

Scout doesn't deny my accusation. Instead, he taps the pen thoughtfully against his nose. "Hmm...so what's the problem, then?"

"Where to start? My best friend looks like she's two steps away from another breakdown. My mother looks as if she's terrified about you coming to take somebody else again. Dad's gone silent. Ollie's locked himself away and is acting more like a moody adolescent than the reasonable adult he is... And I don't know what to do anymore. I don't know where to go."

Scout looks at me a little warily. "You mean, whether you should go home or not?" There's a little shred of unease in his voice that I can't quite miss. Perhaps that's why I only nod, instead of braving real words. He purses his lips, glancing at the calendar. "This far after your death it would be tricky. For them, I mean."

"It's already tricky for them," I find myself snapping. Instantly, I regret it and sigh heavily. "Sorry, I just mean... That's the problem, Scout. I don't know which situation is less tricky. When you gave me those keys, I was so sure that I wanted to go home. Now...what if it doesn't work? What if me appearing is just what Violet needs to fall right over the edge? What if Mum and Dad can't forgive me?"

Scout's expression has become almost apprehensive. It seems as though he doesn't have the answer and he's scared to admit it. Which is why I stand up, force a smile. I don't want Scout to feel any more guilty for me being stuck here than he already does. "It's fine. Don't worry. Do you need any help?"

His piercing gaze stays on me for a moment, then he shakes his head. "Just catching up on filing."

I nod. "OK. I'll be around if you need me." Then I leave, before I can make him feel worse. Because I've long since stopped blaming Scout for what happened to me—I've seen how complex this system is and it's a miracle there hasn't been more cases like me, really.

Not wanting to spend the next period of time just moping about a situation I haven't yet worked out how to fix, I try to distract myself with a book. That's always worked for me in the past. Usually I would find one of those easy-to-read crime books but I've read all the ones in our makeshift library so I settle for *Alice In Wonderland*. Mum used to read it to me all the time.

It doesn't take Scout long to reappear which, to be honest, I'm grateful for. Alice has not helped me at all and I've mainly spent the time glowering at the page.

Scout seems a little apprehensive when he steps into the room. "Hey," he says, voice weirdly quiet.

"Hey," I return, closing the book. He catches sight of the front cover and wrinkles his nose. "What?"

"Lewis Carroll. Strange guy." With this judgment passed, he sits silently for a moment and I let him be, sensing that he's formulating his next words with great care. Finally, after a minute or so, he speaks again. "So," he begins, a little softly, "I think you should go home."

For a moment, I'm stumped. I really wasn't expecting those words to come from his mouth. "What?"

He shuffles forward on his seat, enough that he can take my hand in his. Our fingers automatically tangle with each other. It's a habit we've picked up since New York, one that I haven't quite been able to explain yet. I also haven't been able to resist it yet either. "Daisy. Violet's your best friend and she's struggling without you, yes?" He waits for my nod, then continues. "Then you should go back to her."

"What about you?" I find myself asking, the question slipping out almost instinctively.

Scout sighs, then shrugs a little. "I don't want you to leave me but there's things more important than what I want. Daisy, on that roof in New York I finally realized that what my head has been muddled up with recently is this…this overwhelming determination to help you be happy. If that means I have to lose you then…" He pauses, expression intensely serious as he draws in a deep breath. "Then so be it. Because I care about you, Daisy. And caring means making you happy, even if it makes me sad."

Silence falls between us because I can't quite fathom the right response yet. I've just seen Scout show me something he has never come close to before: a totally selfless concern for somebody else. Me. Daisy Cooper, who not that long ago he considered nothing more than an irritant.

"Well," I begin, my voice somewhat hoarse from the shock of this moment, "that's…" I stop, because sentences just aren't coming to me. Shaking my head to clear my thoughts a little,

I decide to settle for something a little more simple. "That means a lot, Scout. Really."

He shrugs good-naturedly, smiling again with a sense of relief. It would seem that he's been carrying that speech around for a while.

"What if it makes things worse?" I ask after a moment of just watching him grinning to himself. Because, as nice as it is to have Scout's blessing, it doesn't actually change anything. I still don't know if appearing to my friends and family will help.

"It will work."

I laugh wearily at his unwavering certainty. "How can you be sure?" I ask with incredulity.

He shrugs, a fond smile firmly stuck to his face. "Because I know how much you care about them. And that's always been your superpower, Daisy. You care so damn much. So just show them."

"That simple?" I ask, feeling a strange warmth spreading across my skin. Like my body's getting ready to appear once more.

Another shrug, this time paired with a squeeze of the hand. "It's the best I've got."

I consider it for a moment. A quite intense moment, where my brain rattles off a thousand different possibilities at once. But Scout is probably right. There are many things I feel that I don't do very well—meeting new people, remembering capital cities, letting others have the last word. But I think I know how to show I care. I suppose now is the time to put it to the test.

"OK," I murmur after my moment of thought. "OK, I'll try."

Scout nods and, though he's smiling with me, I see the sadness in his eyes. And it does make me pause a little. But he spots this and shakes his head, standing up abruptly. I feel his fingers slip away from mine, leaving my hand feeling cold all of a sudden. "I'll be fine, Daisy. Don't you start fretting over me. Now, let's get you home."

Rule Twenty

Change Is Sneaky

THERE WAS A TIME when getting to another country would take you months. There was a time when people went to bed when it was dark because there was nothing to light their nights. There was a time when dying of cholera was as common as dying in a car crash.

There was a time when I was miserable and alone.

Change, then, can be a blessing. Of course it can. Nobody wants to spend months getting to their holiday in the Maldives. Nobody wants to go to bed early. Nobody wants to die of cholera. And nobody wants to be miserable and alone.

But do you ever think about how these changes came about? We didn't just wake up one morning and suddenly find that there were airplanes and night-lights. Change is sneaky, slow and steady. We don't notice it until it's happened and we can't do much about it. That's the change you have to watch out for.

That's the change that also destroys societies, that gets people killed while others stand by. That's the change that stops you noticing the downward spiral of a family member until said family mem-

ber has spiraled their way right into my office. Like the turning of the seasons, it comes gradually and quietly until, suddenly, it's there.

I know, I'm being negative again. Lots of change is for the better. A pleasant surprise like a secret birthday party. Lovely. Until there's poison in the punch and you realize you haven't noticed your other half slowly turning against you.

So, tonight, remember one thing; remember to check for the differences in your life when you wake up. Examine your family members' smiles, check whether your other half grimaces when you kiss them. Check that the person you trusted yesterday still deserves that trust today.

You never know what you might find.

❋ ❋ ❋

"This isn't my flat."

The words are out of my mouth the moment we leave the lift, so fast that it's like they're instinctive. Almost as if part of me can't stop thinking this is some sort of trick. As though Scout really can't care about me this much.

Scout steps out beside me, shooting me an amused look. "No, it's not. Congratulations on your sterling observation skills as usual, Cooper."

It takes me a somewhat alarming amount of time to clock where we are, considering that I had agreed to move in here not that long ago. But, then again, Eric's flat has never been that identifiable. He takes minimalism to the very limit sometimes. And when we're standing in a sitting room with a gray sofa, a flat-screen television and very little else, it's tricky to confirm that this is indeed his home.

"Why are we here?" I ask finally, once I've definitely confirmed that this is Eric's flat.

Scout's arms cross over his chest as he leans against the lift. "Because I figured Violet could use a break from seeing you appear out of nowhere. I mean, I'm pretty sure this is going to work, but, just in case, I figured that this guy was a safer choice to start with?"

I have a sneaking suspicion that Scout likes to pretend he doesn't know Eric's name. It's not the first time he's referred to him as "this guy," after all. Perhaps it has something to do with New York. Whatever it is, I'm not rising to it. Besides, he's got a good point; poor Violet certainly does not need another failed attempt from me.

So I nod. "All right, fine," I say, feeling a little flurry of nerves in my stomach. I really don't know how Eric will react. Last time he mainly swore and then shortly after kissed my best friend. Hastily, I try to put that thought out of my head. It's still a sore point and I don't want my first act as a visible person to be slapping him across the face.

But I don't quite push the thought away quick enough and, a moment later, doubt wriggles its way to the front of my mind. "Are you sure about this?" I whisper.

Scout looks a little perplexed at my whispering. "There's nobody here. And if there were they wouldn't be able to hear you," he reminds me with an indulgent smile, before nodding. "I'm sure, Daisy. This is the right thing to do."

Deciding not to give me another moment to fret, he reaches across and puts his hand into my dress pocket, pulling out the keys that I've been carting around for the past few weeks. Then he fumbles through his back pocket and pulls out a tangle of string. He loops the keys through the string, dangling them in front of his face. "You'll need to be in contact with the keys at all times or you'll risk disappearing," he explains. "This should keep them close enough." He spins one finger, indicating for me to turn round. When I've done that, he steps forward and ties the string around my neck. I feel his fingers fumble a little, skating across my skin. Then they come to rest on my shoulders, squeezing a little. "All set?"

I turn around to face him and I'm momentarily taken aback by our close proximity. This close, his eyes are almost bottomless.

"Daisy?"

Jolting back to the present, I nod. "All set."

He smiles and his forehead briefly comes to rest against mine. It's unexpected, but not altogether unpleasant. "It was a pleasure, Daisy Cooper," he says once he's pulled back. He's saying goodbye. Is this it, then? No more Scout? Back to my life, as if nothing ever happened? It's been my aim for the last few months, but now it's finally here, it feels a little terrifying.

Scout seems to sense this because he pats my back with an encouraging smile. "It's never going to be quite the same, Daisy. You're changed, irreversibly. And this isn't a reset button. You're not being brought back to life here. Just…creating a pretty good illusion of life. But I know that when you're back with your friends and family, you'll find a way to make it work. Now go. Live well." He pauses, and it looks like he's going to say something else. But he brushes it away and nudges me forward.

"Scout…" I begin, though I have no idea how to end this sentence. Maybe he senses this too, or maybe he just doesn't want to hear it, because he shakes his head and brings my sentence to a halt.

"Off you pop," he says, painfully gentle. But I can't quite make myself move just yet. I know I have to go, I know that this is what I want. But it's only now, with the prospect of leaving him so imminent, that I realize how much Scout has come to mean to me. How unprepared I am to leave him.

"Wait," I say, almost to my own feet as they make the move to turn. "I… I just want to say thank you. For helping me get home. And for being such a good friend. I won't forget you and, well, it was a pleasure to be your assistant, even if I wasn't a very good one."

Scout's expression reminds me of someone seeing a firework go off for the first time. Wonder, awe and shock crackle in his eyes. Then he grins, that sheepish grin that I've always found myself looking at for a second longer than necessary. "You were more than just an assistant, Daisy. And I loved every second of it." With those words barely out of his mouth, he leans in, hesitates. But this time I can't find the will to turn away. His eyes meet mine, he takes a deep breath, then he kisses me.

For a second all I feel is the heat of his lips gently pressed against mine and the growing tingling sensation of shock. Then there's heat against my chest which I distantly identify as the keys, coupled with a buzzing that feels as though I'm wearing a hive of angry bees around my neck. Scout must sense it too, must feel the opportunity for visibility arriving. Because he pulls back, shoots me one final smile. Then pushes me away.

In an instant, he's gone. Or perhaps it's more accurate to say I'm gone? Either way, I can no longer see him which can only mean that I've crossed over into the world of the living. It's worked. The keys have worked.

My lips still feel warm somehow. A shadow of him left behind, a reminder of why my mind is suddenly awash with conflict. Because I know that when he kissed me, I kissed him back.

There's no time to consider this, though. I hear the door opening behind me and I whirl around, not feeling ready for this at all. How could I be? Someone else has just kissed me and, if I'm brutally honest, I'm not mad that he did.

Then I see Eric. It's all very different seeing him when I know he's going to be able to see me back. I feel frozen as he steps into the flat, pulls his keys from the lock with a distracted frown on his face.

A second later, he looks up and, immediately, his eyes land on me. A definite confirmation that I'm visible and I feel a triumphant grin arriving on my face. Eric, on the other hand, is not quite so overjoyed. Instead, he lets out a yell of shock, drops his keys and stumbles back out the flat, slamming the door behind him.

My triumphant smile drops. "Perfect," I find myself muttering, which is perhaps a little uncharitable. Maybe I really have spent too much time around Death. "Eric! Eric, it's me!" I yell, moving over to open the door. But he's holding it firmly from the other side. "Eric, open the door!"

"You're dead!" he hisses through the wood and I can hear his voice trembling. "How the hell can you be here if you're dead?"

I bite down on my lip, trying to work out the answer to an impossible question. Scout always told me to keep it vague, to not give much away. But can I really do that for the unforeseeable future? Just keep things vague? Maybe that's the cost to come back. One of the costs.

"I—I can't really explain. But it's me and it's OK. Please, Eric, come inside. I'm not going to devour your soul or whatever. Please…?"

Perhaps he hears the desperation in my voice or perhaps he recognizes something in my humor. Whatever it is, it's enough to make him release the door handle. I hear the metal squeak as his tightly gripped fingers relax and I take that as a sign to slowly open the door.

And there he is. Backed right up against the opposite wall. My boyfriend, just about. He's a little unrecognizable without his shining confidence, his well-groomed hair, his healthy and bright skin. But he's still Eric.

"Hi."

Eric swallows, eyes wide like two glowing moons. "Hi," he rasps after a long few seconds. He blinks once, twice, straightens up slowly. "Daisy...is it really you? If, if I'm going mad I'd rather just know outright."

I have to laugh at that and the blunt way in which he says it. I've always admired him for saying things as they are.

Apparently my laugh is enough to convince Eric that I am really there, because he straightens up, stumbling a little as he comes toward me. Eyes still wide, he seems to cast his gaze over every inch of me. Like he's looking for the clue, the hint, the confirmation. That I am definitely here.

I step forward, holding out both hands toward him. "Me. See?"

His hands come to rest in mine, fingers wrapping around my palms and pressing gently against the skin. It still feels a little like he's pushing through plastic wrap but he doesn't seem to notice this as he lets out a gasp of acceptance. "You're really here." He practically hobbles forward, pulls me into a hug that feels like it's been years in the making. God, I've missed this so much. Nobody can make me feel safe like Eric can.

Well. Nearly nobody.

"Where'd you go, Daisy?" he breathes against my ear before pulling back, meeting my gaze. His thumbs skid underneath my eyelashes, trembling and clumsy, as he wipes away tears I hadn't noticed falling. A second later he's swooping in for a kiss I've been waiting months to feel again.

I'm expecting it to be wonderful. And it is, sort of. No, it *is* wonderful. But I was expecting more; I was expecting fireworks and magic. But of course there's none of that. With or without keys, I still do not inhabit quite the same world as him, and there's still that barrier between us. A barrier that wasn't there a moment ago when somebody else kissed me.

As I'm considering this, Eric has pulled away and is guiding me gently into the flat. Gently, like he thinks I'm made of porcelain. "It's OK, Eric. I'm not fragile. I'm just…me."

Eric smiles a little shakily. "Right, just you—except for the coming back from the dead part."

We both manage a laugh at that, as he shuts the door behind us, places his bag on the floor, and then goes back to looking at me with borderline awe. It makes me feel a little uncomfortable, so I lean across the gap between us and prod his chest. "Hey, you don't need to gawp at me like that. Like I said: just me."

Eric bites his lip, almost guilty, and looks away. "Sorry," he mutters.

Instantly I feel my own rush of guilt. "No, it's fine. I—I guess this is sort of weird for you."

"Sort of." His words are a little blunt but I can forgive him for that, funnily enough. He rocks back a little on his heels, casting his eyes around the flat for the next thing to say. "You're in white," he finally says, gesturing at my dress.

I glance down at myself, then back up at him. "Uh, yeah, I am."

"You hate white."

I shrug a little as I consider his words. Do I hate white? Is that some part of myself I've forgotten? "Do I?"

"I remember you got a white sweater from an aunt for Christmas and you took it to the thrift store without wearing it."

The memory brings a grin to my face. "Eric, that was because there was a shitting singing penguin on the front."

Eric matches my grin, seeming to relax a little at that.

Maybe this was some subtle test of his, to check that it really is me with all the same memories, likes and dislikes, feelings. It would seem that I've passed, as he hastily pulls me into another hug again. "Sorry," he murmurs into my hair as I wrap my arms around him. "I've just missed hugging you so much."

"You don't need to apologize, idiot," I whisper into his chest with fondness, smelling the familiar scent of his shirts even through our invisible barrier.

"God, I missed your disparaging tones!" He chuckles against my hair, stroking it gently. He pulls back a moment later, holding my cheeks with immense care. "I could never quite believe you were gone...hey, maybe that helped bring you back?"

He's joking, I know that. But for some reason it sets off a little prickle within me. A sense of irritation because his belief had nothing to do with it. It was *me*, *my* keys and *Scout's* shove. One could argue that even Natasha had more to do with it than Eric—it was her idea, after all.

But of course I can't tell him any of that without opening up a huge can of worms. So I can't blame him for his rather naive idea. I can, of course, feel guilty for getting secretly irritated by it in the first place, though.

In an attempt to distract myself from said guilt, I gently pull back from his hold and lead us toward the sofa. "So..." I begin, frowning at how difficult it is to think of what to say next. That's probably to be expected after what we've both gone through. But Eric and I have never been particularly awkward around each other, the time he asked me to move in being the recent exception. Even when we were having our little break, we dealt with it efficiently, like adults.

Now it's all changed. It feels like we're teenagers on our

first date. Eric sits beside me, still a little cautious. "So," he echoes, looking across at me, "are you going to tell me?"

"Tell you what?"

He rolls his eyes, though it's good-naturedly. "What happened, Daisy. How you're here."

I can feel months' worth of pain in his voice but I can't give in. I can't tell him what has happened because I know it's not for him to know. No living person should know what comes afterward: it would alter every tiny thing they do. Besides, if I did tell anyone, Scout would probably find a way to properly bring me back to life just so he could kill me himself.

"I can't, Eric. It's not for me to say. Just—just let's make the most of me being back now."

"OK…" He sighs, sitting back on the sofa. His fingers pleat together, eyes resting on them a little thoughtfully. With slight horror, I realize we've settled into what can only be described as awkward silence. When the hell did this happen? When did we forget how to converse with each other? When did we become two awkward people stuck in a silent room together?

Then we're saved by the buzzer. I glance over, feeling a sense of foreboding settling over me.

Some of this must show on my face because Eric shoots me an encouraging look. "It's OK, it's just Violet."

He obviously means to make me feel better but it does quite the opposite. Violet never came to Eric's flat before I died. Not with me and certainly not on her own. Perhaps it's just an innocent visit to check up on him, but my brain has started replaying that kiss over and over, convincing me that there's no such thing as Violet Tucker innocently visiting Eric Broad's flat. I find myself frozen to the sofa as Eric moves away to the intercom button.

"Violet? Come on up—I've got some good news for you!"

He turns back to shoot me a grin as he releases the button. "She's been freaking out a bit since last time you popped up— that was real, right?" I nod mutely, my voice suddenly lost. He watches me for a moment, waiting to see if I'm going to offer any more information. When I don't, his slight disappointment is all too easy to spot.

He brushes it off a few seconds later as Violet knocks on the door, moving over to open the door just a crack. "Hey," he says, voice a little hushed. "Listen, don't freak but—but someone's here."

"What the fuck are you on about?" I hear Violet grumble, then watch as the door gets pushed open the rest of the way. She steps inside, dressed in leggings and a sweater. The sort of almost-pajama look she always adopts when she's coming back from rehearsals. She's carrying a bottle of wine in one hand and a pot of olives in the other.

Both go flying toward the ground when she lays eyes on me.

Rule Twenty-One

Some Words Will Hurt More Than Death

THERE'S A STUPID RHYME *you people like to teach your kids when they're little that really grinds my gears. "Sticks and stones may break my bones but words will never hurt me." God, what a load of horse manure. Like the fact that there isn't a medicine for being called a horrible name somehow means it doesn't cause damage. But it does.*

You know it does, that's the worst part. You've all had a moment when somebody says something and it stings against your skin like you're swimming through a forest of jellyfish. And it stays rooted there, regardless of how much cream you put on. A scar that won't disappear easily.

So why do you pretend they don't? Is it so you don't have to restrain your mouths all the time? I know, I know—I'm hardly one to talk. And I don't have an excuse for that other than me being a bitter hypocrite.

Some words, though. Some are the verbal equivalent of somebody pulling your fingernails out one by one (apologies for that particular mental image). Lucas has been fired. I can't believe I cared about you, Death. You've taken everything from me.

To name but a few.

I've watched words cause death. But a lot of the time that almost seems like a dodged bullet. Because if some words are left to fester, to lodge deep into your head, they can be some of the most painful forces in this universe.

By some miracle, Eric actually catches the wine bottle before it smashes all over his polished wood floor. It's either a miracle or a testament to his almost fatherly love for his flat, but it saves the day anyhow. The tub of olives, meanwhile, hits the ground and rolls off, coming to a halt beside the sofa, intact thankfully.

With both items rescued or halted, our focus can fully return to each other. Well, more precisely Violet can return to me and I can return to her. Poor Eric doesn't get much of a look in at this point. Not that that should come as any sort of surprise to him.

"Daisy…" Violet breathes across the space.

I don't know what to say; I don't know how to convey everything running through my head right now. It's like trying to pick one specific bee out of a beehive. Maybe Violet understands this or maybe she just doesn't need to hear anything right now, because she's stumbling over and hugging me before I can fret about it for a second longer. Her arms feel bony, too bony, and immediately I want to pull her away and force her to eat a sandwich. But there's plenty of time for that now. If Scout was right about these keys, I won't ever have to leave her.

"Hey Vi, I'm back," I finally manage to murmur as I wrap

my arms around her, her curls tickling against my nostrils. "I'm sorry it took so long."

Violet pulls away, shaking her head. Her eyes are damp but there's a twinkle of cautious happiness there. "Don't be ridiculous. I'm guessing it's quite hard to get back from death?" she asks, giving me one of her trademark smirks. Then she laughs, shaking her head. "Wow, that's a ridiculous question to seriously ask someone."

Laughter slips from me, surprisingly freeing. Trust Violet to walk into this surreal situation and just accept it. She always did have a healthily relaxed attitude toward the unbelievable. I remember when we actually had a whole discussion about whether our flat was haunted or not, something she found alarmingly exciting. The irony of that hasn't quite missed me.

"I know," I finally reply with another laugh. "Totally insane."

Violet grins, hugging me tightly once more before stepping back. She appraises me for a moment, then nods. "Definitely a story to be told. So are you back, Daisy? Properly?" There's a slight tone of almost complaint in her voice but I can't blame her for it entirely, even if it does hurt a little.

I nod, finding one of her hands and squeezing it tightly. "Prospects are looking good," I murmur, not wanting to firmly promise anything just yet. She gives me a final searching look then nods, squeezing my hand back before pulling free and moving over to the sofa.

She sits down, shoots me a weak smile. "I hope so. I—I've really fucking missed you."

I don't know what to say to that. Or if there's anything *to* say. "Me too" doesn't cut it, neither does an apology. Violet seems to sense this as well, though, because she shakes her head a little at me. A silent declaration that she's not expecting any response.

And then the moment's gone as Eric returns. It seems that, during our little reunion, he'd slipped into the kitchen to give us a moment of privacy and now he's back with two glasses of white wine in his hands. One has ice cubes in it which must be for Violet, who can't stand white wine if it hasn't got a practically Arctic chill to it. I know this, of course, but I don't remember Eric knowing it.

Violet doesn't bat an eyelid. Smiling gratefully she takes the glass before glancing to me. "What do you think about drinking now?" She looks back to Eric, grinning a little. "Last time she came she wouldn't have tea because she wasn't sure how drinking would react with her...state." She says the words lightly but the trauma behind them is obvious.

"Yeah, might make a mess."

Violet giggles at that, shaking her head. "Which would make such a change, right Dee?" Her pet name slips out with relief; she's been waiting months to use that again, I imagine.

"Are you implying I'm clumsy, Violet Tucker?"

Violet matches my grin, face shining with joy. "I'm implying that there's a reason we're not getting our deposit back when we leave that flat, Daisy Cooper, and it has everything to do with your addiction to carpet staining."

"So, drink or not?" Eric's voice breaks abruptly through our exchange, as clunky as ever. You would think he'd have got better at that; he's had plenty of practice.

Still giggling, both of us turn toward Eric with matching expressions of sheepishness. It's so reminiscent that I feel tears rising up in the corners of my eyes. But then I shake my head, distracting myself by finally answering Eric.

"Probably best not to risk it, not yet anyway."

Eric frowns. "So...you're *not* alive again?"

I glance down at the keys dangling from my neck, at my white dress. When I look back up, they're both watching me intently. Even Violet's lost a little of her laughter. "Not fully, no. Alive enough, though. I'm still me." I can see Eric chewing on his lip as he takes this in but then he finally nods a slow acceptance.

"It's something, at least," Violet reasons, patting the space beside her on the sofa.

"So," I say, after we've suffered through a moment of somewhat awkward silence. "What's been going on?" It's not meant to be prying but I'm sure I spot a look pass between the two of them. "What?" I ask, perhaps a little sharply. "What is it?"

Eric shakes his head. "Nothing. Just wondering where to start."

Violet takes a sip of her wine, then shoots me a small, hesitant smile. "There's been a lot going on since you left. As I'm sure you can imagine. Your death...well, it sort of—"

"Fucked things up," Eric finishes, which earns him a mild look of rebuke from Violet, seconds before I get there myself.

"Eric!"

"What?" he grumbles, before looking back to me with a slightly sheepish smile. "It's not a reflection on you, Daisy. It's just true. Your death, funnily enough, fucked things up a little bit."

Violet shakes her head, shooting me an apologetic look. It doesn't help at all.

"It's fine," I finally say. "I would be a little offended if it hadn't." It's meant to be a joke, but I can hear that my voice doesn't quite have the right tone necessary. It just ends up sounding hollow, false.

Eric takes another sip of wine, clearly thinking hard about a change of subject. He finds one a moment later. "Vi's show is going well, though. Right, Vi?"

Violet tuts, shaking her head. "It's not my show, Eric. You

make it sound like some amateur production being done at the local town hall. It's at the National, as you well know."

Eric snorts, grinning all the while. "Yeah, you sure don't let me forget that little nugget of information."

It's like watching your old tennis partner play perfectly with a new one. Somebody else has come along and expertly taken over a role that you thought only you were made for.

Maybe that's why my mouth takes on a life of its own and spits out the next words, before I've even really thought about it. "Why did you two kiss?"

Boom. Just like that. Silence. The same silence I imagine comes after a bomb goes off. Who knew words could cause that same reaction?

Violet speaks first. I can hear the croak in her voice and I can imagine how dry her mouth has become. "Daisy, h-how did you know about that?" she asks softly.

It's not the answer I want from her. I wanted an apology before anything else. So my response is sharp. "I saw it. I came down to try and appear to you guys again, after it went wrong that other time—"

"You saw us, without us seeing you?" Violet interrupts, voice a little hard. When I nod, she looks away with a mutter that sounds a lot like, "Basically spying then."

"I wasn't intending to spy. It just happened. Trust me, I really didn't plan on seeing my best friend's tongue down my boyfriend's throat."

Eric's cheeks have flushed red but Violet isn't quite so easily cowed. She shifts a little away from me, crossing her arms. "You're overexaggerating, Daisy. It wasn't like that."

"Wasn't it?" I ask, standing up and looking between the pair of them. "What was it like?"

Eric clears his throat a little awkwardly. "Well, for starters, we were both really bloody upset."

"Yeah, I saw that too."

Violet's eyebrow raise even higher. "What? How much have you been watching, Daisy?"

Her words prickle against my skin with their painful sense of accusation. Does she think I could have come back earlier but decided it would be far more fun to just spy on her and Eric? "Not much! It's just, well, I didn't have much other choice. I couldn't stay properly yet and... I missed you."

Eric grasps onto these words and leans forward a little, desperation in his eyes. "Exactly, Daisy. We missed you too. We were devastated!"

"Oh, so I should just let you make out with my best friend as long as you're upset at the same time?"

"That's not what he's saying, Daisy!"

Funnily enough, seeing Violet back up Eric doesn't do much to calm me down. It does quite the opposite, in fact. Anger begins to build inside me, so much so that I'm somewhat worried that it might cause me to disappear again, like some sort of reverse effect. I try to keep myself calm, try to stop my mouth from going down its own dark and aggressive path. But I can't. It's too late for that. "Isn't he, Violet? What *is* he saying then? Seeing as you clearly know him so well these days."

Violet places her wineglass down with such force that the wine slops over the edge and spills onto the coffee table. Out of the corner of my eye, I see Eric wince. "I'm saying, Daisy, that you're the one that died. So don't start twisting this around to be all our fault."

Bomb number two.

Silence once more. The walls start to feel as if they're crumbling down around me, rubble pressing on my chest. Violet's staring at me with an almost unrecognizable anger and a wholly unavoidable betrayal. Her words are taking root within me, digging sharp and unforgiving claws into my sides. I know those words won't leave me for a very long time.

"I didn't choose to die that night, Violet," I whisper, my voice barely there. Like a ghost, except now she hears every single syllable.

"Is that meant to make it less painful, Daisy?" She stands up, then shoves past me, heading for where she left her coat and bag. She grabs her coat, then whips around to face me, her curls seeming to grow along with her anger. "*You* left *me*, Daisy! You left me on my own and he was the one person stopping me from following after you."

That's it. That's the sentence that strikes me silent. Those are the words that feel like a pavement has smashed into the back of my head all over again. I feel my mouth open, I feel the emptiness in there as every word in the English language departs my brain. She watches me for a moment, eyes searching every crease of my face almost desperately. I don't know what she's looking for but clearly she doesn't find it. Because a moment later she sighs with disappointment, shakes her head and turns away.

A second later the door slams shut. And silence descends.

Rule Twenty-Two

Every Friendship Has A Weak Spot

I BET YOU'RE WONDERING *what happened with Natasha. What really happened. I'm sure you're dubious, suspicious even. You feel like you know Natasha now, know her and her steely efficiency. Would me refusing to take her to one funeral really cause such a rift?*

No. Probably not. Except for the fact that Natasha had never asked for much. Her funeral took some time to organize, around three months. Complicated reasons like family feuds and raising enough money delayed things, and in all that time, Natasha never asked me for any favors. She worked hard, she got jobs done to an excellent standard, and she even managed to look at me without complete disdain.

But I missed the signs. I missed the signs that she was desperately lonely and desperately worried for her husband and her children. She had a weak spot there, one that I didn't see at all. So when I tried to protect her by keeping her away from the people she most wanted to see, everything broke.

Ours wasn't a friendship like Violet and Daisy's, nowhere near. But it was something that was worthwhile and something that should not have been broken.

The thing is, that in my years of service, I've noticed something. A weak spot in a friendship isn't reserved for weak friendships. Quite the contrary. It's a universal thing. Every friendship has something. The strength of a friendship lies in how well you protect that weak spot and how well you patch it up when something does rip through it.

Natasha and I never quite patched our spot up properly. Now, in an empty office with nobody to keep me company but an overloud telephone, I'm beginning to regret that a little.

People always talk about breaking up with your boyfriend like it's the worst sort of breakup you can go through, a painful punch to the gut. But I can tell you, the breakup of a close friendship is much worse. That's not so much a punch in the gut but an amputation of a limb. A limb you can't stop reaching for, only to experience that nasty stomach-drop of surprise when you remember it's gone.

Here I am, then: limbless. Door slammed, silence settled. Violet gone. Stormed out into the night with vicious words left behind that won't stop circling around my head, an out-of-control whirlwind. They're so loud, so unwavering that it takes me a moment to notice that Eric is calling my name.

Then everything snaps back into place.

"Daisy?" he calls again and, finally, I manage to turn away from the door.

"Uh-huh, yeah, sorry… What were you saying?" My words feel thick, clumsy.

"I wasn't saying anything, just your name and asking if you were OK."

I'm silent for a moment, resisting the urge to snap at him because of course I'm not OK. "Is—is she right?" I finally ask, not quite able to meet his gaze.

"She's… I don't know, Daisy. It's really messy and complicated. But I do know that berating her about this isn't necessary, not when…" He trails off, looking at me hesitantly.

"Eric?" I prompt, as foreboding begins to grow inside me.

"It isn't necessary when she feels guilty enough as it is." He squeezes my hand, taking a deep breath. "Daisy, the whole reason she was coming over tonight was that she didn't want to be alone in the flat because she's scared about what she might do."

He says those words so matter-of-factly, as though he's reading out one of his meeting agendas. Except his meeting agendas have yet to send dreadful fear down my spine. All of a sudden, the only thing I can think of doing is finding Violet.

"I need to go. I need to find her."

I race down the flights of stairs, push my way out of the apartment door and stumble onto the street, eyes already darting around in the hope that she's still in view.

Of course she's not, but that doesn't mean I'm giving up. I know Violet and I know her instincts. Both our instincts, in fact. In times of trouble, we head for the river. Back home it was the tiny stream running alongside the church, here it's the River Thames. So that's where I head. Eric's flat is just five minutes' walk from Tower Bridge but even that seems too long when I know Violet could be in danger.

It's a rather murky evening, with almost foggy clouds lurking around the tops of the taller buildings, so it's not too busy once I get down to the riverside. This means I spot her instantly, curled up on a bench with her hood tugged up over her curls, eyes almost burning through the mist.

The relief in seeing her OK (relatively speaking) is enough to make me temporarily forget all my anger toward her. But I approach her cautiously; after all, she's had no reason to forget her anger toward me.

She spares me a brief glance, somewhat suspicious, as I sit down beside her. Then she looks back out to the river, expression set in stone. Clearly she's not going to be giving me any help starting this difficult conversation.

"I wanted to check you were OK," I say finally, wincing at how lame that sounds.

"Well, I'm not," she replies, short and sharp. Her gaze snaps across to me, cold like the fog around us. "Satisfied?"

"Violet—" I try, but she cuts me off almost immediately.

"I know what you're thinking, Daisy. You're thinking that this is some awful betrayal of mine, that I should know better after what happened with my dad." She glares at me. "Tell me I'm wrong, go on?" But I can't. I can only reluctantly shake my head, causing her to look away with a huff of irritation.

"It was just...a shock, I guess."

"So was losing my best friend."

I wince, looking out across the water as if the passing boat might offer me some guidance. Unsurprisingly, it does not.

"So tell me, help me understand..." I finally whisper, reaching across and linking her pinky finger with mine. An action we have repeated time and time again since we came up with the idea, aged eight. Splayed out on her sitting room floor, watching cartoons. Back when the world was simple and the sensation of pinky gripping pinky was enough to make us feel safe.

I feel her finger curl around mine, though her face is still fairly thunderous. "You've spent your whole life trying to keep me alive," she murmurs a moment later, "making me go to counseling, making me take my medication, stopping me from freaking out or whatever. We both spent so much time preventing my death that we forgot to prevent yours." A crack has wriggled into her voice now. Her pinky finger clenches a little tighter. "And I—I used up the milk. You had to go and get more milk because of me. It was me, Daisy. And you were just gone. In a blink of an eye. The flat was empty but your bedroom was full of your life and—and I had to live next door to that. Do you have any idea what that feels like? No, no you don't. Because you think the worst thing to happen is one slightly drunken kiss at the end of a godawful birthday party." She sighs, rubbing her nose with her free hand. "You don't have a clue, Daisy."

Each second she speaks feels like she's battering down this wall around me. A wall I'd built up around myself so I couldn't see just how much pain my death has caused.

"I didn't spend my whole life trying to keep you alive." It's not exactly the first words I expected to leave my mouth but clearly some part of me decided it was what needed to be said. "Is that what you think our friendship is?"

It's hard to read Violet's expression in the increasing gloom of the evening but I do hear an exhausted, shuddering sigh from her as she uses one hand to wipe at her cheek. "Don't put it like that! I'm not saying our friendship is just some one-sided act of survival… But you have to admit you've always focused on keeping me safe. Or did you keep secretly visiting me for some other reason?"

Well, I can't deny that. I did keep visiting her out of worry for her well-being. There might have been other reasons, like simply missing her, but first and foremost was me wanting to know she wasn't about to do something dangerous. But that's not the point. "OK, so maybe I was looking into whether

260 / Tamsin Keily

you were safe or not. But that doesn't mean my whole life with you has been about keeping you alive. All those stupid in-jokes and ridiculous stories we have wouldn't exist otherwise. And I would never have interacted with the rest of the world if you hadn't been there dragging me out into it." She glances over at me a little dubiously, though I can see that her eyes are filling with tears from the way the nearby streetlight dances in the reflection. "Violet, I may have been helping to keep you alive, but at the same time you were helping me to *live*. You know that, right? You know that everything in my life I'm proud of is somehow thanks to you?"

Her face crumples then. Clearly I've struck the nerve she was trying so desperately to hide behind angry words. "That's bullshit," she mumbles as tears dribble down her cheeks and onto her leggings.

"Do you want the proof? Because you know I'll get out an itemized list of evidence." She shakes her head slowly, but doesn't look convinced yet. "Well, for one thing, I would never have got to this city without you. Can you imagine me finding a London flat to rent on my own? No chance. And who made me go to all those parties so I actually made more than one friend? You did. And who slapped Robbie Carter in the face when he laughed at my new bangs? I mean, granted, the bangs were hideous. But you had my corner. Violet, you're my fucking hero."

As I've been speaking, I've been feeling my own tears rising up inside me once more. By the end, it's like trying to talk with a mouthful of toffee. She's looking at me with shock, but also relief. Like the words I've spoken have begun to soothe some dreadful terror within.

And I realize that my ever-present fear of being the dead-weight friend is exactly matching with hers. That all this time

I've been worrying that she puts up with me out of pity, she's been thinking the same thing.

It's natural, then, for us to fall into each other. For arms to tangle around torsos and for cheeks to meet cheeks. Maybe I'm imagining it, maybe it's wishful thinking, but the ever-present barrier of life and death seems to melt away for us. I can feel her tickly curls so vividly, can feel the so-familiar sensation of her nose nudging against mine. Her tears feel damp against my cheek, her soft breaths brush against my ear. It's all so real.

I don't know how long we stay like that; maybe it's seconds, but then again maybe it's hours. We let the world pass by around us and just revel in the fact that somehow, against all the odds (deaths and kisses and fights included), we've found each other again. When we do finally pull away from each other, there's a change in the air. We've acknowledged something about our friendship that perhaps we should have acknowledged long before my death forced us to. We've acknowledged that even in our friendship, our sisterhood, there are weak spots that need to be respected. Hopefully, now they're out in the open, they can be.

The acknowledgment is silent yet somehow I know it's a mutual thing. The clue's in her soft smile, in her weary but relieved eyes. "We should be making the most of this, this miracle," she finally croaks, gesturing in my general area. "You're back, I can see you. Let's not waste another second crying or fighting or whatever…"

After a second, I nod. There's a slight hesitation because that kiss still stings and I can also see in her gaze that she's not fully moving on just yet. But for now, I'm happy to put things on hold. She's right, after all, this *is* a miracle.

Violet smiles with relief at my nod, hops up. "And making the most of it starts by us going home. Walk or Tube?"

The slip back into almost normality is surprisingly easy to go along with. I glance down at my white dress then up at her once more. "No money or card," I point out, standing up as well and taking her arm. "Let's walk."

So, for a while, we do just that. Violet texts Eric to let him know we're headed home and then we fall into companionable silence for a few moments as we walk down the river, arm in arm.

Then, suddenly, Violet speaks again. "There's something different about you, y'know."

I glance over to meet her curious gaze, raising one eyebrow. "Yeah, no shit. No heartbeat, no breath...where do you want to begin?"

She waves that away impatiently, bumping our shoulders. "No, it's something else. You're all..." Her hands twirl through the air as she searches for the right word, seeming to snatch it from thin air a moment later. "You're all assertive all of a sudden."

"No I'm not."

She grins, spotting the defensiveness in my voice with ease. "Yes, you are. Usually when you're pissed about something you just let it stew until you can pretend you were never pissed off in the first place. But back in the flat it was like hell hath no fury like a dead Daisy."

She gets an elbow in the side for that. "Not funny."

Violet chuckles, rubbing her side with a smirk. "No, it's probably not. But still, something's happened to you, Daisy. In between you dying and you coming here you've—"

"If you say blossomed, I swear to God I'll launch you into the bloody river."

Chuckling, she shakes her head before wrapping her hands around my arm. "Come on, then. I demand answers. Tell me. Properly, not like the vague summary I got last time."

"I can't go into the details, Vi. It's not fair for you to know," I begin, before sighing heavily because that won't wash with her. "God, I'm going to regret this... So Death— death isn't just a thing that happens, Death is also a person. A person who I thought was an asshole but who isn't."

Violet stares at me. "Right. Well, now you've *got* to spill the beans."

There's no getting away from it. Besides, it's not like I haven't been dying to tell her anyway. So I tell her all about Death. The person, not the process, because I still firmly believe that there are some things you shouldn't know before you die. Anyway, explaining Death and the odd companionship we've formed is story enough. By the time I've trailed off to a slightly uncertain end, the streetlights are flickering on and we're moving away from the river, back toward the bustle of London roads.

"Shitting hell," she finally murmurs, after a moment of silence. "So, you have feelings for him?" Her eyes have narrowed as we cross the road, and she spares a second to shoot me a suspicious look.

"What? No, of course not."

Violet does that all-too-familiar thing where she purses her lips to try and hide a smile, before looking away, expression one of intensely irritating smugness. It's a good thing I love her or that look would not go down too well. Sure, maybe Scout and I have grown closer and found some sort of understanding. And, sure, we did kiss right before I came back here. But that doesn't mean that there's anything going on. Certainly nothing worthy of Violet's expression.

But, of course, curiosity gets the better of me. "Why do you ask?"

Violet shrugs. "Call it best-friend intuition. You mentioned the fact that this Death guy has a soft side, like, a gazillion times in that story of yours. Almost more than you mentioned how hard it was without me, which I'm just about letting you get away with."

I roll my eyes. But mainly to try and escape having to give a proper answer. Thanks to the hurricane of emotions and conversations I've gone through since returning to this world, I haven't had a chance to properly think about that kiss that was pressed against my lips, probably no more than an hour ago. About how, when I concentrate, I can still feel its warmth…

"Dee?" Like a crocodile, that's how I used to describe Violet and her determination to hold on to things.

"It's nothing." My voice is firm but, like buildings and, as we so recently discovered, friendships, it has a weak spot. One that Violet seems insistent on prodding. "Besides, it's irrelevant now. I'm back here and he's up there. And I've got Eric."

We've reached the corner of our street now. Violet stops, twisting around on the balls of her feet so she's looking at me properly. "Right, of course." Her voice is steady, but there's something hidden underneath its apparent agreement. A little hint of disbelief. But she doesn't push it, not when the scar of our recent argument is still fresh and raw. Instead, she jerks her head down the street. "Home?"

I nod. "Home," I agree.

But as we start down the street once more, I can't help but notice how that word sits on my tongue. Uncomfortable, almost like it doesn't fit anymore. I brush it away, of course, and yet it still leaves behind a sense of unease.

And, like the bite of a crocodile, that unease grips on firmly and refuses to let go.

Rule Twenty-Three

A Home Can Be Hard To Find

HOME IS WHERE THE heart is—that's what you people always say, right? Of course, biologically speaking, that's impossible. Your chest is where the heart is. Home is where the food is would be more appropriate, or where your collection of furniture and meaningless garbage is. Apparently, though, I'm missing the point. But it is cute how you people place so much importance on a building you sleep in. Then again, placing importance on meaningless things is your specialty, really. Just watch a superstitious person have their path blocked by a ladder and you'll see.

The problem is that I've never had anything like a home. My office is the closest I've got and that doesn't really count. I mean, if I came back and found it gone one day I wouldn't shed too many tears. I would just call up Natasha and ask her what the hell had happened.

So no, that doesn't count. When I visited Daisy and Violet's flat, and stood in the midst of that hideous birthday party, I was struck by how much of their friendship was represented in their home. How you could tell, even months after her death, that Daisy was an irreplace-

able chunk of Violet's life. Photos everywhere, capturing momentous moments like graduation and birthdays and not-so-momentous moments like selfies in a wintery field and miniature versions of themselves sprawled out on a picnic blanket.

After that my office felt as homely as an empty trash can. I tried to make it better. I found a potted plant and placed it on the desk, ignored Daisy's bemusement when she noticed it. I watered it, adjusted its position around the room. Even tied a piece of ribbon around the pot in case that it made it seem more important. But, eventually, I just threw it away. It wasn't doing anything.

Because a potted plant does not make a home. Neither does nice furniture or a selection of photos. You probably all know this, this probably isn't that groundbreaking for you.

The problem is that when these things aren't the key to a home, and when there doesn't seem to be a definitive guide, finding a home is as easy as finding a crow in the night's sky. For a moment you may think you've discovered it. Then it will swoop away, leaving you lost in the dark.

Hibernation is something that Violet and I have always thoroughly agreed with as a concept. Winters are cold and dark and usually draining—why do we as a species insist on battling through them? Even when we were children and there was the exciting prospect of snow and ice outside, we would always prefer to stay firmly on the other side of the window, watching with blankets swathed around us like fluffy royal cloaks.

Immediately, we slip back into these habits. For Violet, there is an infinite solace to be found in our place being at maximum occupancy once again and, while I do feel that as well, I'm also hoping that hibernating makes the flat feel like a home again. Since I've stepped inside, I've felt a little as though I've returned to one of my old classrooms. Nothing quite fits like it used to.

But for now, I'm determined not to think too hard about that. What does it matter anyway, when I've got Violet? So I don't think about it. I lose myself in the infinite comfort of almost ordinary conversations. We talk about stupid, random things, like how I'm so lucky I'll never have to get my wisdom teeth removed because Violet's seen the videos and, boy, does it look horrific. We sprawl out on the sofa, catch up on documentaries that Violet was upset I missed the first time. I watch as Violet drifts in and out of peaceful naps and wish that napping wasn't something reserved for my past.

But it's still nice. Peaceful. It's just different, no matter how many traditions we reenact. Then, sometime after midnight, Violet has to go to sleep properly. And I'm left alone. Eyes permanently open, brain permanently switched on.

That's when the flat feels a little less welcoming. In the gloom of the night, things that should be comforting twist into quite the opposite. Our joint calendar, which Violet has belligerently kept up, taunts me with its one blank side. The fridge seems to whisper in my ear how I'll never get to enjoy the taste of anything again. I start to try and picture how my favorite foods like bacon would taste on my tongue but it's useless.

My bedroom, meanwhile, is a treasure trove of shitty feelings. Makeup that won't do anything on skin not really of this world; a wardrobe of clothes that I can't wear because this stupid dress seems impossible to remove; even my fucking tampons bring on a strange sense of wistfulness.

The problem is that this home, for obvious reasons, is not built for the dead. And as I spend another hour trying to read one of the books I never got around to finishing, I can't help but think of the other world I've left behind. A world where the dead don't get constant reminders of what they're missing out on.

But then morning returns. Light streams back into the flat, Violet wakes up once more, and then it's all too easy to pretend such thoughts haven't entered my mind. They're whirled away as we watch the breakfast news just as we used to before work and I can pretend we're back to our ordinary routine.

As Violet is trying to decide whether to call in sick for work, Eric arrives. He's already called his own office to tell them he's not coming in today, which seems to settle it for Violet.

"Well, I can't hang around here while you two make up for lost time," she scoffs, as Eric settles himself down on the sofa beside me. She disappears to get changed for ten minutes, leaving us in slightly awkward silence as presumably both of us consider just how much lost time we'll be capable of making up for when one of us is still technically dead.

When she returns, dressed in her waitressing uniform, she spends another few minutes fussing around in classic Violet procrastination.

"Vi, it will be bloody lunchtime by the time you leave. Go," I finally say with a laugh as she almost gets herself into another conversation with us.

"I'm going. And you'll be here when I get back?" she asks, eyes wide.

I nod. "I'll be here."

Something passes across her face; I suppose you could call it suspicion. And I suppose that's fair enough. But she says nothing more. Nodding, she hugs me tight, nods to Eric, then dashes out the door.

I shift back around on the sofa to face Eric, find his eyes on me. He still seems a little wary, like he doesn't quite believe it's truly me and I'm not about to steal his soul.

"How was last night?" he asks, after a pause.

"Long," I reply, then go on as he tilts his head a little curiously. "I can't sleep."

"I'm sure you'll settle back in eventually."

I shake my head. "No, Eric, I mean literally. I can't sleep. The dead don't sleep." He winces visibly at my words. Shit. Probably best not to mention the dead thing too often. "Sorry. I didn't mean to—"

"No, it's fine. I just…it takes some getting used to. All this."

"Well then, let's talk about something else? Tell me about work or your family or—or anything that's not to do with me being dead."

Eric casts his eyes around the sitting room, brow furrowed. "Um, work's fine, I guess. I got a promotion."

"Oh, cool! Well done."

He smiles at that, the first real smile since I've returned. His eyes seem a little glittery as he gently wraps his arms around my shoulders, drawing me close. "I've missed that, you know, more than anything. Missed telling you these things and hearing you sound so excited and proud."

Resting my head against his chest, I can just make out his heartbeat. It should probably be comforting, but it mainly fills me with jealousy. The silence of a still heart is something I'd got used to, but now I realize how lonely it is…

"Daisy?" he prompts, when I don't reply.

"Sorry…was listening to your heart." I sit up then, before I get lost in my own longing.

He smiles a little, presses a kiss to my forehead with extreme care. "How does it sound?"

"Alive." The word slips out automatically, laced with wistfulness.

Eric doesn't quite know what to say to that so starts rambling on about something else instead. And that becomes the pattern of our morning's conversations. We start talking about one thing and when it somehow, inevitably, ends up back at my death, he diverts us hastily and often awkwardly.

I don't want to talk about my death but it seems that all lines of discussion end up back at that fact. It starts to feel as if my entire identity has been replaced: I am dead and that is all.

Perhaps Eric picks up on this frustration because he suggests we go out for a walk. That helps for a bit. The sun is shining and the city looks glorious, practically glowing with spring beauty.

But after a while, all I can focus on is life. There's so much of it buzzing around me, so many people with thumping hearts and breathing lungs. At one point I think I hear the shrill whistle of life leaving and I turn toward it, shamed to be almost hopefully looking for a death. Because that's my world now, not this world of people blithely living their lives with no regard for the finiteness of it.

We put on a good show, though. We go through the motions of spending the day together while Violet is at work. We go to the aquarium, we visit a museum, take long walks. We giggle at the lazy penguin, stare at the volcano exhibit, admire the spring blossom. It's nice. But it's not life, not really.

On the third day, as we sit waiting for Violet to return for dinner, Eric turns to me with a hesitant expression and I think I know what's coming.

"This isn't going to work. Is it?"

I glance up from the potato I've been trying to peel with a peeler that keeps seeming to slip through my fingers. "The dinner?" I ask, trying to be lighthearted, because reality is starting to bleed through the cracks and I'm not ready.

"Daisy," he sighs, fondly exasperated, "I can't keep doing

this...pretending anymore. What are we trying to do? I mean, zoos and parks are fun but that's not...we can't do that for the rest of our—" He pauses, afraid to say the word.

"The rest of your life," I finish for him, putting the potato down along with the peeler.

"I'm sorry," he blurts out, face pale in the gloom of the shitty kitchen light.

I shake my head. "Don't be," I say, taking one of his hands in mine. I can feel a slight tremor coming through his fingers as he wraps them around my palm. This is truly hurting him. I can understand that; it's hurting me too. It hurts to know that I've been handed this miracle path back to him and yet it's not enough.

He pulls back after a moment, his eyes a little red. "I just don't know where we fit anymore," he whispers. "I'm sorry, I shouldn't be doing this to you, not when you've tried for so long to come back to us, to me. But there's this—this barrier between us and I don't think it's fair."

"On either of us," I agree softly, finding that my own eyes are staying mostly dry. Perhaps I knew all this already, deep down. Too much has changed. Eric has been learning to cope without me and, in doing that, no longer knows how to let me back into his life. And perhaps I've been doing the same, learning to be dead and so forgetting how to live.

My agreement seems like a great relief and he buries his face in his hands, trying so desperately to hide the heartbreak that my death has caused (and that my return has unwittingly brought back to the surface). I wrap my arms around his waist and gently draw him close, rest my head on his shoulder just as I've done so many times before.

"It's OK, Eric. It's OK for us to move on. You're going to have a great life, I know it." It's just not our life to share. And maybe that's OK.

We stay like this for a while. Eventually we share a final kiss and he touches my cheek, my shoulder, committing little things to memory in case he doesn't see me again. Something which is starting to become a possibility, I think.

Before too long, as Violet's arrival time draws closer, it's time to leave.

"I'll look after her, Daisy," he says at the door. "Whatever happens, I won't stop looking after her."

I've not asked for this reassurance but it helps, somehow. But also really doesn't help. If I know Violet's being looked after, am I any use to her here? Am I just a deadweight, literally?

Straying to the sofa once the door is closed and Eric has left, I sit in a slight daze. I know I should feel sad but I don't, not really. In a strange and twisted way, I feel relieved. Relieved that Eric is free to continue to heal without me holding him back, and relieved that I'm free to become someone new without him making me hesitate. Because Violet is right; death has changed me, and not just by stopping my heart.

Violet knows something's wrong the moment she gets home. I know because she closes the door slowly and keeps her hand clenched tightly around it, eyes shutting for the smallest of moments. I hear her shuddering sigh, even from my spot by the sofa. It hurts so much to know that I can cause this reaction from her.

She turns around to face me, places her bag by the door. "Hey," she says, trying to keep her voice light. "You OK?"

I don't think there's an answer to that. It's not that I'm *not* OK, but I also don't think "yes" is exactly truthful either. "Um, Eric and I just broke up."

"Shit. I'm really sorry, Daisy." She moves over to sit down, wraps an arm around my shoulders.

"It's fine. It was a mutual thing. We just…don't really fit anymore."

Violet's silent for a moment. "Because you're still dead. And he's alive," she finally says, voice soft.

I nod slowly, feeling the horrifying revelation I've been trying to keep at bay beginning to rise up my throat. I don't want to admit it aloud because then it's real. And I don't want it to be real. Not when I know how much it's going to hurt us both.

I shift away from her arm so I'm facing her more directly, take both of her hands and squeeze them tightly. She meets my gaze and I can see a defiant attempt to be brave shining through her eyes. It can't quite snuff out the lingering fear, though. Which just makes my next words even more difficult to say.

But here they are. Determined to exist despite how unwanted they are.

I sigh, close my eyes for a second.

"It's OK, Daisy," she whispers, "whatever it is, you can say it."

A small shiver leaves my belligerently dead body. And then, buoyed by her soft encouragement, I let the words free.

"Violet, I think I need to leave."

Rule Twenty-Four

Beware The Words Not Said

THERE COMES A MOMENT for us all, both living and alive, where certain words are difficult to say. Of course some words are difficult to say simply because of how they're spelt. Otorhinolaryngologist, for example. Not that you're likely to say such a word that often, unless it happens to be your job or if your ears, nose and throat have all stopped working as they should.

Sometimes, though, it's not so much about the spelling but about the meaning. An otorhinolaryngologist (an ear, nose and throat doctor, in case you haven't looked it up yet) may find it very easy to say the title of their job but may find it very difficult to tell someone that they're going deaf. A scuba diver may happily state that they've visited an anemone without any struggle but may struggle to tell their girlfriend they've fallen in love with their diving instructor.

And, let's face it, the majority of people in this world are cowards. If we know we can get away with not saying some words, we're probably not going to say them. I could have told Daisy a lot of things before she left, like how nobody has ever understood me so well since

Lucas left, like how she's brought an entire new side to my job and, well, my existence. But I didn't see that having any value (that would be floccinaucinihilipilification, by the way. I'll leave you to check that one out for yourself).

The problem, of course, is that the words we don't want to say are often the most important. If we are never told we're going deaf, we may not take necessary precautions when crossing roads. If we are never told that our partner has fallen in love with someone else, we may waste our time in a fruitless relationship.

And if we never tell our best friend how much it hurts for them to leave, they may never stop doing it.

I remember when we were at school, Violet and I used to read each other's reports. Both of us were high-achieving, anxious young girls who found the idea of bad reports absolutely terrifying. So we decided one year to read each other's out loud. Usually sitting at the bus stop, waiting for the bus to whisk us home for the holidays.

A lot of the time, it was like reading a mirror image of ourselves. Mine would always say I needed to speak up more in class, as if that was somehow stopping me getting the right grades (it wasn't). In contrast, Violet's would always mention her inability to stop speaking up in class. Our history teacher always joked that if he could find a way to keep her silent, he'd patent it and make his millions.

Well, guess what, Mr. Anderson? Turns out it's pretty easy to render Violet speechless. Just die, then come back to her, then tell her you're leaving again. Simple.

Except, of course, it's not. It's a complicated mess.

Violet gathers her coat around herself, staring at me. We're nearing a minute of stunned silence. A record for Mr. Anderson, I'm sure.

Finally, she speaks. "Leave? Leave where?"

I bite my lip. I don't want to have to say it so explicitly. "Life," I manage to say at last.

Violet moves a little closer, frowning. "You—you mean go back to Death?" I can hear the capital letter there, some-how. It's funny, because I hadn't thought of it as going back to him. Of course I've thought about him these past few days, even missed him. But it's not so much about Death; it's about being in a place that can actually acknowledge my existence, that I actually belong to.

"To his world, yes," I correct, as gently as I can. "I think we both know that there's not really anything left for me here. These days have been lovely, but what next? What about after a week? A month? A year? I can't just spend the rest of eternity in this flat, watching your life move on while I'm frozen, stuck."

Violet swallows, fixes me with her most piercing and ex-amining gaze. "You've had this look in your eyes...last night and this morning. Roxy used to wear it when we couldn't take her for a walk."

"Wow, thanks for that complimentary comparison to your dog."

Violet smiles just a fraction, lifting her chin a little. She always does that when she's trying to be brave. Right since her first Christmas play when she played the honored role of First Sheep. "So. How are we doing this?"

"Doing what?"

Violet moves around into the kitchen, pouring herself a glass of water and draining it in one gulp. Wiping her mouth, she takes a deep breath before turning back to me. "Do I need to like, shoot you or something?"

Tears rise up in my eyes at that. She doesn't even hesitate in considering helping, even if it means she's going to lose me. Even if it means bloody shooting me. There isn't a word to adequately describe that sort of friendship and loyalty.

With a deep, deep sigh I move over and pull her into a hug. One of those bone-crushing hugs that we're such specialists at. She presses back against me and I can hear her heart thudding fast and hard, so loud that it's like she's got two of them going off in there.

"I think I knew it was coming," she whispers a second later, pulling back a little to look me straight in the eyes. "I mean, you haven't asked once about visiting your family so I think you've known you weren't going to stay. It will be fine. It's not like it's the first time someone's left me." She smiles thinly, knowing she's not convincing anyone.

"I—I'm not leaving *you*, Vi; I'm s-so sorry." I find myself stumbling over these words, each one thick with tears. Her words, so full of truth, are not helping me to keep calm. How does my best friend know me so much better than I know myself? Because she's right; I have been holding back from going to see my family because I didn't want to put them through the shock of seeing me if I wasn't staying for certain. And I think I've known for a few days now that it wasn't certain, not at all.

Violet sniffs back her own tears, still trying to pretend that this is all normal and fine. Denial, a Violet and Daisy specialty. Then she steps back, holding my arms firmly. I can almost convince myself that I can feel her fingertips properly. "You listen to me, Daisy. Shit happens, people die. Most people don't get the chance to see them again. I am the luckiest person in the world in that respect and I will be forever grateful that you came back. And now it would be my honor to help you get back to the best place for you right now." She stops, takes another shaky breath. Pulls herself together with the finest thread.

"It's not fair," I whisper hopelessly. "I don't want to have to leave you, I don't want to feel out of place here. I want to *stay*."

Violet presses her forehead against mine, hands now resting on my shoulders. "Tell me what you'd say to me," she whispers.

"What?"

"Tell me. If I was in your position right now, and you knew the right thing for me to do was to leave, what would you say?"

I lift my head, vision a little blurred by tears that refuse to be dried out by death. "I don't know."

"Bullshit. You're Daisy Cooper, you always know what to say to help me."

Closing my eyes again, I try to imagine what it would be like to be telling Violet to go back to a place where I will no longer see her, knowing full well that it was the best place for her to be. "I know it's scary," I whisper a second later, almost absentmindedly. "But it won't be. Once you've done it, you'll see so clearly that this was right for you. So go do it."

I open my eyes and Violet's smiling at me, though the smile has sadness tugging at the edges. "I know it's scary, but it won't be. Daisy, once you've done it, you'll see so clearly that this was right for you. So go do it." Then she winks, squeezes my shoulders. "Knew you'd know what to say."

Before I answer, I have to give her one final hug. She lets out an impatient huff but tolerates it for a few seconds, then wriggles back with an expectant gaze. "Come on then, Dee. Tell me what we need to do."

"We need to find the lift," I whisper, voice a little shaky. "There's a lift that takes the dead…up. It's a nightmare to find, though."

Violet nods, stepping back and rolling her sleeves up. Like

she's about to bake a damn cake, not help a friend get back to the afterlife. "Well, how do you summon it?"

"You just sort of feel it out. It tends to appear when you need it."

Violet rolls her eyes at this. "God. It's good to know the afterlife is so well organized."

"It's always worked in the past." I glance around the flat, hands hovering up to the keys still tied around my neck and holding them tightly. They're my talisman for life but they're also part of my death too. Perhaps they can help bring me back both ways? With the sharp edges of the metal digging into my fingers, I close my eyes and try to call out for the lift in my head. After a moment of presumably looking like an idiot, I open my eyes again.

A quick glance around the flat and I can see that nothing has happened. The lift is damn hard to spot, but over the months I've developed a slight knack; the point where the two doors meet has a slight shimmer to it, almost like the light within is trying to escape through. If I can spot that, I can usually find the button to press nearby. But there's nothing.

"Maybe I have to take the keys off," I murmur. But I don't want to do that, because what if I still can't see the lift but then can't get back to Violet? I don't want to be invisible down here and unable to get back up there. That would be torture.

I'm just trying to decide if I have the courage to give it a go when Violet lets out a soft gasp and points to somewhere behind me. I whip around and, sure enough, a set of doors are sliding open to reveal the interior of the lift. "It came!" I exclaim, before turning back to Violet as a rather obvious thought catches up with my excitement. "You—you can see that?"

Violet nods, eyes a little wide with alarm. Understandable. "It's probably just because you're with me, or something." I hope I sound more convinced than I feel because, in truth, I have no idea why she can see it. The only people I've known to be able to see it are the dead and Scout. Violet is neither of those.

"Yeah, something like that," Violet replies, voice soft. She takes a step toward the lift, somewhat entranced. "So…that's death?"

I don't like how she sounds. Not quite wistful but also not exactly scared by the prospect of it. Like she's seeing a roller coaster that's nowhere near as frightening as its commercial makes out.

"No," I say, a little sharply. "That's just the journey up to it. I don't think even Death properly knows what death is."

Violet seems to notice my discomfort because she dutifully takes a step back, shooting me a slightly awkward smile. "So is this…is this going to be goodbye?"

It's a simple question with a presumably simple answer. Yes or no. But now the door is in front of me and Violet is there, waiting for my response, it all feels a bit more complicated. "I'm coming back," I reply finally. "I'm going to go but this isn't it. I can still come back and visit, just like now."

Violet looks at me for a few, long seconds. Sometimes she can be a completely open book but sometimes, like now, she's closed off, an enigma. She could be thinking anything. And that's where the danger lies with Violet; it lies in the words she doesn't say.

"Vi?" I prompt.

She shakes her head. "You said before about not wanting to stop people moving on. That applies to you as well, you know. We will miss you, of course we will. But if it's become better for you to stop coming then…that's OK."

Violet doesn't often have the patience for wise speeches like this, but when she does, she tends to be exceptionally good at them. She pulls me into another hug then. I rest my chin on her shoulder, she tucks hers around my ear. Just like always.

"Love you, tit," she murmurs.

"Love you too, dickhead," I reply. Just like old times.

We pull back a moment later. I smooth down the shoulders of her sweater, she adjusts the loop of keys around my neck. Then she nods toward the lift. "Now or never, then. I've gotta get dinner on."

"I peeled the potatoes."

She laughs. "Thanks. I'm still shit at that."

"I know. Eric told me."

"What a snitch."

We laugh together, but it's bittersweet. We know we're stalling for time here. Delaying the inevitable. And I can't quite step back, I can't quite make that first movement away from her. It goes against every instinct in my bones because no part of me ever wants to leave Violet. Not since the day she entered my life.

Of course, Violet knows this. I can tell from the way she takes my arms and gently pushes me away toward the lift. "Go. Before I shove you in myself."

Her hands leave my arms and it feels a little like she's taking a bit of my heart with her.

It takes another few seconds for me to gather the bravery I need to step inside. It's more of a stumble than a step, and I can't hold back the small sob of despair that this choice has had to be made.

But the moment I step into the lift, I can't deny the warm sense of relief that begins to wash over me. That same feeling you get when you open the door to your home after a long, stressful day at work. I'm back in a place that accepts and acknowledges my existence.

When I turn back to Violet, however, and see her desperately trying to hold back tears, all I can think about is what she'll do when the doors close and she's alone once more. That thought is enough to make my feet stumble back toward her again.

"Oh no you don't!" Violet says, voice firm as she comes right up to the doors. She meets my gaze, finger coming to press the exterior button. Another impossibility. The doors shudder into life and she shoots me a smile. "Go get him, tiger!" she calls.

I have to laugh at that, full of admiration for my formidable best friend managing to make a joke at this moment. "Fuck off!" I call back, managing a little grin.

"Terrible last words!"

The doors shut slowly and I watch her until the last second. She's grinning, laughing at her own joke. And I'm filled with relief, a sense of confidence that she'll be OK.

Until the last second, the last centimeters between the doors. When she thinks I can't see her anymore and I watch as she lets her face drop. A balloon, pricked with a pin.

The lift eagerly hums into life and I feel it lifting away from the ground, taking me up. But I'm scared. Scared that Violet has not told me how she really feels about me leaving, has protected me from the truth and sacrificed her own safety in the process. And I'm scared because if that is the case, I don't quite know what I should do.

The lift comes to a halt. My fingers hover over the button that will send me right back down to my flat again, but it can't quite commit to pressing it. Because I can't say for sure that going back will make it any better.

As I'm hesitating, the lift doors suddenly whoosh open. And, in one shocking and thought-scattering wave, chaos rushes in to meet me.

Rule Twenty-Five

Kindness Is A Superpower

WHAT DOES IT MEAN to be alive? Is it the thump of the heart? Is it the breath in your lungs? Is it walking through the street and feeling your impact on the flow of the world, in tiny, mostly insignificant ways? Or is it something more complicated than that, something that can't be put into words?

I'm more inclined to go toward that final one. I've been taking it away from people for years and I still don't really understand what it is. I know it screams when it leaves, I know people take it for granted until it's gone, and I know it is terrifyingly short. Other than that, it's a real mystery. A conundrum.

But I think I'm beginning to understand what it means to be human. You always puzzled me. Until I spent enough time with one of you and learned that humans just care so damn much. You fill your heart with this intense sense of compassion and determination to love until you're transformed into something entirely new.

I know there's darkness in the world. Trust me, I see plenty of it. But for every dark cloud, I think there might be a ray of kindness

*chasing it away. Blood donors queuing around corners after shoot-
ings, firefighters put everything on the line for a family they've never
met, the person who stands at the railings of a bridge and asks the
person on the other side if they can help.*

*I used to not see the point. I used to think it was just an act of
self-service. But perhaps I was wrong. Perhaps the hope for our future and our world lies in our ability to care.*

And perhaps it's my turn.

✳ ✳ ✳

A cacophony of noise and movement invades my senses. The
all-too-familiar MDS alarm is blaring furiously and I'm sure
it's louder than before. White-uniformed people are running
up and down the corridor, shouting to each other. I recognize
a few from the times I've passed them in the hall. The head
of Road Traffic Accidents rushes past me, deep in a frantic-
sounding conversation with someone from the Sea-Related
Accidents department. Hurrying the opposite way is a cluster
of people from Poisoning, who all seem to be highly riled
up about something.

Stumbling out of the lift, I hastily jump back to avoid being
trampled by one of these staff members. They barely notice
me. This makes me panic for a moment about my visibility
up here and I hastily remove my keys, placing them in my
pocket for the moment. Just in case.

As I'm doing this, Natasha herself appears. At first she
storms past me, muttering furiously under her breath, before seeming to properly register my identity and stopping.
"Daisy!" she barks, rounding on me. "What are you doing
here? I thought you were gone?"

"Um, I came back but I'm not sure I should have."

Natasha waves this away with a noise of great impatience
and irritation. "You're just the person we need, so you're not

going now. We've got an MDS going on and everything is in complete disarray. Death has gone off somewhere." She pauses to shoot a furious look heavenward before going on, "Told us he could handle the first group on his own and would tell us what needed doing on his return. But he hasn't come back and we don't know why."

There's a lot to take in there, so I decide to tackle the simplest question first. "What's the MDS?"

Natasha gives me an almost approving look. "Boat caught in a storm. Unfortunately, we've got some young casualties as well. It was some sort of ferry, by the looks of things."

I frown, staring at her. "And Death's down there?"

Natasha shoots me a bemused look. "Yes. I just said that. What's the problem?"

Shit. I can't tell Natasha the secret fear Scout has, that's not my place. But if he's gone down to an MDS with children, and he's still not back… "Natasha. Tell me. How bad is it?"

Natasha watches me suspiciously for another moment, then looks at her watch. "We've got twenty minutes to get this event locked down before we start backing up. I've set aside enough people to keep up until then but after that we're going to start having people dying unattended."

Twenty minutes, right. "OK. I'll go find Death and find out what's going on. You deal with everyone else, like you normally would."

Natasha looks rather impressed and even shoots me a small smile. But she doesn't let it linger unnecessarily. "Fine. Good. Get moving." It's as close to a thank you as I'm going to get.

So I turn and go right back into the lift. The button I need flashes urgently at me; clearly MDS are too important for trying to sense out the right button on your own. For a moment I battle with the temptation to try sending the lift back home again. But there's a lot of people up here relying on me. Violet will have to wait.

The moment the doors open again, the lift is filled with a howling wind, followed swiftly by a horizontal rain, which spatters angrily against the walls.

Outside, the world is in the midst of an almighty tantrum. Through the murk, I can just make out the towering funnel of a ship stretching determinedly up into the furious sky. A second later, a bolt of lightning crackles above me and for a moment I see the unnatural angle of the ship's deck. Then everything falls back into rainy darkness again.

I start to scramble uphill toward the other end of the ship and, as I stumble along, I become increasingly aware of other people rushing around me. Passengers are yelling for their friends, their family, trying to no avail to be heard over the wind. The whistling of imminent deaths soon join their shouts.

"Scout?" I bellow into the wind, but there's no answer. Clinging onto a nearby pole, I squint through the rain, trying desperately to spot something.

Then I catch a snatch of conversation, drifting over the wind. "Kids, you need to listen to me, OK?"

It's a voice I would recognize anywhere, even in the midst of a furious and deadly storm. And I'm immediately racing toward where I think I heard it, stumbling over my feet as the gradient of the boat's deck continues to tip.

Around the corner, bathed in the flickering glow of the boat's malfunctioning emergency lighting, is a scene so unexpected that I come to an abrupt halt.

Scout is leaning right over the railings of the boat, holding what looks like a thick rope. His hair is sodden from the rain but his face is set with grim yet unwavering determination. Clustered around him, shivering in varied forms of white clothing are two children. One girl, probably about ten and one boy, who seems considerably younger and who is crying desperately into the side of the girl.

As I continue to watch, Scout gives the rope an almighty heave and pulls another child into view. Another boy, dripping wet and also dressed in white. A third victim of the ocean, who Scout untangles from the rope and places down beside the other boy. Immediately, the group of children fall into a relieved embrace.

And still, Scout doesn't notice me. He won't take his eyes off the children.

"Right, is that all of you?" he calls over the wind, voice calm except for a very slight tremor.

The girl pulls herself from the hug, wiping at her cheeks before nodding slowly. "That's all of us. Thank you for getting us out." There's something about her voice which suggests she's already worked out that this isn't a miracle rescue. Which is perhaps why Scout shakes his head a little.

"Oh, it's fine. Couldn't leave you in all those beastly waves, eh?" He pats the shoulder of the smallest boy, who shoots him a slightly hesitant, very tiny smile.

The concern he has for this group is palpable, but unfortunately it is this concern that has delayed the entire MDS.

So I clear my throat, stepping forward. It brings a strange swooping sensation to my chest when Scout looks up, meets my gaze. I really did miss him after all.

"Daisy? What—what are you doing here?"

"I came to help," I say simply, because now's not the time for the full story. I gesture at the small group of shivering children, who are now watching me with slight suspicion. "What's going on?"

He lifts his chin a little. "I'm helping these children. They fell out of the lifeboat," he explains, pointing out to sea. I can just make out the dim orange shape of a lifeboat and the desperate flashes of a searching torch. He watches the waves for a moment. "I heard them calling and... I had to help them."

The smallest boy starts to cry again, Scout's words clearly sparking some awful memory in his head. I step forward but Scout gets there first. He takes a deep breath to steady his own resolve before kneeling down to the boy's level.

"I can carry you, if that would help?" he asks slowly, testing the waters.

The boy is desperate for any sort of comfort and falls into Scout's arms almost immediately. I watch as Scout's eyes close, briefly. Those long years of fear claw at him for just a second but it seems like he will not let it beat him, not today. He stands, bringing the child up with him.

"I've got you," he murmurs, holding the boy securely, if a little awkwardly, in his arms, "don't worry."

I feel a single tear trickle down my cheek. Scout notices this, smiles. "Daisy Cooper, you appear to be crying."

I wipe the tear away. "Scout, you appear to be carrying a child," I shoot back.

I want to carry this conversation on, particularly when it seems to be helping the children. But there's business to attend to. "Natasha's freaking out up top. Apparently you were meant to let her know what you wanted everyone else to do and now the system's close to backing up."

Scout only partly seems to listen, focused on shifting the smallest boy so he's in a piggyback position, before offering his now free hands to the two other children. "Oh, the system will be fine. She's such a drama queen," he scoffs, using his head to gesture for me to follow him as he starts back. "And you, Cooper, would surely not encourage me to rush helping children just to keep the system running smoothly, now would you?" He glances back to me, grinning knowingly.

I can only grin back at him.

A calm has settled over the children that I instinctively know has nothing to do with Scout's magic touch and all to do with the unfaltering care he is showing them. A true display of magic that seems to lighten the darkness swirling around us, as we head back toward the lift.

We stop a moment later and Scout turns to the boy holding his hand. "Right, Kabir. You get to help me with the next bit. I need your finger." Kabir tentatively offers his hand and Scout gently pulls it forward a little. It immediately hits the button of the lift, which lights up in the gloom. The children's gasps of surprise are audible even with the wailing gales.

Scout has them in the palm of his hand after that, and I can only watch with bemused wonder as the man who hid among the ruins of a plane from one child goes on to expertly process three of them, without another moment of panic from any of them. Even the little one, Krish, manages to get processed without much trouble. Once Scout lets him sit on his chair and tick the boxes on the form, he's pretty content.

When the time comes for them to go through the door, I notice that a sense of reluctance has settled around the children, and also around Scout.

I guess this is the downside of allowing yourself to be compassionate.

So it's my turn to be kind. Stepping around the desk, I come to kneel at the children's level. "Right, that's the boring bit over," I say, shooting them all a steady smile. "You're going through this door now. You don't need to be scared. Someone will be expecting you and they'll make sure you're safe. No more scary storms."

Pari, the oldest, looks somewhat suspicious. She's old enough to know that grown-ups don't always tell the truth, especially if they're trying to prevent children from crying. But she's also a big sister and she's not going to let her siblings get anxious again. So she accepts my words with a slow nod.

"Will we see you again?" Krish asks, the question mostly directed to Scout.

Scout wrinkles his nose, then shakes his head. "I wish you could, but I have other people to help, kiddo."

Once the door closes behind the three children it suddenly seems very still and quiet in the office. I glance over to Scout, eyebrows rising. "Well. That was unexpected," I say, before taking a step toward him and squeezing his arm. "Well done."

Scout wrinkles his nose with a sheepish shrug as he moves to sit down. "Three children. Hardly groundbreaking."

"Better than last time," I point out. "You weren't hiding in the wreckage of a plane so I call that definite progress."

Scout straightens up a little. "Yeah. That's true. I just didn't want to let them down. And when I heard them crying... well, it was as if I forgot I was scared."

Smiling, I move to sit down in the opposite chair, then lean across to squeeze his hand. "That's called kindness, Scout. Takes away the fear. You just wanted to help, so that's all you thought about. Like firefighters. Or heroes."

He looks so proud when I say those words that I can't help but grin. It's like a little boy learning to ride a bike for the first time.

Of course he notices the grin. "What?"

I shake my head. "Nothing. It's just...nice to see you. I missed that goofy smile of yours."

Scout sniffs a little at that. Then levels his gaze on me. "So, you came back." A statement, but there's definitely a question mark in it somewhere.

I hesitate, then nod. "Yes."

Scout nods as well, surveying me just as a scientist might survey a brand-new species. This is all new for him. "I thought you wanted to go home?"

"So did I." I bite my lip, glancing down at my fingers as they instinctively begin to tangle together. "But…" I pause, looking up as Scout's phone begins ringing in his pocket once more.

Scout looks like he's considering not answering it but then he relents, tugging it from his pocket. He has pushed Natasha to her limits already today, after all. "Yup?" he says as he places the phone to his ear.

I watch as the lightness leaves his eyes in one fell swoop, like someone's crawled inside and flipped a switch. He frowns, standing up and pushing the chair in behind him. "I'm on it. Thank you, Natasha."

Then he hangs up, looks over to me. His expression immediately fills me with foreboding. "Daisy, that was Natasha," he begins, voice slow and careful. "She's just been sent an emergency file, an unexpected death that's just come in."

My stomach churns. In my mind, I see the lift doors closing again and I see her face fall. Balloon popped with a pin.

"Daisy, the file belongs to Violet," Scout says.

And maybe it's my imagination, or maybe it's some distant part of Violet reaching for me, but suddenly all I can hear is the howling whistle of a kettle beginning to boil and a life beginning to leave.

Rule Twenty-Six

Sometimes We Need To Let Go

WHEN LUCAS WAS LOST, there was nothing left to prove he ever existed. Except for this one piece of paperwork. I hadn't processed it before he went, but he had signed it. All wobbly letters and wonky spacing but it was his name and his handwriting. Sitting on my desk. Proof that once there had been a boy called Lucas who had brought laughter into my days and taught me how to be brave.

I carried that bit of paper with me everywhere. Folded it tightly and stuck it in the pocket of my trousers, even if it was meant to be filed away. I couldn't lose that last scrap of Lucas, I couldn't let it go. Because if I did, then I was accepting that he was really gone.

That piece of paper become worn and crumpled and faded from all the times I held it to my chest, wept into it, threw it across the floor in rage.

Then, one day I lost it.

I still don't know how. It had been a busy day in the middle of one of your countless wars and it could easily have slipped out of my pocket in the commotion. Though I can never quite shake the feeling *that someone just sneaked it away from me, someone who wanted me to forget Lucas and stop questioning the system I was entrenched in.*

Of course I didn't forget. But the loss of that paper did allow for the beginning of something else. Closure. Because without that piece of paper, I was forced to let go. Let go of the idea that he was coming back. It didn't mean forgetting him, it just meant allowing myself to start creating an existence without him. I can't say that existence is perfect, not by a long shot. But it is better than spending day after day crying over a piece of paper.

Letting go is never easy. Sometimes we need that push to get us there. It's just a question of what else gets knocked when that push comes.

✳ ✳ ✳

The first time Violet tried to kill herself, she was eighteen years old. That was before she was officially diagnosed with depression, before she got the medication and the counseling that she needed to help her cope.

Back then, death wasn't a guy with a stupid name label and a dorky sense of humor and a rare yet glorious smile. Back then, death was dark and ominous. A shadow reaching out, ready to snatch my best friend and steal her away from me. And I fought tooth and nail to bring her back. Maybe that's why I got taken in the end. Maybe the system doesn't like being cheated.

She had had a fight with her dad—it wasn't long after he'd left—then she got some harsh criticism from her dance teacher. She was worrying about her exams, she was trying to prove to her mum that she had done an amazing job without her dad around, she was stressed at some friends for not inviting her to a party. And so on. But it wasn't about any of that, not really. People tried to say it was, tried to say she was just a high-achieving girl who needed a reality check.

But those people didn't understand that depression worms its way into minds and cruelly twists the smallest moments into something they're not. And something dark had twisted into Violet's mind, had been quietly whispering in her ear that her life wasn't worthwhile. That night, the voice got too loud and she tried to shut it up.

Twelve hours after she overdosed, she woke up. Her mum had been visiting her grandma in London, so there had only been me and my parents to look after her. I held her hand until her mum arrived, willed her eyes to open. When she did finally open them, all she could do was cry. She never did tell me why she cried so hard that night, but part of me has always been afraid that she was crying because she hadn't succeeded.

So here we are, attempt number two. Somewhere between me leaving her and me returning from a sinking ship, that dark voice has been let back in to wreak its havoc once more.

The flat was empty when we were deposited inside it. Front door kicked open, Violet's bedroom in disarray, blood on the bed sheets, pill packets on the floor, a broken razor. And an ambulance waiting outside, its flashing lights managing to illuminate the flat through the kitchen window. Scout stays silent beside me, though his hand never leaves mine. He just lets me lead him from the sitting room, to Violet's room, to the street, to the ambulance.

We sit in the corner. Two ghosts, watching a medical drama take place before us that neither of us want to see. And there she is. My poor best friend, laid out on a gurney in front of us, tears dried on her cheeks and eyelids fluttering. Holding on. A horribly thick tube snakes down her throat, a monitor beeps out a painfully slow heartbeat. Both wrists are wrapped in thick bandages, which explains all the blood on the sheets. That's a new one for Violet, I find myself thinking in a fruitless attempt to distract myself from reality.

Scout just sits and watches, looking a little uncomfortable. After all, this is not his forte; he's more at home with monitors that don't beep, with patients who no longer breathe. But Violet's not gone yet. And I've fought her way back from the edge before. Now I know exactly who to fight, I'm not letting her go anywhere.

As though it's reminding me of how powerless I am here, the whistling starts in the ambulance, the whistling of an imminently leaving life. It continues all the way to the hospital, all the way through the emergency department, all the way to the little room they put her in. Low but persistent. A whistling kettle placed on a tiny fire that can't quite boil. Yet.

We can only wait as the doctors do all they can. We stand guard outside the room as she has her stomach pumped, we watch grimly as she's given blood to replace the pints lost. But judging by the whistle, it's still going to be close.

Finally, we're left alone in a tiny private room. Just the dead and the near dying. I sit in the chair beside Violet's bed, hand wrapped around her arm. Holding her in place, desperately trying to keep her pinned to this world.

"Daisy…" Scout finally says, but I won't let him go on. I don't like the tone, full of gentleness. That here-comes-the-shit tone I've heard far too much of recently.

"Shut up."

"Daisy," he tries again but I shake my head, lips pressed together so tightly that they feel like they might break. He falls silent. But I can still feel him there, as though he's just waiting to snatch her and take her away from life, from me. He's not taking her. No chance.

I stand up, rounding on him and advancing rapidly. Understandably, he looks rather stricken. All light has gone from my voice, it's just hollow darkness. "If you have a shred of respect, of consideration for me you will leave her alone. You will not touch her. You won't come anywhere near her."

"You know it doesn't work like that."

I shake my head. "I don't care. You find a way to fix this because I will not let her die, I will not let you take my best friend. I will not let her die!" My voice cracks, almost snaps in two. Then I feel the inevitable tears roll down my face in big, fat drops and there's no way I can stop them.

Scout hesitates, then pushes away from the wall and draws me into a hug. One of those firm, steadying hugs that are meant to protect you from the world.

"I'm sorry, Daisy. I'm so sorry this is happening." He sounds genuinely apologetic but that doesn't help. I can still hear the low whistling, the constant, unforgiving reminder that Violet is inches away from dying. Hugging and apologizing is doing nothing for her.

So I push away, shoot him a scowl. "Tell me, then. Tell me you will leave her alone."

He's about to answer, presumably to tell me some more bullshit about the system or whatever. But he doesn't get a chance. There's a coughing sound from behind me and I turn around, desperate to see some good news.

It's not quite that. Her eyes are open but just slightly and the monitor continues to beep at a rate I just know isn't healthy. She may be awake, but she's nowhere near OK. For one thing, her eyes flick right to us and then focus. She can see us.

I glance to Scout, confused and panicked. Perhaps we're too late after all. "She must be halfway between," he murmurs, hand resting on my shoulder now. "Not quite dead, not quite alive. I doubt she's appearing conscious to anyone but us right now."

Feeling a little sick, I step forward and come back to sit beside her. "Vi?" I whisper.

Her eyes struggle to focus, then flick over to Scout. "Who's that?" she croaks, fear weighing down each word. I think she knows deep down who it is.

Which is why I turn back to Scout. "Can you give us a moment?" I ask. "I think you're scaring her."

He doesn't like it, but after a moment of hesitation he nods. "OK. Five minutes."

I nod, turn back to Violet and wait until I hear his footsteps leave the room. "Violet, what happened?" I ask, trying my best not to sound like a disappointed schoolteacher. I know it's not her fault. I know it's not as simple as "what happened." But it's all I've got right now.

She licks chapped lips, rests her head back on her pillow. "Guess I did it properly this time if I can see you and His Nibs back there."

"Answer me properly, Violet." My hand comes to find hers, pinky fingers automatically interlocking like always.

She looks away, a horrible rattling sound coming from her mouth as she tries to breathe. "It all just got too loud, Daisy. And…you kept leaving me." She shoots me a worried look, presumably because she knows her words are going to hurt.

And they do. Like a slap in the face. "I—I wasn't leaving you, Violet. It was never about you."

Violet looks down at our clinging hands. "But that's how it felt, Daisy. You came back, you and Eric broke up, and then it was as if—as if I wasn't good enough for you." She wipes at her eyes with trembling fingers. "I'm sorry."

I shake my head, holding her whole hand now and not just one finger. I don't like how well I can feel the dips and rivets of her palms so clearly. That barrier between us feels too thin, too fragile. "Violet," I begin, my own voice trembling. "It wasn't like that. If that's how it felt, then..." I trail off, a little helplessly. What is the end of that sentence? If this is how I've made my friend feel then what sort of friend am I? Not a good one, that's for sure.

Violet, even in the fog of pain and sorrow, manages to see some of this on my face and she squeezes my hand fiercely. "Stop it. Stop thinking whatever is making you look like that. You weren't to know."

"I should have. I'm meant to be your best friend."

"You *are*." She rests her head back against the pillow, almost whimpering with exhaustion. I've seen how draining her depression can be for her and that's without severe blood loss. "You just...didn't realize that your death had happened to us all." She smiles weakly, eyes still closed. "You've spent your entire life being selfless when it came to me, Daisy. Some might call this progress."

"I don't. Not if it's led to this."

She shakes her head. "I'm just tired, Dee. I'm tired of fighting every day for a scrap of peace, for a moment when I feel good enough. And now you're gone, there's no reason to keep fighting. You were always my trump card, Daisy. Whenever it got dark, I fought on for you. What's the point now?" Coughing, she shifts away a little. "Anyway, it doesn't matter anymore. It's done."

"Don't talk like that!"

She cracks open an eye, gives me a rueful look. "I just saw Death loitering in my hospital room. That's not boding well for me."

"I won't let him take you."

Violet laughs at that. It sounds like creaking floorboards. "My best friend Daisy, telling Death to move along. Sounds about right."

"I mean it."

"I don't doubt it."

We fall silent for a moment. The whistling fills my head again, now there's nothing to distract me from it. Except now it seems to whisper to me how this is all my fault, how if I'd just, for one second, thought about how much she needed to be given space to move on, she wouldn't be in hospital now. I didn't *mean* to do this, I just wanted to see her. I just didn't want to accept that I only got twenty-three years to enjoy the unique sisterhood Violet and I had. And that desperate desire made me forget that this sisterhood was broken on two sides, not just one.

"He seems all right. I can see why you like him," Violet suddenly whispers, breaking through the silence.

Despite everything, I roll my eyes. Trust Violet to start discussing my future prospects on her deathbed. She spots this and smirks weakly. "What? Now Eric's out of the picture, you might as well have a go."

I don't answer. But for Violet that's enough. She smiles knowingly, then rests her head back on the pillow. "You'll have to watch out. Now I'm coming your way—"

"Violet," I snap, "this isn't a joke!"

She shoots me a fierce look. "I'm not joking, Daisy. This is what I want. I want to be with you."

I shake my head. "It doesn't work like that. It was different for me, I wasn't meant to die. But you—you're on his list. You'll go through his door and that will be it. You won't see me again." I'm not entirely sure that's completely true, but if it helps convince her to stay alive, then that's fine by me.

Violet looks at the ceiling for a long time. I see tears pooling in her eyes, like two little thunderstorms. "Fine. What difference does it make? I won't see you anywhere. But I'm not staying here anymore. I can't fight it anymore."

As if her words have some sort of power, the whistling

steps up a notch. It makes me wince, as though reality has slapped me in the face. We're not just having some hypothetical discussion, curled up together on the sofa. We're in a hospital and she's minutes, maybe seconds, away from dying. "Don't you start saying things like that," I warn her. "You can't give up, Vi."

She doesn't answer, looks away stubbornly. Perhaps it's just me, but I'm sure there's a little crinkle of fear in the corner of her mouth.

"Just—just wait here. Don't go anywhere," I growl, jumping up and backing out of the room. I need to find a way to fix this. She's acting tough, but I know the truth. Or at least I think I do.

Scout is hovering right outside the door, so I almost crash into him. He hurriedly stumbles back, giving me space. "How—how are things going?"

I decide there isn't time to answer that. "Is there any way? I mean, she's not dead yet. She—she made a mistake. Or rather, *I* made a mistake." I stumble over the words, drawing in a trembling breath. Scout frowns at that, hesitates before placing a hand on my shoulder again. I shake my head, stepping away because I don't want to hurt anyone else. "It was my fault for visiting her all the time and I should have known it would screw her up. It's my fault and she can't die just because I was a shit friend, she can't!"

"Hey, easy, Cooper." With a soft sigh, he steps forward and opens his arms up, a little tentatively. But it's an offer nonetheless and one I'm all too happy to take. I stumble forward, press my face against his chest. "You're the furthest thing I've ever seen from a shit friend, Daisy. And I've seen a lot."

I feel my chest shudder with a sob. I wish I could believe him, but the evidence speaks for itself. I didn't see that Violet needed space and now we're here.

"I shouldn't have seen her. You shouldn't have let me, so you've got to help me. There...there must be something. Some sort of loophole, like the keys. You helped me make this mess, you have to help me fix it."

There's a look of almost betrayal in his eyes and it breaks my heart all over again. I don't want to put this on Scout, to make him feel any more guilt. But I have to help her.

Finally, he looks away and curses softly. He has an idea, though he doesn't like it.

"Go on," I prompt. "You've clearly got something cooking in that brain of yours."

Scout hesitates. Then nods very slowly. "The system—it's all about balance. Violet needs to die if the balance is going to be kept. But if somebody else was to set the balance instead, somebody like you..."

"Me?"

Scout nods. "You died at the wrong time, but you haven't gone through the door yet. So technically your life is still... available. We can swap things around. Your life for hers."

I don't even need to consider it. I'm nodding straightaway, already turning back to Violet's room as if I can just hand my life over to her like a cup of tea.

"Woah! Hold on, Daisy." He grabs ahold of my arm, pausing me in my tracks. I turn back to him, to a face full of concern. "You need to think about it. You would be dead, properly. No more appearing to the living. No going back."

I think of Violet, driven to this point because I wouldn't leave her alone. I think of Eric, trying his best to move on but haunted by a girlfriend. I think of my parents, confused and angered by grief that only got worse when I turned up. It all seems pretty obvious when you look at it like that.

It's time to let go.

"I choose Violet. I died already."

"At the wrong time, though," he points out. "There could still be a chance, somehow, to get you back."

I shake my head. "It doesn't matter."

"She chose this, Daisy. She chose to die. Do you really want to risk your last remaining part of life? You'd be properly dying, Daisy." One hand comes to rest on my cheek. "We might not even be able to see each other again. And for what? What if she just tries again?"

I shake my head and I can feel determination practically steaming from my pores. It chases his hand away instantly. "No, she won't. I know she won't. Because I'm going to let her go and then—then she can rebuild things properly. It was me that caused this. When I'm gone, she can get help and move on properly."

Scout doesn't look entirely convinced by that, so I go on, "Between me and her, it has to be her. I'm a lot more use up there than down here. It's time to let go. I've died, Scout. Wrong time or not, my life is over. But it doesn't have to be for her. Please Scout, help me do this for her. Do this for me."

Scout hesitates for a long few seconds. Then, finally, he sighs with defeat. "Have you got the keys?" he asks.

Nodding, I pull them out from my pocket and hold them out to him. But he shakes his head, then presses a slightly hesitant yet surprisingly needed kiss to my forehead. "As always, Daisy, it's you, not me who can do this." With my forehead tingling, I give him a questioning look and he goes on, "Your remaining part of life resides in those keys, remember? That's how they helped you appear for so long. Unlike you, though, she's still got enough life clinging on to make up the rest. Give the keys to her and it should work."

"Should?"

He gives me a sad smile. "It's the best I've got."

Rule Twenty-Seven

The Greatest Gift You Can Give Is Another Chance

I'VE ONLY RECEIVED TWO gifts in my life before. One was the pen from Lucas, when he was planning to make Christmas a long-standing tradition and continuing to exist for more than a few months. The other was, strangely enough, from Natasha. Probably about three years ago now, when the relationship between us was still pretty frosty. Until one day, she decided that she was ready to try a bit of forgiveness. So she came to my office after a busy shift and offered me an innocuous-looking envelope. Inside was the very name tag I wear today. Believe it or not, up to this point I'd been surviving without one and just introducing myself every single time. I'm sure you can imagine how tedious that had got.

But no more of that. Now I had a name tag, neatly typed, with a little doodle of a skull beside it. I didn't know Natasha could have a sense of humor like that. I also didn't know she could draw so well.

I sought her out, thanked her in a typically awkward way, which she received with her typical stiffness. Then life, or death, went on. We kept on working, kept on pushing through the deaths. But now *it was different, because I knew that Natasha had not just given me a name tag, she'd given me another chance—another chance to prove that I wasn't an entirely heartless monster.*

I'm not sure whether I've proved that, yet. I mean, we are on speaking terms, though half of that speaking takes place in sarcastic tones. But it's still something. And I will forever be grateful for that gift she placed in my hands.

Second chances aren't for everyone. Some people don't deserve them; they're too precious. And I'm still not convinced that I did deserve one, not really. So now it's my turn to give someone another chance, to take a risk on a person who, I'm not entirely sure, will make the most of it.

After all, if I get to have another chance, I cannot deny it to Violet Tucker. And I certainly cannot deny it to Daisy Cooper.

Time is short.

In an ideal world, I'd want to hear more information from Scout about this plan of his and any possible flaws in it. But there's no time. So I step back toward Violet's room with this plan sitting a little uneasily atop my shoulders. I can feel Scout following right behind me, but that's OK because I feel like he's on our side now. A little act of defiance against the system he's been tied so tightly to all his life, albeit with a touch of blackmail on my part. The guilt for that is already starting to blossom, but there's no time for it now.

Inside the hospital room, Violet's lying back with her eyes closed, so still that she could be dead. But, thankfully, I know better. She's not dressed in white for one thing.

Indeed, the moment she hears the door close, her eyes flicker open. "So, have you made a deal with the Devil?" she whispers with a wary smile toward Scout.

"Sort of," I reply, as I come to sit beside her again, my

keys digging into my palm. Then I jerk my head back toward Scout. "He's a lot more amenable than the Devil." I hear a snort behind me but I decide to ignore it, focusing instead on Violet. "I've got something that can help. It can save you."

She shifts a little, so she's sitting a little more upright. "I told you. I don't want saving."

A sigh from behind me this time. He doesn't think she's worth it. That's the problem, people never think Violet's worth the time because she pushes and pushes. But she just wants to know you care enough to keep trying.

"Violet, you said that last time. Remember? We sat in that hospital back home and you told me that there was nothing you wanted to live for. You told me you were worth nothing and you were just dragging me down. And I told you that you were wrong. And I told you to give it one month. One month for me to prove how wrong you were. And then you started on that medication and going to see that therapist who you decided was too fucking sexy to be a therapist." A ghost of a smile at this and I push on, buoyed by that apparition. "And things started making sense again. Then you smashed your dance exam and we had that amazing day here in London—and you started to remember how to be happy again."

Another small smile. "We sat by the river and ate ice cream and you accidentally told that tourist totally wrong directions," she murmurs, and we share a laugh, the memory vivid enough to chase away some of the shadows around Violet's eyes.

"You'd just forgotten, Violet, what it feels like to be happy. Even if just for a few moments. You'd forgotten that a few moments of happiness can be worth all the shit. Just like you've forgotten now. You've stopped taking your meds—yes, I know about that—and you've been haunted by someone who should have left you alone. You just need to remember again." I fall silent for a moment, watch her closely. Watch as the cogs in her mind slowly turn. Time to go for the trump card. "And one month after that first time, we went for breakfast. And do you remember what you said?"

Violet closes her eyes, tears slowly trickling down her cheeks. "I said—I said I could never repay you enough for saving my life."

I nod, my own vision blurred by tears. "Well," I begin, voice thick, "here's your chance. Time to repay me."

"What?"

I sit forward, take her hand and squeeze it tight. "I want you to do something for me. I want you to take your meds again like you're meant to; I want you to get some help; and I want you to take care of these." I hold out my keys, hand surprisingly steady considering the tears rising in my eyes.

"Your keys?" she asks, looking suspiciously between me and Scout.

"It's my life, Violet. What's left of it, anyway. Remember how I told you that I wasn't fully dead yet, because I hadn't died at the right time? Well, the rest of my life is held in these and I want you to have it. I've got no use for it but you do. You've got a whole lot of stuff left to do down here. I need you to show the world what Violet Tucker can do."

Violet slowly shakes her head. "I... That's... I can't... No, it belongs to you, Daisy. I don't deserve that. Look at me, I can barely look after my own life."

"Violet, I'm not asking you to be perfect. My life wasn't, not by a long shot. I'm just asking you to do the one thing I can't do anymore. And live. Besides, I cannot think of anyone who deserves another chance more than you." I give the keys a little jangle. "Take them. Live well, live outrageously like only you can. Live for the both of us, Vi, you always knew how to get me to make the most of my life—this is just cutting out the middleman."

Violet's eyes stay on the keys for a moment and I can see her thought process slowly clicking away. "Do—do I get to see you again?"

I hesitate, then shake my head slowly. "This is it. Proper death. And it's for the best. We've got to let go, Vi."

Violet is silent for a moment, staring at her hands. Then she glances up again, looks past me and over to Scout. "Will you look after her?" she asks, her voice full of sisterly protectiveness.

I hear another snort from Scout, the squeak of his shoes as he moves a little closer. "She doesn't need looking after."

Violet scans his face for a moment, then sniffs, nods briskly. "Right answer," she murmurs, before looking back to me. "I'm not sure I can do this, Dee."

"I know. Me neither."

She hears the crack in my voice and tugs my hand rather hard, until I almost fall against her chest. Her arms immediately wrap around me, holding me close. "I'm not going to really ever let go of you, Daisy. You know that, right? You don't just move on from someone like you. But I'll try to make you proud, how about that?"

"OK," I croak, resting my head against her shoulder, taking in that familiar scent of hers that even hospitals can't hide. The coconut oil she uses on her hair and the lavender spray she puts on her wrists, supposedly to calm her down. "I'm going to miss you so much," I find myself whispering, allowing the bravery to slip for just a second. I feel so damn small. Like the little five-year-old kid who shuffled into a new class and didn't know anyone, until another five-year-old with wild curls and wilder eyes took them under her wing.

Violet's hand finds my other hand, the one with the keys.

Her fingers curl around them and I let go, ready for her to take them. Because if she's reaching for them on her own, then I'm taking that as a good sign. A sign that she's ready to give her life another chance. "I love you, Daisy."

"And I love you, Violet. Now go live the crap out of your life, OK? Because that's the most worthwhile thing you can do."

"Fantastic last words," she whispers, and then the keys are gone. For a second, there's nothing. No change. Then my little scrap of life finds a new place to call home and we are pulled apart. One of us to life, one of us to death. I feel her fingers graze across mine for one precious second. Then I'm gone.

So, once again, death goes like this. Unconsciousness, darkness, tumbling out, whiteout. This time, it happens rapidly. A series of changes in the blink of an eye. I hear the whistling intensify, but it's not for her this time. It's for me.

White fills my vision. Nothing but white and silence, crushing and endless. I don't remember it being so horrifying last time. I'm filled with an irrational terror that the white will never leave, that Scout won't get to me fast enough and I will be stuck here.

Of course, he comes. Distantly, I feel his hand on my shoulder and, just like that, the whiteout is gone. A blizzard halted in its tracks. Some things he will always get right and this part of his job is certainly one of them.

My eyes slowly open and I see the world from the floor of the hospital room. I must have fallen to the ground. Around me there are the feet of nurses and doctors as they help Violet with her newly recovered life. I have become truly irrelevant to this world but, as I hear the coughing and gasping of Violet returning, I know that I've done the right thing.

Time to let go. Time to move on, so my eyes search for the person who I am still significant to. At least, I hope so.

Scout's eyes are full of unashamed pride. A forest blooming with life. "Hello, Miss Cooper," he says with a boyish grin as he offers me his hand. "I believe you need a ride."

Feeling a little woozy, I allow him to help me up. He wraps one arm around my middle, keeping me upright as I clumsily turn myself back toward Violet's bed. "Did it work?" I croak.

"See for yourself," he murmurs, and I can hear the smile in his voice.

Violet's trying to sit up in bed, surrounded by frantic doctors. She looks as woozy as I feel but she's alive. Her heart beats steadily on the screen of her monitor and she manages to croak a thank you to the nearest doctor who is helping her sit back against the pillows.

"Stay still, Violet. You've lost a lot of blood. You need to rest," the doctor says, her voice kind but firm. Another doctor comes to her side, murmurs something in her ear. "Violet? Your mother's outside. Would you like to see her?"

Violet rubs at her eyes, lets out a small whimper. "Is she angry?"

The doctor lets out a soft, understanding laugh. I get the sense she's dealt with people like Violet before. "Of course not, Violet. She's just so worried about you. She'll be so glad to see you're awake."

Violet's face crumples and her eyes close, then she nods. Slowly at first but then with increasing speed. "Yes, please. Please let me see her."

One of the nurses hurries out and a moment later Aubrey Tucker is racing into the room. She must have come straight from bed, judging from the rather eclectic collection of clothes she's wearing.

The person who is accompanying her brings me a slight shock. It's my own mother, which in hindsight isn't that surprising. She's probably the best equipped to help Aubrey with this situation. She's also dressed half in pajamas, half in clothes—and, despite it being the middle of the night, I'm comforted by the fact that she looks better than the last time I saw her. It gives me confidence in my theory that what Violet needs right now is space.

Still, I find my stomach twisting at the sight of Mum. I will never be able to speak to her ever again, not while she is alive. That door is closed, well and truly.

With that thought whizzing around my head, I find Scout's hand is currently rested on my hip and helping me stay upright. I gently pry it away and then wrap my fingers around it. "Let's go," I murmur, though my eyes stay glued on the scene. But I know I need to leave, I know seeing my mother is the equivalent of finding a gingerbread house in a forest.

I feel Scout's fingers wriggle between mine, then gently tug at my hand. "Good idea, Cooper." He gives me a second more, then chuckles, pulling me a little firmly. "Come on, time to trust Violet Tucker to live without you."

It sounds so daunting when it's put like that, and I shoot Scout a look. "That wasn't helpful, just so you know."

"Noted." He meets my gaze steadily, then jerks his head toward the door. "Ready?"

I give myself ten more seconds. I watch as Violet sobs desperately into her mother's arms, watch as Mum holds one of each Tucker woman's hands, grounding them both to this room, this world.

So we leave. In the lift, Scout keeps silent but also does not let go of my hand and I drift to his side and find my head resting against his chest. His chin comes to rest atop, a simple act of support that doesn't smother me, just reassures me that I'm not alone.

Back up in the world of the dead, order has been restored well and truly. The corridors are blissfully empty once more and Scout's office is gloriously still. We step inside but Scout pauses by the door, pulling it closed with a thoughtful expression. Then he turns toward me. "How do you know," he asks, "that she won't try again?"

There's only genuine curiosity in his voice, which is how he gets away with the question. But that doesn't mean I have an answer for him. "I don't," I say finally. "Just because I gave her a bit of my life and told her to live her life to the fullest, doesn't mean that her depression will let her. It's never going to be that simple. But she's worth taking that risk for. And I believe in her. I believe that she can do it, if she's just given the chance. Maybe that will be enough."

Something flashes across Scout's face, I can't quite place it. "Yeah, I think it will be. You did a good thing there, Daisy. You know that, right?"

I shrug, smile a little sheepishly. "She deserved another chance. It was the least I could do. Besides, it was time to let go, for both of us," I say, like it was the easiest thing in the world.

"The Daisy who came into my office all those months ago wouldn't have known where to start with that."

I grin, take the compliment with surprising ease. "No. Probably not. Thanks, Scout."

He pushes away from the door, comes toward the desk. But he stops before he gets there, turning around once again. "I was sort of eavesdropping a little, out in the corridor," he admits, watching me with understandable worry.

I feel my eyebrows raise. "Totally inappropriate, but go on," I reply, voice steady. Because I'm intrigued as to what Scout wants to say next that is worth him admitting to this misdemeanor.

He shifts a little sheepishly, teeth worrying against his lip. "Violet. She said: 'I can see why you like him.' What did she mean by that?" Scout looks determinedly at a spot behind my head, fiddling with one of his shirt buttons.

For a moment I have to rack my brains to work out what he's talking about, but I get there eventually. "Oh," I say, and Scout's gaze flicks up to meet mine as if he can sense that something important is coming. "Just Violet being stupid. She likes to think she's an expert on those sorts of things."

"What sorts of things?"

"Sometimes you are so damn obtuse," I grumble, but there's fondness in my words and he grins a little. "Things like… love."

"Oh," he says, straightening up a little. "So…you love me?"

It's moments like these that remind me of how inescapably nonhuman Scout is. Of how much he still needs to learn. Like the art of subtlety.

"Um…" I finally say, after a number of excruciating seconds in which I flounder for the right words and Scout watches me expectantly. "It's not quite that simple. For anyone, I mean. It takes time to really know those sorts of things."

Scout nods knowledgeably, as if he actually has a damn clue. "So, you don't know?" he prompts after a moment. "I mean, that's fine because I don't really know either."

It's hard not to smile at that, especially when he sounds so sincere and so considered. "Maybe that's fine for now, then. We both don't know."

Another smile, this time a little wider. For someone so clueless, he does manage to hit the nail on the head surprisingly frequently. I take a step forward, press a light but confident kiss against his cheek. "Well, if it helps, I do know that dying is a lot easier when it's with you."

He looks at me intently, as he methodically works through

these words and what they mean. Then he grins, a little sheepishly. "Well then, Daisy Cooper, welcome to death."

We both laugh. It's a little "first date" awkward but there's warmth and comfort in there too, enough to begin to chase away the shadows of trauma left behind from the hospital ward. Enough to make me believe that it's not only Violet who can move on.

"Well, back to work, I guess," Scout declares a second later, bumping his shoulder against mine. Then he turns and strides toward his desk, humming a little under his breath. "Though I don't think we'll be needing that," he comments, picking a file up off his desk. I just about catch Violet's name stamped across the top, before he drops it into one of his drawers with a satisfied flourish.

Grinning a little, I step forward. "Who's the other one?" I ask, pointing to a file that's been sitting just under Violet's.

Scout's eyes narrow, then he tilts his head. "Hmm…" he says, which is Scout-speak for "oh shit." I come closer, frowning as he hurriedly picks up the file, effectively taking its name out of my eyesight.

"Scout…"

He bites his lip, hesitates for a moment. Then slowly turns it around. I see the name, but it doesn't quite sink in. Not until Scout confirms it for me, his voice bitter like cyanide.

"It's yours."

Rule Twenty-Eight

Sometimes Rules Need To Be Broken

ONCE THERE WAS A girl called Daisy. She lived an ordinary life filled with ordinary things like takeout and book clubs and best friends. Her life was nothing special but she was happy. She was pretty sure she was happy. Then, one February evening, she tripped on uneven pavement and died.

Once there was a man called Death. He lived an endless life filled with identical things like death and death and more death. His existence was crucial and he was miserable. He was extremely sure he was miserable. Then, one February evening, Daisy tripped on uneven pavement and died.

It all sounds pretty simple when you put it like that. But it wasn't. Life is messy, death is even more so. The rules you use to govern your life and make it somehow easier don't just stop when that whistle begins. Daisy's bumpy road from that icy pavement has made that fact increasingly clear.

Yet somehow, we've reached this point. Where Daisy has managed to set the balance right all on her own and made her death *worth something. There's not many people who can truly say that. Violet's heart has found its rhythm and Daisy's heart has let go of that final spark.*

So she's dead, properly now. She's gone. Like none of her ever happened.

Except Daisy doesn't go anywhere without leaving her mark. A crack in the pavement. A determination to try again in the heart of Violet Tucker. An understanding that it's OK to cry in Eric Broad. And then there's me. What has Daisy done to me?

It's hard to tell. But I do know that I've never once allowed for any deviation from the system. Reliable to the end. And yet, here we are: A Daisy, a Death, and a file.

❋ ❋ ❋

Technically speaking, I should be gone. That's the rule. The living in one place, the dead in another. Death and Admin in between. Now I'm dead, I don't belong with him anymore. There's a different door for me in his office, and a system waiting to be followed.

I fully expect it to go like that. I fully expect Scout to sit down at his desk, flip open my file and go through the motions. But he doesn't. He makes an exception. Perhaps it's all the high emotions we left behind in Violet's hospital ward. Perhaps it's the relief that another MDS is finished. Perhaps it's the lingering kiss on his cheek. Or perhaps Scout has simply changed.

His fingers grip the file tight, making the paper creak. "Now?" he asks, eyes fixed determinedly on me.

"What?"

"Shall we do this now? Or later?" He jerks his thumb back toward the door behind him, the one I have yet to be able to step through.

I don't need more than a few seconds to make this decision. "Later. But won't that—I don't know, make the universe explode?"

Scout smirks as he carefully places the file in the drawer with Violet's. "Maybe you're worth it," he comments, almost to himself, a comment I'm not sure I'm meant to hear, so decide not to respond to. He looks up, meets my gaze. "I'll fix it. Natasha can enter you into the system as an Admin worker."

"Natasha?" I ask, a little dubiously because I can't imagine Natasha flouting the rules so willingly, just for me.

Scout must pick up on this because he grins knowingly. "She's got a bit of a soft spot for you, y'know. Apparently I'm a lot more bearable with you around—who knew? I'm sure with a little bit of groveling she'll help us out."

And, to my pleasant surprise, that's exactly what happens. We visit Natasha, who seems to conveniently have all the paperwork ready, though still pretends that the idea is horrifying and highly irregular. She makes us plead a little bit, then agrees to help, on the condition that Scout explains what the hell went on with the MDS.

I leave Scout to that conversation, whispering him a reminder to tell the truth as I go. Natasha is stern but she's also a human—I predict she'll appreciate Scout admitting to having a fear like the rest of us.

It's a comforting feeling, knowing that there is a death waiting for me when I'm ready (perhaps when Violet comes through at the right time, hopefully old and fabulously eccentric). There's no ties, no expectations for me here. Just a mutual understanding that, for now, Scout and I are both better off together. A partnership worth bending the rules for.

Inevitably, work returns. A new routine settles around us. We pick up the dead, we pick up each other when the job seems particularly heavy. Sometimes Scout reads a file and wrinkles his nose, and I take it for him. Sometimes he does the same for me. But when there's a child, we square our shoulders and take it together. It doesn't make it easy, but it certainly makes it bearable.

Violet's file doesn't come up again. I keep checking on her, though, just in case. She can't see me anymore, of course, no chance of that. But that's fine. It's quite freeing to know that I can keep an eye on her but, at the end of the day, there's nothing I can do.

To give her credit, she battles on. She takes time off work and moves back in with her mum for a few months. She lets the procedure following a suicide attempt happen and tries to let it help her as much as it can. Sometimes, when I pop down, I think I see some edge of that dark cloud looming near her. But next time, it will be gone, filed away carefully. She's fighting back, slowly but surely.

After those few months, she returns to our flat and packs up my things. When I come down to find the empty room, I allow myself a moment of sorrow and longing. But I know it's the right thing to do. It's her flat now. Time to make it her own. She rents out my room to a guy from work (restaurant, not theater). He's from France, speaks limited English, but makes excellent poached eggs. They bond over crime dramas and their equally shoddy attempts to learn each other's languages. If I'm going to be replaced, he seems like an acceptable substitute. Especially when I witness the moment he catches her crying over my set of keys one evening. I watch with a proud smile as he carefully coaxes her back to calm with a patience that will get him far. Yes, he'll do.

I notice that I start visiting her less and less after that. It doesn't become as necessary and, when it still hurts to do it, there doesn't seem much point in it. Scout asks me once why I've stopped and when I tell him the reason he nods and smiles. "Still human, then," he says, and hands me another file to sort, fingers grazing over mine for a millisecond longer than necessary.

Sometimes, I'll go back to my family. In a way, they're easier than Violet. But in other ways they're harder. I don't worry about them as much because they've surrounded each other with such love that I know they'll be fine. But I feel the missing of moments more keenly around them. I want to join my brother in hugging Dad when he plants a patch of daisies in the garden. I want to help Mum when she has a crisis at work and needs someone to help with the paperwork. I want to be there to congratulate Ollie when he meets a guy and brings him over for dinner. Little moments that I don't get to celebrate, that's when death hurts the most.

As always, though, time passes on. Summer in the northern hemisphere rolls by in a hazy heat wave and we're kept busy with dehydrated pensioners who have nobody but us to care for them, and then the unfortunate victims of wildfires and flash floods. We're treated to a relative lull after that, as autumn and spring settle over the respective halves of the globe. Everybody seems to calm down a little during those months. Fewer grisly murders for us to sweep up, fewer results of careless accidents in the sea. A chance to catch our breath, so to speak.

Before we know it, winter is gripping over my home once again. I battle through my first set of Christmas deaths, try to ignore the sadness when we walk past lit-up windows on our way to pick up some poor soul with no shelter on a freezing night, or when we hear Christmas carols playing in the crumpled remains of a crashed car.

I have to admit to being relieved when January comes around. Scout congratulates me for getting through the festive season as only he would—by giving me my very own name tag with a wobbly daisy drawn beside it.

A month later, I come back from helping a victim of leukemia and Scout is hovering anxiously in his office. It's highly distracting and the poor young man I'm dealing with gets a rather rushed service because Scout keeps hurrying me along in not the most subtle of ways.

When the man is finally shipped off through the door, Scout is dragging me to sit down almost immediately.

"So, big day," he says, once he's positioned me in a seat and shushed my complaints.

"It is?"

He nods, pulls the calendar off the wall and places it in front of me. He jabs the day, currently only partly filled with the little tallies he likes to do to keep track of his jobs. It hits me like a jolt of electricity. The 3rd of February. The day I died.

"Oh," I say, before looking up at him. "That's why you were dancing around me like a demented bear?"

Scout bites his lip, then shakes his head. "Not exactly. There's…something I'd like to show you. To—to do with the date."

He's acting like he's asking me to come to a school dance with him or something. This is probably the equivalent for him, to be honest. "OK. Show me."

Nodding with a relieved smile, he stands up, comes around the table and takes my hand. Now it really is like a damn school dance. Except Scout and I don't really know how to be awkward around each other anymore, even when he's oddly nervous. He asks about the job and I tell him about getting

320 / Tamsin Keily

lost in a Tokyo hospital which he finds predictably amusing. That leads to him telling me about the time someone got murdered in Hampton Court maze and he spent ages trying to find the guy and then get him back out to the lift again.

The story is so entertaining (or rather the mental image of Scout cursing and storming around a maze is so entertaining) that when we step out of the lift, it takes me a moment to work out where we are. But then I hear the hiss of a bus stopping, smell the grease from the nearby takeout restaurant.

I'm home.

My street, where I lived and where I died, is identical, almost, to how it looked a year ago. Same bus stop with same meaningless graffiti on the seats. Same lamppost with the smashed bulb that still hasn't been fixed. The cat from number thirteen stretches out on the fence with his usual sense of luxury. The trees are bare, the branches shivering in the rough wind. Just like they were that night.

But gathered around one cracked pavement slab is a deviation from the street's normal order of business: a small group of people, huddled together.

I immediately recognize an escaped dark curl from under one hat and let out a small gasp, looking questioningly to Scout. He nods slowly, lets go of my hand and nudges me forward. "I think you should listen."

With a slight sense of apprehension that I can't quite understand, I move closer to the cluster of people. I see Violet's face now, half dipped under a scarf and cocooned in curls, pressed down by her hood. Beside her is Claude, the new flatmate. He looks suitably awkward, but he flicks quick looks across at Violet every so often, checking how she's doing, until she catches him and shoots him a mock glare. Then there's Eric, of all people, standing very straight and fiddling with his tie, adjusting his work coat. He doesn't look entirely comfortable there, which makes sense considering the somewhat suspicious looks Mum keeps shooting him. Backing me up, however unnecessarily, even after all this time.

My family finish up the circle. My brother, looking tired and wearing his gym gear. The lazy bugger couldn't even smarten up for my anniversary, though to be honest it's a little comforting to know that some things never change. Then there's my dad, holding my mum's hand and shifting a little from foot to foot. Mum is positioned the closest to the cracked pavement and seems to be the head of the circle. Again, nothing changes.

But, as I slide into the small gap between her and Violet, Mum nods toward my best friend. "Go on then, Violet. Off you go."

Along with everyone else, I look to Violet. As always, she doesn't shy away from the attention. A born performer, she pushes back her hood with a flourish to let her curls free. She looks around the circle, takes in her audience before smiling. It's small but warm, hopeful. "So, we all know what today is. And part of me thought I'd just let it go by and not make a big deal out of it because, for me, it's not what I want to think about when I think about Daisy. But I also wanted to do something that showed what a mark she left on all our lives, and today seemed like the most appropriate day to unveil that something."

She pauses, looks across to Eric and nods encouragingly. He jumps into action, twisting around to his rucksack and digging around inside until he finds a small brown package, which he pulls out and hands across the circle to Violet. She smiles gratefully, then carefully unwraps the package before holding it out to the middle so everyone can see.

Inside is a small bronze plaque. At the top is a delicate etching of a daisy and below there is a neatly written inscription: "Live life like each day is your last, just in case it is." I read it and swallow, feeling emotion swirling at the back of my throat.

Mum lets out a shaky breath. "Oh Violet…it's perfect. She would never have wanted some quaint little memorial. She would have wanted others to take her death as a lesson."

Violet nods, a proud smile on her face. "That's what I thought." My dad pats her shoulder, though words seem to be a step too far for him right now. Violet shoots him an understanding look, before passing him the plaque. "Off to work then, Mr. Cooper," she chuckles. Her voice sounds so light, so free. A bird that is learning to soar after being freed from a cage.

My dad takes the plaque and carefully places it on the wall. Mum pulls a set of tools from her bucket of a handbag, handing them over. We all watch in silence as Dad drills, hammers and screws, until my plaque is set into the wall, right by my pavement. Everyone stands back, surveys the plaque in silence for a moment.

Then Violet speaks again: "Then we were talking to Ollie a week or so ago and he pointed out how Daisy always liked to find a way to make light of the shit, usually with inappropriate jokes." She grins across at Ollie, who nods his vehement agreement. And I find myself glancing back to Scout with a smile of my own. They're right, after all.

Violet holds out her hand to Eric again. Once more, he digs about inside his bag and then pulls out another package. She cautiously unwraps it and then holds it out to the group once again.

Mum lets out a somewhat disapproving sigh, paired with a

slightly reluctant chuckle. Dad takes the plaque with a smirk, shakes his head as he centers it on the wall, just below the other one. I squeeze around Eric so I can get a look myself, then catch Scout's eye as I read what it says. He's grinning too.

The plaque is smaller and has only words on it. It's Violet's handwriting, carefully copied onto the metal: "Give Death hell, Daisy."

My brother leans in, squinting (stubborn idiot never wears his glasses) before letting out a hoot of laughter. "Nice."

"Private joke?" Mum asks, her expression one of fondness. The poor woman spent her life dealing with those.

Violet smiles, sharing a secret with an invisible best friend. "Yeah, private joke."

By this time, Dad has secured this plaque to the wall and stepped back, wiping his hands on his trousers as Mum takes the tools back from him. Everyone stands in a little semicircle, surveying my memorial in a comfortable yet still somber silence.

It lasts around two minutes, then Mum lets out a little sigh and nods briskly. She never was comfortable with public displays of emotion. Time to go. My dad, of course, spots this and shoots her a gentle smile. "Shall we, love?"

"I think so," she replies, before moving to pull Violet into a tight hug, shaking hands with Eric and Claude politely, if a touch awkwardly. "This was lovely. Well done, Violet. She'd be so touched. See you soon."

Then she beckons my brother to follow them toward the train station. I watch as he presses one finger to my plaque, just briefly, then hurries after them. Eric gives Violet a quick hug and I catch the grateful smile he receives in return.

"Thanks for coming," she says. "Want to come in for tea? Claude's still learning how to brew it right."

324 / Tamsin Keily

Then Violet leads the way with her two boys in tow while my family round the corner and disappear into the London evening. Now it's just the cat, the clouds and the ghosts. Scout sidles over from where he's been loitering a few steps away, giving me space.

"Give Death hell…" he murmurs, arm coming to wrap around my shoulders in what has become an entirely natural act of affection recently. As natural as it is for my head to come and rest against his chest. "Think you'll make them proud in that respect."

I make a small noise of agreement, brushing away a few tears from the corners of my eyes.

"You OK, Cooper?" he asks after another moment of silence.

"Yeah," I reply and I'm pleasantly surprised to find that I actually am. I turn, press a kiss to his lips. Another increasingly natural act. "Thank you, for bringing me here."

Scout accepts both words and kiss with a poorly hidden pride.

A wind begins to scurry down the narrow street, paying us very little attention. The weeds poking through the cracked pavement shake but my plaque stays firmly stuck to the wall. Down the road, I watch as Violet's lights go on in her flat and I can practically hear the switch of the kettle, the whoosh of the fridge door as she hunts out the milk. A cycle beginning again and I am OK not to be part of it.

Above the howl of the wind, a new sound flits over to my ears. A butterfly tickling at my ears, it's barely noticeable. It's the distant whistling like another kettle boiling, yet the world of the dead knows that it's nothing of the sort. I turn back toward Scout and, like clockwork, he steps away and offers up his hand.

"Back to work?" he asks.

I smile, take his hand and tangle our fingers together. "Back to work."

We turn, walk away from the tightly packed street of houses with all their different lives buzzing away inside. The living are moving on, but so are we. And we have work to do.

★ ★ ★ ★ ★

Acknowledgments

There are so many people who have made this book a reality. I'd like to first thank my beyond inspiring mother, the late Deborah Keily, who was kind enough to pass on her writing genes and was also determined enough to make sure I used them. Thank you for teaching me how to be brave and for showing me how to find light in the darkest of times.

Thank you to Morwenna Banks for always having faith in me, even during the early days of over-complicated plots and dubious character development. Thank you also for helping me get the book to the right people—it really wouldn't exist without you and I am so grateful for all your help and support.

A huge, huge thank you to "Team Daisy":

My incredible, brilliant and wonderfully encouraging agent Jo Unwin, who managed to find some potential in the very early, very rough version of this story, and who taught me that stories can be interesting without explosions in them, and who has guided me through this whole new, sometimes slightly daunting world. The amazing Deborah Schneider at Gelfman Schneider who helped this book travel across the pond to the US—something that I still can't believe is a reality. The wonderful team at Orion Fiction—Victoria Oundjian, Olivia Barber, Kati Nicholl and the wondrous Harriet Bourton, who all had such amazing belief in Daisy's story. The ever-helpful Milly Reilly and Donna Greaves for answering all my questions and helping me through the more confusing aspects of publishing a book! And of course the awesome people at Park Row Books, especially Erika Imranyi, who understood what I wanted this book to be and helped me reach its potential. Thank you also for sifting through all of Daisy's Britishness! It has been such a delight and honor to work with you all, and I am forever grateful.

To my gorgeous friends—thank you for dealing with my vacant stares when I was lost in plotting and for showing me the amazing power of female friendship. Special mention to Alice Keane, Stephanie Dallison, Hannah Wise, Jessie Ravenscroft, Emily Winter, Lucy Stephens, Hannah Worth and Megan Francis. Thank you also to the ever supportive and wonderful Cranbourne team.

Then there's my family:

My incomprehensibly wonderful husband, who has been an incredibly calming influence throughout (which was definitely needed). Thank you for the love and the numerous cups of tea over the years. The Brown family, for helping me to the finish line in France. And of course the KBD family—Dad, Mummy Lynne, Alice, Jack, Miles. Your pride, your love, your 5am messages after finishing the draft, your questions about Death's fashion choices, or in my sister's case actually finishing the book, made all the difference. And thank you for living with my obnoxiously loud typing for all these years.

A special mention also to Auntie Ruth, for keeping me typing during my hectic year of teacher training.

But there is one person without whom this book would just not have existed. The Violet to my Daisy, the gorgeous Vix Jensen-Collins. Thank you for having faith in this story, right from its infancy, for listening to endless versions of various chapters and for giving me so much material to work from. Daisy and Violet are the heart of this book, and you are the heart of Daisy and Violet. I am so damn lucky to have you in my life. Thank you.